Take Me Home

Take Me Home

Nancy Herkness

Montlake
Romance

Text copyright © 2012 Nancy Herkness
All rights reserved.
Printed in the United States of America.

Published by Montlake Romance
P.O. Box 400818
Las Vegas, NV 89140

ISBN-13: 9781612186030
ISBN-10: 1612186033

To Joe.

You are missed.

Acknowledgments

I WOULD LIKE TO THANK THE FOLLOWING PEOPLE WHO have helped make *Take Me Home* the book it is:

My agent Jane Dystel, who found this book the perfect home at Montlake Romance.

The discerning Miriam Goderich, who saw my novel's potential and plucked it from the slush pile.

My editor, Kelli Martin, who believes in my work and gives it the kind of attention an author usually only dreams of.

My developmental editor, Andrea Hurst, who understands how to strengthen both story and emotion with the subtlest of touches.

My copy editors, Tara Doernberg and Ashley McDonald, who keep me on the straight and narrow when it comes to the all-important details.

The whole dream team at Montlake, for all they do to make this author happy.

My brilliant critique group: Miriam Allenson, Cathy Greenfeder, and Lisa Verge Higgins, who know where I was when I joined them and where I am now. Enough said.

My pony Papoose, who was my original whisper horse.

As always, my family: Jeff, Rebecca, and Loukas, who celebrate and commiserate with me with equal love.

Chapter 1

REATHING IN THE SCENT OF FRESH HAY AND SADDLE soap, Claire felt the knots of tension loosen their grip on her shoulders. She stood just outside the stable door, her face tilted up to let the early summer sunshine stroke her cheeks and forehead, its warmth suffusing the cotton of her T-shirt and the denim of her jeans.

The stable had become her refuge in the past few weeks. The well-kept brick buildings, the bluish-green mountains rising behind them, and the constant motion of powerful, glossy horses pushed her problems away for an hour or so.

"Hey, Claire, over here." Sharon, the owner of Healing Springs Stables, waved to her from halfway down the stable's central aisle. "Got a horse I want you to meet before you go riding."

"Another candidate for my whisper horse?" Claire called, smiling. Her friendship with the horsewoman was another reason Claire came here. Sharon had become the rock she clung to in her sea of failure.

Thick pine bark muffled the fall of her boots, but the barn was far from silent as the clank of halters against water buckets and the affectionate banter of stable hands with their charges drifted around her. She took another deep, grateful breath before she joined her friend.

"I'll make a believer out of you yet," Sharon said, her flyaway copper hair a blazing halo around her face.

Claire fell into step beside her, almost jogging to keep up with her six-foot-tall companion's athletic stride. "Is the horse one of your rescues?"

"Yup. Just came in this morning. She's a Thoroughbred, a former racehorse. Ought to be a sympathetic listener for your troubles."

"If you say so." Claire wasn't clear on why a former racehorse would understand her problems with her ex-husband or her younger sister, but she humored Sharon.

"Here she is," Sharon said, stopping in front of the stall door and easily looking over the top. Her eyebrows lifted in surprise. "Oh, hey, Dr. Tim. You sure got here fast."

"You said the horse was in bad shape, so I made time for her." The voice emanating from within the stall was deep, with a touch of the local West Virginia drawl.

The stall door swung open, and a man the size of a small mountain stepped out. Backlit by a slanting shaft of afternoon sun, the ends of his straight hair glowed deep red while the edges of his plaid shirt blazed blue and gold. In one large fist, he hefted an oversized tan duffel bag with *Sanctuary Veterinary Hospital* embroidered on it in dark-green letters.

Claire had heard about the new veterinarian in Sanctuary, but she hadn't encountered him in the few weeks she'd been back in her hometown. No one had mentioned he wouldn't look out of place on a football team's defensive line. Yet something about the calm, deliberate way he moved inspired a sense of security rather than a threat of physical dominance. She could picture him holding up the world if Atlas got tired.

"Dr. Tim, this is my friend Claire Parker," Sharon said. "She works at Davis Honaker's art gallery in town. She just relocated here from up north of the Mason-Dixon Line last month. Worked in a fancy gallery before, so Davis feels real lucky to have her."

"Nice to meet you," Claire said, blushing slightly at Sharon's praise, as she stepped forward with her hand extended. The vet's duffel hit the ground with a thud and a puff of pine bark dust. For an awkward moment, Claire stood with her hand out, while Dr. Tim seemed frozen.

"Sorry, ma'am, it's a pleasure," he said, finally moving to wrap his strong, callused fingers around hers. "For a minute there, I thought I'd met you before."

As Claire Parker stepped out of Sharon's shadow, Tim saw Anais. He knew his mind was playing tricks on him, but something about the dramatic lighting and the way the woman moved evoked the image of his wife as she had looked onstage, maybe because that was how he kept dreaming about her.

He looked desperately for the differences there must be between this woman and his dead wife. Yes, Claire had shining dark hair smoothed back into a sleek bun, the way his wife had often worn hers, and they shared a certain husky timbre to their voices. But Anais's eyes were blue, while Claire's were velvet brown, and under her T-shirt and jeans, Claire had more curves than the slender actress would ever allow herself.

Yet he, the rational scientist, was blindsided by the resemblance. He thought leaving New York would save him from the constant reminders, yet even here in the wilds of West Virginia, he got yanked back into the nightmare.

Claire looked up at him with a question in her eyes, and he realized he was still holding her hand. He gave her an apologetic smile as he released his grip.

Her gaze became intent, as though she was trying to read something in his face. With a sense of disquiet, he wondered what his expression revealed. Most people had given up on offering sympathy that thinly disguised their curiosity about his wife's death, but Claire Parker was new here. She might not know he preferred to avoid the subject.

"Excuse me, ma'am," he said, giving Claire a polite nod before he turned away to face Sharon. He pulled a prescription pad and pen from his pocket and began to write, covering three sheets before he tore them off and held them out. As he refocused on the condition of the mare he'd just examined, clean, strong anger boiled up again. "Whoever owned this horse should be prosecuted for criminal negligence."

"You won't hear any argument from me." Sharon took the papers with a sigh. "Add this visit to my monthly bill."

"This one's on me," Tim said. "I can't charge you in good conscience when you'll never get any useful work out of this horse. She'll just eat your feed and take up a stall."

"She'll help Claire. That makes her worth the room and board."

He caught Claire's little gesture of embarrassment from the corner of his eye and turned back to her. "Is Sharon trying to match you up with a whisper horse?"

"Oh, so you know about Sharon's theory," she said, looking relieved. Then her eyes lit with a gleam of mischief. "Do you have a whisper horse yourself?"

"Not yet," Sharon interjected.

He shook his head. "I figure the animals I treat have enough problems of their own without adding mine." Even his worst enemy didn't deserve to listen to what he'd have to say.

"At least there's no danger they'll post your true confessions on Facebook," Claire said.

"That's an advantage I hadn't considered," he admitted, his attention caught by the undercurrent of laughter in her tone.

"You two aren't taking this seriously," Sharon said. "Everyone needs someone to tell their troubles to, and horses have broad backs to help carry your burdens."

"I know, just whisper your worries into your horse's ear and they'll magically disappear," Claire said, throwing a smiling glance in Sharon's direction. "Is there a horse who knows all your secrets, Sharon?"

"I have a whole stable full of whisper horses," Sharon said with a grin as she unlatched the stall door. "Let's see what you think of Willow."

"Now?" A shadow of discomfort crossed Claire's face as her gaze cut toward him and back. "Isn't it supposed to be a private thing, just me and the horse?"

So the self-assured Claire Parker didn't want to meet her potential whisper horse in front of a stranger. Maybe she wasn't quite the skeptic she pretended to be.

Or maybe she was desperate for someone to talk to.

He didn't want to get tangled up with that kind of neediness again. "I'll look in on your pregnant mare and then come back to discuss Willow's diagnosis."

"Sounds like a plan," Sharon said.

Claire's brown eyes were warm with appreciation, and he was startled by the little flicker of heat they kindled in his gut.

"Thank you," she said. "I'm not sure what happens when one finds the right horse. It might not be pretty."

"There will be weeping and gnashing of teeth," he quoted.

With a chuckle, she bared her teeth and clicked them together a couple of times before slipping into the stall.

He was left to think about how the shape and color of her lips remained crystal clear in his memory.

Claire relinquished the veterinarian's company with a strange reluctance. His smile came slowly but held the same warmth as the afternoon sunshine. She found his solidity comforting; it would take a disaster of epic proportions to throw Dr. Tim off balance. However, his calm rationality seemed incompatible with whatever mystical connection she was supposed to make with Sharon's abused racehorse, so she was grateful for his tact in withdrawing.

As she stepped into the dimly lit stall, she laid her hand on the horse's flank to let the mare know she had company. Willow's brown coat was rough and prickly, her tail a mere stub. As she slipped her hand forward, Claire felt the sharp jut of the horse's hip bone. "She's awfully thin."

"Her owner neglected her after she pulled up lame in a race. Once we get her healthy, she'll be a beauty."

"I'll have to take your word about the beauty. Right now, she looks terrible, poor thing." As Claire gently smoothed the horse's brittle coat, pity and rage twisted together in her chest. "How could someone treat a living creature this way?"

"Yeah, I'd like to lock the bastard in a stall without any food and see how he liked that kind of treatment for himself."

Claire ran her fingers along Willow's neck. The mare stood with her head hanging down as though it was too heavy to lift. Claire knew that feeling; she'd felt that way after her divorce. "I think maybe Willow needs a whisper human. She doesn't look capable of taking on any more worries than her own."

It's not that Claire wasn't willing to discuss her problems, even with a horse, but she had never had much luck with counseling. Her high school guidance counselor had advised her to go to secretarial school when Claire asked for college scholarship forms. Her marriage counselor had been helpless in the face of the relationship's death throes. The divorce mediator had been unable to prevent her ex-husband from walking off with most of her small but precious art collection.

Now Sharon thought she should use a horse as a therapist. *Well, at least Willow wouldn't charge for her time.*

"Why don't you give her a treat?" Sharon suggested.

Claire had forgotten the baby carrots she'd shoved in her jeans pocket as she walked out of her rented house for her precious afternoon ride. Her life in New York City hadn't allowed for horseback riding, and now it was the one indulgence she permitted herself between work and helping out her sister.

Claire dug out one of the carrots and held it on her flattened palm. "Go ahead, sweet girl, just enjoy it."

Willow blew a moist breath against Claire's skin, but didn't take the treat.

"Do you think her teeth are bothering her, so she doesn't want to chew on something so crisp?" Claire asked.

"I'll ask Dr. Tim when he comes back."

"Does he have a last name?"

"It's Arbuckle, but no one calls him that. He took over Dr. Messer's practice about six months ago. I'm surprised you haven't heard all the talk around town about him."

"I guess I'm not part of the grapevine yet."

In fact, Claire hadn't gotten involved in Sanctuary's activities at all. When she found out her younger sister Holly had acute Lyme disease, Claire had come back to her old hometown to take care of her, hoping to mend their strained relationship at the same time. Despite all the time and energy she expended on both tasks, she wasn't much nearer her goal than when she'd arrived three weeks ago.

Claire wanted to know more about the veterinarian, but Sharon was interested in her relationship with the horse.

"Willow looks less tense now. You're doing her good. Now you have to let her take care of you in return."

As Claire scratched gently around the base of Willow's ears, the horse gave a deep sigh and leaned her head against Claire's midriff, making her stagger slightly. She felt a prickle of tears behind her eyes at this small sign of trust. If only she could get Holly to feel the same faith in her.

"Now look at Willow's eyes," Sharon said. "That's what will tell you."

Since the horse's head was still drooping, Claire dropped to one knee in the deep, fragrant straw. With what looked like a huge effort, Willow lifted her head slightly, and Claire saw her eyes: dark, liquid, with a plea in them.

Claire wanted nothing more than to pour words of comfort into the mare's heart and soul, to tell her she didn't need to have that look in her eyes ever again. Claire leaned her forehead against Willow's and squeezed her eyes shut against the tears threatening to roll down her cheeks.

She knew then what Sharon was talking about. This was her special horse, whether she needed Willow or Willow needed her.

Chapter 2

*D*R. TIM," SHARON SAID, TURNING AWAY FROM THE stall, "how's the expectant mom doing?"

As the vet's voice rumbled on about palpation and the chorionic vesicle, Claire swiped her sleeve across her eyes and quickly pushed up to her feet. "Okay, Willow, how do I explain to Dr. Tim that I believe in whisper horses now? He'll think I've lost my mind." She gave the mare a hug and walked to the stall door, cracking it open to slip out.

Tim stood with his head bent, listening to something Sharon was saying. A curve of auburn hair fell onto his forehead, and it looked so smooth and shiny Claire had an urge to brush her fingers through it.

"Let me get Claire's riding horse for her, and then we'll take a good long look at Willow together," Sharon said. She strode away from them before Claire could offer to come with her.

"How'd it go?" Tim said, sliding his hands into his jeans pockets. "Is Willow the one?"

"It may sound silly, but there was some kind of connection." Claire waited for a jibe, but he just nodded. She flashed him a wry smile. "However, she has her own problems to get over before she can handle mine, so I'm counting on you to fix her up."

"I'll do my best, but Sharon's the real miracle worker when it comes to horses. I've seen her save some I thought were hopeless." He contemplated the scuffed toes of his tan cowboy boots for a few moments before looking up. "I guess you have some pretty weighty problems."

Claire was taken aback by his directness, but the sympathy in his gray eyes disarmed her. She thought about her ugly divorce and her sister's ongoing reluctance to let Claire help her. "No more than most people. They just seem piled on top of each other right now."

"Well, I sure hope Willow can help you out."

"I thought you didn't believe in that."

"Oh, I never disagree with Sharon about horses. She's forgotten more about them than I'll ever know."

Claire found herself liking his modesty. "She's very picky about who handles her livestock, so she must think you're quite knowledgeable yourself."

The muffled thud of hooves and creak of leather announced Sharon's return.

"Salty here is your ride for today," Sharon said, running the stirrup down the leather so Claire could mount.

"He's really big." Claire eyed the gray gelding dubiously. He had to be over seventeen hands tall.

"I'll be happy to give you a leg up," Tim's voice rumbled from behind her.

"Thanks, but I can—" Claire gave up her protest as he bent and laced his fingers together at knee height.

The slanting sun laid a brushstroke of light across his face, making the dark gray of his eyes turn luminous and the surface of his skin look warm and tempting where it stretched over his jaw. It was all Claire could do not to lay her palm against the plane of his cheek to test its texture.

"You can handle him fine," Sharon said.

"What?" Claire was startled into a blush by what seemed like her friend's mind reading ability.

"Salty. He's strong, but he's got a mouth like silk."

"Oh. Right," she said, pulling herself together enough to grasp the reins and saddle before bending her knee into the cup of Tim's fingers.

"Ready?" he asked.

All she could manage was a nod.

Suddenly, she was hurtling upward as though she weighed no more than a cornhusk doll. She swung her free leg over the saddle as the vet halted her flight at just the right moment.

He wrapped his fingers around her calf and shifted her leg forward in order to check the security of the girth. The gesture was so automatic for anyone who rode that it steadied Claire. "Thanks for the leg up. It felt like I was being launched by NASA."

Tim looked up from his task. His height made Salty seem like an average-sized horse. "Sorry about the overkill. I just came from inoculating a several-hundred-pound sow, so my muscles are still in pig-wrestling mode. Not that you look anything like a sow."

"I can't tell you how relieved I am." Claire grinned. She shortened the reins to let Salty know she was ready to move.

The vet was still holding her knee and gave it a gentle squeeze. "Don't you worry about Willow. We'll make her strong enough to handle your troubles."

When the horse took a restless step sideways, and Tim let go, she felt it as a loss. The warmth and strength of his grip were strangely reassuring. With just his touch, he had convinced her that her whisper horse would be in good hands.

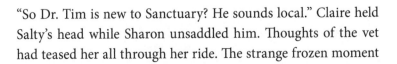

"So Dr. Tim is new to Sanctuary? He sounds local." Claire held Salty's head while Sharon unsaddled him. Thoughts of the vet had teased her all through her ride. The strange frozen moment while she waited to shake his hand and the feel of his fingers locked around her knee kept replaying in her mind.

"He grew up here, but he was so smart he finished high school early. I guess that's why you don't remember him. Anyway, he got scholarships to every college he applied to. I heard some schools even sent folks down here to beg him to study with them. Anyways, he's got more letters *after* his name than I have *in* mine."

Sharon's last name was Sydenstricker.

"With all those credentials, why would he come back to a little town like Sanctuary?" Claire asked.

"The usual. A broken heart."

Claire was surprised. For some reason, she had expected something less trite. "So who broke Dr. Tim's heart?"

"His wife."

A weird sense of disappointment jangled through Claire.

"Well, I guess she's not his wife anymore," Sharon corrected herself, "since she passed away a little over a year ago."

So the vet was mourning the love of his life. Whatever she thought had sparked between them must have been entirely in her own mind, given his recent tragedy.

"How sad for him," Claire said, "to lose his wife so young."

"She was a pretty famous actress too. Committed suicide right on an empty Broadway stage."

"You mean he was married to Anais Tremont? I remember hearing about her death on the news." Claire tried to imagine the emotional damage he must have sustained when his beautiful, talented wife killed herself. "It sounds to me like Dr. Tim needs a whisper horse more than anyone."

"Aunt Claire!" Kayleigh squealed, throwing her arms around Claire's thighs and squeezing.

Her enthusiastic greetings always sent a tingle of pleasure through Claire, especially since the eight-year-old had only recently warmed up to her city aunt.

"Hello, sweetie." Claire put down a grocery bag on the kitchen's russet Formica counter and bent to return the child's hug. "Where are your mom and sister?"

"Brianna's reading, as usual." The little girl rolled her eyes. "Mom's in the office on the computer. What are you fixing for dinner tonight? Can I help?"

"I'm counting on you." Claire opened the door of one of the pine cabinets and quickly stowed away a box of sugary cereal before Kayleigh spotted it. "It's a very gourmet menu—tortellini with butter and cheese, green beans amandine, and brownies with ice cream and hot fudge sauce."

"Yummy! Except for the beans." Kayleigh grimaced. "I'll stir."

"Let me just go say hi to your mom, and then we'll get going."

Kayleigh climbed onto a plastic step stool and began unloading the groceries, her long sun-streaked braid flicking back and forth across her back as she moved.

Claire took a deep breath and went in search of Holly. She hesitated a moment by the mantel that held her sister's Royal Doulton china figurines, one-half of the collection their mother had divided between Claire and Holly when she moved to Florida.

Claire traced her finger along the smooth, flowing folds of a pink ball gown. When they were young, Holly used to beg to play with the pretty ladies like they were dolls. Claire only wanted to examine the graceful turn of one figurine's neck or the subtle colorations of another's swirling cape. It was the beginning of her appreciation of art.

She felt a stab of guilt as she remembered her china ladies were packed up in a cardboard carton. Her ex-husband, Milo, had dismissed them as being without artistic merit, refusing to have the statuettes on display in their apartment.

"I should have put up a fight," she murmured, touching the arc of a hat brim. "These have lines just as beautiful as Milo's abstract sculptures."

She frowned as she noticed one of the figurines was missing. Maybe her sister had moved it to a different room.

Leaving the comforting familiarity of the statues with a sigh, she found Holly hunched over the old typing table that served as her computer desk, her face lit an eerie blue by the laptop's screen.

"Hey, sis! I thought I'd check on you before I start dinner." Claire closed the door before she leaned down to give Holly a peck on her pale cheek. It still shocked her to see the "pretty Parker sister," as Holly had always been known, with limp, matted curls and dark circles under her brown eyes. Despite a course of intravenous antibiotics, the Lyme disease refused to ease its grip on her. "Holding up all right?"

"I'm okay, thanks. Tired, as always." Holly pushed back the workstation chair and swiveled to face Claire. "Frank just e-mailed to say he's coming home tomorrow at lunchtime, so you don't have to come in the evening. He can fix dinner."

"I'm glad Frank will be home to see you and the girls," Claire said, although she was dubious about the meal. Holly's husband was a sales representative for heavy construction equipment, so he traveled extensively for work. Maybe it was guilt at leaving his sick wife alone so much, but he treated her illness as an inconvenience and rarely did more than order in pizza when he was home for the weekend. "Why don't I cook something extra tonight, and Frank can warm it up tomorrow?"

"I said Frank will make us dinner," Holly insisted with a sharp edge in her voice. Claire almost welcomed the little spurt of anger; it made her sister sound stronger. Then Holly seemed to deflate again as she said, "I'm sorry. I didn't mean to sound ungrateful."

"Hey, don't worry about it. I understand completely." Claire was pretty sure Frank would be thrilled not to have to prepare a meal. But she wasn't going to argue any further—she had a more important issue to raise. "I saw on the kitchen calendar that you have a doctor's appointment tomorrow. Why don't you let me drive you this time?"

"I canceled it. Frank's coming home early."

"O-kay." *Why couldn't Frank take his sick wife to the doctor?*

Holly's anger flashed again. "I can go to the doctor another day, and I want to see my husband. So don't make that big-sister-knows-best face at me."

Claire bit back the hurt rejoinder she wanted to blurt out. She remembered the days when she and Holly would joke about their husbands' little quirks and foibles. Now she had to walk on eggshells around the subject of Frank.

Ironically, Holly returned the favor by not bringing up Milo, just when Claire would have welcomed the chance to discuss her ex-husband with brutal honesty.

"I didn't know I was making a face" was all Claire said. "Can I bring you some tea before I start cooking?"

Holly looked up with tears in her eyes. "I didn't mean that. I just, I don't know…I'm so tired I can't think straight."

"And I'm worried about your health, so sometimes we see things differently. But we both have the same goal, and that's to get you better. So no more arguments or apologies."

As Holly looked down at her hands, Claire did a surreptitious scan of her sister's arms, relieved to find no fresh bruises. One of the disturbing symptoms of the Lyme disease was that it made Holly so tired she banged into things. Ugly, livid marks would appear on her arms and hands without her being aware she'd hurt herself.

"I met the new vet, Dr. Tim, today," Claire said, trying to defuse the tension with some local gossip. She even found a certain comfort in just saying the man's name. "Have you ever seen him? He's a big guy, but he makes you feel kind of safe, like nothing can hurt you when he's around."

"I've heard about him. You know Frank's allergic, so we can't have pets."

"He's taking care of a really sick horse at Sharon's stable." Claire debated whether to go into the whisper horse story with Holly and decided not to. Their relationship was tenuous enough as it was; if she thought Claire was crazy, it wouldn't help matters.

Holly took a deep breath and lifted her eyes to Claire's. "How much longer are you staying in Sanctuary?"

Claire blinked and took a step backward. The question seemed hostile, yet her sister's tone was neutral. Once again, Claire struggled to say the right thing. "I…I don't know. It depends on how you're feeling."

She thought of the new position waiting for her at the Thalman Art Gallery in New York City. Henry Thalman couldn't hold it for her indefinitely. She needed to give him an idea of when she would be back. Not to mention the flood of e-mails from friends and colleagues in the art world inviting her to various openings and exhibits. She hoped they wouldn't drop her from their lists since she kept declining.

As though she heard Claire's thoughts, Holly said, "I don't want to keep you from your life in New York."

"You're more important than anything there." Which was true up to a point. Milo had darkened that world for her. Even the gallery position, which should have been her dream job, was tainted by his scorn for her ability to recognize good art when she saw it.

Holly shook her head. "You worked awful hard to get where you wanted to be. You shouldn't stay here too long, or all that effort will go to waste."

Claire couldn't tell whether her sister said that in order to get rid of her or if she really meant it. She hadn't told Holly about the job because she didn't want her to feel pressured into pretending to feel better. Frank pushed his wife that way enough. "Nothing's going to waste. The Gallery at Sanctuary is a great place to work."

"Really?" Holly's skeptical glance said she didn't believe her.

"I've always loved matching people with the right art for them. The challenge is the same in Sanctuary as it is in New York." Of course, the budget here was one-tenth that of the gallery in New York.

"I guess that makes sense."

Claire watched her sister carefully as she braced herself and asked, "So, do you want me to stay here longer?"

Holly looked at the computer screen, then at her hands, then at the opposite wall. When she turned back to her sister, tears streaked her cheeks. "I don't know."

Chapter 3

$\mathcal{A}$S SHE STOOD IN THE GALLERY'S BACK ROOM THE NEXT morning, Claire continued her internal debate as to whether Holly wished she would leave or wanted her to stay. Shaking her head, she decided it didn't matter—she was staying until Holly was better.

That decision made, she brought her attention back to the painting displayed in front of her. It was by Kay Fogler, a new artist Davis was considering for an exhibit in the gallery. He had asked Claire to give him her opinion on whether the work was ready to show, but she kept putting off her answer. All the niggling doubts her ex-husband had planted in her mind undermined her ability to make a decision.

The buzzer announced that someone had entered the gallery, and Claire heaved a sigh of relief. Wiping her damp palms on her slim black linen skirt, she went out to greet her new customer.

Although the man had his back to her, she was sure it was Tim Arbuckle. Among the swirl of color and shape in the gallery's main showroom, the gravity of his presence drew her eye straight to him. He was standing in front of an expansive landscape by Len Boggs, one of the gallery's most popular artists. The vet had good taste.

As Claire walked up behind him, he turned and said, "Morning. I thought I'd stop by and give you an update on Willow."

"That's very kind, but you shouldn't have gone to the trouble." Claire halted several steps away so she didn't get a crick in her neck from looking up at him. Even in her sky-high pink suede pumps, she only came to his shoulder. She liked the sense of rootedness he projected, like a grand oak tree that could withstand any storm.

"No trouble. There was a parking space right in front of the gallery." He pushed his hands into his jeans pockets in a gesture she was beginning to recognize. "Your whisper horse is going to be okay, but you'll never be able to ride her. Her owner seems to have raced her while she was injured, because she's got some fractures that didn't heal properly. Then he quit feeding her."

Claire was shocked by the strange ragged sound issuing from her throat.

Somehow Tim appeared to understand and nodded as he said, "Willow's lucky Sharon rescued her when she did. She might not have survived too much longer. I've reported her owner to the racing association."

"Will they do anything to him?"

"They'll have to investigate, but it's probable he'll be banned from racing."

"I suppose I'll have to be satisfied with that, even though it doesn't seem nearly severe enough. He should be banned from ever coming near a horse again."

"You're right, but unfortunately, the law doesn't offer animals anywhere near the protection it should." He ran his hand through his hair in a gesture of frustration before a smile made the corners of his eyes crease. "It's nice to meet someone who cares so much."

Something about that smile touched off the tug of attraction she'd felt the day before. He seemed so comfortably uncomplicated, in his plaid shirt with the sleeves rolled up to expose the muscles of a man who routinely handled large, uncooperative animals.

She felt a yearning to run her fingers over the contours of his forearms and brush back the forelock that once again fell over his right eyebrow. Maybe it was just that he was the antithesis of Milo's smooth sophistication and effete slimness.

She firmly clasped her hands behind her and turned toward the Boggs landscape. "Do you enjoy Len Boggs's work? This is one of his new paintings."

"Actually, I'm partial to pictures of horses. I heard you have a Julia Castillo painting here, and I've been meaning to come by and take a look at it."

Surprise flicked at Claire. The man's speech was pure West Virginian until he spoke the artist's name, and then his pronunciation turned classically Spanish. Add to that the fact he knew Julia Castillo painted horses. She reminded herself that he had been married to a prominent stage actress; he must have rubbed shoulders with some of the artistic set.

"You're more than welcome to see it," she said, "but it isn't for sale."

"And here I thought this was an art gallery, not a museum." Tim's gaze swept the paintings spotlighted on the white walls of the gallery.

"The painting belongs to me," Claire said, "but I feel such a beautiful piece of art should be shared. You may not be aware of this, but Ms. Castillo has not produced any new work for well over a year. Therefore, we have none to sell."

And it was the only painting her ex had left her with in the divorce settlement, so she treasured it beyond its artistic merit.

Claire doubted Dr. Tim could afford a Castillo anyway. Since there was no new supply of paintings, the value of the existing ones had skyrocketed, another reason she kept hers at the gallery.

Davis had recently upgraded the security and fire prevention systems, so she didn't have to worry about theft or damage.

"The painting is this way," Claire said, starting toward the back of the gallery, where a windowless room with extra alarms held the most valuable inventory.

As Tim followed her down the hallway, she actually felt the floorboards vibrate as his feet hit the old oak planks. Never before had she been so aware of a man's presence through nothing more than his footsteps.

She glanced at her companion and caught him doing the same to her.

"So Sharon said you're from up north."

"Actually, I grew up about ten miles south of Sanctuary," she said.

"From your lack of accent, I'd say you'd moved away for some time, then," Tim said.

"You'd be correct." Refusing to be drawn into a discussion of her time in New York, she reached the door to the "Castillo room" and punched in the alarm code. "Are you a collector?"

"I like pictures of horses. I have a couple by Larry Wheeler, a very minor George Stubbs, as well as a few of Lionel Edwards's humorous drawings. I've never been a fan of Munnings, but I have one nice pencil sketch by Degas. I've always wanted to own a Castillo, though."

Claire kept her jaw from dropping, but she knew her eyes had gone wide. He had just punctured her unconsciously judgmental balloon with his list of well-known equine artists. He'd done it on purpose too, just as her ex-husband had in their fateful first meeting six years ago. Except Tim wasn't trying to snow her with his knowledge. With a mental shake, she gathered up her professional persona. "Perhaps I can help you. I have contacts with other collectors."

She swung the door open and gestured for the vet to precede her into the room, but he didn't move.

"After you, ma'am."

It still surprised her when the scruffiest of rednecks would hold a door for her or offer her a seat at the bar. She had been too young to receive such courtesies when she'd bolted from her home in the middle of nowhere right after high school. Yet Dr. Tim's courtly manners were just exaggerated enough to be touched with irony. He had caught her out in her inadvertent snobbery.

All irony dropped from him when he caught sight of the work of art hung in the place of honor. It was a large canvas with a group of five horses standing together in the middle of a land-scape of meadow, mountains, and sky. The vibrant colors were both softened and heightened by the slight haze of a low-slant-ing, late-day sun.

His eyes narrowed into a look of intense concentration, and she heard the intake of breath as the full impact of Castillo's gen-ius hit him. He took a few steps toward the painting, as though drawn by a magnetic force, then stood still.

Claire loved to watch people react to art. She could learn so much about them. This man understood what he was looking at. She could see it in his stance, at once respectful and attentive. She could tell by the way his mouth turned up in a smile of pure delight.

Finally, he let out a low whistle of appreciation and turned back to her. "This is one of her best."

Claire almost purred with gratification. "Thank you. I think so too."

"You can see the distinct personality of every horse in the herd," he said, gesturing toward the picture. "You can almost hear them talking to each other. And the light is extraordinary."

Claire nodded as pleasure at *his* pleasure washed through her.

"May I ask how you came to own it?"

"Pure luck," she said. "The artist's uncle Carlos Castillo brought four paintings to the gallery in New York where I was working. No one in the city art world had heard of Julia Castillo then, and Carlos was trying to expand her market. Luckily, I was the first person he showed the paintings to. I bought three of the paintings for the gallery without even consulting my boss. The fourth—this one—I bought for myself."

She didn't mention that her boss at the time was Milo and that he had hated the paintings, telling her they were trite and out of step with the gallery's vision. Of course, she had thought they shared a vision for the gallery.

She didn't argue with him, though. Bowing to his opinion, she offered three of the paintings to Henry Thalman and kept this one. Henry had sold all three within a week while his clients clamored for more. Milo accused her of all sorts of ugly things it still made her cringe to remember. In hindsight, that had been the beginning of the end for their marriage.

"You made a smart investment," Tim said.

Claire had to choke back a wry laugh before she could answer. "Not really. I simply *had* to have this. I knew I would never sell it."

"Never?" He gave her a slow smile.

She shook her head. "Never. Some things are too precious to let go."

Tim's gaze swung around to the painting. She'd seen the same look in the eyes of clients before. He wanted the Castillo for himself. He needed to lose himself in the artist's vision every day. She braced herself to courteously but firmly turn down whatever offer he was about to make.

"Hmm. Could we discuss it over dinner?" he said.

"Excuse me?" The invitation threw her completely off balance.

"Would you have dinner with me so we can talk about the painting?"

"I...er...I'm not sure. I mean, I hadn't thought about it." Claire was shocked when her first impulse was to say yes.

"I expect not, since I hadn't asked you yet."

"Thank you, but I can't accept," she said, pulling herself together. "I have no intention of selling the painting, so there's no point in discussing it."

"We can talk about other things." He was enjoying the fact that he'd flustered her.

"*What* other things?"

"The weather. The price of corn. The hat Mrs. Callison wore to church on Sunday." Tim gave her a disarming smile. "Why the person who discovered Julia Castillo works at an art gallery in Sanctuary, West Virginia."

That clinched Claire's decision. He would ask questions about her life in New York that she would have to find a polite way to avoid answering. "Most definitely not," she blurted out, then added with an apologetic smile, "I appreciate your invitation, of course."

"So you disapproved of Mrs. Callison's hat? Too many sunflowers?"

"Mrs. Callison's hat had tiger lilies on it, and I liked it. It made a statement."

"I had to deliver a foal, so I missed church last Sunday and only heard about the hat—from an unreliable source, evidently. I wouldn't have pegged you as a churchgoer."

"I sing in the choir."

His eyebrows rose. Finally, she'd been able to surprise *him*.

In fact, she wasn't a churchgoer, but Holly had been a stalwart in the choir for years. When she couldn't muster the strength to sing, she asked Claire to be her stand-in. How could Claire say no?

"A woman of many talents. Are you free Friday night?"

"A man of great persistence," she echoed.

"I learned young that when you want something, you keep after it. It works nine times out of ten."

"What is it you want—the painting or the date?"

"It seems to be a nice package deal, so both."

His eyes glinted with both humor and a challenge. Claire hadn't had this much fun flirting since…well, since she'd married Milo. Temptation slithered through her brain. Frank was always home on Friday nights, so Holly wouldn't want her there. She'd be all alone in the converted barn she rented.

"All right, I'm free Friday night, but there will be no false expectations. I'm not going to sell the Castillo to you."

"I'll pick you up at six thirty. You're renting Ms. Hauser's place, aren't you?"

"One thing about small towns—no one needs GPS." Claire rolled her eyes. "Where are we going?"

Since only four restaurants in Sanctuary didn't serve fast food, she would be familiar with whichever one he named.

"Not sure yet. I'll let you know if you give me your number." He pulled out a silver cell phone and typed in the digits she gave him. "No need to show me out."

She nodded. She wanted to spend a few moments alone with the Castillo anyway. She'd been looking at the man more than at the painting. "Thanks for stopping by to keep me posted about Willow. I'll see if I can locate another Castillo for sale before Friday."

A low chuckle rumbled in his chest. As he reached the door, he looked over his shoulder and said, "One other thing I learned young—never say never."

She waited for the sound and vibration of his footsteps to recede before attempting to engage with the painting. Shoving away thoughts of anything other than Julia Castillo's brushstrokes, Claire fought her way into the tranquil world of the artist's vision.

Just as she could almost hear the swish of horsehair and the buzz of lazy bees in the sunshine, the phone shrilled. Claire jumped and let out a startled "Oh!" before crossing the room to pick up the handset from the wall. The caller identification said it was Holly, and Claire's throat went tight. Her sister never called her on the business phone, only on her cell.

"Holly, are you okay? Are the kids all right?"

"No…I mean, yes, I'm fine, or I'm not hurt or anything. The kids are fine. I just…I just heard…I mean, Frank just…"

"Is Frank okay?" Holly's voice was so choked with tears that Claire could barely understand her.

"Yes…I mean, no, I hate him, but he's fine."

"What?"

"Frank just told me he wants a divorce."

Chapter 4

OUTSIDE THE GALLERY, TIM CLIMBED INTO HIS PICKUP truck. His vanity had gotten the better of him during his conversation with Claire. He could tell she thought he was a simple country horse doctor. Which shouldn't have bothered him, since he worked hard to project something close to that image. But it had, so he'd name-dropped his catalog of artists and invited her out to dinner just to show he was as sophisticated as she was. He shook his head at himself as he put the pickup truck in gear and eased the big vehicle out into what passed for traffic on Washington Street.

Last night, he'd dreamt about Anais for the first time in a month, and he was sure it was because of his encounter with Claire Parker. As he lay awake at two a.m., staring at the shifting shadows on his bedroom ceiling, he decided the only way to put Anais's specter back to rest was to face Claire again. He would prove to himself she was nothing like his dead wife.

So when he saw an empty parking space right in front of the art gallery, he'd followed up on his middle-of-the-night decision and pulled in.

His resolution had wavered as he stood waiting in the empty gallery. In fact, when he heard Claire's footsteps behind him, he had taken a deep breath and braced himself before turning.

But this time it had not been Anais standing in front of him.

Today he'd seen a woman with glossy dark hair that fell sleekly to her elbows and a serene oval face lit by deep-brown eyes. Her outfit was straight from the streets of East Side Manhattan, with heavy gold jewelry, an off-white silk blouse, black skirt, and bright-pink shoes with very high heels. All the city fashion didn't conceal the figure he had noticed yesterday, a figure with a lushness his wife would have considered professionally unacceptable.

He realized her voice, too, was different from Anais's. Now that he could listen without the overlay of a ghostly echo, he heard a whisper of the South in some of Claire's words. Yet her phrasing was clipped and northern.

What had made him react so strongly to her when they'd first met? He had encountered other dark-haired women since his wife died. None of them evoked nightmares.

To get to the bottom of the problem, he had done what worked for him as a scientist: he kept asking questions and making observations.

The request to look at the Castillo had started out as a way to keep probing. Then he'd seen the painting, and buying it became more than a ploy. He wanted it—no, he *coveted* it for the living room of the house he was building halfway up Flat Top Mountain.

As he pulled into his parking slot at the Sanctuary Veterinary Hospital, he realized he was looking forward to an evening with Claire Parker.

His receptionist, Estelle Wilson, greeted him at the back door with his white lab coat in her hand. "You're late, and you've got two emergencies on top of your regular appointments."

Estelle was a retired first-grade teacher who believed in punctuality. She also knew everyone and everything about Sanctuary, so she was an invaluable resource.

"Do you still have the private phone number for the Aerie?" Tim asked, washing his hands. "The one Adam Bosch gave me?"

Estelle threw him one of her gimlet stares. "Of course I do. He's the chef with the German shepherd. If you tell me when you want to eat there, I'll call for you."

"This is personal, not business."

"I've never been one of those folks who is too uppity to do an occasional personal chore for their boss."

Tim reflected that he'd never had any personal chores for her to do before this. "Well then, I'd appreciate it if you could get a reservation for two at seven this Friday."

"*This* Friday?" Estelle looked daunted.

"Adam said he'd get me a table anytime I wanted one."

"Yes, but even the rich people wait months to eat there. Still, you did save his dog's life."

A couple of hours later, he had worked his way through the patients lining the walls of his waiting room and was making follow-up calls.

Estelle poked her head into his office. "That Adam Bosch fellow really loves his dog. He swore it was no problem to get you in this Friday."

"You're a marvel," Tim said. He felt again that surprising lift of anticipation at the prospect of the dinner.

As Estelle left his office, Tim dialed Claire's cell phone. It went to voice mail, and his fizz of anticipation faded slightly. He'd wanted to hear her reaction to his choice of restaurant.

"Claire, this is Tim Arbuckle. I've got reservations at the Aerie for Friday night. Looking forward to seeing you then."

Tim hung up the phone and scooped up the keys to his pickup truck. It was time for his farm visits. As he walked up front to get the appointments from Estelle, she looked at him strangely.

"You're humming," she said. "I've never heard you hum before."

❖

Claire found Holly in Brianna's room, sitting on the bed with her shoulders hunched over, wearing a sheer pink baby-doll nightie. When her sister raised her head, Claire saw blotches of red on her skin and mascara smeared under her eyes.

Claire crossed the purple rug with the unicorns dancing on it and sat down beside her sister, turning to wrap her in a gentle hug. "Oh, Holly, sweetheart, I'm so sorry. I'm so very sorry."

"Frank told me to make sure we were alone today. I thought he wanted...well, you know." Holly fingered the filmy fabric brushing her thigh. "That's why I'm wearing this stupid nightgown. Instead, he wanted—"

An ugly moan tore out of her mouth, and Claire hugged her sister tighter. "Do you want to talk about it?" she asked softly. "You don't have to."

"No. Yes. I don't know. Oh God, what am I going to do?" Holly's sobs shook the bed they sat on.

"You're going to get through this tough time and come out stronger on the other side." Claire restrained herself from calling Frank all the names she wanted to. She'd learned the hard way that sometimes people changed their minds before a divorce was final. Then they remembered your unkind comments about their almost ex-spouses, which made things awkward.

"He actually looked disgusted when I walked out wearing this, like he hated the sight of me. He *gave* me this on our last anniversary. He said I looked like a Vegas showgirl in it, and it made him hot for me. Not anymore."

"You look fantastic in it," Claire said, remembering how insecure she felt when her marriage disintegrated. "Like a Victoria's Secret model."

"Not unless I was a foot taller."

"If you can joke about that, it proves you're going to make it through this."

Her sister gently shrugged out of Claire's embrace and sat up straight. "Maybe, but I don't know what to do now."

"Well, some people go to a marriage counselor to see if they can fix things." Claire had believed in that once.

"No," Holly said with a finality that surprised Claire. "There are things that…Well, it has to end."

Claire didn't push her to explain, but her sister suddenly slumped over again. "Frank says we have to sell the house. He needs the money to buy an airplane."

"What the hell does he need an airplane for?"

"He says he'll be able to cover more territory and make more money for alimony and child support. But I don't want to sell the house." Holly looked around her daughter's tiny room, decorated with brightly colored fantasy creatures. "I stenciled every one of these pictures on Brianna's walls. I did the ones in Kayleigh's room too. This is my family's *home*, and I made it, not Frank."

Claire remembered how excited Holly had been when she and Frank bought the brand-new ranch house, built in a subdivision that had once been a cornfield. It was small and looked like every other house on its treeless street, but Holly was thrilled that Brianna and Kayleigh would have their own rooms, a luxury Claire and Holly hadn't had. Almost as important had been the mantel where Holly could display the treasured Royal Doulton figurines.

"We'll figure something out," Claire said with sudden fierceness as she thought of her sister's carefully arranged china statuettes. "I promise you. We'll buy out his half of the house."

Claire's comment set Holly off again, and the day's events tumbled forth piecemeal between bouts of crying. It wasn't an unusual story, Claire thought grimly. His wife was ill, and Frank didn't have the guts or the decency to go through it with her.

Of course, what he'd said to Holly was they'd married too young, had children too young, and now he wanted some freedom to "be himself." Claire suspected he wanted to be himself with other women—and in fact, would bet he already had—but she didn't share the conviction with her sister.

According to Holly, Frank had made his speech and then bolted out of the house. She didn't know where he had gone.

Claire made sympathetic comments and let Holly cry. God knew she could empathize. The day Milo told her he wanted out of their marriage, Claire had felt like a mule had kicked her in the belly.

When Holly flopped back on the bed and announced she was wrung dry, Claire stood up. "Sweetie, go wash your face and put on a robe while I open a bottle of wine. If you're sure there's no hope of saving your marriage, we need to do some preemptive paperwork so you and the girls get everything you deserve. We're not going to let Frank waltz out of this marriage with more than his fair share."

Claire might as well use her hard-won experience to keep Holly away from the traps she'd fallen into. Her naïveté had allowed Milo to abscond with all of her paintings except the Castillo, and the only reason he hadn't taken that was because he thought it was junk. She hoped he was kicking himself now that it was worth more than all the others put together.

Claire persuaded Holly to let a neighbor pick up Brianna and Kayleigh at school and have them sleep over. Then she and Holly combed through all the papers in the family file cabinet. As they sorted through the bills, Holly was shocked by how much Frank spent.

"He always said we were saving as much money as we could, while he was buying iPods and netbooks and fancy cell phones I never saw," she said. "Did you notice this charge for clothes at Macy's in Detroit? No wonder he always looked so sharp. If I spent that kind of money on my clothes, I'd look a hell of a lot better too."

Claire kept quiet about her suspicion that not all of the items had been for Frank's personal use.

After they gathered as much information as they could, Claire refilled their wine glasses until they'd polished off the bottle.

Holly gulped down the last of the chardonnay and put her glass down on the kitchen table. When she spoke, her voice was so soft Claire had to lean in to hear her. "I'm sorry I never talked to you about it."

"About what?"

"Your divorce. When it was happening. I'm sorry."

"It wouldn't have changed anything." That was true, but she would have welcomed Holly's emotional support.

"Frank and I, well, we were having some problems even back then." She turned the glass around and around on its base without looking at Claire. "I felt guilty asking you about your marriage when I couldn't admit to what was happening in mine."

So Holly hadn't been uncaring; she had just had troubles of her own, troubles she wasn't prepared to share. Claire felt as though several tons of misery slid off her shoulders and splintered into tiny fragments at her feet.

She put her hand over Holly's to still the turning of the glass. "Don't worry about it, sweetie. I understand."

"Thank you," Holly said with a hiccupping sob. "Thank you for staying. Now I think I need to go to sleep."

A ripple of disappointment ran through Claire. She wanted to keep talking until all the constraints and barriers between them had been battered down. She sighed and stood up, bracing her sister when she staggered under the combination of emotional trauma, Lyme disease, and wine.

Tucking a nearly comatose Holly under the comforter, Claire's heart ached. She wished she could spare her sister the pain of having her world shattered by the divorce, but all she could do was help her through it. She smoothed the hair back from Holly's forehead as tears trickled down her cheeks. Her sister looked so small curled up all alone in the middle of the king-sized bed.

Chapter 5

"So, Sprocket, why hasn't she answered my voice mail?" Tim took a beer out of the sleek stainless steel refrigerator.

The miniature Doberman pinscher raced in circles around his feet, barking with excitement.

Tim looked down and shook his head. "A man of my size should have a Newfoundland or a Saint Bernard, not a crazed little ball of energy like you. It's not dignified."

When the injured Sprocket had been brought into the veterinary hospital by a distraught woman whose car had hit him when he ran in front of it, inquiries had brought forth no owner to claim him. Since the dog wore no collar and was undernourished, Tim assumed he had been abandoned. By the time Sprocket had healed enough to be adopted, he had become deeply attached to Tim.

He reached down and scooped up the little creature, letting him lick his face as he strolled to the newly delivered sofa in his freshly painted living room. The only other habitable rooms were the kitchen and the master suite. The rest of the house was still a construction site.

"She probably didn't play my message yet. She's a busy career woman, after all." Tim sat down and stretched his long legs out with a sigh of pleasure, while Sprocket curled up against his hip.

The sofa was positioned so he could gaze out the wall-sized picture window at the soft undulations of mountains rolling away into the distance, their hazy blue-greens darkening rapidly as the sun slid down the sky. These ancient mountains, their once sharp contours softened by eons of wind and water, helped him put his life into perspective.

He took a swig of beer and skimmed his hand over Sprocket's sleek skull as he considered how right it felt to be back here.

He had lived in New York for Anais, who had to be there for her stage career. He, on the other hand, could do his research almost anywhere. He had the financial resources to build and equip his own laboratory right here among the hills of West Virginia, if he wanted to.

Not that he had done any research since he'd come here. The veterinary hospital kept him busy. Which had been the point. It gave him less time to remember.

The surprise was how much he enjoyed the hands-on work of dealing with whatever creature, large or small, needed his help. Not to mention soothing their owners. Slowly but surely, he was being drawn back into the fabric of his hometown.

Now his carefully constructed refuge was being jarred by Claire's presence. She reminded him of the things he might miss about his old life in the city, like having someone recognize the names of the artists whose work he collected, all of which was in storage right now. He'd had fun surprising her with those, but it only worked because she understood what he was talking about.

Yet for all her big-city sophistication, she believed she could tell her troubles to a horse. Not just any horse, but a broken-down Thoroughbred she couldn't even ride. Tim finished the beer in one long swallow.

Maybe it would have helped Anais to have a whisper horse.

❖

The next morning, Claire woke up with the sense that something needed her attention. As she lay on the sofa bed in Holly's living room, she heard a tiny ping emanating from the handbag she'd tossed on the kitchen counter when she'd raced in the door the day before. She had a voice mail.

With a groan, she hauled herself up and retrieved the phone before collapsing back on the bed with it held to her ear. The thin mattress didn't quite cushion the wire coils, so she felt stiff and a little bruised.

Tim Arbuckle's deep voice thrummed through the receiver as his message played.

"The Aerie!" Claire said out loud, forgetting her aches. "He must really want my painting."

The Aerie was the most expensive restaurant in the area, the brainchild of a chef from Washington, DC, who fell in love with Sanctuary on a visit five years before. It was situated halfway up Two Creek Mountain and had its own helipad for the convenience of the ultrarich clientele who flew in from all over the country.

The town residents had resigned themselves to the constant buzz of chopper blades at mealtimes, mostly because the fly-in diners shopped in the local stores often enough to boost the economy. Claire had sold paintings to several of them herself.

She had never been to the Aerie and had always heard it was impossible to get reservations less than two months ahead of time.

She groaned again. She couldn't leave Holly alone while she went off and enjoyed a fabulous gourmet meal at a fancy restaurant. Every bite of food would taste of guilt.

Yet how could she cancel when Tim had somehow managed to do the impossible and get a table on such short notice? Had he spent money to bribe the maître d'?

As she tried to figure out how she could cancel the date without betraying Holly's secret, she replayed the message. Maybe it was because she was wiped out by the emotional wringer of her sister's disintegrating marriage, but Tim's voice was like his physical presence; it made her want to wrap herself in it, to ward off the troubles of the world.

She played the message a third time with her eyes closed and then resolutely hit the erase key. It was too early to call him back anyway.

It wasn't too early to call Sharon, though. Horses were early risers. "Hey, sorry to bother you in the middle of morning chores, but I need a good lawyer."

"That ratbag ex of yours isn't going after the horse painting, is he?"

"No, no, I need one for my sister. Frank wants a divorce, and I want to take Frank to the cleaners."

"Jesus H. Christ, what kind of a rotten bastard dumps his wife when she's seriously ill? I'll call Paul Taggart myself and tell him to leave Frank Snedegar with nothing more to his name than a pair of dirty boxer shorts."

"Paul Taggart?" Claire was surprised by the name of her old high school friend. "He's a good lawyer?"

"Can't think of a better one. He golfs with Judge Hardy."

"*A good lawyer knows the law...*" Claire started.

"*A great lawyer knows the judge,*" Sharon finished. "You know Paul?"

"I went to high school with him, and we played foosball at the Sportsman. He was smart and had great reflexes. Even back then, he knew everyone."

"I can't picture you playing foosball, especially not in such a dive."

"The entertainment possibilities in Sanctuary were limited in those days. We used to drive forty minutes just to go to McDonald's. By the way, don't mention this to anyone," Claire said. "I don't want Frank to start draining bank accounts or anything."

"You got it."

"How's Willow doing? I was so upset when Tim told me how badly she'd been abused."

"Willow's going to be just fine, don't you worry," Sharon said. "So when did you talk to Dr. Tim?"

"He stopped by the gallery to give me an update on her condition." Claire wanted to gloss over their encounter, so she kept talking. "Too bad Holly didn't marry someone like Dr. Tim. He wouldn't desert her when the going got rough."

"Yeah, although you have to wonder…"

"About what?"

"A man whose wife committed suicide."

"For all we know, she was clinically depressed and went off her meds."

"You're probably right. Dr. Tim sure seems solid." The volume of Sharon's voice ratcheted up to a level that made Claire jerk the phone away from her ear. "Hey, Lynnie, don't put Jojo in there! Sorry, I have to go."

Claire hit the *End* button and cradled the phone for a moment. Somehow she had put the whole tragedy of Tim's wife out of her mind. He seemed so normal, so straightforwardly who he was.

Dropping her phone on the bed, she got up and found Holly sitting at the kitchen table, drinking coffee out of a mug with *#1 Mom* in hot-pink letters. As Claire sat down across from her, Holly said, "I don't even remember going to bed. Thanks for getting me in my jammies. And everything else."

"That's what sisters are for," Claire said. "Remember it! And I'm taking you to the appointment I'm going to make with Paul Taggart to start the divorce."

"Okay. That would be good." Holly traced the writing on her mug with a fingertip. "After seeing all those bills yesterday, I realize I was stupid. Frank didn't spend all the money on himself, did he?"

"There's no way to know for sure," Claire said after hesitating a moment.

"You know the worst part? I still love him." Holly slopped coffee onto the polished pine of the table. "I've loved him since the moment he walked up to me at the bowling alley and asked me to dance. In a bowling alley! It was the most romantic thing anyone had ever done."

Claire came around the table to smooth Holly's uncombed hair. "Sweetie, there are lots of other romantic men in the world. You'll find one who dances in the bowling alley *and* sticks around when you need help the most."

Would Tim Arbuckle dance in a bowling alley? Claire shoved the question out of her mind.

Holly wiped her eyes. "If you don't mind, I'd like to leave soon so I can pick up the girls and take them to school myself. I need to see them for a little while."

"I'll call my boss and Paul's office while you're showering."

"Pick out anything you want from my closet," Holly said as she disappeared down the hall. "I think we still wear the same size."

The offer made Claire's throat tighten. In the way of sisters, they had argued about sharing clothes, but when the occasion was important, one always handed over the perfect dress to the other.

When Claire explained to her boss that she had a family emergency, Davis offered to open the gallery himself. "Take all the time you need," he said. "Family's important."

Her second call got them an appointment with Paul Taggart in a couple of hours.

Now Claire was staring at the selection of high-waisted mom jeans and floral-patterned knit tops that constituted Holly's wardrobe. She didn't want to insult her sister by preferring to wear the wrinkled, tear-stained clothes from yesterday, but Claire decided when Holly was strong enough, she was going to take her shopping. It was one of the things they used to love doing together.

Spotting a pair of black jeans squashed in the far corner, she pulled them out and rooted around for a solid-colored top, finally locating a simple white T-shirt with a slightly scooped neck. Not what she would have chosen for a first meeting with an attorney who was also an old friend, but it was Holly's divorce, after all, not hers.

"Did you find something?" Holly asked, coming in with a towel wrapped around her head. When Claire held up the jeans, an odd expression crossed her sister's face before she said, "I haven't worn those in a long time."

"Why not?"

"I don't know. Because moms don't wear tight black jeans."

"You're right. Black jeans just reek of sin and devil worship."

Holly looked startled and then began to giggle before she faked throwing her brush at Claire. As she ducked, Claire felt closer to her sister than she had in several years.

Chapter 6

"ELL, I'LL BE, IT *IS* MY CLAIRE PARKER." PAUL TAGGART was as tall and lean as she remembered him from their days as foosball partners at the local bar. "I heard you were back in town, but I didn't believe it."

Ignoring her outstretched hand, he drew her into a hug and then held her away from him, his long fingers gripping her arms with all the strength he'd developed spinning the game's rods. His familiar lightning-fast grin flashed white teeth against an olive complexion. "You look good," he said.

"You too, Paul. In fact, you haven't changed a bit." Seeing him sent her reeling back to the days of fake IDs and cheap beer. "You know, I always wondered how you finished at the foosball nationals."

"Eliminated in the quarterfinals," he said.

"Too bad. I was sure you'd go all the way."

"I thought so too, but those guys were good." He gave a rueful wink before turning to her sister. "Morning, Holly. I understand you need some legal assistance. Have a seat."

As Holly talked, Claire watched Paul. Sitting there in his tie and shirtsleeves with his suit jacket draped over the back of his chair, he looked confident and professional without being intimidating. The sharp angles of his face hadn't changed, but he had grown into them.

His office projected the same reassuring qualities. The golden oak desk was large but not overwhelming. Matching bookshelves held framed photos and knickknacks scattered among the thick legal tomes. None of the photos showed what might be a wife or children, which surprised Claire.

She'd occasionally wondered what Paul had done with his life. Seeing her high school friend well established professionally was satisfying, especially after the time she'd seen another schoolmate—one of the smartest boys in her class—bagging groceries at Kroger. The man had barely raised his head when she said hello. The incident reminded her of the reasons she'd done everything in her power to leave Sanctuary behind.

Claire forced her attention back to the process required for divorce in West Virginia. A few details were different from her New York experience, but most of it sounded depressingly familiar. However, her old school chum was handling Holly's questions and concerns with a gentle clarity that kept the ugliness to a minimum.

"Have you ever held a full-time job?" Paul was asking Holly. "Do you have any professional training?"

"Just waitressing at Joe's Drive-In. Frank and I got married before I finished college, and then Brianna came along."

"Frank has a good job, so that shouldn't be an issue," Paul said, but there was a line between his brows as he jotted something on his legal pad.

Claire remembered the statistics about the drop in the standard of living for divorced stay-at-home mothers. She thought of Holly's cozy little house and the unicorns dancing across Brianna's walls. She leaned forward. "Paul, I'm counting on that killer instinct that made you a nationally ranked foosball player to get the maximum child support and alimony for Holly. Frank's the one who's walking out, so he needs to suffer the consequences financially."

Paul sighed. "Unfortunately, the courts don't much care why a couple is divorcing. It's all about dividing up the assets equitably and making sure the children are reasonably well provided for. I'll do my best, though."

As they stood to leave, he came around in front of his desk and said, "Claire, can I talk with you privately?"

"I'll be right there, Holly." As soon as her sister closed the office door, Claire turned. "What is it? Is there a problem?"

"No, no, nothing like that." Paul drummed his fingers with machine-gun speed against his thigh, a nervous gesture she remembered from the old days. "It's just really good to see you, and I wondered if you'd like to have lunch one day this week. To catch up on things."

"That would be fun, but I need to be sure Holly's okay before I schedule anything."

"Of course. Let me know when you're free."

He seemed oddly constrained, but Claire put it down to the passage of so many years. Even though she felt as though they could pick up their easy friendship right where they'd left off, he might not. On an impulse, she rested her hands lightly on his shoulders and kissed him on the cheek. "I'm happy you're doing so well. I'm sorry we lost touch."

"I expected it. I knew after what happened to Mr. Van Zandt, you'd never look back."

Having Paul stir up painful old memories made Claire long for the comfort of Willow, but she didn't want to leave her sister alone. As she drove Holly through town, inspiration struck. "Let's grab some grilled-cheese sandwiches at Joe's and eat them at Healing Springs Stable, if you feel up to it. Maybe Sharon can find you a whisper horse too."

"A what?"

"I'll explain when we get there."

"Well, I was thinking of picking up the girls for lunch," Holly said, looking at her watch, "but all right. I wouldn't mind some french fries."

Twenty minutes later, they were sitting in Sharon's office, tearing into hot sandwiches that almost dripped butter and slurping extra-thick milk shakes through wide straws.

"Christ, I can feel my arteries clogging," Sharon said as she wadded up her greasy sandwich wrapper and tossed it in the tin trash can.

"But it's worth it," Claire said. "I used to dream of Joe's milk shakes when I was in New York."

"Sharon, what's a whisper horse?" Holly asked, pushing away the remaining half of her sandwich.

"I'll show you." Claire stood up and pulled Holly to her feet and toward the door. "Come on, sis. I have to warn you that Willow's not pretty. She was abused and starved by her former owner. But she has a kind spirit."

Holly had taken riding lessons for a year before she had decided she would rather play with smaller, less scary things, like dolls and puppies. Her tone was dubious when she said, "A horse with a kind spirit."

"It's in her eyes and the way she rested her head against me. You'll see."

When they arrived at the stall, it was empty, though. "Oh dear," Claire said, "where do you suppose she is?"

"If you're looking for Willow, Dr. Tim took her out for a stroll," a young woman lugging a hay bale down the aisle volunteered.

Claire's disappointment flipped to anticipation mixed with worry. Sharon hadn't mentioned Willow having any new problems, so hopefully the vet was just checking up on her.

She grimaced as she remembered that she needed to cancel their dinner date. However, she didn't want to do it in front of Holly, so she would put that unpleasant chore off until later.

Turning toward the barn's back door, she saw the silhouette of a man leading a horse, recognizing Tim by his long, steady stride.

"Is Willow all right?" she asked as he came closer.

"She's fine, all things considered." He pulled up the mare a few feet away and ran his hand down her neck. "I wanted to see if she showed any active pain when she was moving."

Claire watched his square hand glide soothingly over the horse's dull coat. "So how does she seem?" She stepped forward to greet her whisper horse. "Hey, girl. How's it going?"

Willow butted her head gently against Claire's chest, just as she'd done before.

"She's not in any pain, but she can't handle much more than a slow trot. Those old injuries give her trouble if she goes any faster."

"You poor girl! Do you think she misses being able to gallop?" she asked, looking up at Tim and feeling a little zing of awareness when she met his eyes. "Sharon says she's a Thoroughbred, so she's got speed in her genes."

"Well, right now, I'd guess she's happy just to be fed. Once she's stronger, she may have the luxury of wishing she could gallop again."

"That breaks my heart. We should all be able to do what we're meant to." Claire rested her forehead against the mare's. "I'll take you for lots of walks, sweet girl, I promise."

"Being cared about should more than make up for the loss of a gallop or two," Tim said.

She glanced up to find sadness in his eyes. What on earth had she said to make him look that way? Oh God, was it something about his wife?

Holly cleared her throat loudly.

"Oh goodness, I'm sorry," Claire said. "Holly, this is Dr. Tim Arbuckle. Tim, my sister, Holly Snedegar."

Holly hesitated a moment before she put her hand in Tim's. "I heard you'd come back to town and bought Dr. Messer's practice. My neighbor Janet Bostic says you took real good care of her cat Chuck."

"Glad to hear she was happy. Was that the calico who swallowed the squeaker from his cat toy?"

"Wow, you have a good memory!" Holly said.

"Well, to be honest, it stuck in my mind because it was kind of funny. Every time the poor cat moved, he set off the squeaker. Then he would spin around to see where the noise had come from, which made it squeak again. He was pretty exhausted by the time Mrs. Bostic brought him in."

Claire stifled a laugh. "Poor fellow. I assume the story had a happy ending."

"I'm only telling it because it had a happy ending. First, I removed the squeaker." The humorous gleam in his eyes winked out. "Then I contacted the toy's manufacturer and read them the riot act about putting such a small part in a cat toy."

"Did anyone seem to care?"

"Well, with a little persistence, I got transferred to the CEO, so at least he heard my complaint."

"I know you can be very persistent," Claire said, harking back to their conversation at the gallery.

She enjoyed the deep bass of his chuckle. Then she glanced at Holly and found her watching the two of them intently. Claire was embarrassed to realize that she'd almost forgotten her sister's presence. Tim seemed to fill her entire field of vision.

She looked back at Willow, only to see the vet's fingers absently combing through the horse's scraggly mane. His touch was so gentle it barely moved the loose skin at the crest of the mare's neck.

"Tim came into the gallery to inquire about buying the Castillo," Claire explained, both to distract herself and to include Holly in the conversation.

"It's a pretty picture," her sister said in a colorless tone.

"Definitely pretty," Tim said, "and it matches my sofa, so I'm planning to purchase it."

Holly looked startled. "Claire hates it when people say that about her art."

"I imagine so," Tim said.

"You're pulling my leg, aren't you?"

"You caught me," he said with a glinting smile that invited her to join his joke.

That won an answering smile from Holly. "Shame on you."

Claire was delighted to see her sister shed the dazed look she'd been wearing since the night before. Evidently, Dr. Tim hadn't become a vet because he couldn't deal with humans.

"I—" Tim began and then reached into his jeans pocket to pull out a cell phone. "Excuse me, my office is calling."

Claire signaled that she would take Willow. Tim nodded his thanks before he turned and walked away, holding the phone to his ear.

"Can I be honest?" Holly asked, her eyes tracking Tim as he moved away.

"About what?" Claire braced herself for a comment on the subject of Tim.

"This horse. She looks terrible. She's all skin and bones. What does it mean that she's your whisper horse?"

"It means I can whisper my troubles into her ear and she'll share them with me."

"Why would you pick her?"

"I didn't. She picked me." Claire turned Willow's head toward Holly. "Look at her eyes. After all that she's suffered, there's no meanness, no bitterness there. And she trusted me the first day she arrived. Me! I have no idea why."

"Horses have good instincts." Tim's deep voice startled her. She spun around to find her nose almost touching one of his shirt buttons. "Sorry, I didn't mean to surprise you. Generally, folks hear me coming," he said, moving toward the horse. "I've got an emergency call, so I'll say good-bye. See you Friday at six thirty."

He gave Willow a scratch behind the ears and, with a polite nod, strode off toward the opposite end of the barn.

"He's scary," Holly said as Tim vanished through the barn door. "And what did he mean about Friday?"

"Tim? Scary? Why would you say that?" Claire ignored her sister's question.

"Did you see his face when he was talking about the cat toy manufacturer? His eyes got all flinty, and his jaw muscles were twitching. You have to watch the quiet ones. They hold in a lot and then blow up. You don't want a boyfriend who goes ballistic."

"This is only the third time I've talked to him, so he's not even close to a boyfriend," Claire said. "Come on, Willow, let's put you in your stall."

As she swung the door open, she warned Holly to step back to avoid any new bruises. When the mare didn't immediately follow her, Claire tugged gently on the halter.

"She wants to know what the vet meant about Friday too," Holly said. "A whisper horse needs to know all your secrets."

"I'll explain it to her another time."

"No, you go ahead and talk to her. I'll wait in Sharon's office. It's nice and cool in there."

"Are you sure?" Claire was torn. She wanted to give Willow some attention, but her sister was her first priority.

Holly nodded. "It's nice to be out of the house, but I need to sit down for a minute or two. Go!" She flapped her hands at Claire and walked away.

"Thanks, Holl!" Claire led the mare into the stall. "Let me grab a brush and give you a little TLC."

She jogged to the tack room and back, picking up a brush and some soft horse treats. When she began to run the stiff bristles over the horse's scruffy coat, the mare gave a deep sigh and dropped her head, eyelids fluttering closed. "I guess you like this, girl," Claire said, feeling the horse's contentment seeping into her own body. The rhythmic motion freed her mind to wander, and it veered toward Tim Arbuckle.

"Guess what? Dr. Tim reported your rotten owner to the racing association. Let's hope the creep never sets foot in a stable again." That reminded her of Tim's story about Chuck the cat. "He yelled at a CEO about a cat toy too. You have to admire a man who goes to all that trouble to defend you and Chuck."

She worked the brush up behind Willow's ears, and the mare's head dipped even farther toward the ground as she gave a low grunt of pleasure. "You also have to like him for appreciating the Castillo so much he wants to buy it." Her pleasure at Tim's reaction seemed out of proportion, and she frowned. Was she thrilled because Dr. Tim collected horse art, giving his opinion the weight to counterbalance Milo's dismissal?

Willow reached around to nudge Claire's motionless elbow with her velvety nose. "Oh, sorry, girl, I got distracted," she said, resuming her sweep along the mare's neck. She glanced at her watch. "I really have to take my sister home."

She dug in her pocket for the treats, holding them out on her palm. Willow lipped them up and chewed contentedly. "Wonderful!" Claire said, wrapping her arms around the horse's neck and laying her face against her cheek. "You're feeling better. Dr. Tim said he'd take care of you, didn't he?"

She drew back and smiled into the depths of Willow's eyes. "Your vet seems to succeed in whatever he sets his mind to. Maybe I should worry about hanging on to my painting."

After returning the brush to the tack room, Claire found her sister reading *Blood Horse* in Sharon's office. "Are you taking up a new career in breeding racehorses?" Claire teased.

Holly's smile was faint, but it was a smile. "It has pretty pictures, and besides, there wasn't anything else to read in here."

"Sorry to leave you alone, but Willow thanks you for letting me brush her. She was so relaxed she nearly fell asleep."

"I hope the grooming made her look a little better too." As they walked toward the parking lot, Holly said, "So tell me about when Dr. Tim first came to the gallery."

Claire almost deflected the question, but then she remembered their heart-to-hearts about boys in the rhododendron thicket behind their house. Maybe some girl talk would bring her sister closer.

"He came in yesterday, and I showed him the Castillo."

"You told me the painting wasn't for sale, that you just exhibited it at the gallery."

"I told him that too, but he was, well, persistent." Claire took a deep breath and confessed, "He asked me out to dinner for Friday."

"I *knew* it!"

"Not what you think. He was trying to soften me up to get the painting."

"Uh-huh," Holly said in the tone of voice that meant she thought the opposite.

"Don't worry, I'm not going."

"He doesn't seem to know that."

Claire blew out a sigh. "Yeah, I need to tell him."

Holly leveled a look at her sister. "You're going to cancel because of me, aren't you?"

"I didn't want to go anyway. He surprised me, and I couldn't come up with a good excuse to say no."

Her sister fiddled with the hem of her floral shirt. "I don't want to stop you from going, but there are things about Dr. Tim you should know."

"You mean about his wife?"

Holly's gaze jerked upward. "You've already heard that she killed herself?"

Claire nodded.

"And you still want to go out with him?"

Anger tightened the muscles of Claire's jaw. "Yes."

"I think you should be real careful. You don't know what drove her to it."

"No, and neither do you."

Holly sighed. "Don't get all huffy. I'm just concerned."

Now Claire felt like a heel. "I know, but it seems wrong to pass judgment on someone without knowing all the facts."

"Do you like him?"

Like wasn't the right word. She was strongly aware of him. "Yes, and he cares a lot about Willow."

"Well, Lord knows I'm not the best judge of men," Holly said with another sigh. "Anyway, please don't cancel your dinner. I'd feel horrible knowing you'd missed out on it because of me."

"It's no big—"

"Go! The girls and I will watch Disney movies. It's our favorite Friday-night date."

Although she knew that was true, Claire was still torn when an idea struck her. "Will you and the girls help me pick out what to wear?"

Chapter 7

THE NEXT DAY, CLAIRE STOOD IN FRONT OF THE Castillo painting, letting the color and light and movement flood through her and wash away the ugliness of the last couple of days.

"Earth to Claire?"

She jumped and turned at the same time. "Paul! You scared the heck out of me."

"I called from the front gallery, but obviously you were farther away than just this room." He stood in the doorway of the secure room, a seersucker jacket hooked on his finger and slung over one shoulder. "What has you so fascinated?"

He strolled up to stand beside her, his lanky frame so similar and yet so different from the teenaged boy she remembered.

"This painting by Julia Castillo. Are you familiar with her work?"

He shook his head as he examined the painting. "It's nice. Very scenic. Could I afford it?"

"It's not for sale," she said, disappointed by his lukewarm appreciation of her treasure. "It belongs to me. Davis says it adds cachet to have it in his gallery. And frankly, it's gotten so valuable that I don't want to keep it in my house. There's a state-of-the-art alarm system here."

"So I couldn't afford it."

"I'd have to see your Form 1040 before I could answer that."

He grinned. "My accountant tells me I can afford lunch at Food and Folks. Join me?"

"I have an appointment in forty-five minutes," she said, glancing at her watch, "but that should give us enough time for a sandwich."

"If that's all you've got, we'll make it work," he said.

As they walked the four blocks to the restaurant, Claire felt a smile curve her lips as virtually everyone they passed said hello to her companion.

He deftly avoided being buttonholed by two older men, but made a little boy giggle by producing a quarter from behind the child's ear. She remembered that Paul had always been good at sleight of hand, hiring himself out as a magician at kids' parties to earn some extra cash. Some things hadn't changed.

The café's hostess knew Paul too and escorted them to a quiet corner table covered with a red-and-white-checked tablecloth.

"I think you should run for mayor," Claire said after they had placed their orders.

"Been there, done that."

"Seriously?"

"Two terms. It was good for business, but bad for my social life. Too many committee meetings at night." Paul was twirling a spoon through his fingers at lightning speed. "I know you weren't a big fan of Mayor Wickline, so you'll be happy to know I defeated him when he was running for his fifth consecutive term."

"Mayor Wickline," Claire said slowly. "I'd forgotten he became mayor."

The name sent her back to the high school classroom, where she watched the only person who understood her love for art packing up his belongings. As Mr. Van Zandt taped his last box closed, her art teacher had looked up at her and said, "This place destroys people like you and me. If you want to survive, get out of Sanctuary."

It took years before she found out why he had left so suddenly; George Wickline had been the cause.

"Claire? Do you want another glass of iced tea?"

"Oh, sorry!" She shook her head apologetically at the hovering waitress. "I got caught in a time warp for a minute there."

"My fault." Paul's smile was rueful. "I shouldn't have brought up such an unpleasant memory at our reunion lunch."

"Don't apologize. Sometimes it's useful to be reminded of harsh reality."

"Not today, though," Paul said. "This meal is about happy times."

Shaking off her dark mood, she pointed the conversation back to him. "I didn't see any family photos in your office. Why hasn't some smart woman snapped you up?"

The spoon ceased spinning. "I guess the women around here aren't that smart."

She was taken aback by the irritation in his voice. "I'm sorry, I shouldn't be so personal."

"No, no, it's fine," he said, but he looked away. "What about you? No smart men?"

"I was married briefly," she said, "and divorced at length."

"You should have hired me as your lawyer."

"Tell me about it! How does it look for Holly?"

"I can't really talk to you about it. Attorney-client confidentiality," he said with a regretful gesture. "However, I'm going to make it as painless as possible."

"For Holly. Make it agonizing for Frank."

He laughed, and the discussion turned to former high school classmates; Paul kept track of virtually everyone. Not all the histories were happy ones.

"Okay, I think you should run for *president*," she said. "The way you keep everyone's life stories straight is truly impressive. You'd be a natural campaigner."

"Actually, I've been approached about running for the state senate." The spoon was in motion again.

"Go for it. You'd be the best senator the state's ever had."

"I'd take that as a compliment if I didn't know so many senators personally."

Claire chuckled. "It's so great to see you again."

"Same here. I should have come to the gallery sooner."

"Why didn't you?"

The spoon went still. "The same reason you didn't come to my office."

Claire considered why she hadn't looked him up. "You mean because you were afraid we'd say hello and a long awkward pause would follow?"

"Yeah," Paul said with a half smile. "And because I was afraid New York would have changed you deep down, but you sure seem like the same Claire I knew way back when."

She traced a path around the checks of the tablecloth with her fingertip. There were aspects of her younger self she wanted back, and some she couldn't seem to shed.

"Claire?" Paul was slouching down in his chair in an effort to see her expression.

"I was wondering if I really am the same Claire," she said, looking up. "There's been an awful lot of water under various bridges in my life."

"You are." Paul's pale-silver eyes were locked on her. "You've got a lot of big-city polish with the sleeked-back ponytail and the mile-high heels—which I like a lot, by the way. But I see my old friend behind it all."

"If you say so." Claire caught sight of the time on Paul's big wristwatch. "Oh Lord, I have to get back to the gallery. I have a couple coming in to look at the Len Boggs exhibition. They flew in to have lunch at the Aerie first."

"They could buy three Boggs paintings with what lunch will cost them," Paul said, taking the check out of the air before the waitress could lay it on the table.

"You've still got the quickest hands in the East," Claire said as he waved away her offer of a twenty-dollar bill. "Do you ever play foosball anymore?"

"Only when I've had too much to drink. You?"

"Not since college."

"I challenge you to a match," he said, holding the door for her, "at the Sportsman Saturday night. Loser buys."

She hesitated. She still felt guilty about her Friday dinner date with Tim, but a late-night foosball game on Saturday wouldn't have the same freight, since Holly always crashed in bed by nine o'clock.

Glancing at Paul, she found anticipation blazing in his light eyes. She remembered that look, and suddenly, she wanted to feel the rubber grip of a foosball handle against her palm and the slide of cold beer down her throat. She grinned up at him. "Make it after nine, and you're on."

"Just like the old days."

"Except this time, I'm going to pound you into the bar floor."

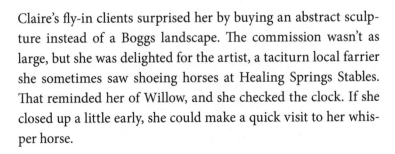

Claire's fly-in clients surprised her by buying an abstract sculpture instead of a Boggs landscape. The commission wasn't as large, but she was delighted for the artist, a taciturn local farrier she sometimes saw shoeing horses at Healing Springs Stables. That reminded her of Willow, and she checked the clock. If she closed up a little early, she could make a quick visit to her whisper horse.

Thirty minutes later, she slipped into Willow's stall, having changed only the sky-high heels Paul had commented on. The mare whinnied and abandoned the hay net she had been picking at, gently butting her head against Claire's chest and then rubbing it up and down.

"Hey, I'm glad to see you too, but this blouse is a Diane von Fürstenberg. Just because I got it on sale doesn't mean you can use it as a face rag," she said, laughing as she grabbed Willow's halter to hold her still. She dropped a kiss on the white star on the mare's forehead. "You've got more energy now, don't you, girl? And your ribs aren't quite as easy to count. Maybe Sharon's right. Maybe you will be a beauty."

Willow stamped a hoof, sending the earthy fragrance of the thick straw bedding swirling around the stall. "Mmm," Claire said, closing her eyes and pulling in a deep breath. "Warm, clean horse. Straw just out of the bale. Fresh-cut hay. It smells like home."

Her eyes flew open. No, that wasn't right. Sanctuary was *not* home; it was the place she had left behind for all kinds of good reasons. For the first time since she'd returned here, she was feeling the pull of her roots. This was Paul's doing; he had sucked her back into the past where she didn't want to be.

"Forward, I need to look forward," she said, combing her fingers through Willow's stubby mane. Which reminded her of her upcoming date with Tim. "I'm going to eat at the Aerie. It makes me feel guilty that I'm excited."

She lowered her voice to a murmur. "Truth is, I'm kind of excited about seeing Dr. Tim too. He's...well, intriguing." She thought of the strength that sent her hurtling onto Salty's back and the way his hand wrapped around her knee as he checked the girth. Her body set up a happy little hum at the thought that he might touch her again.

"It's just a little harmless flirting. He wants my painting; I get to have a gourmet meal with a nice guy."

Willow snorted.

"You don't think it's harmless?" Claire stroked the mare's nose. "You might have a point. My track record with men is not impressive. But this relationship has an ending date already. I'll be leaving Sanctuary, and Tim will be staying."

Willow shook her head, her ears flapping.

Claire knew the horse couldn't possibly understand her, but guilt still knotted in her chest. "You have lots of good people to take care of you besides me," she said, wrapping her arms around Willow's neck. "You don't really need me."

The truth of that twisted a strand of regret in with the guilt, and she turned her face into the horse's warm, solid neck, trying to erase the sense that she had failed yet another being she cared about.

Chapter 8

CLAIRE'S MOOD LIFTED AS HOLLY AND THE TWO LITTLE girls pulled clothes and shoes out of Claire's closet with abandon, oohing over some and giggling over others.

Holly had hesitated before accepting Claire's impulsive invitation to help her pick out an outfit, but now she seemed to have gotten into the spirit of the occasion. Her sister had always loved fashion, so Claire thought a little clothing consultation might distract her from her health and marital problems.

Even the usually quiet and studious Brianna had her small feet half-filling a pair of black pumps accented by purple patent leather heels. Claire draped a shimmering gold chiffon scarf around the little girl's head and shoulders, and Brianna's face lit up as she flapped her arms to turn the sheer, floating fabric into rippling wings.

"Okay, we have to get serious, girls," Holly announced. "Aunt Claire brought us here for a purpose. We are on a mission to choose the perfect outfit for her date."

Kayleigh slid a jeweled Lucite bangle onto her wrist, then looked at her mother with a puzzled expression. "I didn't think grown-ups went on dates. Or is it just because you and Papa are married that you don't?"

Claire's gaze flew to Holly's face. A stricken look darkened her sister's eyes, but she said, "No, it's just that I haven't felt well enough to do things at night since I got the Lyme disease. Papa and I used to go bowling on Saturday nights, but back then, you were in bed before we left home."

"Oh good, because I want to go on lots of dates," the little girl said, turning the bracelet so it sparkled, "especially if I get to wear pretty stuff like this."

Claire let out the breath she'd been holding. Unfortunately, Kayleigh's question had quenched all of Holly's animation.

"You know, it's nice to be in West Virginia where you can wear pretty colors," Claire said, steering everyone's attention back to the clothing.

Brianna looked at the garments strewn over the bed. "But your clothes are almost all black."

"That's because in New York you're required to wear black at least six days a week," Claire said.

"Really?" Kayleigh asked, wide-eyed.

"No, she's kidding," Brianna said. "I can tell by the way the corners of her mouth sort of tilt up. They always do that when she's joking."

"Wow!" Claire said. "I didn't know. Thank you for warning me."

"I like it," Brianna said. "It makes you look like an elf."

She felt absurdly pleased to seem otherworldly to a child. "Maybe I can grow points on my ears."

"Hey, back to your job!" Holly admonished them, her hands on her hips. "Now I'm going to work on Aunt Claire's hairdo."

"What?" Claire protested as Holly tugged her toward the slipper chair in front of the taffeta-skirted dressing table.

Claire had rented the former barn furnished, so the bedroom reflected the tastes of its owner—a retired poodle breeder—complete with a pale-pink canopied bed, rose-splashed wallpaper, and a dressing table with lighted mirrors fit for a Hollywood starlet. It was not appropriate for an ex-hayloft, but the little girls loved it.

"I can do my own hair."

Holly picked up a brush and made a sweeping gesture with it. "Silence! I control the Brush of Doom."

It seemed only Claire detected the forced tone in her sister's voice because Brianna and Kayleigh looked up from their task in surprise. "Mommy's bossing Aunt Claire around," Kayleigh stage-whispered.

"Your mommy has always been very bossy," Claire said, rolling her eyes to play into Holly's act. "I feel sorry for you guys, having to put up with her all the time."

"You're undermining my authority," their mother said, shaking the brush at Claire. "They'll never listen to me again."

The conversation deteriorated into a tickle fight, which left all four of them sprawled at various angles across the bed. Holly's wrist lay about six inches from Claire's nose, and she noticed a new bruise discoloring her sister's pale skin. The fresh evidence of Holly's Lyme disease hardened the lump of dismay in Claire's stomach.

"I hope Brianna and I have fun like this when we're old," Kayleigh said.

"You will, honey," Holly said, pushing off the bed. "It's a sister thing."

Longing speared through Claire. If only this lighthearted play wasn't all for the benefit of the little girls.

Claire busied herself with rehanging the items Holly and her daughters had rejected. Eavesdropping on the debate amongst the three made her smile and blink back tears at the same time. She remembered how wrenching her divorce had been, and she had no children to worry about shielding from the ugliness.

"Aunt Claire, your outfit's ready," Brianna called out. "Close your eyes and I'll lead you."

Claire braced herself as she let Brianna pull her to the foot of the bed. Opening her eyes, she relaxed. Except for a few more pieces of jewelry than she would ordinarily wear, the outfit was great.

"This is fantastic!" Claire turned to her sister. "You didn't tell me that we had two fashion mavens in the family."

"We like to cut out the clothes from *Vogue* and *Elle* and rearrange them so normal people could wear them," Holly said. "It's one of our games."

Claire turned back to the bed so Holly wouldn't see her tear-filled eyes. Laid out like a magazine display was a purple full-skirted dress fastened down the front with giant black buttons, the black-and-purple pumps Brianna had been wearing, and a narrow black belt to cinch the waist.

Kayleigh had added several slim black-and-gold bangles and gold hoop earrings with jet drops dangling from the bottoms. There was even a white scarf with black polka dots, which Claire was dubious about until she put the dress on and Holly wrapped the scarf over her head and around her neck. It was the perfect touch of whimsy.

After a session with the Brush of Doom, Holly declared Claire's ensemble complete.

"Wait!" Claire said. "You all deserve a reward for your outstanding work."

She scooped the gold chiffon scarf up off the bed and wrapped it around Brianna. "For your soaring imagination."

The glinting bangle was slipped back on Kayleigh's wrist. "To match your sparkling eyes."

She reached up on the closet shelf and took down a bright-red Kate Spade handbag Holly had been strutting in front of the mirror with earlier. "To hold the memory of tonight."

"I can't take this," Holly said, pushing the bag away. "I know what these cost."

"You know that credit card commercial about what everything costs until you get to the last item and it's priceless? Well, this evening has been priceless for me. When I see you carrying this bag, it will remind me of it."

"I shouldn't, but thank you," Holly whispered, cradling the leather bag as though it were spun glass.

Claire hadn't given away anything that mattered to her, yet the three recipients looked at their gifts as if they were made of solid gold.

"Girls, why don't you go downstairs and watch the Disney Channel?" Holly said abruptly. "I'm going to help Aunt Claire straighten up here."

"Yay! Maybe *Wizards of Waverly Place* is on," Kayleigh cheered as she and her sister dashed for the door. Holly limited their television watching, so this was a rare treat.

"You sit right down and watch me clean up," Claire said. "I know you're exhausted. And I notice you have another bruise. I wish you'd take it easier."

Holly crossed her arms so the bruise was hidden. "It doesn't hurt."

"Well, that's good. Now sit and rest."

Holly dropped onto the dressing table's chair without further argument. "I wasn't sure whether I should tell you this, but I decided you should know."

Her sister's tone was so serious that Claire put down the belt she'd been rolling up. "What is it? What's wrong?"

"I looked up Anais Tremont online. There were a whole bunch of news stories, but none of them answered the most important question."

"Which is?"

"Why she did it. There was a suicide note, but it was never released to the press. Dr. Tim refused to comment. Ever."

"Who could blame him?" Claire said. "Imagine what he was going through! His gorgeous, talented wife blew her brains out in an empty theater. Why would he want to talk about that, especially to a bunch of reporters?"

"Yeah, but you can't help wondering."

Claire would never admit it, but Holly was right. She did wonder what could have driven Anais Tremont to such despair that her only option was death.

Chapter 9

CLAIRE HAD FORGOTTEN THE POTENT THRILL OF NERVES and anticipation a first date could deliver. When the doorbell rang, she dropped the black leather clutch into which she was tucking her cell phone and lipstick.

"Get a grip!" she said as she knelt to scrape everything back into the purse's narrow opening. When her hasty sweep sent the lipstick rolling under the couch, she muttered a curse and then shouted, "Come in! It's open."

She was half-kneeling, half-lying on the braided rug with her arm extended under the sofa when Tim's amused voice said, "May I help?" and the heavy piece of furniture tilted onto its back legs.

She grabbed the errant plastic tube and sat up, shoving the lipstick into the clutch lying beside her on the floor. "Got it! You're a handy man to have around."

His chuckle came from behind her as the sofa was lowered gently back into its normal position. "Was it something very valuable?"

"It's Rarer than Ruby," Claire said, pulling her full skirt out from under her knees and bracing her other elbow on the cushion to push herself up.

She felt his hands come around her to grip her waist, pressing against the belt Kayleigh had picked out. Then she was weightless, soaring upward like a ballerina in her partner's arms. Startled, she grabbed for an anchor and found his wrists, her fingers wrapping around what felt like warm girders of muscle and bone.

"What's rarer than a ruby? A blue diamond?"

She wobbled as he set her down on her purple heels, and his grip tightened slightly. Her fingers were still locked on his wrists.

"A what?" Claire was too caught up in the experience to grasp what he was talking about.

When she was steady on her feet, he turned her to face him by reaching around to take her opposite hand in his and gently pulling it, like a continuation of their balletic pas de deux.

"What were you so determined to retrieve from under the couch?"

Her spin brought her around to eye level with his chest. He was wearing deep-blue woven silk, not plaid flannel. The silk was framed by the lapels of a pale-gray blazer. She raised her gaze higher, scanning up the strong column of his throat, to find his eyes glinting with a hint of mischief, while the corners of his mouth turned slightly upward.

"My lipstick. The color is Rarer than Ruby."

He tilted her chin up farther with a nudge of his finger and considered her mouth. "Mmm. I like it."

She couldn't help it. She licked her lips, an involuntary reflex.

The glint and the smile disappeared, and in their place was a look she'd never seen nor expected from Tim. It was as though a huge lens were pulling all the light from the sky and focusing it on one thing—her mouth. She could almost feel the heat, and it shocked her. She had thought of him as big, slow, and safe, but right now, he seemed coiled and ready to spring.

She waved the lipstick tube around to distract him and said, "Maybe I'll let you borrow it for our next date."

Now why had she said that about another date? She let out her breath as his eyes lost their laser intensity.

"I don't think it would work with my skin tone," he said.

Her laugh was hearty with relief. "Nor your muscle tone."

"Thank God!"

"Let me grab my wrap, and I'm ready." If she didn't fumble her purse again.

As they walked out the front door, he took her elbow in his warm, enveloping grasp. She had always thought of herself as an independent woman who didn't need a man's support. Yet she found herself savoring these little demonstrations of Tim's physical strength. It made her feel…cherished. It was an old-fashioned word, but Tim seemed a bit of a throwback to her, like a knight protecting those weaker than he was, whether they were abused horses or cats named Chuck.

"Oh," she said, doing a little stutter step when she saw the car on the gravel driveway. A dark-green Range Rover, shining as though newly waxed, stood where she had expected a pickup truck. "Nice car."

"It's big and useful."

Like you, she almost said.

"I really wanted a Porsche," he said, "but I got leg cramps during the test drive."

Claire's laugh was pure amusement as she pictured Tim levering his substantial frame into the tiny interior of the sports car. "I think you'd have to get one custom built."

"Now why didn't I think of that?"

She was surprised to see his eyes light up with serious intent. He truly *did* want a Porsche. She realized that being so large imposed limitations she had never considered. Flying coach must be sheer torture for him.

He walked her around the car and opened the door for her, giving her a little boost up onto the high step. When he carefully tucked the voluminous folds of her skirt out of range of the doorframe, her delight at the gesture put extra warmth into her thanks.

He responded with one of his slow, safe smiles before he closed the door.

As he came around the car, she settled herself in the capacious leather seat and traced the elegant woodwork while admiring the fancy sound system. This was a high-end model—and a new one. Maybe Tim *could* afford the Castillo. Not that she was selling it.

The other door opened, and Tim slid into the driver's seat without bothering to use the car's running board. He started the engine before reaching into his jacket pocket and sliding a pair of tortoiseshell glasses onto his nose.

"I've never seen you in glasses before," Claire said.

"Just for driving. Too much staring at the computer screen, according to my ophthalmologist," he said, turning to give her a rueful look.

"They suit you." The transformation was striking. Between the tailored clothes and the stylishly intellectual glasses, he looked like a man with lots of initials after his name. Even his unruly forelock seemed to fall onto his forehead in a more restrained fashion. She still had an urge to brush it back, but his altered appearance and the intense moment by her couch had pushed the intimidation factor up several notches. Her impulse to touch him was easier to squelch.

"You're not really a simple country vet, are you?" she said as he put the big SUV into gear. "I mean, look at these speakers! They probably cost more than my entire car did."

Tim slowed down so he could look over at his passenger. Her brown eyes were smiling, so he decided she wasn't criticizing him.

"What about you?" he asked. "You look like you're from the big city, but you have that little touch of country in your voice. There are some hidden layers there too."

"I thought I'd lost my accent," she said. "Everyone here says I sound like 'one of those uppity New Yorkers.'"

"They aren't paying as much attention as I am."

He saw her look down at her hands where they clutched her purse amidst the billows of purple skirt and realized he'd made her nervous for the second time tonight.

The first time had been when she'd licked her lips. As a scientist, he knew it was an unconscious response triggered by his half-joking scrutiny, but as a man, it had made him want to follow her tongue with his own. He'd seen the flicker of hesitation in her eyes and tamped down his reaction. He had learned that his physical size sometimes made his mental sharpness overwhelming to people. He'd have to be more careful, or Claire would run right away.

"That's a real pretty dress," he said to defuse the tension. He didn't know much about clothes, but he knew this outfit was different from her usual sleek, sophisticated gallery attire. It reminded him of glamorous old movie stars. He liked the softness and grace of it.

Anais had been a chameleon, changing her persona daily even when she wasn't onstage. She would transform everything: her gestures, her posture, her speech patterns. He was never sure who he would wake up with every morning.

He was reassured that Claire still moved and sounded like herself.

"Thank you. My nieces helped me pick it out," she said, fiddling with one large black button. "That reminds me—Holly was curious about how you got reservations at the Aerie on such short notice. You said you called in a favor?"

"The chef has a German shepherd who tangled with a bear last year. I sewed up a few gashes, and he told me to call anytime I wanted to eat there."

The dog was nearly dead when chef Adam Bosch had carried him into Tim's office with tears streaming down his face. Tim had worked on the bloodied creature for three hours before he was sure the dog would pull through. Bosch had sent him a case of Opus One wine and an open invitation to dine at the Aerie anytime he wanted to.

This was the first time Tim had taken him up on the offer.

"I guess being the local vet has its advantages," she said. "It's sort of like the town doctor. People are grateful to you for taking care of their loved ones."

"It's better than being the town doctor because people don't have to be embarrassed that I've seen them without their clothes on," he said.

"Oh yes, as a teenager, I always blushed when Dr. Wiley said hello to me anywhere outside of his office."

"My patients, on the other hand, greet me with big, sloppy kisses."

Her laugh was silvery, a contrast to the slight throatiness of her speaking voice. He was emboldened to shift to a more significant topic. "Since I can't have the Castillo, you're going to have to find me something just as good for my new house. When I chose a building site with a great view, I set up a problem for myself."

"Competition?"

"In a nutshell."

"That happens a lot in Manhattan apartments. The spectacular views of the cityscape make mediocre art hanging near them look even worse. Here most people find Len Boggs's work a complement to the scenery."

"Don't get me wrong, I think the fellow's got plenty of talent, but I'm a scientist, and his style is a little too impressionistic for me."

"Hmm, I can think of a couple of possibilities that I can pull out the next time you're in the gallery. So where is your great view?"

"Near the summit of Flat Top Mountain. The house is still under construction, but there's enough finished so I can live there."

"Doesn't the noise and mess drive you crazy?"

"I'm not there during the day, and at night, it's quiet. I like coming home to my own place and seeing the mountain ridges stretching out to the horizon. It makes my troubles feel smaller."

He hadn't meant to say that.

"Sharon says that's why they call it Sanctuary," Claire said. "People come here to take refuge from their troubles."

"And the folks who already live here, what do they do?"

"I guess they tell their troubles to one of Sharon's whisper horses," she said, her skirt rustling as she shifted in the seat.

A faint scent of citrus and rose tantalized his nostrils. Tim took a deep breath, savoring the clean floral fragrance.

"It felt good to come back here," he said. "Like wading into a cool mountain stream after being hot and sweaty and chewed up by horseflies."

"Not for me," she murmured, turning away to stare out her window.

"What did it feel like to you?"

Dozens of trees flashed past before she said, "An admission of failure."

He understood that she had admitted something to him she didn't let on to many people, so he thought for a moment before speaking. "I don't see it that way."

"I'm sorry. I don't know why I said that," she said, touching his sleeve in a feather-light gesture of apology. "Home doesn't mean that to most people."

"I'm not offended. I'm interested. You held a trusted position at a big art gallery in New York City. You came here to help out your sister when she became ill. Where's the failure in that?"

"Didn't you work very hard to get into college? Didn't you think that, once you left Sanctuary, you would never come back? Didn't you believe that you really didn't belong here?" Her voice grew more passionate with each question.

"Yes, but I see things differently now. I have different resources to draw on."

"I guess I don't. As soon as Holly is on the mend, I'll be heading back to the bright lights."

He was surprised at the stab of regret he felt. Claire intrigued him. He liked the New York edge softened by her mountain twang. She was smart and sophisticated, but grounded in ways most of his wife's friends in the city hadn't been.

"I have a dream job waiting for me there," she continued, "opening a new branch gallery for Henry Thalman."

"No wonder you want to get back. He's top of the heap in art dealers." He considered how powerful the lure of that position would be to someone in Claire's field. She wouldn't linger in Sanctuary with that prospect in her future. He slowed down to negotiate an especially sharp turn and changed the subject again. "How's your sister doing?"

"She still has a lot of joint pain, and she gets exhausted very quickly. The doctor says it may take a year to get back to normal. I guess you know that Lyme disease is hard to diagnose, so she didn't start on antibiotics until it was pretty advanced." She seemed about to say something more, so he waited. Then she gave a tiny shake of her head and remained silent.

A sign indicating the turn to the Aerie flashed white in the dusk, and he steered the big car onto the narrow road. A muffled trill of electronic notes sounded from Claire's purse.

"I'm so sorry," she said, digging out a cell phone. "I leave this on in case Holly needs me."

The number on the phone's screen had her pushing the *Answer* button immediately. "It's Holly. She wouldn't call if it weren't urgent. Hello?"

It wasn't Holly; it was Brianna, whispering. "Aunt Claire? I'm scared Papa's going to hurt Mama. He's yelling at her, and I just heard a noise like glass breaking."

For a moment, Claire couldn't grasp what the little girl was talking about. "Brianna, sweetie, where are you?"

"In Mama's bedroom. She told us to come here after Papa came in. Now they're in the kitchen, but I can hear them. I'm afraid he's going to hit her again."

"He hit her?" She was still trying to comprehend what Brianna was telling her.

"Not yet, I don't think. It was another time when they had a fight."

Suddenly, the bruises Holly blamed on Lyme disease took on a horribly different significance. Claire shook her head to clear the panic that threatened to cloud her thinking.

"Brianna, I want you to take Kayleigh and go to that little secret storage space in your closet. Be very quiet when you go down the hall, and take the phone with you. Tell me when you've gotten there safely."

"Okay."

Claire was concentrating so hard on what she was hearing through the phone that she had forgotten she was in a car until it swerved sharply. She looked up to see that Tim had reached a slightly wider spot in the road and was turning the big vehicle around as quickly as he could in the limited space. She threw him a grateful glance.

"Brianna, are you there, sweetie? I just wanted to let you know that I'm on my way over there. Everything will be all right."

Claire winced as the muffled sound of a man shouting came through the receiver. She braced herself against the door as Tim took the mountain road's sharp turns at a significantly higher speed than he had during their leisurely ascent. He must have figured out the urgency of the situation from her side of the conversation.

"Okay, Aunt Claire, we're in the closet," Brianna whispered. "Mama and Papa didn't notice us."

"You did really well, sweetie. You're a very smart, brave girl. I have to hang up for a few minutes so I can get there faster. If you get scared or something else happens, call me back. I'll be there very soon."

"All right, but hurry. I don't want Papa to hurt Mama."

"Oh God!" Claire said, dropping her head in her hands for a brief moment after she disconnected. Holly's situation was so much worse than she had ever dreamed. The car banked hard left, and she grabbed for the Jesus handle, saying, "Thank you for turning around so quickly."

"No problem," Tim said as he finished manhandling the SUV through an S curve. "Where are we headed once we get off the mountain?"

"Rolling Meadows. The new development. Holly's on Cornsilk Lane. We need to get there fast. Evidently, Frank has hit Holly before, and Brianna is afraid it's going to happen again. He's shouting and throwing things."

"I know a shortcut there, but it's going to be bumpy."

"As long as your car will survive, I'm good with that. Should I call the police? Oh God, Holly will hate me for dragging them into her private affairs."

"Did Brianna say anything about Frank having a gun?"

"No, and I know my sister made him get rid of his hunting rifles when Brianna was born."

"Then I think I can handle him, if you're afraid it would upset your sister to have the police involved."

Claire looked over at her companion. His gaze was locked on the road unspooling crazily back and forth in front of them. His hands seemed to envelop the steering wheel, holding the heavy SUV steady as they raced down the mountain.

Even in the roomy interior, Tim took up a lot of space. "You can certainly handle him, but the police might get there faster."

"We'll be there in under ten minutes. Hold on," he said, wrenching the car off the asphalt and onto an old dirt logging road.

Claire's teeth snapped together as they hit the first bump, so she remained silent until they made it to the blessed smoothness of pavement again.

"Just so you know, Frank asked Holly for a divorce two days ago," she said as Tim turned into Rolling Meadows. "She hired Paul Taggart to represent her. I don't know what Frank would be upset about, since it was his idea to split up."

"The man's wife is seriously ill and he can't hold off on the divorce until she's healthy? What a bastard! Which house?"

"Third one on the right."

Tim was opening his door before the car had stopped rolling. Claire kicked off her high heels and followed him at a run up the front walk. He gestured her to stop as they reached the front door. He turned the knob gently and cracked the door open so they could get an idea of what was happening inside.

Holly's voice came through the opening with horrifying clarity. "Please, Frank, no! *Please* put her down!"

Chapter 10

CLAIRE BOLTED INTO THE HOUSE, IGNORING TIM'S PROtest. All she could think of was that Frank was threatening one of his daughters.

She skidded on the polished marble tiles in the tiny entryway and felt Tim's steadying hand on her back, but she wasn't stopping. She burst into the living room to find Frank standing by the fireplace, brandishing one of the Royal Doulton figurines. Her knees nearly buckled with relief when she realized Holly was pleading for the china, not a child.

"What the hell are you doing here?" Frank demanded, lowering his arm and staring blearily at Claire. "You weren't supposed to be here tonight. Holly told me you wouldn't be. She lied to me again, that slut!"

"I'm just here to help out while she's sick," Claire said, inching toward where her sister cowered in an overstuffed armchair.

"Why the fuck didn't you stay in New York with your stuckup husband and all your stuck-up friends? I told Holly not to let you come here, but she didn't listen to me. We don't need you messing up our lives."

He seemed to have forgotten that he was messing up his own life. He also seemed to have forgotten the china lady in his hand, much to Claire's relief.

"I'm not trying to mess up anything," she said calmly.

"The hell you aren't, you damned bitch." He staggered before bracing his legs wide apart. "I come home to see my children, and my wife tells me she's already been to a lawyer. Have you fucked him yet, you whore?" he snarled, turning to address his wife. Moving his head upset his balance again, and he grabbed at the mantel with his free hand. "Then she accuses me of having a girlfriend. You ungrateful bitch, I work my ass off to put a roof over your head and food on the table, so I deserve some appreciation every now and then. I can't get it from you, that's for sure."

"That's enough of that kind of talk," Tim said in a firm voice Claire suspected he used to deal with difficult pet owners.

"What? Who the fuck are you?" Frank asked, swaying as he turned toward Tim. "It's a goddamned party here, ain't it? Did you come to screw my wife too? Or are you screwing the New York bitch?" Frank's face contorted into an ugly leer. "Or both of them together? Wait, you're the one whose wife shot herself. You must be a real bastard to drive a woman to that."

Claire flinched and looked at Tim. His expression didn't waver, nor did his slow but steady progress toward Holly's drunken husband.

Claire took advantage of Tim's diversion to scoot over to Holly. Her sister had one hand cupped around her left cheek, and tears streaked what Claire could see of her face.

"Frank, why don't you and I take this outside?" Tim said.

"Do you think I'm crazy?" Frank said. "You're a goddamned giant. You stay away from me, or I'll break this whore's ugly statue." He turned it upside down and squinted at the bottom. "Lauren, that's its name. My wife loves this thing more than me. Don't you, sweetheart?"

"No, Frank. I've always loved you." Holly's voice quavered, but she didn't stop talking. "I've never looked at another man. You know that."

"Liar!" Frank screamed, raising his arm and hurling the figurine straight at Holly and Claire.

Claire tried to push Holly out of the way, but her sister resisted, lifting her hands to catch the flying statue. It bounced off her fingers and struck Claire on the cheek before hitting the wall and shattering into pieces.

Claire bit off a cry that was as much shock as pain, and Holly shrieked, "Oh my God, no!"

"I'm okay," Claire whispered to her sister, hoping not to provoke Frank further.

"I think it's time for you to leave," Tim said. His voice had swelled in volume and held an undertone of menace.

Frank seemed abashed by the havoc he had wreaked. He stood with his mouth slightly open, still braced against the fireplace.

Tim took another step toward him.

"You can't throw me out of my own house," Frank said, straightening and pushing away from the mantel.

Fear flooded through Claire as she saw him glance at the rack of fireplace tools. She willed him not to pick one up and go after Tim.

"I wouldn't bet on that," Tim said, dragging Frank's attention away from the potential weapons.

Claire watched in fascination as Tim transformed into an aggressor. He shifted his feet into a wide fighting stance, his hands curled into fists, and his head came forward. He looked ready to charge at Frank like an enraged bull. Stalking to within two feet of Holly's husband, he slammed his clenched fist against the wall beside him, making all three of them jump.

"It's time for you to leave," Tim repeated.

Frank swallowed visibly before he took a few stumbling steps toward the door. "You got no call to throw me out of my own house," he mumbled, bouncing off the arm of the love seat and nearly falling. "I got the right to see my children."

"You forfeited that right when you came in here drunk and violent," Tim said.

"If you were married to a boring slut like her, you'd be drunk too," Frank said, grabbing the doorjamb for balance. He pitched his voice in a falsetto. "She's too sick or too tired or the children might hear." His voice dropped to its normal register. "No wonder I looked somewhere else for a little bit of fun. You can't blame a man for that."

"Get out before you lose the option of leaving without my help," Tim said.

Claire glanced down to find her sister watching the exchange with wide, frightened eyes.

"Fuck you!" Frank yelled as he scuttled out of the living room. No one moved until the front door slammed. Claire realized she'd been holding her breath and gulped in a lungful.

As she relaxed, Tim's posture changed too. His fists uncurled, his shoulders dropped and almost seemed to decrease in breadth, while his chin came up to a nonthreatening angle.

Holly dropped her face into her hands and began to sob.

Claire was about to lean over to comfort her sister when Tim stepped in front of her. "Are you all right?" he asked, tipping her chin up and making a swift survey of her face.

"I'm fine," Claire said, although her cheek was starting to throb. "Maybe a bruise, but that's all."

"Does it hurt here?" His touch was feather light, but she winced when he grazed the spot where the statue had made contact. "I see it does."

She looked up at him. What she saw in his dark-gray eyes sent a tremor of shock rippling through her. Anger blazed in their depths with an intensity that would have been frightening had it been directed at her. She gasped, and he turned away. But she saw that his hands had clenched back into fists.

Holly was staring at Claire. "Did Lauren hit you? I'm so sorry." She started to sob again. "Everything's going wrong. Everything! I'm so sorry."

"It's okay, Holly. We'll get through this." Claire bent to touch her sister's shoulder.

Tim knelt at Holly's feet. "Are you hurt?" he asked. "Did he hit you?"

Holly lifted her head as her hand crept back up to the side of her face. "No…yes…I'm not hurt."

Tim scanned her face just as he had Claire's. When he raised his hand, Holly flinched slightly, but let him run his fingers over her cheek and jaw.

"I think you both need ice packs, but first, we should call the police."

"No!" Holly nearly shrieked. "I don't want anyone to know."

Tim remained placid. "Your husband is driving in an impaired condition that's dangerous to himself and to others. He needs to be taken off the road."

"Oh," Holly said. "I hadn't thought about that. So you'll just report him for drunk driving?"

"If that's all you want me to say."

Holly turned to Claire, who said, "He's right. Frank could kill himself and anyone in his way."

"All right," Holly said with obvious reluctance, "but nothing else."

"Nothing else." Tim questioned Holly about Frank's car and license plate before pushing up from the floor. "I'll call from the kitchen and fix up those ice packs for both of you."

Claire saw Holly shrink back into the chair as Tim straightened to his full height, and it made her want to cry. What had Frank done to her sister?

Claire suddenly remembered the two girls hiding in the bedroom. "I'm going to go check on the children," she said.

Her sister rocketed up from the chair with a cry of distress. "Oh my God! Brianna! Kayleigh!"

"They're okay. They're in Brianna's closet," Claire said.

"How do you know?" Holly asked. "In fact, why are you both here?"

"Because Brianna was worried and called me."

"Brianna overreacted," Holly said. "Frank doesn't mean it. He just can't hold his liquor."

"Holly, you have to tell me the truth," Claire said. "How many times has Frank hit you? I know that's where those bruises came from."

"No, those are from the Lyme disease. He's never hit me before tonight," Holly said, but she was turning away as she spoke so Claire couldn't see her face. "I have to go get the girls."

Claire let her sister shuffle down the hallway toward Kayleigh's bedroom.

Why was Holly still lying?

Chapter 11

"AMA! ARE YOU OKAY?" CLAIRE HEARD BRIANNA say before Holly shut the door to the bedroom. Anger and pity roiled inside her, an unsettling stew of emotion that reminded her of her feelings about Willow's abuser. Except she found she was angry at Holly as well as at Frank.

She turned and started toward the kitchen just as Tim emerged with a dishtowel-wrapped bag of ice in each hand. "This one's for you," he said, handing her one bag. "Your cheek is starting to swell."

"Oh great," Claire said, pressing the bag against her face and sinking onto the sofa.

"Don't worry. The cold will take it down," Tim said. "Where did your sister go?"

"To Brianna's bedroom, second door on the right. That's where I told the girls to hide."

"Let me give this to her, and I'll be back."

Claire sat there with the ice numbing her skin, staring at the shards of the china statue littering the rug. She knew she should get a dustpan and clean them up before the children saw them, but she couldn't summon enough energy to move. An indistinct murmur of voices issued from the bedroom before the door opened and closed again.

Then Tim was kneeling in front of her, his eyes lit with concern. "How's it feeling?" he asked.

"Cold," Claire said. "It's fine, really. Do the girls seem all right?"

"As well as can be expected. Your sister's doing a good job of calming them down."

"I'm really worried about their safety," Claire said. As Tim shifted up onto the couch, it dipped under his weight. The tilt of the cushion slid her up against his big, solid body, and she let herself savor the feeling of security it gave her.

"Changing the locks might be a first step," Tim suggested.

"I'll suggest it to Holly." Claire was dubious, though. Her sister seemed to be in denial about the seriousness of the situation. She slanted a glance at the man beside her. "You're quite an actor. I thought you were going to fold Frank in half and stuff him up the chimney."

"Fortunately, he thought so too."

"Actually, I was terrified he would pick up a poker and slam you with it." She suddenly remembered Frank's comment about Tim's wife. Should she bring up the ugly words or pretend they had never been said? She decided on an oblique approach. "Frank said some horrible things about Holly, which I know aren't true."

He slewed around so he could look at her. "I don't pay much attention to what a drunk says."

"I'm glad." She didn't believe him, though, because the shadows were hovering in his eyes. "Thank you so much for your help. I don't know how I would have gotten Frank out of here without you. You were amaz—oh my God, the dinner reservations! It's way past time. You'll never be able to get a table there again. I feel terrible!"

"Easy, Claire," he said, engulfing her free hand in both of his. "I'm not worried about whether I can eat at the Aerie or not."

Milo would have been. Claire gave her head a little shake to rid herself of the thought of her ex-husband. The warmth of Tim's hands seemed to radiate up her arm and through her body.

She could feel her nervous tension ease, even as a new set of sensations sprang to life.

She left her hand in his as she said, "I feel really guilty about dragging you into this situation, especially on a first date. It's not quite the evening you were expecting."

"Hey, none of that," Tim said. He raised the back of her hand to his lips and brushed the lightest of kisses across it before releasing it.

The tender gesture sent little curls of pleasure dancing over her skin.

"Now," he said, "we need to discuss how to keep everyone safe tonight."

"I'm going to barricade the doors and stay here." *Whether Holly wanted her or not.*

"I'm staying too."

"I can't ask you to do that."

"I don't recall your doing any asking." Tim's smile was easy, but his tone said he wasn't budging.

"It's not me you have to convince, anyway. It's my sister."

The sound of a door opening ended the debate. Claire stood up as Holly appeared. For the first time, Claire noticed her sister was wearing a dress and high heels. It infuriated her that Holly would still dress up for her creep of a husband.

"The girls and I are going to bed soon," Holly said. "They're going to sleep with me in the master bedroom. I'm sorry you both had to see all this, but it's over. You can go on to dinner now." Holly's eyes went wide. "Oh no, dinner!"

When she started toward the kitchen, Tim held up his hand to stop her, saying, "I turned off the stove when I was making the ice packs."

"Thanks," Holly said, her sudden burst of energy fading so she looked pale and drained. "I was making a nice family dinner for all of us before Frank and I…"

"Before you what?" Claire prompted when Holly's voice petered out.

"Frank came over because I wanted to talk to him about how we would tell Brianna and Kayleigh we were getting a divorce." Holly's eyes filled with tears. "We were going to have dinner with the girls first and then discuss how to handle our announcement after they went to bed. But he showed up drunk."

"Holly, we have to talk," Claire said firmly.

"Not tonight," Holly said, massaging her temples with her fingertips. "I'm exhausted."

"I'm sorry, but there are certain things that can't wait." Claire kept her tone gentle. "We have to tell the police about Frank being violent when he's drunk. Paul can get a restraining order first thing tomorrow. And you have to change the locks on the doors."

"I…No, it will just make Frank angry again." Holly sank into a chair. "He was mad tonight because I got a lawyer already. He said I was in a big hurry to get rid of him."

"He wants to control you, even in the divorce," Claire said. "It's classic abusive behavior."

Holly's gaze skittered sideways. "I got mad too and mentioned his spending habits. That's when he started yelling and calling me a slut."

She looked so sad and defeated that Claire debated whether it was right to push her any more. Then she thought of Brianna's frantic phone call. "You don't want Brianna and Kayleigh to see another scene like this one, or even worse, do you?"

Holly gave an almost imperceptible shake of her head. Claire went over to kneel by her chair. "Tim and I will stay here tonight, but we have to leave in the morning. I'll be crazy with worry, not knowing if you and the girls are safe."

"All right." Holly's voice was a mere thread of a whisper.

Claire wanted to leap to her feet and pump her fist. Instead, she stretched up and touched her lips to Holly's uninjured cheek. "Attagirl, sis. We'll handle this together."

As Claire straightened, Holly reached out and gave her hand a quick squeeze, murmuring, "Thanks."

"I'll talk to the police, if you'd like," Tim said. "The chief and I are acquainted."

Holly nodded, and Claire mouthed her own *thank you* as Tim headed back toward the kitchen.

"I'm going to say good night to the girls," she said, turning to head down the hallway.

The two children were huddled together under a patchwork quilt on the big bed, their curly hair wisping out of the braids hanging over the shoulders of their princess pajamas. Claire had given Holly and Frank the quilt as a wedding gift, commissioning its creator to embroider their names and the date along the border. She wondered if Frank's name could be ripped out without damaging the fabric too badly.

"Aunt Claire!" Kayleigh shrieked, hurling herself across the bed and into Claire's arms. "I was so scared."

Claire shifted the little girl to her side and held out her free arm to Brianna. The older girl scooted across the quilt and snuggled in against her.

"Thanks for coming," Brianna whispered. "I was scared too."

"You did the right thing by calling me." Claire watched Brianna's face lose some of its pinched tension. She wanted to reassure the child, since she suspected Holly had reprimanded her for involving others. "It was important for me to be here tonight. I think you know that."

Brianna nodded before she buried her face in Claire's shoulder and began to sob. "Mama says Lauren got broken. She was my favorite Royal Doulton lady."

"You can have Genevieve. She's really pretty too." Kayleigh's little voice quavered slightly.

Tears welled up in Claire's throat. She and Holly had done the same thing when they were young—spent hours debating which of the china ladies they each liked the best.

"No, Genevieve is yours," Brianna said, lifting her tear-streaked face. "I'll pick a different lady."

"Maybe we can find another Lauren," Claire said, mentally crossing her fingers for good luck. "My job is to locate beautiful things for people, so you can hire me to help you. For free."

Brianna sniffled and straightened up. "Thank you, Aunt Claire, but I like Laurianne too. She's reading a book."

"That's nice of both of you," Claire said, admiring her nieces' generosity toward each other. "I want you to know that you are two very smart, brave girls. You did exactly the right thing tonight, both of you. I'm proud of you."

"Aunt Claire? Mama says you have a whisper horse that you can tell anything you want to," Brianna said.

"That's right. Her name is Willow."

"Can two people have the same whisper horse?"

"I don't see why not, but the real expert is my friend Sharon. Why don't we visit the stable tomorrow and ask her?"

"Me too?" Kayleigh asked. "Mama says they have kittens there."

"Of course you too," Claire said, pulling the girls close to her again.

As she hugged them, she thought how small and light their child's bones were beneath the brightly colored pajama fabrics, almost like a bird's. A desire to protect them from all the ugliness in the world surged through her with fearsome power. How could Holly even think of exposing these two precious beings to Frank's violence? Claire could feel anger welling up inside her again. She fought it down by dropping her nose into Brianna's hair and inhaling the sweet powdery scent of innocence.

"I love you so much," she murmured against the curve of her niece's skull. "And I love you," she said, shifting to Kayleigh's little head.

She felt something shift deep inside her as her feelings for these two little girls seemed to expand and strengthen second by second. "I won't let anyone hurt you ever again."

Oddly enough, she had said almost the same thing to Willow.

Chapter 12

"How did it go with the police chief?" Claire asked Tim. She had tucked two clean, pajama-clad little girls in bed next to her sister before she found him sitting at the kitchen table eating the casserole he had rescued from the oven.

His blazer was slung over the back of the chair, and he had rolled up the sleeves of his shirt. As he leaned forward to take a bite, the familiar errant lock of hair fell onto his forehead. She wanted to slide onto his lap and burrow into the expanse of blue silk spanning his chest, hiding from the disaster of the evening.

"Hungry?" he asked. "I'll heat up a plate for you."

"Thanks, but I'll pass for now." The spike and drop of adrenaline had killed her appetite. Claire sank into the chair across from him, her full skirt spilling over the arms.

Putting down the fork, he wiped his chin before speaking. "They're going to send a patrol car by here regularly. He also promised to send the locksmith over first thing in the morning."

"Thank you!" Claire slumped back in her chair. "I tried to talk her into changing the locks on the day Frank announced he wanted a divorce. She wouldn't hear of it."

"Sometimes it takes a while to come to terms with a harsh reality," Tim said, his tone sober now. He reached across the table and opened his hand palm up, an invitation to comfort. Claire hesitated only a moment before placing her hand against the warmth of his palm. She felt the calluses on his fingertips brush her skin as he carefully closed them.

That was all it took, just that minor point of contact, and she became aware of him across every inch of her body. Why had she never before noticed that his lower lip had a full, sensuous swell that made her want to trace it with her tongue?

"Folks don't always want to admit things have gone wrong in their lives, and it's especially hard to admit it to family," Tim was saying, his low rumble of a voice sending delicious little vibrations dancing along her spine.

Claire shivered as the heat of his hand licked up her arm and melded with all the other sensations his presence fanned into being.

"Are you cold?" he asked, letting go of her hand and reaching around for his jacket. "Take this."

He stood and draped the jacket over her shoulders. "Mmm, much better," she said, pulling it close around her so she could feel the body heat where he had sat against it and smell the scent of clean male. It was as close as she could get to having his arms around her. "I think it's relief. You've just solved all my short-term problems."

"Maybe I'm your whisper human," he said, his big hands cupping her shoulders and his mouth close to her ear. "Tell me your troubles and they'll go away."

Claire shivered again as his breath feathered over her cheek. "That's a nice thought, but more burden than I'd ask anyone else to bear."

He gave her shoulders a gentle squeeze before he released them. "I'm in better shape than Willow is for bearing burdens." He returned to his chair and picked up his fork again. "My apologies for eating when you're not. It takes a fair amount of fuel to keep me going."

"I feel terrible. You should be eating four-star haute cuisine instead of mystery casserole." She watched the play of muscles in his throat as he swallowed and thought about feeling them move against her lips.

"The casserole is right tasty. Why don't we try for the haute cuisine again tomorrow night?"

Claire yearned to say yes so she could sit across another table and bask in the quiet power of this man. "It sounds great, but I have another commitment tomorrow night. May I have a rain check?"

"Sure. We'll aim for next weekend," he said, but she sensed a slight withdrawal.

She felt compelled to offer an explanation. "I've been challenged to a foosball match by an old friend." Of course, she was going to cancel it, in light of Holly's situation. However, she didn't intend to tell Tim that since he might insist on staying with Holly again.

"You play foosball?"

It was the first time she'd seen him look startled, and it pleased her that she'd been able to ruffle his usually placid exterior. "Why are you so surprised? Do I seem like a klutz?"

"You look like a woman who doesn't frequent that sort of a bar. Are you playing at the Black Bear?"

"No, the Sportsman."

"Seriously?"

Claire knew why he said that. The clientele at the Sportsman left something to be desired. She had never gone there without Paul's protective escort. Even with his company, she had once been accosted by a drunken patron who had outweighed Paul by about a hundred pounds. Luckily, the bartender had intervened, and both of them had emerged unscathed. However, they avoided the place for a few months following the incident.

"It's where I learned the game. Did you ever play?"

"In grad school."

"Not college?"

"I didn't go to bars much then." Tim picked up his empty plate and carried it to the sink.

"Too much homework?"

He rinsed the plate and fork and opened the dishwasher door. "I couldn't afford a fake ID."

"You got carded in college? That's hard to believe, given your...er...height."

"Well, I was younger than your average freshman, and pretty skinny."

"How old were you?"

Tim closed the dishwasher and straightened. "Fifteen."

Claire rocked back in her chair. "That's why I didn't remember you from the high school. You graduated before I got there."

"I was just good at science, and I ran through the courses at the high school pretty quickly." He shrugged. "College seemed to be the next logical step."

"Where did you go undergrad?"

"Boston," he said. "How about you?"

"New York University, but only part-time. I had to get a job." He was avoiding answering her question, and she couldn't figure out why. "Boston College or Boston University?"

There was a long moment of uncomfortable silence.

"Jesus H. Christ! You went to Harvard, didn't you?"

All her assumptions about Tim Arbuckle fractured, and she struggled to rearrange them into a new pattern.

"That's why I don't tell people," he said, pushing his hair back with a gesture of irritation. "They get the wrong idea."

"You mean you're not brilliant? Never mind. You can't answer that honestly and still pretend to be a humble country veterinarian." Claire wasn't sure why she was unsettled by this. He had never lied to her; he'd just given her a misleading impression.

"I don't *pretend* to be a country veterinarian. It's what I do for a living."

"You forgot humble." She suddenly remembered his catalog of equine artists and the way he had pronounced Julia Castillo's name. And Sharon had mentioned colleges trying to recruit him. "I'm sorry. I'm just surprised. Like you were about my foosball habit. Except going to Harvard at age fifteen is a little more impressive."

She tilted her head back to offer an apologetic smile. He didn't smile in return, but he did come back to the table and lower himself into the chair. It creaked slightly as he settled into it. He laced his fingers together on the tabletop and stared down at them.

"Your secret is safe with me," Claire said.

That brought his gaze up to her face. She regretted her outburst when she saw the lines of strain around his mouth. He shook his head. "It's not a secret. Enough folks remember me from high school to know where I went to college and how old I was." He huffed out a breath. "Sometimes I'd just like to be normal."

Claire had a sudden vision of a skinny, teenaged version of Tim, fresh from the hills of West Virginia, arriving on the campus of moneyed, tradition-steeped Harvard. Even worse, he was three years younger than his fellow freshmen, a huge gap of experience at that age. He must have felt like a total outsider.

She reached across the table and laid her hand on top of his clenched fists. "I never belonged here, either. I cared about useless things like paintings and statues. That's why I left for New York as soon as I could."

"I imagine that's why I ended up in New York too. We're not misfits there, just New Yorkers." His smile was twisted, but it was a smile.

Headlights flashed through the window. Tim was instantly on his feet and peering through the dark glass. "It's a police cruiser," he said.

"That was prompt. Let me guess, you saved the police chief's Saint Bernard."

"His Chihuahua."

Chapter 13

"Aunt Claire! The chocolate chip pancakes are ready."

Claire opened her eyes to find Kayleigh standing by her bed in Brianna's room, wearing blindingly pink Hello Kitty pajamas. She squinted at her wristwatch: it read 7:10 a.m. Stifling a groan, she said, "They smell yummy. Who cooked them?"

"Dr. Tim. C'mon!"

"You go ahead, sweetie. I've got to put some clothes on." Claire had stripped down to her bra and panties before sliding between Brianna's lavender sheets.

She wondered what Tim had worn to sleep in Kayleigh's pink-polka-dotted bedroom and how far his feet had hung off the end of the child's bed. She started to giggle at the image of Tim in his boxers with the fluffy kittens quilt draped over him. Her giggling came to an abrupt halt as her imagination conjured up the expanse of bare, muscled chest it would expose. She threw the covers back and scooped up her dress, fumbling with the huge black buttons as she wished she'd thought to borrow some jeans from Holly's closet.

After a quick wash and a muttered curse at Frank over the bruise on her face, Claire followed the aroma of warm chocolate and buckwheat into a kitchen crammed with activity. Tim stood at the stove, also dressed in last night's clothing, while Brianna and Kayleigh took turns sprinkling the chips in the pancakes.

Although she had circles under her eyes, Holly was pouring milk into the Pokémon glasses arrayed at the five table settings. She must have put concealer over the bruise on her cheek, because Claire couldn't see any sign of it.

"Morning," Claire said, feeling guilty that she had slept through all the preparation. "What can I do to help?"

"You can sit down and start eating," Tim said, reaching for a plate piled high with steaming pancakes. "My fellow chefs like the cooking more than the consuming."

The slow smile he gave her made all the commotion fade away. For a long moment, she saw nothing but his gray eyes accented by the unruly lock of hair. She felt her lips turn upward in a smile to match his as warmth bloomed deep inside her.

"Girls, come over here and sit," Holly commanded, breaking the fragile spell. "I'll let you squirt whipped cream on your pancakes."

That sent the children scrambling for their chairs as their mother shook the can of Reddi-wip.

Claire walked over to take the plate from Tim, feeling oddly shy about being close to him.

"Just a minute," he said, putting his finger under her chin and turning her face upward.

She thought he was going to kiss her, and held her breath with shocked but delighted anticipation. Instead, he bent down to examine the bruise left by the flying figurine. "No swelling," he said with satisfaction. "It may be tender for a while, though."

Disappointment doused her little flare of excitement. She tried to summon the nerve to stretch up and brush her lips against the angle of his cheekbone. However, she was too aware of three extra pairs of eyes to risk it.

She turned to the table and presented the platter with a flourish. "World's greatest pancakes!"

As breakfast was consumed with noisy relish, Claire could almost forget the ugliness of the night before. The little girls' innocence sluiced away the stains of violence. Tim's calm, solid presence banished fear.

"I'll pick you up as soon as I finish work, and we'll go to the stable," Claire promised the girls. "That should be about four o'clock." Davis would cover the rest of the afternoon for her.

"Okay, young ladies, clear your plates and go wash up," Holly said, starting to push out of her chair.

"Sit—"

"Stay—"

Claire and Tim spoke and stood together.

"All right!" Holly said, smiling and sinking back onto the seat. "I'm outnumbered."

Her sister's smile lightened Claire's spirits even more. Why couldn't their relationship feel like this all the time?

As she and Tim worked side by side while bantering with Holly, Claire wanted the time to stretch out like a long summer twilight. However, Tim was extremely efficient, and the kitchen was tidy all too soon. Holly excused herself to check on the girls.

"Can I give you a lift home?" Tim said, drying his hands on a Disney Princess dish towel he had slung over his shoulder.

"Thanks, but I'll stay here a little longer and hitch a ride with a neighbor. The gallery doesn't open until ten."

"I'll give you a call about that rain check," Tim said, hanging the towel up on its rack.

Claire screwed up her courage and walked over to him. Rising up on her tiptoes, she put her hands on his shoulders, marveling at the sheer mass of them under her palms. Still, she couldn't reach the cheek she was aiming for. He bent his head, and for a moment, they locked gazes. Then he stooped further and kissed her on the lips.

She dug her fingers into the muscle curving over his shoulder, letting her eyes close as she savored the touch she'd been craving since the night before. He kissed the way he did everything else, slowly and with thoroughness. Her skin seemed to light up with the desire for his mouth to slide over every inch of it, and she moaned softly.

His hands came up to her waist, pulling her against him just as Kayleigh's voice rang out. "I want to say good-bye to Dr. Tim."

Tim moved them apart with a speed she hadn't thought him capable of. She caught sight of the blaze of raw hunger in his eyes just as he turned away to greet Kayleigh and Brianna. It set another match to the tinderbox of frustration he had created in her.

After the farewells were said, Claire walked beside him to the front door.

"Good luck with your foosball match," he said.

"Oh Lord, I'd completely forgotten about that," Claire said. "I'll have to call and—"

"You're not canceling it on my account," her sister piped up from the living room.

Tim mouthed, *Sorry*, and Claire gestured, *Don't worry about it*, before thanking him aloud and waving a chaste good-bye.

The moment the door closed behind him, she felt the void of his absence and hustled into the living room to distract herself by discussing the situation with her sister.

"You're not changing your plans because Frank had too much to drink last night," Holly said in a low voice. "Dr. Tim told me the locksmith is coming as soon as he opens. Besides, the police are watching the house."

Claire opened her mouth to argue when the doorbell rang. She and Holly exchanged a worried look as Claire gestured that she would answer it.

She raised her voice to say, "Be right there," as she made her way to the front door. She took a deep breath before she twitched the curtain away from the sidelight to see who the visitor was.

Relief coursed through her as she saw a dark-blue police uniform. "Holly, it's okay," she said, pulling the door open with a smile. As she looked up past the uniform to the officer's face, her grin widened. "Robbie? Robbie McGraw?"

"Yes, ma'am," he said, smiling back at her. "I heard you were back home."

"Am I allowed to hug you when you're on duty?"

He rubbed the back of his neck. "Maybe not with my partner watching."

Claire laughed. "Later, then. It's so good to see you."

"Is something wrong?" Holly asked, appearing beside Claire. She seemed to shrink back when she saw Robbie.

"No, ma'am, Mrs. Snedegar. The chief asked me to stop by."

"That's real nice of you, Robbie," Holly said, her voice forced. "Call me Holly. After all, you and Claire were in the same grade."

Claire eyed Holly with bemusement. Then she remembered. Holly had had a crush on Robbie McGraw—quarterback, Eagle Scout, and all-round nice guy—in high school. He, being two years older and the darling of every cheerleader on the squad, had never encouraged her. It must be mortifying to have her old crush know about her marital situation.

"Can I get you a cold drink?" Holly was asking. "And something for your partner?"

"No, ma'am, but I appreciate the offer. The chief wanted me to advise you to call nine-one-one, even if you're not sure there's a danger. A false alarm is better than a real disaster."

"I promise to do that," Holly said, her cordiality slipping at the reminder.

"We'll be patrolling the neighborhood frequently, so we can get here fast if you need us," Robbie assured them.

"You've made me feel a heck of a lot better," Claire said. "Thanks for taking the time to come by."

As she watched him stride back down the walk, Claire reflected that her old classmate hadn't changed all that much. He was still as trim and fit as when he'd led the football team.

"Is he married?" she asked Holly as he ducked into the driver's seat of the cruiser.

"I thought you liked Tim."

"I do." Claire was startled by Holly's reaction. "I mean, I was just curious about Robbie. I haven't seen him since high school."

"No, he's not," Holly said, "but it's not for lack of the ladies trying. Twyla Bradford was bragging that he had bought her an engagement ring, but it turned out to be a cameo ring for his mother. Twyla was good and embarrassed."

Claire was savoring the normalcy of her sister's little tidbit of gossip when the light faded from Holly's eyes. "Anyway, Robbie's still a bachelor and seems to want to stay that way."

Holly went back to the couch in the living room, and Claire followed. "Listen, when I take the girls to the stable, I want you to go right to bed. I'll run them to Joe's Drive-In for dinner, so you don't have to fix anything. Okay?"

"You don't need to do that."

Claire blew out a sigh of exasperation. "I know I don't need to. I want to. I like Brianna and Kayleigh. I like being a real aunt to them."

"You really do. It just surprises me." Holly looked up from tracing the welting on the couch cushion. "Claire?"

"Yes?" An odd note in her sister's voice made her sit down on the couch. "What is it?"

"I've been so stupid," Holly burst out as tears traced glistening tracks down her cheeks. "I believed everything Frank said about you. He told me you were a snob and you didn't care about Brianna and Kayleigh. He tried to get me to stop you from coming down here. He said you were just doing it to play the grand lady helping out her poor little sister."

Each sentence seemed to jab Claire in the heart. She sat stunned as Holly kept talking.

"That's why I kept pushing you away all the time—to make Frank happy. I even thought that's why he asked for the divorce, because he was mad at me for letting you come. You've been so good to me, and I've been horrible. I'm so sorry." Holly's sobs shook her whole body.

"Holl, it's okay. Take it easy," Claire said, leaning forward to take her sister's hands in hers.

"Frank made me doubt you, and I believed him."

Claire remembered how thoroughly Milo had convinced her she was a failure at work and at marriage. She loved Milo, so she trusted him; Holly had done the same with Frank. Both men had abused that trust. "You should have told me Frank didn't want me here. I didn't mean to stir up trouble between you."

"There were already problems between us; that's why I tried to keep you at a distance. I didn't want you to know my marriage was in trouble."

"Jeez, I'm divorced myself. I would have understood."

"I know it doesn't make any sense, but I've been all alone here since you went to New York and Mama and Daddy moved to Florida. Frank has been my world."

"Oh, sweetie, I know exactly what you mean," Claire said. "I've been there too."

All her sister's strange behavior made sense now. She could feel the barrier between them crumble. There might still be a few bits of hurt lying around, but she could deal with those. She pulled her sister into a fierce hug and received the same embrace in return.

Claire waited until Holly loosened her hold before she said, "There's one question I've been wanting to ask you. When you told me you didn't want to go to marriage counseling, you said it had to end. Why?"

Holly dropped her face in her hands for a few seconds before she sat up and squared her shoulders. "You know all those charges we found on Frank's bills?"

Claire nodded.

"I shouldn't have been surprised by them. Frank cheated on me before. He swore it was a one-night stand because he was drunk and lonely on the road, and it would never happen again. He implied it was my fault because I was always so involved with our children."

"Oh no, sweetie, tell me you didn't believe that!" Claire was furious on her sister's behalf. "What an asshole!"

"I realize that now, just like I realize it wasn't the only time."

"I wish I could have helped you through that."

"It was too humiliating to talk about," Holly said.

"I get that, but I hate the idea of your blaming yourself for his infidelity." Now that Holly had admitted to this much, Claire wondered whether she should challenge her sister about the physical abuse she was convinced had also taken place. Frank's strategy of isolating his wife and discrediting anyone who might help her sounded like a textbook abuser. Brianna said her father had hit her mother before. Yet Holly continued to maintain that this was the only incident.

As Claire hesitated, Holly spoke again. "Anyway, he promised it would never happen again, so I let it go." She looked down at her hands before she lifted her head to gaze straight into Claire's eyes. "I did it for the girls. So they would have a mother and a father together while they grew up. Can you understand that?"

Claire nodded. She too felt a fierce desire to make Brianna and Kayleigh's world a perfect place.

But would her sister ever admit that the price might have been too high?

Chapter 14

CAN TWO PEOPLE HAVE THE SAME WHISPER HORSE?"
Brianna asked.

Sharon shot a querying look at Claire, who was holding Brianna's hand as they stood outside the tack room. Claire gave a tiny nod.

"I don't believe anyone's ever asked me that before." Sharon rubbed her chin with her free hand. "Some horses can handle more than one set of secrets, but the horse has to be very special."

"Is Willow very special?" Brianna asked.

"Willow? Willow could handle *four* sets of secrets."

Brianna's look of relief was profound. Claire hadn't realized how much the little girl wanted to unburden herself.

"Okay, then," Claire said. "Let's go see Willow."

Claire left Brianna just outside Willow's stall while she clipped the lead line on the mare's halter and tied her to her metal feed basket. Stroking the horse's neck, she touched her forehead against Willow's and said, "You've got a big job to do. You have to take care of a little girl's troubles. I'm counting on you."

Opening the stall door, she called Brianna in and handed her a horse treat. "Make your hand completely flat like a plate. Now offer it to Willow."

"It tickles," Brianna giggled as the mare's whiskers brushed against her palm.

"Willow, this is Brianna. She needs your help." Claire positioned Brianna in front of the big Thoroughbred. She was pleased when the child showed no fear as she reached out to pet the horse's soft nose. "Just stay here where Willow can see you. It helps to look into her eyes while you talk to her."

"Where will you be?"

"Just outside. Call me when you're finished, and I'll come in to untie her."

"Will you be able to hear me?"

"Not if you're just talking to Willow. Only if you call out loudly," Claire promised. As she said it, she crossed her fingers behind her back, hoping the childish gesture would salve her conscience. She had every intention of eavesdropping on Brianna's confession.

At the child's nod, she slipped out of the stall, latching the door. Then she quietly opened the door to the adjacent stall, where a placid gelding named Ozzie was munching on his hay. As she came in, the buckskin horse turned around to look at her before going back to his chewing. Claire gave his flank a gentle pat and tiptoed to the wall adjoining Willow's stall.

"Mama and Papa had another big fight last night."

Horror welled up inside Claire as she heard the confirmation that this wasn't the first ugly scene Brianna had witnessed between her parents.

"I think they're going to get a divorce like Janelle's parents did. She had to move away, even though she didn't want to. I don't want to move away, either. Kayleigh and I would have to decide who would go with Mama and who would go with Papa."

Tears blurred her vision at the quaver in Brianna's voice.

"But maybe it's better if they get a divorce, because I'm afraid Papa will hurt Mama the next time he gets mad."

Suddenly, it felt terribly wrong to listen to Brianna's most private thoughts, even if Claire had done it with good intentions. She put her hand over her mouth as a sob caught at her throat. Stumbling to Ozzie's stall door, she swung it open and bolted across the barn's aisle.

After swiping her shirtsleeve over her eyes, she leaned one shoulder against the wall across from Willow's stall so there was no chance of overhearing her niece's words. She was mulling over how she could tactfully convince Holly to tell her children about the divorce without Frank's presence when she heard Brianna call her name.

"Did Willow help?" she asked as she walked in the stall.

Brianna nodded as she stood stroking the mare's nose. "Her ears move around, so I know she's really listening."

Claire knelt in the straw beside the little girl and the big horse.

"If you ever feel like talking to a person, I'd be happy to listen. Of course, my ears don't wiggle, but I'd still hear you."

Brianna nodded again, but asked, "Do you have another treat to thank Willow with?"

So the child wasn't yet ready to let her aunt in on her heartbreaking secrets.

Even the mouthwatering scent of Joe's Drive-In's hand-cut french fries couldn't keep Claire from choking up as she remembered Brianna's overheard confession. Fortunately, Kayleigh was intent on describing every one of the kittens in the litter at the stable while Brianna interjected occasional questions. They didn't seem to notice that their aunt barely tasted the creamy chocolate milk shake.

She closed her eyes and rested her head against the car's window.

"Do you have a headache?" Brianna asked, leaning forward between the seats.

"No, sweetie, I'm fine. Just a little tired. I had a busy day at work."

"Did you sell any pictures?"

Claire swiveled around to look at her niece. She was surprised the little girl understood what she did at the gallery. "Two big ones by an artist named Len Boggs." Which meant a very handsome commission check, which she planned to use to buy a replacement Lauren statue for Holly.

"Are they pretty?" Kayleigh asked.

"Very beautiful," Claire said. "They're paintings of real places all around West Virginia. The painter lives not too far from here." She kept debating whether to mention Len Boggs to Henry Thalman. The man had real talent, but maybe it wasn't good enough for New York. Milo's scorn for the Castillos still haunted her, and she couldn't bring herself to risk her reputation with her future boss.

"Can I see some of them?" Brianna asked.

"Sure. I'll drive you by the gallery on the way home so you can see the ones in the window display." Maybe seeing them through a child's eyes would help Claire make up her own mind about Boggs's work. "We'll talk to your mom about coming over tomorrow to see the ones inside."

Kayleigh made a face. "Isn't it kind of like a library where you have to be quiet and behave yourself?"

"I'll arrange a special private showing so you can make all the noise you want."

"Okay, I'll come," Kayleigh said, her face brightening.

Claire reflected that it was hard to brood around children. As they finished their delicious but health-destroying meal, Claire flipped on the radio to the Disney Channel, and all three of them sang their way home.

When they pulled into her sister's driveway, Kayleigh bolted out of the car, while Brianna slowly unfastened her seat belt.

"Aunt Claire, thank you for sharing Willow with me."

Claire had a few things she'd like to discuss with Willow right now. "Tell me anytime you want to talk to her, and I'll take you there."

They went inside to find Holly sitting at the kitchen table as Kayleigh described the kittens for a new audience. Claire's eyebrows rose as she noticed that Holly was wearing jeans and a floral-print blouse rather than the usual sweatpants and baggy T-shirt. "You look nice."

Holly flushed. "Since the police are checking in on me, I thought I should get dressed."

"Good idea," Claire said. After letting Kayleigh rattle on a little longer, Claire interrupted to mention her promise of a gallery visit the next day. "On Sunday, we're only open from noon to four, so I'll take them over at ten for a private tour."

"Okay," Holly said after a beat of hesitation, which worried Claire.

"Have there been any problems here today?" she asked.

Holly shook her head, pulling a ring hung with two shiny gold keys out of her pocket and offering it to Claire. "These are your copies of the new keys to the front and back doors. The locksmith talked me into getting deadbolts to be really safe."

Claire felt a little glow of warmth because her sister had thought to get her the copies without prompting.

"I got lots of rest today, thanks to you, so I can put the girls to bed," Holly said. "We're rooting for you to win your big foosball match tonight."

Claire leaned down to hug her sister, savoring the fact that she could do it without any constraint. "Thanks, Holl, I'll do my best."

"You always do," Holly said.

Claire turned those three words around and around in her mind like a beautiful sculpture as she drove back to Healing Springs Stables. Just three little words, and yet she felt like a champion already.

Her joy in the healing relationship with her sister was tempered by the pain of Brianna's revelations. She needed to figure out how to approach Holly about that, and a chat with Willow would help her think more clearly.

It was strange to realize that she and Brianna truly shared a whisper horse.

Claire didn't have time to socialize, so she bypassed Sharon's office and headed straight for Willow's stall. Stopping outside the tack room, she scooped up a couple of carrot bits from the bowl Sharon kept there.

"You look mighty dressed up for a visit to a barn." Tim's voice came from behind her, making her jump.

"Don't sneak up on me like that," she said, turning to find him standing with his arms crossed over his chest. He was wearing an olive-green polo shirt, neatly pressed khakis, and loafers whose polished surface was marred only by a thin film of pine bark dust. "I could say the same about your outfit. What happened to your flannel wardrobe?"

"Those are my work clothes, and it was my afternoon off." He was smiling at her in an unsettling way.

Maybe it was his change of style that was making her antsy, but she was strangely intimidated by the new Tim. "If you're not working, why are you at the barn?"

"Because you and I have some unfinished business from this morning," he said, reaching for her wrist and towing her toward an empty stall whose door was standing open.

"What bus—oh!" Claire gasped as Tim closed the door and pulled her against him, his mouth coming down on hers. He gave her the same thorough kiss he had in the morning, but now he went on to explore the pulse just behind her earlobe and the arc of skin exposed by her scooped neckline. Claire arched backward as he moved aside the ruffled fabric so his lips could skim her collarbone.

"Oh yes, there!" she hissed when his tongue began to trace the same path.

He shocked her by yanking the back of her blouse out of her linen trousers and sliding his hand up underneath the fabric to splay against her bare skin. She wove her fingers into his hair and tilted his head up so she could nip at the full lower lip that so tempted her. The heat of his hand branded her back, and she felt her nipples harden.

"Pick me up," she said, sliding one knee up the side of his thigh as a cue. He was too tall for her to fit against him the way her body demanded.

"Good idea." He slid his hand out from under her blouse so he could cup her behind, lifting her in one fluid motion.

She wrapped her legs around his hips and moaned his name as she felt his erection between her legs. He took a step forward so she was braced between the warm wall of his body and the wood of the stall. He shifted his grip so his hands were wrapped around her thighs as he pressed against the most sensitive spot on her body.

"Oh dear God," she whispered as the pressure and friction sent pure arousal streaking deep inside her.

A muffled groan tore from Tim, and he went still, his forehead touching the wood beside her ear. "This is more business than I expected to do here."

She could feel his heart pounding and knew he was exerting the self-control she couldn't muster. Then he seemed to snap; his hands skimmed up to her breasts, where his thumbs circled her aching nipples, and his mouth skimmed up to her earlobe again. "Come home with me now," he rasped.

Claire's body was vibrating with nearly electric sensation. A niggling little voice insisted that she couldn't say yes, but her mind was so fogged with pleasure that she had to think hard about why. "Can't. Foosball match."

His thumbs stilled. She indulged herself in one flexing circle of her hips that made them both gasp before she unlocked her ankles from behind him and let him lower her feet into the straw bedding.

Once she was safely down, he braced his forearm against the wall and dropped his head onto it. "Give me a minute, and I'll help you tidy up," he said.

She wanted to run her hands over his broad, muscled back displayed so invitingly in front of her. Instead, she forced herself to tuck her blouse back into the waistband of her navy linen trousers.

"How did you know I'd be here?" she asked, pulling bobby pins out of the intricate bun now hanging halfway down her neck and plaiting it into a simple French braid.

"Some research and a lucky guess. I called Holly's house, and she said you'd just left," he said, pushing away from the wall. "After last night, I figured you might want to consult your whisper horse."

She brushed a few stray wisps of straw off her trouser legs.

"Turn around," Tim said, "and I'll do your rear."

"That's what got us in trouble to begin with," Claire said, slanting him a heavy-lidded glance.

Tim held up his hands in the gesture of a scrubbed surgeon. "As a doctor, I'm trained to use my hands in a purely professional way."

"You're trained to use your hands on horses and cows," Claire said. "And you claimed I didn't look anything like a sow."

The teasing light in his eyes dimmed for a split second before he ran his palm down the curve of her hip, finishing with an affectionate pat on her bottom. "I'll try to think of you as one, if you'd prefer."

"No, I'm fine with the way you think of me." She directed all the heat seething inside her into the look she threw him.

"Then I get another rain check. This is the second one you owe me." He drew his finger down the center of her nose to her lips, which he traced with a deliberation that made her close her eyes and whimper. He smiled. "I'll take that as a yes. Have a good talk with Willow."

He flicked her cheek with his finger and walked out of the stall, leaving Claire to sag against the wall. How was she supposed to tell Willow her concerns about Holly when Tim had left every nerve ending in her body standing at attention, demanding satisfaction. All she could think about was the feel of his mouth…and his hands tracing the swell of her breasts…and his erection pressing between her thighs. She shoved away from the wall and stalked out into the barn's wide corridor.

She'd lost the carrots during her encounter with Tim, so she detoured back to the bowl and scooped up some more. Slipping into Willow's stall, she held them out. "Can you handle these yet, girl?"

Willow whinnied a greeting before she crunched through all three of them with enthusiasm. Some of Claire's frustration drained away as she savored this small triumph in the mare's recovery. "You know, your friend Dr. Tim is a tease. He's got me all revved up with no place to go except a foosball game. How am I supposed to concentrate on a little white ball rolling around a table when I feel like…well, this?"

Claire couldn't even admit to her whisper horse what she was feeling about Tim right now.

Maybe it was a good thing she had this foosball match to distract her. When she considered it more rationally, she'd kissed

Tim exactly once before she nearly had an orgasm up against the wall of a barn. That was probably moving too fast to be healthy.

"I'm newly divorced, and his wife committed suicide," she muttered. "We're a couple of emotional disasters."

Except it didn't feel that way. He seemed so grounded, so careful and deliberate. Not the sort to dive in without being able to swim.

"I need to focus on my sister's problems," she said as Willow snuffled at her empty hand. "You're not going to believe what Frank did last night…"

Chapter 15

WHEN HER DOORBELL RANG AT NINE O'CLOCK, CLAIRE took a deep breath before she went to the door. Describing Frank's behavior to Willow had helped clarify her concerns about him, but her body still hummed with the tension Tim had coiled there.

She swung open the door to find Paul standing on her front porch. He was dressed for the Sportsman: jeans, sneakers, a dark-blue zippered windbreaker, and a baseball cap with the John Deere symbol embroidered on it. When she invited him in, he flipped the cap off and rolled it down his arm to catch the bill between his fingers.

"That brings back memories," Claire said. "You spent hours practicing."

Paul grinned, his teeth flashing white against his olive skin. "Got to keep the manual dexterity sharp."

"Oh, so you're using intimidation now." She shrugged into a gray West Virginia University hoodie. She had changed into jeans, a hot-pink T-shirt, and running shoes and added a layer of concealer over the bruise on her cheek.

"You're using distraction," Paul said, eyeing the neon-bright color of the T-shirt.

"I never even considered it," she lied.

"You can't fool me. I taught you that trick."

Claire laughed and threw her arms around him in an impulsive hug. "It's so great to see you, Paul. I should have called you sooner."

His return embrace was like whipcord around her shoulders. "Damn straight you should have." He pulled her in close. Stirred up from her encounter with Tim, her body responded with a little jolt of pleasure. Her response shocked her, and she jerked back.

Paul let his palms slide down her arms to take her hands. "You know, I always wanted to ask you out on a real date in high school, but I was afraid you'd say no."

"Are you serious?" There had been a time when she had wanted her relationship with Paul to become more than friendly. She'd flirted outrageously with him, but he hadn't taken the bait.

Now their lives had diverged, and they had become different people. Paul offered a friendship that was easy and uncomplicated. There was nothing to hide, no need to keep up a facade, because he'd known her before her grown-up identity existed.

"Pretty ridiculous, eh? You were the smartest girl in the school, and I was the screwup."

"I would have cramped your style," Claire said. "And you weren't a screwup; you just never worked up to your potential."

He laughed. "How many times did my parents hear that from the principal?"

"You seem to have made up for it since then." She squeezed his hands and let go. "No more delaying tactics. It's time to show you how we play foosball in New York."

When she walked into the Sportsman, the flash of neon, the sound of pinball machines clanging, and the scent of peanuts spun her back in time. It was still early, but there were enough patrons to give the impression of a crowd. And they all knew her escort.

"Taggart, my man, let me buy you a beer!"

"Paulie, you old bastard! Who's the pretty lady?"

"Watch your mouth there, Fred." Paul's tone was part jovial, part warning. He greeted everyone by name and introduced Claire while making it clear that she was not to be bothered.

The bartender put two chunky glass mugs of draft beer on the counter and, with a wink at Claire, said, "On the house. Next round, you make Taggart pay. He can afford it."

"Oh, I plan to make him pay—at the foosball table," Claire said.

The bartender chuckled and held out two quarters to her. "For the first game. If I was a betting man, I'd bet on you, pretty lady."

"You'd lose," Paul said.

"That's not very gentlemanly," Claire said, handing him the quarters.

"Foosball is not a gentleman's game." He unzipped his jacket and held it wide. His T-shirt read, *National Foosball Championships. Only the best arrive. Only the deadly survive.* A flaming foosball graphic left burn marks on the shirt.

"You don't scare me." In fact, Paul had always been better; his hands were stronger, and his reflexes were lightning fast. She could only hope that pushing paper for a living had slowed him down enough that she could make him work for his win.

"Let's play," he said, putting one hand on the small of her back and steering her toward the far room, where Brad Paisley competed with the clack and hiss of air hockey, the ping of pinballs hitting bumpers, and the thud and pound of the foosball tables.

"Clear the way for the king of foos," someone shouted as Paul propelled Claire toward the center table. "The emperor of spin has arrived."

The four men arrayed around the table grumbled but relinquished their handles when Paul slapped down the quarters on the machine. "Singles," he called out. "Best of three."

Claire walked around to the other side of the table and wrapped her fingers around the handles of the 5-bar and the 3-bar, flicking and rolling them to get a feel for their weight. The spectators erupted into hooting and cheering.

She looked across the table. Paul was smiling, but his eyes told a different story. They were narrowed and intent. She remembered that look so well, and suddenly, she was a teenager again, longing to be part of the crowd. Playing foosball with Paul had given her that, allowing her to be a different person for a few hours. It felt good to step out of herself, even now.

"Ladies first," Paul said, ceremoniously handing her the heavy white ball.

She "foosed" it through the server hole, spinning it so it went to her man. She took a shot on Paul's goal. He blocked it easily, and the game picked up speed.

Her strength had always been her moving defense, and she managed to keep Paul scoreless longer than she had expected. However, he baited her into committing her 2-rod in one direction before he executed a snake shot in the other. His shot streaked past her goalie and into the goal with a bang.

"First blood," she acknowledged.

They played neck and neck up to a tie at five goals each. Winning foosball required a two-goal differential, so play continued. Claire could feel her wrists beginning to tire, so she called a time-out. Someone handed her a bottle of water, which she chugged gratefully before grasping the handles again.

Paul scored twice in succession to win.

"Good game," he said. "You didn't make it easy for me."

"Get the little lady a beer on me," someone shouted. "Hell, get her two of them. I ain't never seen anyone that good lookin' get close to beating Taggart."

"Not until I win," Claire called back with a grin. "I have to stay sober. Then I'll take you up on your offer."

Paul downed the rest of his beer in two swigs. She was pleased to note his T-shirt was sweat stained, proving she had made him work. She tried to step back from the table to stretch her arms, but found herself ringed in by a considerable crowd. Evidently, word had gotten out about the match, and folks had come to watch.

"Time," a self-appointed referee called.

Claire gave her hands a couple of shakes and took up her position at the handles. "Your foos," she said.

She pulled every trick out of her bag to bring the score to 4–3 in her favor. Then a fluky bank shot sent the ball rolling past Paul's out-of-position goalie and into his goal.

Claire threw her hands up and yodeled her triumph to the skies as the room erupted. Even Paul was grinning, despite being on the losing end of the celebration.

"You know you got lucky with that last one," he said.

"Better lucky than good," she declared.

The crowd parted as the bartender shouldered his way through, carrying a tray laden with beer bottles. "You've got a lot of admirers," he said as he held out his burden to Claire.

"You said you'd take a beer if you won," a voice called from the crowd.

"Yes, but I'd like to have a chance to at least stand up through the third game," Claire said, surveying the tray in laughing dismay.

"Hey, I won the first game," Paul pointed out. "Where are *my* admirers?"

"We'd go broke buyin' you beers every time you win," Claire's vocal friend shouted. "Besides, you ain't wearing a pretty pink T-shirt."

That sally met with loud catcalls and several comments on Paul's beauty, or lack thereof. Claire laughed along with the crowd.

"Time!"

All humor drained from Paul's face as he took hold of his rods. "Your foos," he said.

The ball went to her man, she faked Paul out with a dink, and scored. Paul met her eyes over the table, and she knew she was in for it. He bombarded her with shots from all angles, at all speeds, and from all rods. All she could do was defend for her life. The spectators began to coach her, shouting warnings and suggestions.

The score was 4–2, with Paul in the lead. The muscles in Claire's hands were screaming with exhaustion. She tried a palm roll and lost control of the ball.

"Watch his two-rod," a deep, familiar voice called out.

Claire forced herself not to look away from the table, but she felt Tim's voice like a long, slow caress down her spine.

As Tim had predicted, Paul took a shot with his defensive rod. "Time-out!" she yelled after she barely managed to block it with her goalie.

Wiping her palms on her jeans, she scanned the crowd. Tim's height made him easy to spot; his shoulder was braced against one of the columns dividing the bar area from the game room. As soon as she found him, he sent her the slow smile she was coming to anticipate.

As she watched his lower lip curve, she remembered the way his mouth had slid over her skin. Another ripple of awareness shivered through her. Having Tim in the room was not going to help her concentration.

"Nice block," Paul said, yanking her attention back to the table. "I thought I had you."

"My guardian angel saved me that time." She methodically stretched the fingers of each hand backward, playing for time to rest her muscles and her brain. "If I asked nicely, would you consider calling it a draw?"

"What incentive would you be offering when the score is four-two in my favor?" Paul grinned evilly.

Claire rested her elbows on the edge of the foosball table and leaned forward. "The satisfaction of knowing that chivalry is not dead?"

"I already told you there's no chivalry in foosball."

Tim's voice cut through the hooting. "Perhaps I could defend the lady's honor."

Chapter 16

*D*R. TIM?" TWISTING AROUND TO LOOK AT HIS CHALlenger, Paul wore a look of incredulity. "You play foosball?"

"So what do you say?" Tim asked as he made his way through the crowd to the table. "The lady has played hard and well, but she's worn down. Will you accept a new opponent to finish the match?"

Paul's eyebrows drew together, and he gave one of his rods an irritated spin.

"If I had a gauntlet, I'd throw it down," Tim persisted.

The man standing beside him took off his cowboy hat. "I don't rightly know what a gauntlet looks like, but you can use this here ole hat. Hittin' the floor ain't going to do it no harm."

Tim took the hat and neatly sailed it onto the two 5-rods in the middle of the foosball table.

Claire watched, fascinated, as Paul and Tim faced each other across the gleaming metal bars.

"What about it, Claire?" Paul asked, shifting his gaze to her. "Are you willing to let a stranger take over your hard-fought match?"

Claire couldn't imagine Tim's slow, deliberate way of moving would be much of a match for Paul's lightning reflexes. She didn't want Tim to be embarrassed by getting beaten too easily. Nor did she want to humiliate him by turning down his offer of help. She felt stuck between a rock and a hard place.

"If the good doctor can score even one more point for me, I'll be eternally grateful," Claire said, hoping that would save face for Tim.

"Okay, Doc, let's see what you've got." Paul flicked his 5-rod, sending the cowboy hat up into the air, where he caught it and tossed it onto the antler of a stuffed deer's head hanging on the wall. "I'll give you a couple of warm-up shots."

"That's mighty generous of you, but I'm ready."

"Suit yourself," Paul said.

Someone had positioned a barstool at one end of the foosball table and waved Claire over to it. She scooted onto the well-rubbed wood without taking her eyes off the game table.

The contrast between the two men seemed to disappear as they took identical stances, the same electric intensity vibrating in both of them. In Paul, it was familiar. In Tim, it sent a deep thrill of nerves and excitement zinging around inside her.

"Your serve," Paul said.

Tim pinched the ball through the hole, and the contest began with a slam and bang of the rods. Claire held her breath until she realized Tim knew his way around a foosball table. She didn't believe he would beat Paul, but he was not going to be a pushover. As she let some of her tension go, Tim executed a double bank shot that clanged decisively into Paul's goal.

A raucous cheer rose from the crowd. Paul nodded to Tim in acknowledgment. "Nice shot."

Claire slumped back in her chair with relief. Tim's honor would stay intact; he had scored on the town champion.

Her loyalty was divided; careful not to voice support for either, she found herself rooting for both men internally. However, when Tim scored again to tie the game at 4–4, Claire had to slap her hand over her mouth to muffle her whoop of triumph.

Once again, Paul gave credit to his opponent. Tim showed no jubilation; his gaze remained on the table.

Paul foosed the ball and walloped it at Tim's goal. Tim slammed his goalie over and, incredibly, kicked the ball off a corner of the plastic man's boot. It caromed around the table and somehow got behind Paul's goalie, rolling slowly but inexorably into the goal.

"Pure luck—good for me and bad for you," Tim said. "If my memory serves, it's your foos." Since he needed only one goal to win, custom dictated he offer his opponent the ball.

"There's nothing wrong with your memory or your skills," Paul said, his smile a quick baring of teeth. "I think Claire got herself a ringer."

As Paul sent the ball rumbling across the table, Claire found herself even more torn. On the one hand, she wanted Tim to triumph, both because he was the underdog and he was playing out her match. However, Paul had earned a certain respect for his skill at the game table, and she hated to see him brought low in his hometown.

She held the armrests of her barstool in an iron grip when Paul shot at Tim's goal, hoping it would go in and hoping it wouldn't. Tim made the save.

Time seemed to be suspended as the ball zigzagged back and forth among flashing silver bars and blurs of red-and-blue plastic. Suddenly, Claire saw a gap in Paul's defense. She watched Tim brush-pass the ball to get in position. Then she watched him hit it to the opposite corner, where it rattled around harmlessly.

He had deliberately blown the shot.

Her eyes flew to his face, but it showed nothing except alertness. *Had she imagined the opening or anticipated it just because she knew Paul's style so well?* She shook her head. It had been there, and Tim had seen it too. She could tell by his setup. She was sure he had misfired the ball on purpose.

She looked around and realized she was the only person who'd noticed. The crowd had been drinking, so their powers of analysis were clouded. Paul was immersed in the game; he didn't have time to worry about whether Tim missed intentionally or not. Only she was in a position to understand what had happened.

She took her eyes off the table and watched the vet instead. She began to see how fluid his movements were, how easily he controlled the rods, how relaxed his stance was. Yes, his eyes were locked on the game, his face wearing the mask of fierce competition, but he wasn't struggling to keep up with Paul's onslaught. He was directing his play as strategically as his opponent was.

This was a Tim she had glimpsed before but never quite believed. No longer a big shaggy dog, he had transformed into a hunting tiger. The revelation turned her low flicker of awareness into a roaring bonfire. But bonfires could flare out of control easily, consuming everything in their path. Claire tried to tamp down the flames.

Tim lost the game 8–6. Despite watching carefully, Claire had not caught him in any more intentional errors.

"The man deserves a reward," someone shouted. "He came from behind and nearly beat the king of foos."

Claire felt like a deer in headlights as the crowd's gaze swung toward her, and she realized they were expecting her to do the rewarding. Grabbing two bottles of beer and pasting a smile on her lips, she slid off the barstool and sauntered over to Tim with a little extra swing in her hips.

"How about a couple of nice cold ones for that great game?" she said, offering him the Budweisers.

"Hell no! He deserves a kiss from the pretty lady."

Claire looked at Paul with a silent plea for help, but he just shrugged and spread his hands in a *What can you do?* gesture.

When she turned back to Tim, he gave her an apologetic grin, but didn't make a move to stop the situation.

So he was enjoying this. Well, so could she.

She reached her hands up to his shoulders and stood on her toes, tilting her chin up and pursing her lips as though for a kiss. She was careful not to touch any more of him than she had to, and she avoided his eyes. Then she dropped back to flat feet and shook her head in mock disgust. "The man's too damned tall to reward."

Laughter rose from the spectators. The barstool was passed over and set in front of her. She made a show of climbing up two rungs before she lifted her face and offered her mouth to Tim with an exaggerated pursing of her lips.

It was a tactical error. Her shoulders were seized with an iron grip, and her eyes flew open to find Tim's face filling her vision. His breath fanned her cheek as he angled his head to take her mouth in a very real kiss. She thought she heard applause, but it was quickly drowned out by the explosion of sensation Tim's mouth set off. She wanted his big hands to move down and cup her breasts. She wanted to crush herself against his large, warm body. She wanted—

His mouth lifted from hers.

Tim held her steady on her perch and pitched his voice so only she could hear. "I was afraid there'd be a riot if they thought I wasn't getting rewarded adequately."

Claire sucked in a breath and gave him a shaky smile, trying not to let him see how deeply his performance had affected her. "You deserved it. Paul's a pro, and you nearly beat him."

"I was inspired," Tim said. He shifted his grip to help her off the stool.

His words seemed to dance across her skin, flicking little sparks wherever they touched. Her body roiled with arousal.

It made her jump when Paul appeared beside her and wound his left arm around her shoulders in a protective gesture. She wanted to squirm away from a touch that felt all wrong, but he kept his grip on her as he offered his right hand to Tim. "Good game, Doc. We'll have to arrange a rematch. You're a tough competitor."

Tim's hand dwarfed Paul's. "Claire tired you out for me."

"I'm not buying that," Paul said. "You used some damned smart strategy. We'll meet again."

"All I know is I could use a beer about now," Claire said. "I'm wrung out by all the exercise and all the tension."

"How about you, Doc?" Paul asked. "It's on me."

"I wouldn't turn it down."

In the flurry of activity, Claire slipped out of Paul's grasp and turned to Tim. "Where did you learn to play so well? I thought you didn't hang out in bars in your youth."

"In Manhattan. I went through a bar phase once I was legal and out of grad school. Those weren't my finest days, but I learned a few life skills like foosball."

Huge mugs of beer were thrust into their hands, and the crowd surged around them, congratulating all three players. Paul once again circled his arm around Claire's waist to keep the more inebriated well-wishers at bay. She kept wishing it was Tim's big body pressed against her side.

When the press of people finally thinned, Claire looked around for Tim, but he was nowhere to be found. Exhilaration drained from her like the air from a deflated balloon. He hadn't bothered to say good-bye.

"Now that was one fine foosball match," Paul said as he escorted her out to the parking lot. "You played just like the old days. And that Dr. Tim has been hiding his light underneath a bushel basket. I'd never have guessed he was that good."

"Me either. I was lucky he came along to rescue me from abject defeat."

Paul laughed and then sobered. "Hey, I'm sorry about that whole public kissing scene. I tried to think of a way to stop it, but it's the Sportsman. Sometimes you have to let the rowdies have a little leeway so things don't get ugly."

"Oh, it was no problem," Claire lied. "Dr. Tim put on a good show without doing anything ungentlemanly."

Except for making her want to drag him over to the pool table to have her way with him.

"Yeah, but I remember PDAs were not something you enjoyed."

"Oh, I'm not as shy now as I was back then."

"Good to know."

After getting her settled, he slid into the driver's seat and turned to scan her face in the weak light of the car's interior lamp. "Claire, I'd…" he began, then shook his head and turned the key in the ignition.

"What?"

"Some other time."

"Okay." She sank back into the haze of arousal Tim's kiss had thrown around her and was oblivious to Paul's suddenly white-knuckled grip on the steering wheel.

Chapter 17

TIM BANGED OPEN THE BACK DOOR OF THE VETERINARY clinic, setting off a chorus of barking that shattered the deep silence of the closed building.

"Damn, didn't mean to do that," he muttered, flicking on the light switch to bathe the hallway in a fluorescent glare.

After he'd left the Sportsman, he realized there was no chance he would be able to sleep. Adrenaline and arousal were still surging through his body.

Walking quietly, he made his way to the extra room he had converted into a small laboratory, thinking he might do some mindless chores to help his body come down from its high.

As immature as it was, he felt a fierce sense of triumph over the fact that he could have beaten Paul Taggart, the town's famous foosball champion, had he chosen to. In truth, he knew that eight times out of ten, Paul would win, but for that one moment, Tim had been the top dog, the unsurpassed player in the bar, even if only he had known it.

A grin spread over his face, and he did a silent fist pump to avoid disturbing the now quiet dogs.

How ridiculous that he took satisfaction in that all these years later. It just showed how deeply your childhood marked you; being too tall, too skinny, and too brainy had doomed him to eternal dorkdom in his school years. Never would he have been invited to compete with someone as cool as Paul Taggart, let alone be able to best him at his own game.

Yet when the moment had come to fire that shot into his opponent's goal, Tim had decided against it. Taggart had a certain image and reputation as a player in Sanctuary. One defeat at the foosball table probably wouldn't ruin it, but Tim wasn't going to be the spoiler. Maybe he'd challenge Taggart again sometime in a more private venue.

Or maybe not. He'd learned that proving something to yourself was enough.

There had been a few minutes there when he'd regretted his restraint. Seeing Taggart's arm resting around Claire's waist in such a casual, familiar way had put a twist in Tim's gut. The two of them seemed to have such an easy relationship. The memory of it put a damper on Tim's pleasure, especially when he remembered that Claire had looked like she was going to the guillotine when the crowd forced her to kiss him.

Claire's little comedy act about kissing him after the foosball match reminded him of something his wife would have done, and he didn't like the echoes it created in his mind. So he had put a stop to it by taking over the leading role. In one way, it had worked: once his lips touched hers, he knew Claire was the living, breathing woman whose body he wanted to explore from head to toe.

In another way, it had backfired: his own body went right back to the state of frustrated arousal he had fought down after their interlude at the stable. He had done his damnedest not to go to the Sportsman, but his mind couldn't convince the rest of him it was a bad idea.

He hadn't been in a state this volatile since Anais had died. The thought pulled him up short.

He realized he was standing in the middle of the lab, frowning at the toes of his boots.

He had been sleepwalking since her death, and now he was awake.

Was being awake a good thing?

He considered the scuffed leather a few more seconds before he slipped his cell phone out of his jeans pocket.

Claire jumped when the phone rang. It was midnight, and she was alone in her house. She checked the caller ID and saw that it was Tim. Heat sizzled through her as she picked up the phone.

"Claire, it's Tim. Are you alone?"

Claire dropped the phone. "Oh God, I'm so sorry," she said as she scooped it up off the braided rug and put it back to her ear. "I...Well, the phone fell on the floor."

"That would explain the thud." Tim's voice was amused, but an undercurrent of something dark and beckoning ran through it.

She knew what he wanted. A man didn't call at this hour to ask if you were alone for any reason but one.

"I..." She swallowed and sat down in the pool of light the table lamp threw on the sofa. She had made the decision to talk to him. Wasn't that her answer right there?

"Claire?"

"Yes, I'm alone."

"I'd like to come over."

"All right." She couldn't manage any more words than that.

"I'm at my office, so I'll be there soon," he said and disconnected.

She sat with the phone in her lap, frozen by the push and pull inside her. She could feel her nerves starting to hum with pleasure at the knowledge that Tim would be touching her in all the places she craved. Yet she shrank from opening herself to this man she knew just well enough to understand she knew nothing about him.

She should get up and do something—put on different clothes, light a fire or a candle, open a bottle of wine, turn down the bed. *Something.*

Instead, she relived her encounter in the barn and Tim's appearance at the Sportsman. Twice today he had sought her out. What had he said when they were discussing her painting? That if you want something you just keep after it. The thought sent a shiver of nerves and anticipation rippling through her.

A knock sounded on the door. She jumped and cursed softly as she realized she hadn't done anything on her list to prepare for his presence. He was here, and she wasn't ready in any way.

She padded to the door as he knocked again.

"Claire?" His voice was loud enough to penetrate the wood, but quiet enough not to carry to a neighbor's house.

She swung open the door. He stood on the porch, his silhouette outlined by the light of the outdoor sconces.

"Come in."

He came into her house with the same power and certainty he had shown at the foosball table. As the door swung shut behind him, his arms were around her, and she was pinned against the wall with his mouth on hers.

Then sensation swept away all thought: the silky heat of his mouth, the pressure of his chest against her peaking nipples, the hard curve of his erection against her belly. And his hands, the feel of his hands skimming over her shoulders and her ribs and her hips and her thighs. She couldn't keep track of where his hands were, because they seemed to be everywhere while his mouth pulled at her attention.

He slid one hand up her back under her T-shirt and flicked the hook of her bra loose. Pushing shirt and bra upward, he lowered his head to her breasts.

"Oh yes," she breathed, her head falling back to knock against the wall as he licked one aching nipple. Her whole body jerked as his teeth grazed her skin and sent a rope of electric heat spinning down between her legs.

"You know what I want to do, Claire?" he asked, lifting his head.

"Tell me."

"I want to take you here, standing up, like we were in the stall. It's been in my mind ever since this afternoon. But I don't want to hurt you."

Her knees nearly buckled with pure lust at the idea of being open and locked against his hips while he slid inside her. She was so wet and ready she knew nothing he did would cause her pain.

"Oh God, yes!" She unsnapped and unzipped her jeans, dragging them and her panties down to her ankles in one movement. As she untangled her feet and kicked the pile of clothing away, she heard the rip of foil and looked up to find Tim fitting a condom over his erection.

Then her hands were on his shoulders, and his hands were wrapped around her thighs, lifting her and spreading her legs wide. She bent her knees around his waist and reached one hand down to position him against her.

"Now!" she said.

He thrust up at the same time she slid downward, seating himself deep inside her. They both cried out, an incoherent sound of surprise and satisfaction.

She locked her ankles around him, feeling the teeth of his jeans' zipper dragging exquisitely at the tender flesh of her inner thighs. His hands had shifted to cup her buttocks, and she felt the brush of his fingertips against her anus, an additional sensation she found shockingly erotic.

He flexed his hips, and she ground against him, making him groan her name. She crushed her breasts against him, reveling in the feel of her naked skin against soft flannel and hard male muscle.

"That's it, you're in trouble now, lady."

He backed her up against the wall and began to stroke in and out, forcing her legs wider open. The friction of the denim and the zipper and his cock wound the coil of her arousal tighter and hotter and deeper until she felt the first spasm of release and convulsed so hard she nearly screamed. He moved faster and sent her spiraling into full orgasm. As her muscles clenched again, he drove into her fully and shouted with his own climax.

As the afterglow rippled through her, Claire dropped her forehead onto Tim's shoulder. She could feel his heart hammering against her breasts, especially when he drew in a deep gulp of breath.

"Mmm," she said, tilting her hips to add an extra fillip of pleasure.

A laugh rolled through him. "You aren't getting any more from me right now. I'm done—for the time being."

"I don't want to move," she murmured. She savored the sensation of being sandwiched between his body and the wall so no part of her was left untouched. As he began to slide out of her, she whimpered a sigh of regret.

Her mew turned to a startled "Oh!" when he replaced his cock with his hand, playing in the moist, hot place between her legs.

"I can't," she said, but her hips bucked as he kept stroking. "No, no more. Oh dear God!"

Another orgasm ripped through her as he pushed his fingers inside her. She dug her fingers into the bunched muscles of his arms, holding on for dear life as the spasm yanked her body into an arc of explosive sensation.

"I was pretty sure you could," Tim's voice rumbled beside her ear.

She sagged against him, feeling like a rag doll. "Please don't try for a third."

"I could take that as a challenge."

"Only if you want to kill me," she said into his neck.

She felt the brush of his lips against her ear and the shift of his weight. With her legs still wrapped around his waist, he carried her over to the sofa and gently deposited her on the cushions. As he sat down beside her, she burrowed into his side, curling her legs and arms up against him. She felt his movements as he stripped off his condom.

He tugged at the wad of T-shirt and bra rucked up under her armpits. "This looks uncomfortable. Lift your arms up."

"Right, you're only thinking of me," Claire said, but she raised her hands over her head so he could take the last of her clothes off.

She was about to go to work on the buttons of his shirt when he drew his fingertip over her breast with such exquisite gentleness that she gasped.

"You're so beautiful," he murmured.

Every inch of her skin was sensitized, so the touch of his hand made her nerve endings spark. As he pulled her onto his lap, she jerked when the tender spot between her legs came into contact with his denim-covered thighs.

"Did I hurt you?" he asked, starting to shift her again.

"No, just stop moving. Please." She tucked herself against his chest as he ceased trying to reposition her and simply encircled her with his arms. He let out a long sigh as he settled one hand on her hip and one on her shoulder, creating little oases of extra warmth.

For several minutes, she was content to just sit and inhale the scent of him as her body settled into a state of satisfied contentment. Unfortunately, as her physical senses quieted, her brain started buzzing again. She lifted her head. "You deliberately missed that shot."

Tim's head was tipped to rest on the back of the sofa and his eyes were closed. "What shot?" he asked without moving.

"You had Paul's goalie out of position, and you set up for the goal with a brush pass. Then you shot into the opposite corner on purpose."

"Why would I try to lose the game?"

"That's what I want to find out." Now that her afterglow had faded, it hit her that she was stark naked and her companion was fully dressed. She felt self-conscious and reached across Tim to grab a crocheted afghan, pulling it around her bare shoulders.

"Hey," he said, rousing from his torpor, "that blanket is not a good addition."

"Well, then you take all of your clothes off," Claire said, grinning. "It's only fair."

"Okay." He started unbuttoning his shirt, and her eyes went wide as she enjoyed the view.

Then she realized he was trying to distract her from her question. She put her hands over his to stop him. "This is only a temporary delay," she promised. "Why did you blow the shot?"

"I'm not the town's most famous foosball player," Tim said, not meeting her eyes. "I'm pretty sure I did everything I could to win the game."

"That's what I suspected. You didn't want to take Paul's title away from him." She let go of his hands to cup her palms around his face. *How many men could resist the temptation of beating the alpha male?* "You're an amazing man." Then she went at his shirt buttons herself.

"I don't remember saying that, but as long as I get credit, I won't argue." He dropped his hands on either side of her and watched as she worked her way down his shirt. She yanked the tails out of his waistband and pulled the fabric aside to bare the impressive expanse of his chest.

"Wow!" She let her fingers drift over his bared skin, tracing the curve of a pectoral muscle and tickling across the light fur of glinting auburn hair. She flattened her palm on the washboard of his abdomen and felt his muscles contract under her touch.

"Claire?" His voice was ragged. "If you keep that up, you may be having that third orgasm sooner than you want."

She dragged her gaze up from the magnificence of his chest. His pupils were huge and dark, while the tendons of his neck were strained with the effort of controlling his response to her exploration.

Just like that, she was ready for the third orgasm; she could feel the heat and moisture bloom inside her. She started to straddle him, but considered the size of the couch in contrast to the size of the man underneath her. "Why don't we go upstairs, where there's a king-sized bed?"

"Once I get into your bed, I intend to stay until morning."

"I have to get up early," she warned.

"How early?"

His thumbs were circling her nipples, so it was hard to think. Closing her eyes didn't help; it just made the focus on her breasts more intense. She grabbed his wrists to stop him, her fingers barely going halfway around the girders of sinew and bone. "Um, I have to get the girls up and dressed and be at church by nine thirty to get my choir robes on. So seven-ish."

Before she knew what was happening, he had hitched her over his shoulder and pushed off the cushions. The afghan got left behind in the transition, so her bare breasts were flattened against his flannel-covered back, and her naked bottom was in the firm grip of one of his large hands. His other hand was snugged across the backs of her knees, to hold her in place.

"Are you always so Neanderthal?" she asked, giving him a playful thump on his back.

He grunted in caveman fashion before heading for the stairs. "Call me Grog."

Being carried upstairs while inverted was surprisingly interesting. With any other man, she would have been nervous about being dropped or causing him injury. Slung over Tim's shoulder, she relaxed and enjoyed the whimsy of it. His playful side was just one more revelation.

"Turn left," she said as he paused at the top of the stairs.

Her view changed from pine planks to rose-colored carpeting. Tim gave her buttock a pat and bent to drop her carefully onto the bed.

He straightened to strip his shirt off and unfasten his jeans.

"I have an important question to ask you," she said, remembering her conversation with Holly. "Keep undressing," she prompted when his hands froze at his waistband. "Would you dance in a bowling alley?"

He kicked his boots off and stepped out of his jeans before pushing her knees apart and kneeling between them. "Depends on how good the music is."

She had no more questions.

Chapter 18

"CLAIRE, I HAVE COFFEE."

"Wha...?" She heard the voice and she smelled the coffee, but she couldn't figure out what either one was doing in her dream.

The bed seemed to drop out from under her on one side, and she rolled into something warm and solid. The voice rumbled closer to her ear. "It's seven ten. You have to sing in the choir."

Tim. Foosball. Sex. Amazing sex. It all flooded back into her brain. She lifted her head and madly shoved her hair out of her eyes.

He was sitting beside her on the bed, with his shirt unbuttoned and a mug of coffee in each hand. "This is one of the best dreams I've ever had," she said, trying to pull the sheet over her breasts as she scooted into a sitting position. Tim's weight on top of the covers made it impossible, so she grabbed a pillow instead.

"Don't cover up on my account," he said with a smile that made her feel shy and hot at the same time. He held up one mug and then the other. "With milk and sugar or black?"

"Milk and sugar, please." She took the mug and swallowed the nectar it contained. "It's actually sweet enough. You are my fantasy man."

"Hold onto your coffee," he said, making the bed rock as he settled in with his back against the headboard and his long legs stretched out and crossed at the ankles. He had pulled his jeans on, but his feet were bare.

"You have beautiful arches," she said as she took another sip of her coffee.

The mattress shook as he laughed and flexed his left foot to exaggerate the arch. "If it makes you want me, I'm good with that."

She was feeling oddly constrained. In the bright, clear light of morning, some of the things she'd done and let him do to her last night made her blush. It was hard to chat casually when images from their lovemaking kept flashing across her mind's eye. The truth was she'd known him for so little time that she didn't have a lot to discuss with him. Willow? Holly's abusive husband? The foosball game? The Castillo painting? Nothing seemed quite right for the moment.

"You're mighty quiet. Having second thoughts?"

"Oh God, no! Just a bit of morning-after awkwardness."

"I'll get out of your way, then," he said, swinging his legs off the bed. "Just let me grab my boots."

She grabbed his arm. "No, Tim, I'm not trying to get rid of you. I'm trying to, well"—she shrugged—"think of something to talk about. We don't know all that much about each other."

Or we know things we can't talk about, like your wife's suicide.

He kept his feet on the floor, but he turned toward her with a glint of wicked humor in his eyes. "There are a few things I know, like the way you like to be—"

"Shhh," she said with a laugh as she put her hand over his mouth. "I have to be in church in less than three hours, so I need to be in the proper frame of mind."

His tongue traced a slow, sensual circle in her palm, and she snatched it away. "You're not helping."

"All right. You know, I like this place. It's solid and comfortable, even though it's pink," he said, gesturing at the room around them. "Have you thought about buying it? You could use it as a weekend getaway."

"No, I stay with Holly when I visit here, which isn't that often, to be honest."

"Sanctuary isn't a bad place. Why are you so set against it?"

"I feel more at home in New York. Don't you miss it yourself?"

There. She'd approached the eight-hundred-pound gorilla of his wife's death.

"I like it here." He stared down into his coffee. "It's easy."

"Really? I feel the opposite way," she said, sliding her legs out from under the covers and hugging the pillow in front of her. "Sanctuary has its own issues."

"It sounds more like you have issues with Sanctuary."

"Oh, definitely," she said, pulling on her bathrobe. "I really have to shower."

"I don't suppose I could persuade you to save water and shower with a friend," he suggested, a laughing gleam back in his eyes. "After all, cleanliness is next to godliness, and it's Sunday."

"Solo cleanliness."

He reached out and caught her wrist, pulling her in to stand between his knees. Despite the fact that he was sitting and she was standing, their eyes were nearly level.

"Claire, you're as skittish as a new foal." The teasing glint vanished as he cupped his hands over her shoulders. "Last night was a lot of fun, but it wasn't just a romp in the hay. It was a lot more than that. I don't know what exactly, but more."

"Thank you," she whispered. "That's how I feel too, especially the 'I don't know what exactly' part."

He slid his hands up to her face, holding it so he could brush his lips lightly across hers. "We'll work that out as we go." He spun her around toward the bathroom and gave her a gentle smack on the rear.

Tim sat on the bed, elbows on knees as he cradled his coffee mug and listened to the splash of Claire's shower. He felt a stirring in his groin when he pictured water sluicing over the soft skin he'd so recently explored. She would look delicious with her long hair slicked down her wet back.

"Okay, I need to derail that train of thought," he said to himself, shoving off the mattress. He prowled around the room, checking the view out each dormer window, prolonging the pleasure of being in Claire's bedroom.

When the sound of running water ceased, he padded over to scoop up his boots and plunked back down onto the bed. The whir of a blow-dryer picked up where the shower left off, and Tim smiled. She'd be in there a while if she had to blow-dry her mane.

He bit off a curse as his phone buzzed on the bedside table. It was too early for anything other than a medical emergency. Sure enough, when he dialed in to his answering service, a distraught woman sobbed into the phone that her Bitsy had been hit by a car.

He pulled on his socks and boots, buttoned his shirt and tucked it in, and walked to the door. It would be better to write her a note downstairs in the kitchen. That would sidestep her sudden shyness.

He had his hand on the doorknob when he reversed direction, heading back for her bed. Planting one knee on the mattress, he bent to inhale her scent from the sheets.

When Claire emerged from the bathroom, Tim and his coffee mug were gone. Calling his name down the stairs elicited only silence, setting off a waltz of relief and disappointment inside her.

"Not even a good-bye kiss," she said to her reflection in the mirror. She wondered if he had left out of consideration for her ridiculous fit of nerves. "He really is a nice man."

And funny and playful and smart and compassionate and kind and sexy as hell.

"What's not to like?" she asked the mirror again as she pulled on her under-the-choir-robe clothes.

He was building a house in Sanctuary.

His wife had committed suicide.

"Two big problems," she conceded to herself.

They dissolved from her mind when she found the note he'd left on the downstairs hall table. He'd used the preprinted to-do pad she kept by the refrigerator and filled in the blank line before *List* so it read:

> <u>Tim's</u> List—*after he takes care of the veterinary emergency that called him away before he could say good-bye:*
> *1. Kiss Claire in her sister's kitchen.*
> *2. Kiss Claire in an empty stall.*
> *3. Kiss Claire in the Sportsman.*
> *4. Kiss Claire in her living room.*
> *5. Kiss Claire in her bedroom.*
> *6. Find a lot more places to kiss Claire.*

He'd put a check in front of the first five items.

"Oh dear God!" she said, running her fingertip over the list. "I could fall in love with this man."

A fist of panic closed around her throat at the thought.

Chapter 19

HE WAS MAKING LOVE TO CLAIRE. THEY WERE IN A bed, but he couldn't tell if it was Claire's or not. It didn't matter because all he wanted was to touch her warm, curving body. Suddenly, the room around him changed to the apartment in New York City where he and Anais had lived right after their wedding. And the body under his changed to Anais's.

He knew immediately, despite all his concerns about the similarities between the two women. Making love to them was completely different. He was startled because somewhere in the back of his mind lurked the idea that his wife was dead. He laid his fingers against the pulse point of her neck, just to be sure.

"Not yet," Anais said, her mobile face alive with laughter and malice. "Not quite yet." She slid out from under him and picked up a gun off the bedside table. Standing naked and bathed in a spotlight, she held the gun to her temple.

"No!" he shouted. "I'll stay with you through it all!"

"That's not good enough."

She squeezed the trigger, and he jerked awake, the surface under him rocking wildly.

"Holy shit!" He realized he was in the hammock behind his house, and Sprocket was barking.

He swung his legs around so his feet were on the ground and reached down blindly to scoop up the little dog, needing the feel of something warm and alive.

He stared over Sprocket's head to the mountains beyond, orienting himself in the real world, away from the nightmare. The light was building toward midday, so the hills looked more green than blue.

He tried to draw his usual comfort from them, but all he felt was the old guilt rolling over him in waves.

Claire had enlisted a fellow alto's assistance with her sleep deprivation problem. Mrs. Grandison had strict instructions to joggle Claire's elbow if she noticed her nodding off during the sermon.

With Mrs. G's help, she made it through church without embarrassing herself. She gave Brianna and Kayleigh a private tour of the gallery and truly enjoyed discovering which artworks each girl responded to before she drove them home.

She stayed upright through an afternoon of dealing with "lookie loos," browsers with no intention of buying anything. She set her phone to vibrate and then checked it compulsively, hoping to hear from Tim.

Although he knew she was working, she was surprised he hadn't called. It seemed out of character, especially after his whimsically affectionate note.

She checked her watch and decided she could close up ten minutes early since the gallery was empty. Bustling around, she shut down the computer, checked the alarm on the Castillo room, and flicked off the lights. She was rooting through her purse for her car keys when the door chime sounded.

"I'm sorry, we're clo—" she said as she turned to find Paul Taggart standing in the doorway, wearing a white T-shirt, jeans, and a black leather jacket and boots. A motorcycle helmet was tucked under her arm.

Time spiraled backward. How many times had he shown up at the end of her Girl Scout meetings, dressed just like this?

"Hey, Claire. Want to go for a spin on the bike?" he asked. She couldn't tell if he was speaking those words in the past or the present. They were the same in both times.

"Paul?" she said, trying to reorient herself in the here and now.

"You okay?" His grin vanished as he came up and took her elbow in a warm, firm grasp. "You look like you've seen a ghost."

"I have. You!"

"Not me. I'm flesh and blood, and I'll prove it." He leaned down and dropped a quick kiss on her cheek. "Nothing spooky about me."

Claire hated the fact that she wanted to scrub his kiss off. The only person whom she wanted to touch her was Tim, and he still hadn't called.

"What's spooky is that you look exactly the same as you did when we were in high school. Did you sell your soul for eternal youth?"

"Nope, I'm just young at heart. It shows on my face." He gestured toward the door. "So, what do you say to a ride? The sun is shining, and you're off work."

"I need to start dinner for Holly and the kids," Claire said, deciding not to mention her exhaustion from lack of sleep the night before.

"This early? I can have you back in plenty of time to fix dinner."

"I'm not really dressed for it." She glanced down at her lilac silk pants and taupe open-toe heels.

"Since when did that stop you?" Paul's grin dared her to live dangerously, the way it always had.

He was right about it being too early to start dinner. And she was tired of staring at her silent cell phone, willing Tim to call. It made her feel pathetic. "Oh, what the heck! Let's hit the highway."

"That's my Claire," Paul said, looping his arm over her shoulders and pulling her against his side as he steered her toward the door.

"Just let me call Holly," she said, pulling out her phone.

"You're going on a motorcycle ride with Paul Taggart?" Holly's voice rang with shock.

"Just a short one. Unless you need me there."

"No, no, everything's fine. I'm just surprised."

Claire was little surprised too, but she wasn't going to admit it. "Has anyone called for me?"

"No." Holly sounded puzzled. "Were you expecting someone?"

"Mmm, I asked Davis to change my schedule, and I didn't hear from him yet," Claire lied. Maybe Tim had called her at home and gotten the answering machine. Except he knew she was working today. And he knew her cell phone number.

She said good-bye to Holly and hit the *End* button more firmly than necessary. If Tim hadn't called the gallery, or her cell phone, or Holly's house, he didn't want to talk to her.

She pasted a glitteringly false smile on her face and turned back to Paul. "I'm ready."

Paul's Harley gleamed in the sunshine as he handed her the extra helmet. He had always made her wear one, even when they were teenagers. She climbed on the back of the bike and wound her arms around his waist while he kicked on the Harley's big engine. The years rolled back when he roared down Washington Street to the highway. She reveled in the wind whipping the silk of her clothes against her skin and the blur of houses and trees reeling past her vision.

Everything was stripped away: the emotional roller coaster of Holly's situation, the nastiness of her own divorce, even her disappointment at Tim's silence. She was a teenager again, thumbing her nose at everyone's idea of her as a nerd and a good girl. That's what Paul had done for her then—let her live dangerously while being perfectly safe.

Paul turned off the highway and gunned the motorcycle up a dirt road as she held on for dear life over the bumps. He cut sharply to the right and went careening across a meadow until they reached an outcropping of limestone.

Paul locked the kickstand into place and pulled a blanket out of the bike's storage bag, flicking it open on the grass. The blanket made her nervous. Paul had clearly planned this.

"It's Chief Chipaway," Claire said, pulling off her helmet, "the disappearing Indian."

The rock formation had once looked like an Indian chief's head. However, since limestone was soft and easily eroded, the chief's features had vanished one by one until only the locals could find the resemblance to a human being. Paul used to bring her here to drink contraband beer.

"He's lost an ear since you lived here," Paul said, pulling two Budweisers out of the storage bag, twisting off the tops, and handing her a bottle. He clinked his beer to hers. "Here's to old friends."

"Cheers!" Claire tilted her head back and let the nearly cold liquid run down her throat. "Mmm, that first sip is the best."

"Have a seat," Paul said, dropping onto the blanket and tugging at her wrist.

She was afraid she had made a mistake in accepting Paul's invitation. She sank down cross-legged on the plaid fabric and hoped she was misinterpreting his intentions.

Paul shrugged out of his jacket and took another swig of beer before leaning back on his elbows.

"It's hard to imagine you as a two-term mayor when I see you in your biker gear." She twisted her beer in her hands.

"I'm a man for all seasons," he said, grinning at her. Then his smile dropped away. "You know, I heard from Peter Van Zandt after I got elected mayor."

"You didn't tell me that before!" Claire sat up, nearly spilling her beer. "Where is he? What did he say?"

"He said he was glad someone who rode a motorcycle was mayor. He's living in Atlanta."

"Teaching?"

Paul shook his head. "After the incident here, he couldn't get a job in a school."

Claire felt all the old fear and loneliness boil up. Mr. Van Zandt had been her champion; he had understood and believed in her dream of a career in the field of art. When he had been driven out of Sanctuary, she had nearly given up.

"He's a house painter. Likes it, though, he said."

"What a stupid waste of a brilliant teacher!" Claire felt angry tears burn in her eyes. "This town ruined his life."

"Hey! Sanctuary has changed since then."

"Really? Has that aspect of Sanctuary changed?"

"I like to think it has." Now she could see clearly the man he had grown into. His jaw was squared, his gaze level. "I ran for mayor to fix some things I thought were wrong here."

She was still upset, but she took a swallow of Bud and leaned back on her elbows. "I'm sorry. It's ancient history, isn't it?"

"You know, there's something I always wanted to do back in those ancient times, but I didn't want to ruin our friendship." He had rolled onto his side and was looking down at her, blocking the sunlight. Dipping his head, he kissed her, his lips tasting of beer and fresh air.

For the sake of the past they shared, she wished she could respond the way he wanted her to, but all she could think of was how different Tim's lips had felt on hers. She put her palm on Paul's chest and gently pushed.

"Thank you, but we're not those kids anymore," she said as he let the pressure of her hand move him a few inches away.

"No, we're older and wiser and capable of appreciating the people in our lives."

She pushed a little harder, but he had become immovable. She sighed. This wasn't something she'd wanted to say to him. "I'm involved with someone else."

Regret and something she thought might be resentment flashed in his eyes, but he lifted his head. "One of your sophisticated New York friends, I guess. Tough to compete with that."

It seemed easier to let him think that. She wasn't certain whether she was actually "involved" with Tim. It had only been one night, after all, and he still hadn't called. She slipped her hand into her pocket to verify her frustratingly silent cell phone was still there.

"Now I know why you're in such a rush to get back to New York," he continued.

She sat up and wrapped her arms around her knees. She wasn't going to keep misleading him. "I've got a dream job waiting for me in the city. A new gallery to open where I can exhibit whatever artists I choose."

"You could do that here. Davis thinks you hung the moon. He'd probably make you a partner in the gallery."

"That's really nice, but New York is one of the centers of the international art world. It's an amazing opportunity."

"Especially for a hillbilly girl made good."

"You see, you understand."

"You talked about it a lot when you'd had a couple of shots. In fact, you wouldn't *stop* talking after a couple of shots."

"Jerk!" Claire gave him a friendly shove, unbalancing him so he toppled backward onto the blanket.

He called her something equally unflattering, and they fell into their old, friendly banter. Claire wasn't fooled, though. Paul didn't like to lose; he would be riled up when he found out her love interest was a local.

Assuming she still had a local love interest.

Chapter 20

CLAIRE STOOD ON HOLLY'S LITTLE CEMENT-FLOORED porch, collecting herself before opening the front door. When Paul dropped her back at the gallery to pick up her car, she made sure to dodge his attempt to kiss her. She blew out a sigh. Life in Sanctuary was becoming more complicated than she'd expected.

Walking through the kitchen door, she stopped dead. Robbie McGraw sat at the table, with a mug of coffee and a half-eaten slice of pie arrayed in front of him. Holly sat opposite him, dressed in a pink blouse with a ruffle around the collar, her hair falling in shining waves around her face. Even more amazing, she was wearing makeup and a smile.

"Well, I'll be," Claire said, falling into the country speech patterns of her youth, "Robbie's here. And spoiling his dinner with pie first."

He stood as soon as he saw her. "I guess it's okay to get that hug now that I'm off duty," he said with a grin.

Claire laughed and walked over to wrap her arms around him and give him a peck on the cheek. "It's nice of you to come by when you're not working."

"Well, a slice of homemade cherry pie makes it worth the trip."

"Homemade, is it? I think I need a piece too. I'm a big believer in eating dessert first." So Holly felt well enough to make a pie for

Robbie. That was good news. As her sister started to push her chair back, Claire said, "Stay put. I'll get it."

She cut a wedge of pie, poured a glass of milk, and sat down. Holly shifted in her chair and kept her eyes on her mug. "Robbie called to say he would come by to take a look at the locks on the garage windows. I thought the least I could do was make him a snack."

"Excellent idea, since I get to enjoy it too," Claire said, savoring the buttery crust and sweet fruit. "You'll have to drop in more often, Robbie."

"How was your ride?" Holly asked, making Claire choke on a bite of pie. Fortunately, her sister turned to Robbie and continued with a note of censure in her voice. "She went off on a motorcycle with Paul Taggart."

"It was great," Claire said after taking a gulp of milk. "We visited Chief Chipaway."

"Nice spot up there," Robbie said. "I haven't seen Paul on his Harley in a while."

"He and Claire used to roar around on a motorcycle back in high school. It gave Ma and Pop fits."

"Only when you told them," Claire said.

"I was afraid you'd get maimed or killed."

Claire snorted before she grinned at Robbie. "Don't let Holly fool you. She was just using Paul's motorcycle to get the pressure off her for taking Pop's Oldsmobile to the movies without permission. Let's see, which boy was that with?" Claire cocked her head and put her finger on her chin. "Grady? No. Lester? No. I think it was—"

Holly's lips twitched. "Stop that right now, Claire Adele! I never once went out with Grady or Lester, and you know it."

Claire just smiled and shook her head.

"I guess I'd better be going," Robbie said, having polished off the rest of his pie. "It's dangerous to get between sisters when they're fighting."

"That's right," Claire said. "You've got, what, three sisters?"

"All older," Robbie said. "They bossed me around something fierce. Thanks for the pie."

Claire got up to lock the kitchen door behind him and then started to load the dirty dishes into the dishwasher.

"Oh, Tim called for you," Holly said as she stacked some plates for Claire.

A fork clattered onto the linoleum floor. "Oops," Claire said, scooping it up and hoping Holly hadn't seen the grin she couldn't quell. "Did he leave a message?"

"Nope. Just asked if you were here. I told him you'd be at your place around nine."

Claire looked at her sister. Now that she wasn't putting on a bright face for her guest, the dark circles under Holly's eyes stood out against her pallor. She'd put concealer over the bruise on her cheek, but even then, it showed through. Claire tamped down the excitement fizzing through her veins at the news of Tim's call and concentrated on her sister. "Robbie's a nice guy."

"I had a crush on him when I was fifteen." Holly drew a circle on the vinyl tablecloth with her fingernail.

"I remember," Claire said. "We talked about it in the rhododendron cave. That pie was great."

"It was out of the freezer from last summer. I can't even remember the last time I had the energy to bake fresh," Holly said.

"I know, Holl, but you will get better." Claire squeezed her sister's shoulder gently. "Where are the girls?"

"Over at the Defibaughs'. They should be home in half an hour."

Claire hesitated. She hadn't had a chance to think about the best way to approach Holly about what Brianna had said, but this was the perfect opportunity. She sat down across from her sister. "I know you wanted to do this with Frank, but I think you need to tell Brianna and Kayleigh about the divorce."

If Holly had been wan before, she looked like a ghost now. Claire pushed on. "Something Brianna said yesterday made me realize she knows there's a chance of divorce, and she's very frightened. She even thinks she and Kayleigh would have to live with different parents."

"Oh no, I would never let that happen!" Holly said. "I'd let Frank have the girls before I would split them up."

"It won't come to that, I promise you," Claire said fiercely. "Look, if you don't want to talk to them alone, I'll do it with you."

Holly looked like a deer in headlights. "I don't know what to say. I have to tell them their world is going to be torn apart, and it's my fault. How do I explain that?"

Claire flashed back to how Milo had systematically undermined her confidence in herself. Not only had he convinced her that it was her fault he no longer wanted to be married to her, he had convinced the judge that his expertise had guided her in buying the paintings she had acquired, which were now worth hundreds of thousands of dollars. He'd even made *her* believe it.

The memories brought a rush of clean, strong anger. If she could see the error of Holly's brainwashing so clearly, how could Claire continue to let Milo's ugly words undermine her own confidence? She put the question away for later as she reached over and took one of Holly's hands. "Don't even *think* it's your fault. Brianna and Kayleigh's world will be fine because they are lucky enough to have you as their mother."

"Oh God, I'm so scared!" Holly said, clutching Claire's hand convulsively as tears streaked down her cheeks. "How can I tell my children everything will be okay when I don't know what's going to happen myself? I don't understand Frank. He's the one who asked for the divorce. Now he acts like it was all my doing."

"He wants to be in control, and you've taken that away from him." Claire gave Holly's hand a little shake. "Get mad, sis! Frank has no right to treat you this way."

Holly stared at her for a long moment, her eyes liquid with tears. Then she sat up tall. "You're right. I have to fight for the girls."

"Damn straight! Don't let the bastard cheat them out of what they deserve." She knew she was channeling her anger at Milo into firing her sister up. It felt good to use it for something constructive. "Shall we discuss what you want to say to them about the situation?"

Holly's shoulders sagged slightly. "Let me think about it tonight. I promise I'll talk to them tomorrow."

Holly laid her free hand on top of their already entwined fingers. "I'm really, really grateful you're here."

Claire felt her throat tighten with emotion at the trust Holly was placing in her. "You know what I always used to tell myself when I was going through this with Milo?"

"What?"

"It will be all right in the end, because if it's not all right, it's not the end."

Chapter 21

$\mathcal{A}$S CLAIRE DROVE UP TO HER RENTED HOME, HER HEAD-lights flashed on the dark sheen of a big SUV parked in front of the double garage door. Her heartbeat kicked up a notch.

She'd forgotten to turn on the outside lights, but she could see a silhouette sitting in one of the rocking chairs on the front porch.

It was 9:15. Tim was waiting for her to come home.

All the chaotic emotions of her day converged into one searing bolt of joy: He had come to spend the night in her bed again. Practically leaping out of her car, she forced herself to slow down as she approached the porch.

"Evening." Tim's deep voice rumbled through the still night air. She felt it on her skin.

"Hi. I hope you haven't been waiting too long," she said, feeling shy as she walked up the steps.

He was standing now, holding a dark shape out to her. "Here's something to apologize for not calling sooner."

She flicked on the outside light switch. The yellow bulbs threw deep shadows over Tim's face, but sent warm highlights dancing over his hair. She remembered the delicious tickle of it brushing against the inside of her thighs less than twenty-four hours ago. "Queen Anne's lace and black-eyed Susans," Claire said, taking the bouquet. "These bring back such memories!"

"The florists aren't open on Sunday, so I had to make do with wildflowers."

"Wildflowers are better than a store-bought bouquet," Claire said, looking up at him, wondering why he didn't kiss her. "Come in and have a beer."

His hands were shoved in his pockets, and for a moment, she thought he was going to refuse. In fact, he made an almost imperceptible movement toward his car before he pivoted toward her door. "A beer sounds good."

Her incandescent happiness flared and died at his strange response. There would be no throwing herself into the comfort of his arms. Instead, another strand of pain went twisting into the dark tapestry of emotions she carried with her tonight.

For the entire day, Tim had wrestled with his demons, taking such a long tramp through the woods that he had to carry an exhausted Sprocket home. Sanctuary was supposed to keep his ugly phantoms at bay, and here he was, facing ghosts again.

His night with Claire had brought him a pleasure and peacefulness he hadn't felt in months. Today he was paying the price.

He didn't know how to deal with this. He had no idea what he should say to Claire.

He knew he had to say something, offer an explanation or an apology. He flinched away from the thought of delivering either.

As it got later, he paced around his house while Sprocket watched him from the sofa. He picked up the phone and dropped it again. Then he forced himself to dial Holly's number. A flood of relief washed through him when Holly told him her sister was not there.

Now here he was, two feet away from the woman who had let him sleep without nightmares last night. He had watched her expression shift from excited welcome to stunned bafflement, and felt the guilt of it.

He wanted to leave before he said words that would wound her. Last night had included an unspoken declaration of trust and respect. He was about to ruin both of those things.

He followed her into the pine-paneled kitchen. As she bent to rummage in the refrigerator, her pants outlined the shape of her hips and bottom. His hands twitched with the urge to trace those curves again. She turned with a bottle of Molson in each hand, saying with a forced smile, "Hope you don't mind imported."

Something in his face made her smile vanish. "Tim, what's wrong?"

He opened his mouth, but no words coalesced in his brain. He had nothing good to say, so he did what he'd been holding back from since she walked onto the porch.

He took one stride toward her and, with both hands, tilted her face upward. Before she could react, he dropped his head and devoured her mouth. As her arms came around his back, he felt the chilled glass of the bottles through his shirt. She opened her mouth and let him explore at his leisure while she clung to him. Her pliancy threw gasoline on the flames.

He shifted his grip to her behind and lifted her onto the beige Formica of the kitchen countertop, spreading her legs so he could come up against her.

"Tim!" Her voice was part laughter, part shock. "Let me put these bottles down."

He gave her just enough room to twist sideways and slide the beer onto the counter. Then he wrapped one arm around her waist and pulled her to him. The V of her legs rubbing against his erection tore a groan from his chest and snapped any control he might have been holding on to. He wanted to slip into the forgetfulness of being inside her.

"Ahhh, yes," she said, pushing her hips forward to bring the friction to an exquisite pitch.

He felt the tightness spiraling into his groin and brought his hands around to the button of her pants, almost yanking it off in his haste to undress her. He jerked her zipper down and bent to pull at the cuffs while she worked the waistband down over her thighs. She started to toe off her hot high heels.

"Leave those on," he said, unfastening his fly and rolling a condom over his cock.

Her eyes widened in surprise, but he silenced any comment by sliding two fingers inside her. Her head fell back with a gasp as he tested her readiness. Her hot slickness made him harden even more. He withdrew his hand and slid his palms around and under her hips, positioning himself and then driving into her just as he pulled her forward.

"Oh my God!" she yelped as she grabbed fistfuls of his shirt and arched into him. "Oh yes!"

His mind went blank. All he could feel was the gathering, widening pool of electric sensation as he slid in and out. Her knees were braced on his hips as she opened herself farther for him, tilting to give him an even better angle.

Then the pool drew in to a point of infinite pleasure and vaporized in a blazing cloud as he felt her muscles contract and release around him. He threw his head back as his climax hit him like a freight train.

He drove himself inside her as far as he could and then wrapped his arms around her as she came again, holding her tight against him to absorb the power of her orgasm. When she went limp, he kept holding her, feeling the little shudders running through her as her body slowly relaxed. He wanted to stay like that, without the necessity for words, but he knew it had only been a temporary reprieve.

"Wow!" she said, her voice muffled against his neck. "That was not what I expected. But I liked it. A lot."

"I was afraid I'd been too hurried."

She lifted her head on a chuckle. "I used to think you always moved with slow deliberation, but that was a gross misconception on my part."

"You being from New York, I feel I have to keep up," he said, joining her banter with a guilty sense of relief.

"You kept it up quite nicely."

He laughed, a real laugh. This was why he wanted to be with Claire; she brought fun into his life.

He was making this more difficult than it had to be. He should just enjoy the lovemaking, the banter, and not get twisted into knots about any deeper levels. He just needed to convince his subconscious of that.

She slithered sideways and snagged a beer, holding it up to him. "You earned this big-time."

"We did this in the wrong order," he said before opening the bottle and handing it back to her. "I was supposed to get you drunk before I took advantage of you."

"Is that what you were doing? Taking advantage of me? I could have sworn we were just having hot sex on the kitchen counter." Claire took a swig of beer and grinned at him. "Which, by the way, seems to be the perfect height for someone of your… er…stature."

"I figured that out a long time ago," he said, stepping away to dispose of the condom. "Kitchen tables are too low. Bar stools are too unstable. But a good solid countertop makes for a perfect base of operations."

She threw back her head and guffawed. It was the sound of a woman who felt all was right with her world.

As he watched her sitting on the counter, swinging her bare legs so her spike heels tapped the cabinet, her hair spilling out of her ponytail at odd angles, he knew he wasn't going to say one damned thing to ruin this moment.

Because he wanted to stay for the night.

At six a.m., his eyes came open as usual. He never could sleep past six. This morning he was glad to be awake because he had an armful of warm, sleeping Claire. In fact, he had cocooned himself around her in the night so that his front was touching every inch of her back, while his right hand was tucked under her left breast.

As he lay still and enjoyed the feel of her bare skin against his, he checked the recesses of his mind for lingering nightmares, but found none. Once again, Claire's presence kept them away.

So he had two options. One was to spend every night with Claire. The other was to stay completely away from Claire. He didn't have to think much about which he would prefer, but Claire might not agree.

Chapter 22

A POWERFUL SUNBEAM SMACKED CLAIRE AWAKE. SHE rolled away from it and stretched luxuriously, a sense of satisfied well-being humming through her body. She was alone in the rumpled bed, but she expected that. Tim had to go to work, while today was her day off—from everything. Holly insisted she not come over on Monday mornings.

Claire lay on her back, staring at the ceiling. Tim had been so different last night. He'd made love to her with an intensity bordering on desperation. And he hadn't talked.

The night before, it had been all about teasing and playing with each other. Last night, conversation was minimal. If she managed to get three sentences out, he would interrupt her with such a fierce kiss that her words went right out of her head.

She shoved herself up to a sitting position as it hit her: There was something he didn't want to talk about. He almost hadn't come into the house. Had he meant to break it off last night? Was that why his lovemaking had given her the weird sense of being held on to by a drowning man?

It had the unsettling effect of reminding her of Milo. After a business dinner she wasn't invited to, he had come home to find her lying on the couch, reading a book. He'd practically ripped her clothes off. Their coming together had been so violent they had rolled off the sofa and ended up sprawled on the Oriental rug.

The next day, he told her he wanted a divorce.

"Damn it!" Claire said, throwing the covers back and hurling herself off the bed. She stomped around, showering and getting dressed in her riding clothes since she planned to spend the morning at Healing Springs Stables.

Her fury evaporated when she went downstairs to find the coffeemaker primed and ready for her to just flip the *On* button, while a half dozen Dunkin' Donuts and a fresh bouquet of black-eyed Susans in a blue drinking glass stood on the kitchen table.

A new to-do list was propped against the doughnut box. The first three items were the coffee, the doughnuts, and the flowers with checks beside them.

Item number four was, *Persuade Claire to try out my bed tonight.*

She sank into a chair and flipped open the lid of the box. All the doughnuts had chocolate icing.

Even sugar and chocolate couldn't quite melt away her sense of unease. As soon as she got to the stable, she went to Willow's stall and, after giving her a carrot, clipped a lead line onto the mare's halter.

"We're going for a walk, sweet girl. I've been neglecting you, and I'm sorry. Life got crazy on me."

As they passed the paddock, Sharon was working a new colt and raised a hand in greeting. Claire waved back but didn't stop.

Following a trail between Sharon's immaculately painted white fences, Claire led the horse up a slight rise and into an open meadow. She kept walking until they reached a spot where she could see the ridges of the mountains undulating away into the distance, their crests kissed by the morning sun. Even Willow seemed to appreciate the view; she lifted her head and flicked both ears forward. The light made her brown eyes glow like fine sherry.

"You're starting to look like a Thoroughbred," Claire said, running her hand over the mare's shoulder. "Your coat is beginning to shine."

Willow leaned her head against Claire's breastbone and blew out a sigh. Claire had to brace herself against the weight of the horse's head, but she savored the sign of trust. She scratched around the base of Willow's ears, making the horse sigh again.

"I need to discuss something with you." Claire kept stroking the horse's head. "You know your vet? The big guy who gives you shots? Well, I can't figure him out."

Willow shifted to sniff at her pocket.

"Oh, fine, here's a carrot. Anyway, two nights ago, we had a great time together, both in bed and out of it. But last night, something was wrong. He acted like my ex-husband right before he decided to be ex. So what's going on?

"Here's my theory: It has something to do with his dead wife. Do you think I might be the first woman he's slept with since his wife killed herself? Could that be freaking him out?

"Here's another good question: Why am I getting involved with a man whose wife committed suicide? Doesn't that strike you as a bad idea?"

Willow rubbed her forehead up and down Claire's arm. "Easy there, you're going to knock me over. Wait, was that a nod meaning, *Yes, it's a bad idea*? How do whisper horses work? Do you actually talk back?"

The mare dropped her head and started grazing on the long grass. Claire plunked down beside her so she could still see one of the horse's huge liquid eyes.

"But he's such a nice man, and Lordy, he's got good hands. Must come from being a vet and having to figure out what's wrong from just touching his patients."

She tore off a thick blade of grass and tickled Willow's ear with it, making the horse shake her head.

"Here's the thing. I'm only staying in Sanctuary a few more weeks. What harm can it do to enjoy great sex with a hunky guy? I know there's a time limit to the relationship, and he knows it too. So there will be no expectations and no emotional attachments."

Willow shook her head again, this time without the provocation of a blade of grass.

"You're right. I'm kidding myself about the no expectations thing. But it's been so long since I've felt this good with a man. You have to understand, Milo made me feel like crap about myself. So I'm going to override you on this one. I want to see where it takes me."

Willow lifted her head and bent her long neck around to look behind her. Claire followed her gaze and saw Sharon standing by the gate and waving.

"Session's over, sweet girl," Claire said, scrambling to her feet. She rolled her shoulders, feeling how the knots of tension had eased. Flinging her arms around Willow's neck, she rested her forehead against the horse's. "I'm so glad Sharon found you for me. Now, can you help me get Holly a whisper horse?"

Sharon talked her into staying for lunch after Claire had returned from a long, fast ride on the big gelding Salty. She seemed to have developed a liking for oversized males.

Claire slurped up the last drops of a Joe's milk shake and slouched back in the oak armchair in front of Sharon's desk. "If I continue eating Joe's, I'm not going to be able to fit into my jodhpurs."

"Got to keep up your strength," Sharon said. "I hear you were out on the bike with Paul Taggart yesterday."

"Oh God! Small towns!" Claire said, rolling her eyes. "He came by the gallery right as I was closing up. It was a beautiful day, and I couldn't resist the invitation."

"I hear Dr. Tim gave him a run for his money at foosball on Saturday."

"Did you also hear that Dr. Tim was finishing the match I started?"

"Yup. So which one is it that's putting that glow on your face?"

Claire buried her face in her hands to hide whatever telltale glow Sharon saw. "This is why I love New York. No one knows. No one cares."

"You took Willow out to talk to her, didn't you?"

"Yes, and it helped, so you can say, 'I told you so,' " Claire said, dropping her hands to give Sharon a wry smile.

"Having a whisper horse is a good start, but here's the thing: a horse can't make your decisions. Willow can help you sort your thoughts out, but you have to make the choices."

"What are you saying?"

"Me? I'm not saying anything," Sharon said with a grin before sliding her chair back from her desk and walking out the door.

How ironic that Sharon thought she needed to make a choice between Tim and Paul, when her dilemma was so much more complex. Claire gathered up the empty wrappers off the desk, muttering under her breath about gossipy neighbors and nosy friends. As she tossed the last paper cup into the garbage can, her cell phone vibrated in her pocket.

"Hey, Holl—"

"Claire!" Her sister's voice was edged with panic. "The girls are gone, and I don't know where they are!"

Claire glanced at her watch, wondering if she'd completely lost track of time. It was only one thirty. "Holly, sweetie, the girls are at school," she said gently, thinking her sister's memory problems were getting worse, not better.

"No, they're not. The principal just called, wondering why I hadn't let her know they weren't coming back to school after lunch."

"Wait, did you pick them up for lunch?"

"No. The principal claims Frank did."

Chapter 23

FEAR WALLOPED CLAIRE IN THE SOLAR PLEXUS AS VISIONS of Frank crossing the border into Mexico with Brianna and Kayleigh in tow raced through her mind. She took a deep breath and forced herself to sound calm. "Okay, let's think about this. Did you try his cell phone?"

"About five times. It went to his voice mail."

"Has Frank ever taken the girls out of school for lunch before?"

"No, never." Holly's voice quavered.

"Okay." Claire took another deep breath. "Let's think where he might have taken them after lunch."

"Their grandpa's?"

"That's a good thought. Where does he live?"

"On Randolph Street. I'll call him."

"Don't do anything yet," Claire said, already halfway to her car. "I'm coming over, and we'll figure out the best strategy together. Don't worry, we'll find Brianna and Kayleigh."

She sprinted the rest of the way across the gravel and broke every speed limit on her way to Holly's house. If a cop wanted to give her a ticket, he'd have to catch her first.

Holly was standing on the front porch, and Claire raced up the steps to pull her sister into her arms. Holly exploded into great gulping sobs. "Oh God, Claire! What if Frank's taken my babies someplace where I'll never see them again?"

"Hey! No matter where he's gone, we'll find them." Claire unwound herself from the embrace and led her sister back inside. "Holl, we've got to think now. I promise you can cry all you want later."

Holly sat down on the nearest chair and scrubbed her hands over her tear-soaked face.

Claire had been making plans on her mad drive through town. "I'm going to borrow the Defibaughs' car and drive over to your father-in-law's house to see if the girls are there. I don't want anyone to recognize my car and spook Frank."

"I'll come with you," Holly said, starting to stand.

Claire put her hand on her sister's shoulder. "You have to stay here, sweetie, because we hope Frank will bring them home all by himself. And you need to keep working on possibilities. Write down the name and address of everybody you can come up with who Frank might take the girls to."

"Oh God, I don't know if I can think that straight right now."

"You can because it's for Brianna and Kayleigh." Claire squeezed her shoulder. "We'll find them. I swear."

Then she was out the door and jogging down the street to the neighbor's house. She knew Linda Defibaugh well enough to ask for the loan of her white minivan without having to offer too much of an explanation. The car looked like every other mom van in town, so she hoped Frank wouldn't see her coming until it was too late.

Claire wasn't optimistic about finding the girls at their grandfather's. If Frank wanted to scare Holly, he would make it harder. If he had really kidnapped them and taken them far away…Well, that was a possibility Claire tried not to think about just yet.

She parked two houses up the hill from Frank Snedegar Sr.'s house and walked casually down the sidewalk to his front door.

Before she rang the bell, she stood stock-still and listened, checking for the sound of children's voices from either inside or outside the house. She heard nothing.

Her heart sank, but she rang the doorbell.

"Hang on a minute! I'm coming, but I'm an old man," she heard a voice calling from inside. The door opened on a stocky elderly man holding a wooden cane. She could see where Frank Jr.'s square-jawed good looks had come from. "Hello. Who are you?"

"I'm Claire Parker, Frank's sister-in-law. May I come in?"

"I recognize you now. Sure, come right in. It's always good to have a visitor. You look like you've been at the stable. Smell like it too." He gave her a twinkling look that robbed his statement of insult.

Claire forced a smile as she stepped into the small front hall.

She stood motionless again, holding her breath for several seconds, just to make sure the older man wasn't covering for his son. Again, there was only silence.

She peeked into the den, where a hastily folded newspaper lay on the seat cushion of an armchair while a half-eaten sandwich sat on a metal TV table. There was no sign of children having been around.

"So, what brings you here?" he asked. "Seems to me I haven't seen you since Brianna's second or third birthday."

"You're right. I don't get back to Sanctuary much, unfortunately," Claire said. "I came to see if Frank had been by here with the girls today. He forgot to tell Holly he was taking them out of school for lunch, and now the principal's a little upset."

She knew that didn't make a lot of sense, but she hoped Frank Sr. would just answer her question.

"Nope. Haven't seen those little cutie pies in a couple of weeks. Usually Holly brings them around to visit their old grandpa, but

I know she's been under the weather. Whyn't you just call my son on his fancy cell phone?"

"We tried, but we got his voice mail."

"I know all about that. He's always out of batteries, or couldn't get a signal, or didn't have the ringer turned on. I have a suspicion sometimes he just doesn't want to talk to his old man."

"Well, he uses his phone a lot for business," Claire said vaguely. "Thank you! I need to head back to Holly."

She gave him a brief handshake and jogged back out the door and down the steps, turning to give a wave. She hoped he didn't phone Frank Jr. once he figured out her story had more holes than a slice of swiss cheese.

She called Holly and asked who the next person on the list was, calming her sister down, even as she felt the fear roiling through her. Holly gave her Frank's sister's address, where she repeated her lunatic story. The woman looked at her strangely, but said Frank hadn't been there since Saturday morning. Two more stops proved equally fruitless, and Claire decided to head back to Holly's house to regroup.

"Maybe we should call Robbie," Claire said as she slumped in a kitchen chair.

"No, I don't want the police involved. At least, not yet. It's bad enough they know about Frank's drinking problem. I don't want them to think he's a kidnapper too." Holly choked on a sob. "He's just trying to scare me."

"But why?"

"I forgot to tell you. Paul called this morning to say they were serving Frank with the divorce papers today."

"So he's pissed off and hitting you where it hurts, the bastard." Claire really wished Tim had punched Frank in the nose when he had the chance. "I see one more name on your list. Who is it?"

"The last person I thought of, but it might make sense. His great-aunt Judy lives on a farm out near the Dinosaur Cave. I haven't been out there in years, so I don't remember exactly where it is."

Dinosaur Cave was one of the area's tourist attractions. An amateur spelunker had found a mastodon jaw in one of the caverns, so the owners had given the cave its dramatic but inaccurate name and set it up for walking tours. The biggest drawback was the location—several miles from town along narrow, winding country roads.

It sounded like just the sort of place Frank might take his daughters if he wanted to terrify his wife.

"Do you have an address I could plug into the GPS?" Claire asked.

Holly shook her head. "The only one I know is the McElhenny farm. She probably gets her mail at the post office."

Finding the farm wasn't Claire's only worry. She was nervous about the possibility of confronting a furious, vengeful Frank alone and far from help.

"Does Great-Aunt Judy have cows or horses or something?" Claire asked.

Holly looked at her as if she were an idiot. "It's a *farm*."

"Right." Sometimes Claire's brain got stuck in New York mode where farms could be just houses out in the country with empty fields around them. "I think I'm going to call Tim. He makes house calls, so he might know where the place is."

And it would be good to have Tim's large, solid presence behind her if the scene got ugly.

"He already knows what's going on, so I guess that's okay." Holly's voice was shaky.

"Are you sure we shouldn't call Robbie to stay with you?"

"No, no, I'll be fine. In fact, I hope Frank comes back here. I want to give him a piece of my mind."

"Attagirl! That's my sis!" Claire said, pulling her cell phone out of her pocket. She stared at it a moment, trying to decide how to phrase her request. "Hello, yes, this is Claire Parker. I have kind of a personal emergency. May I speak with Dr. Arbuckle as soon as possible?"

It took no more than thirty seconds before Tim's deep voice rumbled into her ear. "Claire, what can I do to help?"

Claire let out the breath she'd been holding without realizing it. She gave him a brief summary of the situation.

"I'm on my way. See you in ten minutes."

That was it. Nothing more was needed to persuade him. Claire's eyes swam with tears of relief that she could shift some of her burden onto Tim's wide shoulders. She had to look away from her sister so Holly wouldn't see her moment of weakness.

True to his word, Tim was there in nine minutes. Claire knew because she checked the clock every thirty seconds.

She went out on the porch to meet him. Just seeing him jog up the steps toward her sent a tendril of calm curling through her. Rising onto her tiptoes, she fisted her hands in his plaid shirt and pulled him down for a quick, reassuring kiss before she said, "I'm so sorry to interrupt your—"

"I'm glad you called me." He held her against him for a quick, frozen moment, then released her. "I brought the clinic's pickup because no one will be surprised to see it tooling along the back roads."

After Tim assured Holly he was familiar with the farm, they headed back out to the truck.

"I got some extra pointers from Estelle Wilson before I left the office," Tim said, putting the pickup in gear.

"Oh my God, she was my first-grade teacher," Claire said. "So she retired and went to work for you?"

"Lucky for me. She knows everyone and everything about Sanctuary."

Claire was silent as she watched Tim steer onto the highway, slipping the big vehicle into a space between two cars that she never would have attempted.

He drove with a fierce alertness that allowed her to let go of the iron control she'd been hanging on to in front of Holly. "I'll tell you the truth: if the girls aren't at Great-Aunt Judy's, I'm afraid Frank may have taken them away somewhere to hide them," Claire said, her voice catching on a swallowed sob. "He got served with the divorce papers today. God, I just hope he's not drunk too."

Tim took one hand off the wheel and covered her fists where she had them clenched together in her lap. His glance never wavered from the crowded highway. "If the girls aren't there, we'll keep looking until we find them. I think our next step should be to call in the police."

"I tried to talk Holly into that, but she wasn't ready yet. She doesn't want the whole town to know about their problems."

"Can't say I blame her."

His voice was tight and hard. Somehow she knew he was thinking about his wife's suicide and all the surrounding publicity. It must have been horrendous for him.

"Chief McClung won't put it out on the radio if we ask him not to," Tim continued. "Let's not borrow trouble, though."

She turned one hand up to squeeze his, loving the warmth of his palm and the toughness of his calluses. "I'd like to hold your hand for the whole drive, but I think you're going to need it. Those country roads have some tight curves."

"I reckon you're right, but we'll wait until I have to turn off this nice straight stretch."

She felt tears welling up again and fought them back. "The good thing is the girls are with their father, so they won't be worried or scared."

At least she hoped that was the case. Brianna had sounded frightened on Friday night, but it had been fear for her mother rather than for the little girls' own safety.

A few minutes later, he pulled their entwined hands over to his side of the front seat, kissing the back of her hand before he let it go. "We're about to turn. Hang onto your Jesus strap."

It was a left turn. Tim cut the wheel and hit the accelerator hard as a gap opened in the oncoming traffic. Claire closed her eyes as horns blared. She was about to compare him to a New York taxi driver but decided not to remind him of his past again.

They followed the footprint-shaped signs for Dinosaur Cave, barreling along the twisting single-lane country roads. Then he took a right onto a gravel road, and Claire was completely lost. She hung on for dear life as they bounced between barbed wire fences containing cows, sheep, and an occasional llama. When they reached an intersection with a paved road, Tim turned onto it and slowed down.

"That field on the left should be McElhenny's," he said. "See if you can spot a mailbox or sign of some kind as we come up on the driveway."

Claire sat forward and scanned along the fence line. "I think there's something up ahead. I saw a flash of red near the cattle guard."

Narrow metal bars spaced a hoof's width apart spanned the farm's entrance road, keeping the livestock in without the necessity of a gate. As they got closer, the red flash resolved itself into a homemade sign with the name *McElhennys* painted on it in white block letters.

"Oh, thank God!" Claire breathed as the pickup rumbled across the metal grate.

She looked over to find Tim examining the layout of the buildings.

"Can you spot Frank's car anywhere?" he asked.

"No, not so far." Claire's throat cramped in panic at the thought of not finding the girls. "Wait, there it is by the barn. The silver Escalade."

"I'll box him in with the truck," Tim said, bouncing over the ruts of the dirt road at a speed that kicked up clouds of dust. "Then he can't sneak away while we're looking for the girls. You know them better than I do. Where should we start—house or barn?"

Claire looked back and forth between the white frame house with its wide front porch and the tin-roofed barn, its open door a dark, blank rectangle. "How about if I take the house and you take the barn?"

"We go together. You're not facing Frank alone." Tim's voice brooked no argument.

She hated to admit it, but she was relieved to have that decision taken out of her hands. Frank wasn't behaving like a rational human being. "Okay, then." She thought of Kayleigh's love of kittens and Brianna's desire to talk to Willow. "The barn."

He drove past Frank's car and swept around a full circle, parking so the pickup faced the road and hemmed in the big SUV. Claire swung open her door and leaped to the ground.

"Leave your door unlatched," Tim said, jogging around the truck's hood, "just in case."

She didn't ask in case of what. She didn't want to think about the implications of needing a quick getaway.

They walked side by side from the sunshine into the dimness of the barn. Claire nearly reached for Tim's hand to bolster her courage as she waited for her eyes to adjust to the change in light.

They stood on a wide, tiled breezeway lined with open stalls sporting shiny electric milking equipment. "No kittens," Claire murmured in dismay as she scanned the empty, echoing space of the dairy barn.

"There are stairs over there," Tim said, gesturing left. Claire started toward them, only to have him catch her wrist. "Let me go first."

She looked up to find his eyes lit with concern, while the lines around his mouth were deep and tight. She nodded, and he gave her wrist a quick squeeze before he let her go and strode to the open wooden steps that disappeared up through the ceiling. He went up the steps quickly and with surprising lightness for a man of his size.

Claire stayed close behind him, reaching the top step just as a woman's voice called, "Dr. Tim? What brings you here? Don't tell me there's another outbreak of red nose!"

"No, no infectious epidemics right now, Mrs. McElhenny," Tim said.

Claire dodged around him to find a tall, thin woman with a graying ponytail standing in an open doorway, a baffled expression on her lined face.

"This is Claire Parker, Holly's sister," Tim said as naturally as though they were at a cocktail party. "We came by to pick up Brianna and Kayleigh."

Judy McElhenny looked even more bewildered. She gave a quick nod of greeting to Claire. "I thought they were spending the night."

"Change of plans," Tim said. "Their mother needs them at home. Is Frank around?"

"He's in the house, pretending to watch the TV but snoring like a buzz saw." A nervous smile twitched at Judy's thin lips. "He's been traveling a lot for work. It wears him out."

Claire noticed the change in Tim's posture; his shoulders dropped and his hands opened out of clenched fists. He had been braced for a belligerent Frank, and now the threat was gone. She felt her own shoulders relax a fraction.

The older woman hesitated a moment before she turned back to the door. "Brianna! Kayleigh! Time to go!"

"But we're almost finished with our house!" It was Kayleigh's voice, and Claire's knees nearly buckled with relief at the sound.

"Your mom wants you," Judy called back. She shrugged at Tim and Claire. "We were building a house out of straw bales."

"So we don't get to bake special oatmeal cookies?" Brianna said, emerging from the door, her hair and clothes sprouting bits of straw. "Hi, Aunt Claire. And Dr. Tim."

Kayleigh came right behind her, and Claire swooped down onto her knees to engulf them both in a bear hug. "Oh, it's so good to see you guys. I missed you."

"We missed you too," Brianna said politely, but with a note of confusion in her voice.

The girls obviously weren't worried by their unusual afternoon off from school, so her greeting made no sense to them. Loosening her hold, Claire felt the tension drain from her. She stood and took their hands in hers. "Let's get them down to the truck before Holly wonders where the heck we all are."

She started down the steps.

"Dr. Tim, there's something I want to ask you about the mastitis," Judy said.

Claire kept going. She just wanted to get the girls safely back to their mother. They clattered down the steps and across the tile.

"Auntie Judy's nice," Kayleigh announced, "but she doesn't have any kittens to play with."

"You can always play with the kittens at Sharon's," Claire said, hustling them over to Tim's truck.

"Can we miss school too?" Kayleigh asked.

Claire laughed as she boosted the little girl into the backseat of the extended cab and buckled her seatbelt. "Probably not."

She helped Brianna in next. "We aren't really supposed to miss school, are we?" her older niece asked.

"Not really, but it's okay if there's a good reason for it."

Claire closed the door and let out the breath she'd been holding.

"What the hell do you think you're doing with my children?" Claire spun around to find Frank rounding the back of the truck, his face scarlet with rage. "I'm taking them home, where they belong," she said, keeping her voice low in the hope the children wouldn't hear.

"They belong with me just as much as with my bitch wife." He bore down on her, his hands balled into fists.

Claire squared her shoulders and stood her ground. "Not if Holly doesn't know where they are. You can't just take them out of school and not bring them back."

"I can do whatever I damn well please. They're *my* children. No piece of paper from a lawyer can change that." An ugly sneer twisted his features. "Don't they say possession is nine-tenths of the law?"

"Maybe with things, but when you take a person, it's called kidnapping."

He grabbed her arm and pulled her within inches of his face. "You tell my bitch wife that I don't appreciate getting handed lawyer papers when I'm working. And you tell her I'll take the children any time I want to until she gets a proper attitude about who's in charge."

Claire flinched as spittle landed on her cheeks.

"Get your hand off her, Frank." Tim's voice was low but pulsated with menace. "You don't want your children to see me knock you flat on your back."

Frank seemed to freeze, his grip so hard she could almost feel the bruise forming. Then he flung her away from him, her elbow banging against the truck. "Brought your tame grizzly with you again, I see."

Tim stepped between them, blocking her view of Frank. If she thought his voice was menacing before, it now emanated cold fury. "If you ever touch Claire or Holly again, I will cause you pain you can't even imagine."

"Are you threatening me? Because I've got witnesses."

Claire peered around Tim to see Frank backing away as he glanced right and left. Judy McElhenny stood in the barn door, her gaze flicking between the two men.

"Witnesses to what?" Tim asked. "Kidnapping? Assault? You're right. You've got witnesses. Go back to the house, Frank. You don't want to make me any angrier, or I might forget I have an audience."

Frank glanced at the truck, where two small faces peered out the back window. A vein pulsed in his forehead. "You'll be hearing from me. Both of you." He stalked away toward the back of the house.

Tim stood still until the slam of a door broke the silence. Then he nodded to Judy. "Nice to see you, Mrs. McElhenny."

"You too, Doc," the older woman said. Her look turned apologetic. "Frank is just upset about the divorce."

"Guess so," Tim said. He turned back to Claire, probing her arm with careful fingers. "Does this hurt? Or this?"

She fought the desire to burst into tears as the fear-induced adrenaline drained from her body. "No, no, nothing hurts. I'm fine."

He enveloped her in his arms and lowered his head to rest it against her forehead. "I shouldn't have let Mrs. McElhenny hold me up in the barn. I should have been here to keep Frank away from you. When I saw him touch you, I wanted to flatten the bastard, but I couldn't in front of the girls. I'm sorry."

"It's my fault. I should have waited. I just wanted to get them home to Holly." She rested against him, wrapping herself in the safety and comfort of his presence.

He pulled her in tighter before letting his arms drop. "Let's get on the road."

Swinging open the unlatched door, he helped her into the high cab. She could see the guilt in his eyes and in the tense set of his shoulders, but she didn't know how to banish it.

"We didn't say good-bye to Papa," Brianna said, her voice small and tentative.

"I know, sweetheart," Claire said, racking her brain for an explanation. "He...um...was waiting for an important phone call for business and heard the phone ringing in the house."

"Oh, okay." Claire was amazed that Brianna seemed to accept her improvised excuse without question.

"Aunt Claire, we got to miss part of school and ride on the tractor with Jake," Kayleigh said, joining the conversation. "But we were supposed to get cookies too. Aunt Judy was letting us help make them."

"We'll buy you ice cream sundaes at Dairy Queen on the way home," Claire said, throwing Tim a rueful glance as he turned the key in the ignition.

"Why don't you send your sister a text message? See if she wants ice cream too," he said.

"Good idea!" Claire said, pulling her cell phone out of her jeans pocket. Before she pressed the speed dial for Holly, she leaned over and said in a voice pitched for his ears only, "I couldn't have found them without you." She laid her hand on his forearm, feeling the reassuring flex and strength of his muscles under her palm. "I don't know how to thank you."

His expression lightened a fraction as he slid her a sideways smile. "I'll write you a list."

Chapter 24

*H*APPILY FILLED WITH HOT FUDGE AND ICE CREAM, Brianna and Kayleigh greeted their mother without any indication they were concerned by their unusual day. As Claire watched her sister hug the girls and calmly ask them about what they had done this afternoon, she started to shake. She walked casually out the back door, hoping no one would notice her crazy reaction.

As she braced her hands on the white plastic patio table, trying to control the tremors, Tim's warm body pressed against her back, his arms encircling her.

"They're fine," he said. "You brought them home safely."

"*We* brought them home safely." She turned into him and buried her face in his shirt, giving in to all the fears that she'd held at bay while she needed to, letting silent sobs rack her. "I was so scared he'd taken them somewhere we wouldn't be able to find them or that he was drunk and violent toward them. I never realized how heartbreaking it can be to love a child."

Her eyes were closed, but she could feel the soft flannel of his shirt against her cheek and smell the comforting scent of warm male overlaid with a slight tang of antiseptic soap from the veterinary clinic. She burrowed into him, letting herself rest against his solidity. The sound of his heartbeat against her ear calmed her.

"We'll do everything we can to keep Frank away from them," Tim said, his voice seeming to resonate all the way through her. "That's one thing about a small town. It's hard to hide."

Claire's trembling slowly eased, and she lifted her face away from his now soggy shirt. "Sorry, I got you all wet."

"I've had worse at work."

She tilted her head back to look into his strong face and reached up to brush at the lock of hair that fell onto his forehead. "You dropped everything and came to help, no questions asked," she said. "You're my hero."

She felt his muscles clench as though he had been struck by a physical blow, but his voice maintained its slow, even drawl. "You're the one who went toe-to-toe with Frank. That scared the hell out of me."

"I wasn't worried because I knew you were there." She scanned his face, seeing the shadows in his eyes. "Why did it bother you when I said you were my hero?"

He bent to kiss her forehead, so she could no longer see his expression. "Someone said that to me a long time ago, and things didn't work out well afterward."

It must have involved his wife, so Claire let it go. She took a step away, out of his embrace. "Thanks for the chest to cry on. I couldn't reach your shoulder." Her weak joke banished a few of the shadows from his eyes. "You must have left a lot of patients sitting in your waiting room. You should get back."

He didn't respond instantly, locking his gaze on her face. Whatever he saw there must have satisfied him, because he nodded and said, "Call me when you're ready to leave, and I'll swing by here to pick you up."

"I don't need a ride. My car is here."

"I'm taking you to my house. Frank knows where you live."

Claire's spirits lifted at the thought of spending the night with Tim before another thought sank them again. "I think I should stay with Holly, in case Frank shows up here."

"I'm going to take care of that possibility with Chief McClung. There will be a cop here all night, I promise you."

"Which is better protection than I would be."

"I don't know about that. Frank looked pretty worried."

His teasing warmed her. She cupped her hand against his cheek. "I'm looking forward to seeing the house you're building."

He turned his head and kissed her palm, then took her hand and folded her fingers inward. "Hold on to that," he said, "until I can add to it."

He pivoted and strode around the corner of the house before she could force any words past the lump in her throat. She stood there until she heard an engine rumble to life and knew he was gone.

Just as she turned to go back in the house, the back door opened.

"Claire? Is everything okay?" Holly came out onto the cement patio. "Tim left?"

"He had to go back to work." Claire hoped her face didn't look as swollen and tear streaked as it felt. She kept talking to distract her sister. "You were great when the girls came home. So calm and normal, like nothing out of the ordinary had happened. I nearly blew it when I first saw them."

"It took all my willpower," Holly said. She crossed her arms and looked straight at Claire. "You were as scared as I was that Frank was going to hide them somewhere far away."

"Okay, yes, I admit it."

"Let's go sit in the gazebo for a minute," Holly said, waving toward the little six-sided wooden structure at the back of the yard. Surrounded by azaleas and mountain laurel, it offered a cool spot to sit and supervise when the girls were playing outdoors.

Puzzled, Claire walked across the neatly mown grass beside her sister, passing the children's pink swing set and yellow plastic playhouse. For some reason, the empty toys made her teary again, so she swiped the back of her hand across her eyes as they settled into the cushion-padded wicker chairs.

"I was scared of something else too," Holly said without preamble. She made eye contact with Claire and then dropped her gaze to her lap, where her hands lay twisted together. "I was afraid Frank might hurt the girls."

Claire sucked in a sharp breath.

"He's never touched them before," Holly hurried to say, "but after the other night, I wasn't sure what he'd do." She lifted her eyes to Claire's. "You were right. He's hit me before this."

Although she'd suspected this, hearing her fears confirmed made Claire feel like Frank had just punched *her*. "Oh dear God!"

Holly turned her face toward the peaceful yard, but Claire got the sense she wasn't seeing anything in it. "The first time, we'd been to the Black Bear, and Frank had too much to drink. When we got home, he accused me of flirting with one of his friends and called me some ugly names. When I denied it, he backhanded me across the face."

Claire flinched at the image.

"I was wearing those tight-fitting black jeans that night. That's why I never wore them again," Holly continued. She looked at Claire with an almost pleading expression in her eyes. "He cried the next day and begged me to forgive him. So I did."

"I understand," Claire said soothingly, even though she didn't. How could her sister have lost her sense of identity to the point that she stayed with a man who treated her with such emotional and physical violence?

"No, you don't understand," Holly said. "I could put up with Frank as long as he was good to the girls and good to me in front of the girls. I did it to keep our family together." As Holly spoke, her posture changed. She sat up, and a fierce light shone in her eyes.

Claire began to see that her sister had drawn on every ounce of her strength in trying to do what she thought was best for her two daughters. "I understand now, but you shouldn't have endured it all alone."

"Sometimes no one can help you," Holly said. "If you put it into words, you won't be able to handle it. You just get through one day at a time."

"The bruises on your wrists?" Claire asked, her fingers curling into fists as she thought of her sister suffering without anyone to support her.

Holly lifted one hand to glance at the livid marks around its base. "When he told me he wanted the divorce, I lost it. After all he'd put me through, he dared to tell me it was my fault he wanted out. I started screaming at him. He squeezed my wrists to get me to stop."

Claire dropped her face into her hands as the terrible situation seared itself into her brain.

"Now you know all of the whole ugly truth," Holly continued. "I pushed you away to try and keep Frank from getting angry. I was stupid to think that anything I did would stop the violence."

"You're not stupid. You're one of the bravest people I know," Claire said, lifting her head and taking her sister's hands. "We're going to make damn sure Frank never has the chance to lay hands on you again."

Holly entwined her fingers with Claire's. "I don't want Brianna and Kayleigh to know. No matter what he did to me, Frank's their father. I don't want to turn him into a monster in their eyes. That's why I didn't want the police involved."

"That's going to be really difficult."

"We have to find a way, for the children's sake."

Claire nodded a silent promise, but she wasn't sure how to carry it out.

"Will you be with me when I tell the girls about the divorce?"

"I thought you wanted to—"

Holly interrupted by shaking her head. "They're going to need your love to help them deal with it. I saw how strong that was this afternoon."

Claire couldn't untangle the ball of emotions inside her enough to speak. She nodded again. Then she and Holly were in each other's arms, crying and saying how they'd missed each other.

"When do you want to tell them?" Claire said, as they sat back and wiped their eyes.

"Tomorrow. I can't handle any more drama today."

Chapter 25

*T*IM WAS RELIEVED TO FIND PATIENTS STILL WAITING for him at the veterinary hospital. The ever-efficient Estelle had rescheduled some and shuffled around others, so for a couple of hours, he was too busy to think about Claire and how he'd felt when Frank grabbed her. Finally, the last patient padded through the exit, and he shrugged out of his soiled white lab jacket and tossed it in the hamper.

"Everything up front is shut down," Estelle said, appearing in the door to his office. "I'm glad the little girls got home safely."

"So am I. Thanks for handling the crisis here."

"Children should not be taken out of school without a very strong reason," Estelle said.

Tim chuckled at her teacher's disapproval of playing hooky. "You're a treasure."

"Pffft!" she said, giving him a dismissive wave as she pivoted on her heel and left.

He scraped a hand through his hair and realized he was both too tired and too wound up to attempt doing paperwork. However, he judged Claire wouldn't be done with her duties at her sister's house for another couple of hours.

That left too much time to remember how he had screwed up and left Claire to face Frank alone. While he was being polite to Judy McElhenny, that slimy bastard had manhandled Claire.

He kicked at the trash can by his desk, making it clatter on the tile floor.

He almost wished Frank had refused to let her go. It would have justified smashing his fist into the man's face, feeling the crunch of bone as he broke his nose. Of course, the person he was angriest with was himself for putting Claire in danger.

"I'm just going around in circles here."

He forced himself to sit down at his desk, swiveling the chair around to face the computer. The door to the bathroom caught his eye, reminding him of the shower Dr. Messer had installed there. Evidently, Messer's wife complained when he came home covered in farm dirt, so the vet had built a roomy stall with a rain showerhead. Tim had never used it since the smellier he was, the more interesting Sprocket found him when he walked in the door.

Right now, a hot shower sounded like just what the doctor would order for himself.

He stripped down to his boxers, draping his shirt and jeans neatly over the desk chair. Then he headed for the bathroom, where he hung his underwear on the back of the door and cranked up the shower as hot as he could stand it. When the steaming water hit his skin, he groaned out loud at the sheer luxury of it, dropping his head forward so the jets pounded the tired, tense muscles in his neck and shoulders.

Once the initial shock of pleasure wore off, his mind wandered. Nothing he did could keep it away from Claire. When he remembered coming out of the barn to see Frank's fist clamped around her arm, fear slugged him in the gut again. If Frank had hauled off and hit her, she wouldn't have been able to avoid the blow. She was like a mother bear, drawing the attacker away from her cubs.

Then Claire had called him her hero. He braced his arm against the tile wall as he felt the kick in the gut all over again.

How many times had Anais said that to him?

Yet she hadn't trusted him to live up to it. He had told her they could win the battle against the disease. He had offered his strength, his medical expertise, and his love, but she had chosen to die instead.

He threw his head back and let the water smash into his face so it would wash away the tears coursing down his cheeks. He'd been battling this anger at his dead wife for so long it felt good to give in to it, to be pissed off that she didn't believe in him enough to stand and fight. He had been there beside her, and she had chosen to give up without a fight. Not like Claire, who stood and looked fear in the face.

He slammed his fist into the wall, making the glass doors rattle in their stainless steel track. "God damn it, Anais! We could have beaten it!" he shouted. "You should have had more faith in me. I was there!"

As the anger drained away, he slumped against the wet tile. Exhaustion swept over him, and yet he felt lighter. Some pain inside him seemed to loosen its talons.

He grabbed a bar of soap and gave himself a quick wash.

As he was rinsing, the bathroom door opened a crack. "Tim? Are you in there?" Claire's voice came through the opening. "Holly and the girls went to bed early. You didn't answer your cell, so I figured I'd just drive over here."

His exhaustion lifted. He felt a smile tug at the corners of his lips. "Come on in."

He heard Claire laugh, and then the door opened wide and he saw her wavering outline through the frosted shower doors. "Oh, darn, the view isn't as good as I hoped," she said.

"I can fix that." He slid open the shower door and reached for the towel he'd hung on the nearby hook. It wasn't there.

"Is this what you're looking for?" Claire dangled the towel from her fingertip. She had changed out of her riding clothes and was wearing a denim skirt, a white T-shirt, and little flat sandals. Her face was bare of makeup, and her hair was pulled up into a simple ponytail that swung down her back. She looked different. Younger. Happier. Sexy as hell.

She dropped her gaze to his feet and let it travel upward with a long stop at about groin level.

"I guess you're glad to see me," she said.

He stepped out of the shower and walked toward her, dripping a trail of water as he went.

"You'll get me all wet," she said, backing up until she bumped against the wall.

"You read my mind."

She thrust the towel out in front of her, her face alight with disbelieving laughter. He closed his fingers around her wrist and moved her arm out of the way so he could sandwich her between his wet skin and the plasterboard.

She gasped as his erection came in contact with her stomach. He bit back a groan as the water soaked through the cotton of her shirt and bra so he could feel her nipples harden against his bare chest.

When she dropped the towel and slid her hands over his buttocks, her palms warm and slick with the droplets from his shower, her nails feathering over his taut muscles, he gave up on self-control and moaned her name out loud.

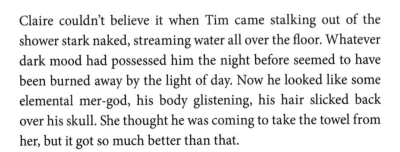

Claire couldn't believe it when Tim came stalking out of the shower stark naked, streaming water all over the floor. Whatever dark mood had possessed him the night before seemed to have been burned away by the light of day. Now he looked like some elemental mer-god, his body glistening, his hair slicked back over his skull. She thought he was coming to take the towel from her, but it got so much better than that.

As he pressed against her, she felt the water soak through her clothes to her skin, transferring his heat to her. She ran her hands over his buttocks, up his back, across his shoulders, and down again, gliding along the gorgeous arcs and angles of his muscles and tendons.

Where drops of water beaded on his skin, she licked them off, savoring the taste of clean male. As her tongue touched his nipple, his hips rocked against her and he groaned.

"This was supposed to be your punishment, not mine," he rasped.

"You consider this punishment?" She licked his other nipple.

He took her head in both hands and tilted it up and away from his chest. "How wet are you?" he asked with a wicked undertone.

"Soaking," she purred back.

He kissed her, teasing her lips with his tongue. Then, without warning, he scooped her up and carried her out of the bathroom and into his office. It was the second time he'd picked her up, and she was starting to enjoy these casual demonstrations of his strength.

He rounded the metal desk and sank into the leather executive chair behind it, cradling her on his lap. Her skirt had hiked up, so all that separated her from his erection was the sheer cotton of her panties. The contact sent a shock of electric pleasure sizzling through her body. She arched backward in his arms, gasping.

He slid one hand up the inside of her thigh and pushed aside her panty with his thumb, slipping one finger inside her. She opened her thighs and pushed against his hand, needing motion and pressure. "More!"

"Whatever you say." He withdrew and then thrust two fingers inside her, while finding her most sensitive spot with his thumb.

She sprawled across his thighs, bucking with the motion of his fingers, feeling the delicious heat building deep inside her. She let her gaze travel up the beautiful contours of his torso to revel in his expression of total focus. He changed the angle of his hand, and suddenly, the pleasure tightened and exploded. "Oh yes! Yes! Yes!" she gasped with each contraction, her muscles clenching so hard her back bowed upward off his lap.

"Easy, sweetheart," he said, shifting one hand to protect her head from the wooden frame of the chair arm.

As the spasms weakened to mere shudders, she sank back down and curled into him. She loved the fact that he put his arms around her and nestled her closer, even though she could feel his own unsatisfied arousal against the back of her thighs. "Give me a couple of minutes," she said. "I think I pulled some internal muscles with that one."

"Take your time." She felt the brush of his lips on the top of her head and heard a smile in his voice. "I'm basking in your afterglow."

"It was the sight of you stepping out of the shower. Like a Michelangelo sculpture come to life. In fact, you're almost the same size as *David*."

"Now there's a comparison I don't mind at all."

She pressed her ear closer against his skin, loving the vibration of his deep voice. "I was talking about your height."

"So was I."

"Liar!" She lifted her head to meet his eyes. A dancing imp of mischief lit their gray depths. That was all it took to set desire stirring in her again.

She squirmed out of his arms, deliberately rocking against his erection for both their benefits. Hooking her fingers into her panties, she pulled them down to her ankles and kicked them off. Then she planted her knees on either side of his thighs, letting his cock spring up between them.

He seized the hem of her damp shirt and stripped it off over her head as she raised her arms. Before she could unhook her bra, he wrapped his hands around her rib cage and pulled her toward him so he could suck on her nipple through the sheer lace. The inner muscles she thought were completely drained of energy revived and tightened at the sensations of heat and moisture and pressure.

She reached down and circled the tip of his erection, making him growl against her breast. She stroked down his length and back up again. He shifted his grip so one hand was splayed across her back to hold her against his mouth while the other pushed her denim skirt up to bunch around her waist. Then his cock was between her legs, and she held her breath, waiting for the thrust that would fill the craving inside her.

"Damn it! I need a condom," he said.

She collapsed against him, stifling laughter, as he reached behind his back to scrabble at the clothes hanging over the chair.

"L-l-let me help," she gasped through her fits of giggling. "I have a better angle."

"In the pocket of my jeans," he said through gritted teeth.

She stretched her arms past him and slipped her hands into various pockets, finally locating two foil packets and pulling them out.

"Now we're in business," she said, ripping one open. "Allow me to do the honors."

"Only if you promise to stop laughing," he said. "It might damage my fragile ego and cause erectile dysfunction."

"Hmm. Not much fear of that," she said, circling him with her fingers and sweeping downward.

"The condom," he reminded her.

She rolled it on and started to move back over him when he took hold of her hips and lifted her into position, holding her poised above him for a long moment and then bringing her down as he flexed his hips up.

She threw her head back and yelped at the rough pleasure of their combined motion. The sensation was so acute it was almost unbearable. "Again!" she begged.

His grip on her hips was nearly bruising as he moved her upward. Again, they came together hard so he was deep inside her. "Stay there," he commanded, reaching around to unhook her bra.

She brushed the straps down her arms and flung the scrap of satin and lace across the room, offering her breasts to his hands and mouth.

With his cock filling and anchoring her and his tongue teasing her breasts, she could do nothing more than hang onto his shoulders and let him send her spiraling inexorably toward another orgasm. As the pressure built, she began to undulate against him, moaning at the deliciously unremitting assault on her nerve endings.

When the first wave of orgasm hit, she dug her fingernails into his muscles and shrieked as her whole body convulsed around him. He pushed upward, and her muscles clenched again.

"Oh God, Claire!" he groaned, his head falling back against the chair. Then his hands were like vises on her waist, moving her up and down until his hips came up off the chair and his cock pulsed inside her while he shouted her name.

After collapsing back into the chair, neither of them moved for some time. Then Tim's stomach rumbled loudly, making Claire giggle. "Typical man. Satisfy one appetite and another one makes demands."

"We just burned a lot of calories. It's no wonder I need some fuel."

He levered them both out of the chair and then turned and eased her back in it.

"Ugh! It's soggy," she complained as her backside hit the clothes that had absorbed the water from his skin. She started to pull her skirt down from around her waist. "My skirt's wet too, and not from what you're thinking about."

Tim's mouth twitched into a wicked grin, but he said, "Luckily, we have a dryer here."

They prowled around his office, collecting damp garments and piling them on the chair.

Claire headed for the bathroom to grab the towel she'd dropped there. Being naked while in the throes of passion was one thing. Lolling around an office without a stitch of clothing was another.

As she emerged with the towel precariously tucked around her, she found Tim standing in front of a closet, pulling on a pair of clean, dry jeans. "Hey, no fair," she protested.

He reached in and pulled out a white lab coat, which he tossed to her. "I think this will be a good look."

She pulled on the coat and dropped the towel. "Oh, right, a white tent," she said as she rolled back six inches of sleeve. Even buttoning the top button left virtually all of her cleavage exposed.

"I like it a lot," Tim said, eyeing the expanse of bare skin appreciatively. "You'll feel less cranky once you have some food in you. Let me get the dryer going."

Shirtless, he gathered up the damp heap of clothes and padded barefoot out of the office.

She wandered around his work space, curious to see what personal touches he had added. The only wall decorations were framed pet care posters from pharmaceutical companies. No diplomas. No photographs. None of the art he collected.

His blond wood desk boasted a state-of-the-art computer, an elegant leather desk set, and a couple of expensive-looking pens, but no quirky paperweights or funky souvenirs. The small round conference table was completely bare. One wall was filled entirely by built-in Formica shelves and doors, so she strolled over to take a look at the book titles.

"Have you read *Macrocyclic Lactones in Antiparasitic Therapy* from cover to cover?" she asked as Tim returned.

"No, but I listened to it on CD."

Claire choked on a laugh. He threw her a grin and pulled open one of the Formica doors to reveal a refrigerator, which he proceeded to empty, spreading an array of food out on the conference table. Adding a basket of plasticware and napkins, he beckoned her over and held out a wheeled chair for her. "What's your pleasure?"

"You go ahead," Claire said, sitting down. She had eaten dinner with her sister, so she wasn't hungry. "Your stomach's making so much noise I'd feel guilty eating first."

"Sorry. I didn't get my afternoon snack." He assembled a multilayered sandwich.

As he took his first bite, she leaned forward. "Thank you again for what you did this afternoon. All the things you did," she added, thinking of his comfort when she fell apart on the patio.

His mouth was full, so he waved a hand in dismissal.

Claire unwrapped a wedge of gouda and cut off several slices, laying them on wheat crackers and offering the plate to Tim. He transferred a couple to his own plate. "How is Holly doing?"

Claire hesitated and looked across the table. Tim's hair had dried in tousled waves with the usual unruly curl falling onto his high, intelligent forehead. His bare shoulders looked as if they could easily hold the weight of the world. He had put down his sandwich and leveled his dark-gray gaze at her. This was a man she could trust with the truth. "She admitted Frank has hit her before."

She could see the muscles in his forearms flex as his hands clenched into fists.

"Yeah, I wanted to smash his face in too," she said. "She stayed with him anyway to keep the family together. What kills me is that she had to suffer through it alone."

"You're here."

"Only because she caught Lyme disease." Claire sat back in her chair and sighed. "It's a long story."

Tim uncurled his hands and picked up his sandwich with the air of a man who was ready to listen as long as she wanted to talk.

"When we were younger, Holly and I were really close. Even after I moved to New York, we talked all the time. Then she married Frank and I married Milo." Oops, she hadn't meant to bring her marriage into the story.

Tim's eyebrows shot up, but he just took another bite and chewed.

"Milo and Frank didn't hit it off, but that wasn't a problem for a while, anyway." Until just before Claire and Milo's wedding. That was really when it started, now that she thought about it— when Holly hadn't come to the wedding. "Then it got so I'd ask her about something that ordinarily we would have shared without a second thought, and she would change the subject. It began to really hurt me."

So Claire had dragged Milo down for Brianna's birthday. The visit was a disaster. Milo had complained about having to sleep on a lumpy sofa bed and use a toilet that required removing a child's potty seat.

Frank seemed determined to provoke Milo into his worst behavior, while Holly did her best to avoid being alone with Claire. The one time Claire managed to pull her aside and ask her what was going on, Holly looked at her blankly and said she didn't know what Claire was talking about.

"I tried to find out what the problem was, but Holly just kept pretending nothing had changed between us. I was involved in my life in New York, and I finally gave up trying to fix things. There was so much unsaid between us that it was almost painful to talk with her."

Tim had finished his sandwich and was simply listening, his hands resting on either side of the plastic plate.

"When I found out Holly had a bad case of Lyme disease, I decided to come down and help her. My marriage had ended, and I took it as an opportunity to reconnect." Claire picked up a cracker and snapped it in half. "From day one, Holly made it clear she didn't want me here. However, I could see she was really sick, so I stayed anyway. Even after Frank asked for the divorce, she'd been pushing me away. Until the day after his drunken rampage."

"I'm guessing that you've been beating yourself up, trying to figure out what you did wrong."

"Pretty much." Claire blinked hard to keep tears from overflowing onto her cheeks. "I know I got caught up in my job and marriage, but I thought we would always be close. I don't understand why she wouldn't talk to me when things went so terribly wrong."

"You know," Tim said slowly, "Frank did what every other abusive spouse does—isolated his victim so she had nowhere to turn but him. I'm guessing he convinced her it was her fault somehow."

"How did you know?"

"It's typical behavior. It gives him leverage. Just like taking the children did."

"It makes me sick that Frank would twist everything around that way, and she believed him." Claire shredded a piece of cheddar. "I know it sounds selfish, but it hurts my feelings that she didn't tell me."

Claire looked up from the little pile of crumbled cheese and crackers she'd created. Tim's eyebrows were drawn together in a frown, and his gray eyes were shadowed with concern. And pain. She reached across the table to give his hand a quick touch. "I'm sorry. You know, as awful as the situation is, it's brought Holly and me back together again, so I can't regret what's happened."

She'd hoped to see his expression lighten, but the darkness continued to hover. "I never had a brother or sister, and I always knew I had missed out on something special. You and Holly are lucky."

"Thanks for listening to true confessions," she said. "Let me fix you another sandwich."

"No, the first one hit the spot. I'm going to check on the clothes."

He rose from the table and strode out of the office. Claire watched him go.

Just when she thought she could relax with Tim, the shadows would cloud his face, and he would withdraw. He seemed so solid, so easy with himself, that she forgot he had hidden vulnerabilities. She kept stumbling into them when she didn't mean to. With a sigh, Claire began gathering up the food strewn across the table and stacking it in the refrigerator.

As she stowed the last package of cold cuts away, Tim came back in with a pile of neatly folded garments. The frown was gone, but his eyes were still clouded with some pain she couldn't decipher. "Warm from the dryer," he said, handing her the top of his stack.

"Mmm, nice," Claire said, holding them against her cheek. What she really wanted to lay her cheek against was Tim's bare chest, but the mood between them had changed. So she simply watched him button his shirt up with a sense of regret.

"If you keep looking at me like that, we'll never get out of this office," he said.

"Sorry, it's just a shame to cover up such a work of art," Claire said, grinning at him. She slipped her panties and denim skirt on under the giant lab coat. Turning away from him, she dropped the coat so she could put on her bra.

"I might say the same thing," Tim said. He threaded his belt through the loops and buckled it. "Manet's *Olympia*."

"Good choice! I always liked her direct stare. I thought you'd go for Goya's *Maja*—the unclothed one, of course." She had pulled on her T-shirt and was finger-combing her hair.

Much to her relief, the atmosphere between them had brightened again. She hated being responsible for bringing the pain to Tim's eyes.

Chapter 26

ISH STOMACH SET UP ANOTHER RACKET ON THE WAY
home, so Claire insisted on picking up a pizza at the
Court Restaurant. The scent filled the pickup truck and kept
his salivary glands working on high. Having Claire on the seat
beside him, with her short denim skirt doing little to cover her
delicious thighs, kept other glands active too.

Now he balanced the pizza in one hand and threw open
the door to his house with the other. Sprocket hurled himself at
them, yipping, so Tim didn't get to see Claire's first reaction to
the slate-floored entrance to his home.

"Sprocket, sit!" he commanded. The little dog put his rear
down for a split second and then bounded up again.

Claire knelt and let the dog sniff her hand. He put his paws
on her knees, trying to reach her face with his tongue. She picked
him up and straightened as he licked her face. "What a cutie!
Hey, Sprocket, thanks for the free facial."

Tim put the pizza box down on the hall table and took the
excited dog out of her arms. "Okay, buddy, that's enough. Only
I'm allowed to kiss her that often."

Claire looked at him and covered her mouth, her eyes dancing above her hand.

"What?" he asked.

She uncovered her wide grin. "It's just that…Well, I figured you'd have a Bernese mountain dog or a…a Great Dane or

something. Sprocket's so...so little, and the contrast just looks...
funny." She kept erupting into giggles.

"She's laughing at us, Sprocket." Tim gave the dog's head an
affectionate pat. "Luckily, I'm very secure in my masculinity. I
used to have a toy poodle."

"You did not!"

"Well, no, but—"

She picked up the pizza. "Where's the kitchen?"

He led her into the next room, which was lined with cherry
cabinetry and dark-gray granite countertops.

"It's beautiful!" she said, standing in the middle and turning
slowly around. She walked to the island and traced a pale-silver
vein in the granite. "Gorgeous! Like a streak of lightning against
the night sky."

He let out a breath he hadn't realized he was holding. This
was a woman who had a highly developed aesthetic sense. He
was worried about how she would react to his taste.

As Claire sat beside him at the counter enjoying pizza and
beer, he realized that being with her made him more aware of
everything around him. Colors seemed heightened, scents were
sharper, voices and music sounded clearer and more distinct.

But he was most aware of her—the intelligence in her brown
eyes, the mobility of her expressive mouth, the fragility of her
wrists, and the shining flow of her dark hair. She brought his
senses fully alive.

Unfortunately, she also seemed to evoke darker feelings,
forcing them up to the surface, where he had to face them. As he
had offered comfort over her strained relationship with Holly, it
had struck him that his words could apply to himself.

Someone could argue that Anais's suicide had nothing to
do with him, but it didn't feel that way most of the time. He
kept looking for what he had done wrong. What else had Claire
said? It hurt him that Anais hadn't told him how deeply she was

suffering. Not to mention the promise she had asked from him in the letter she'd left. He had kept it. The press had never gotten so much as a whiff of why she had killed herself, even though it meant the blame had fallen on him.

She wouldn't let him help her while she was alive, so he had made sure to honor her last wish.

"Tim? Are you all right?" Claire's hand was on his shoulder, and she was peering into his face. "Did I say something to upset you?"

"No, I'm fine. Just"—*Just what? Haunted by my dead wife?*— "just thinking about Frank."

"Oh."

She looked confused, and he realized he had no idea what she had been talking about while he wandered off into his own personal hell. "I was hoping he'd refuse to let go of you, so I could deck him."

"Hmm, and I thought your threats were all an act. I remember what you did at Holly's house, using your voice and body language to intimidate him without having to resort to physical contact. I was impressed."

Anais had taught him that, only in reverse. His height meant he intimidated people without intending to. His actress wife had shown him how to adjust his posture and his gestures to make his size less overwhelming to others. For a moment, he stayed silent. He had worked so hard to keep Anais away from this place and from Claire. Yet he found he wanted to bring his dead wife out into the open, to see if that would banish the darkness surrounding her. "Anais showed me how to change my body language. Her stage training made her an expert."

Claire sat silent, her eyes wide and soft. She gave him a tremulous smile, and he was afraid she pitied him. That was another reason he never mentioned Anais's name. He hated the combination of curiosity and sympathy it brought out in people.

"Why don't I show you the rest of the house?" he said, closing the almost-empty pizza box and carrying it to the refrigerator. "Not much is finished. Just the living room and master suite."

"Thank you for trusting me enough to share that," she said, ignoring his change of subject.

"It was time to stop avoiding the topic." He felt better too, as though he'd cracked open a window to let light and fresh air waft through. He grabbed two more bottles of Molson from the fridge and opened them, giving one to Claire. "Now let me lure you into my bedroom."

She stood, reaching up to cup his cheek with her palm as she pressed a gentle kiss against his lips.

He put his hand on the indentation in her back where her T-shirt met her skirt. He couldn't resist slipping his fingers under the white cotton to feel the warm satin of her skin.

"Beer and a back rub," she said, breaking the tension, much to his relief, "what could be better?"

He fluttered his fingertips against her rib cage, making her squirm and giggle. He loved to hear the trill of her giggle; it contrasted with the sophisticated facade she wore so comfortably.

She angled her arm to bat at his hand. "Not quite what I had in mind for the back rub," she said.

"I find a really good massage requires a certain state of undress."

"Didn't you want to give me a tour of your house?" she asked.

"You sidetracked me." It was true. He wanted to slide his hands under her clothes every time he saw her. He craved the feel of her against his skin because she chased away the cold. This time he offered her the crook of his arm. "Let me show you my etchings."

She snorted and threaded her arm through his elbow to rest her hand on his forearm, tracing the line of his muscle with her index finger. Her feather-light touch sent a bolt of arousal straight to his groin.

"This is the living room," he somehow managed to say as he almost dragged her through the doorway.

He watched her gaze sweep the room and come to rest on the expanse of glass. The moon had risen while they ate, bathing the softly arching mountain ridges in a cool, silver light.

"Ahhhhh," she sighed, releasing him and moving closer to the windows almost as though she were sleepwalking. "Much better than etchings."

He could see her reflection in the glass, overlaid on the view and washed to black and silver just like the mountains. Her expression was rapt and for the first time, he saw her as part of this place, saw that it called to her just as it called to him, no matter how much she denied it.

He stepped up behind her, putting his arms around her and resting his chin lightly on top of her head. "Why do you fight it so hard?"

She relaxed back against him. "I'm not putting up much of a fight."

"I mean Sanctuary. You love the mountains. You love your sister and her kids. You love horses. Why are you so determined to leave?"

He felt her stiffen. "You must have wanted out pretty badly yourself to go to college at age fifteen."

"I just ran out of classes to take. The guidance counselor told me I should apply to college, so I did."

"Did he suggest Harvard to you?"

"It was on the list he gave me."

"You know what the guidance counselor did when I went to talk to him about studying art history in college?" she asked. "He smiled and handed me information on two-year teaching certificates and a practical nursing program. His other suggestion was secretarial school. My parents thought they were all great ideas."

"That obviously didn't stop you."

"No, it made my future in Sanctuary very clear to me. Then my favorite teacher—the only one who believed I had a future in art—quit the next day."

"Who was that?"

"Mr. Van Zandt. He taught art and Spanish."

"I remember him. He was one of the young, cool teachers."

"He was the first person who spoke the word *connoisseurship* to me. I fell in love with that word. It seemed miraculous that you could have a career as a connoisseur of art, but I knew that's what I wanted to be."

This glimpse of her younger self fascinated him, and he wanted to hear more. "Why did he quit?" he prompted.

Her grimace showed in the window's reflective surface. "He was forced to leave by a parent who claimed he made homosexual overtures to his son. Mr. Van Zandt wasn't even gay."

"So why the accusation?"

"The son wanted to join the art club instead of playing football. Evidently, the kid was pretty stubborn, because his father couldn't think of any other way to get him to play quarterback, or whatever position it was. And no one in Sanctuary stood up for Mr. Van Zandt. No one."

"So you lost your one supporter. That was tough."

"It was a total shock. I walked into his classroom while he was boxing up his last few possessions. He told me to get out of Sanctuary before it destroyed me."

There were tears in her voice, and he felt her drag in a shuddering breath. He tightened his hold on her and dropped a kiss on the top of her head. "I can't blame him for his bitterness, but he shouldn't have let it spill over onto you."

"I never thought of it that way, but I guess he shouldn't have. All I knew was that the only person who understood my dreams was telling me to leave, or they would be destroyed." She turned in his arms and looked up at him so he could see the tears start down her cheeks. "I felt utterly alone that day, and that's when I knew I couldn't stay in Sanctuary."

He imagined the teenaged Claire standing in the empty classroom, resolving to find a way out of her small-town life all by herself, and the courage of it took his breath away. He began to understand what Sanctuary represented to her.

"You did it, Claire," he said. "You proved everyone wrong about you."

At that, she shifted away from him, and he released her. "Some things worked out; others didn't," she said.

He knew she was thinking about her divorce. From his standpoint, divorce looked like a minor glitch, not a major failure.

Her story told, she stepped away from him and turned to scan the rest of the room. "I understand now," she said.

"You do?" He felt a clutch of panic at what his living room might have given away.

"Why you want the Castillo." She waved to the blank wall over the sofa. "It would balance the incredible view."

He nearly sagged with relief. "Now that you know what a great setting it would hang in, will you sell it to me?"

She laughed and shook her head, making her hair ripple around her shoulders. "Nope. I promise to find you something else worthy, though."

"Problem is, when I get a notion in my mind, it's hard to shake it loose. I just can't picture anything else in that spot."

"What did you tell me the other day? That when you want something, you keep after it."

"It works nine times out of ten," he repeated. He took her elbow and led her toward another doorway. "This way's the master bedroom."

"Oh my, a fireplace," she said as she stepped into the high-ceilinged room and spotted the rough-cut stone hearth. "I've always wanted one in my bedroom. And you have a glorious view from here too."

"Right now, I prefer the closer view," he said, letting his gaze skim down her legs to her nearly bare feet. She was wearing dark-pink polish on her toenails.

"Really?" she said, turning and giving him a mock sultry look. She took a sip of her beer and deliberately ran her tongue over her lips.

"How about that back rub?" he said, taking the bottle out of her hand and setting it on the mantel beside his. He scooped up Sprocket and put him outside the door before closing it.

She looked small and shy, standing in the middle of his big bedroom, her arms wrapped around her waist. All he could think about was seeing the curves of her smooth, bare skin contrasting with the patchwork quilt spread over the king-sized bed. She would look beautiful against the golds and greens. For a moment, he wasn't sure how to approach her, and then she raised her arms and ripped the shirt off over her head.

"There's nothing I like better than a good back rub," she said and flung the tee across the room.

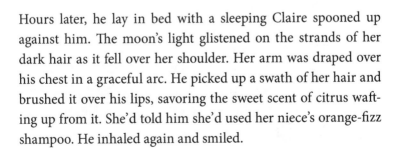

Hours later, he lay in bed with a sleeping Claire spooned up against him. The moon's light glistened on the strands of her dark hair as it fell over her shoulder. Her arm was draped over his chest in a graceful arc. He picked up a swath of her hair and brushed it over his lips, savoring the sweet scent of citrus wafting up from it. She'd told him she'd used her niece's orange-fizz shampoo. He inhaled again and smiled.

It felt good to be awake because he wanted to be, not because he couldn't sleep. He could feel Claire's soft breath ruffle across his skin, her heartbeat against his ribs.

His smile faded as he considered whether he kept seducing her just to fend off his nightmares. No, that couldn't be true, because there were other women who had been willing to keep him company in his bed. None of them had tempted him.

It wasn't until he saw Claire step out from behind Sharon that he began to want something again. Why? Why did Claire do that? The first answer he had come to dug cold, sharp claws into his mind: Claire reminded him of Anais in some dark, unspeakable way.

But there was no darkness in Claire; he could see that now. What she had was the strength to help him fight his way out of Anais's shadow. As he wrapped himself in the warmth of Claire's presence, he almost believed his past could be banished and he could love her with a whole heart. Almost.

The next morning, Tim again woke her by waving a fragrant mug of coffee under her nose. Dressed in a pair of plaid cotton pajama pants, he sat on the bed, kissed her, and offered her whatever she wanted for breakfast, but the darkness was back in his eyes. He kept looking at her as though she might grow fangs and bite him, and not in a sexy way.

"Tim, what is it?" she asked, putting her hand on his arm. She tried a weak joke. "Did I call you by the wrong name in the throes of passion?"

She saw him think about brushing the real question aside, and then he dropped his head, staring down into his coffee. "No, you're pretty good with names," he said. He combed his fingers through his hair. "I reckon I'm just unsettled by how fast we've gotten close."

Claire pushed herself upright against the pillows. Last night, he had spoken Anais's name to her for the first time. A weird jumble of feelings—shock, sympathy, a strange gratification— had held her silent for too long, and the moment had passed. Maybe he wanted or needed to talk about his wife, but couldn't find a way to bring it up again.

"I don't think I responded very well last night when you mentioned your wife's name," she said, wishing he would look up. "I mean, I know what happened with her—"

"No one knows what happened with my wife."

"All right, I know the bare facts of what happened. I can only imagine what you suffered—are suffering. I'd like to help."

"That's a real nice offer, but I don't think I should take you up on it," he said, standing up while keeping his back to her. He towered above her, and she could see the tension knotting the muscles of his shoulders. After a silence, he looked back at her and said, "You *have* helped me. It's easier to think about her now."

"Maybe you should talk to Willow. She's good at keeping secrets, and very sympathetic." Claire knew this might be her only chance to discuss the topic, so she decided to try every angle she could think of.

"As much as I respect Sharon's views on the subject, I'm not going to spill my guts to a horse."

"Maybe Willow isn't your whisper horse. Maybe you just haven't met the right one yet."

He turned then, his face a mask of exasperation. "Claire, a horse isn't going to change anything."

"I know that." She wasn't going to let his skepticism stop her. "It's what you say to the horse that changes *you*. Putting your situation into words gives you a new perspective."

"Words are meaningless. Actions tell you what you need to know."

She gasped as she began to comprehend how deep his pain must run. *How would she feel about herself if Milo had committed suicide rather than divorcing her?* "I'm sorry," she whispered. "I didn't really understand until just now."

"Then you'll understand why I don't think Willow will be of much assistance." He stalked over to the window and took a swallow of coffee.

She slipped off the bed and padded up behind him, wrapping her arms around his waist and laying her cheek against the warm, bare skin of his back. She felt him breathe in sharply.

"Claire, when you touch me, I don't know what helps or doesn't help."

"It has to help," she said, thinking of herself and how cherished she felt when she was with him. "What could feel better than this?"

"I can think of several things," he said, putting his mug on the windowsill to turn in her embrace. He tipped her chin up for a long, coffee-flavored kiss. "We did a few of them last night."

With a sense of unease, she let him put an end to the discussion. She could almost feel the shadow of his dead wife falling between them. When he slid his free hand down to cup her bottom, she put her hands on his chest and pushed. "Easy, buster! I have to get to Holly's house in less than an hour."

"We can manage that," he said, hooking his hand under her knee and pulling it high up on his thigh while bending so his erection rubbed right between her legs.

That was all it took to awaken the craving to have him inside her. She yanked open the fly of his pajama pants and freed his cock. He wrapped her other leg around his waist and carried her over to the bedside table. Dropping her feet to the floor, he pulled a condom from the drawer and rolled it on. She hitched one leg up on his thigh so he could drive himself up and inside her. She flexed her hips as his fingers stroked her in a matching rhythm, and an orgasm slammed into both of them almost simultaneously.

"We may have set a new world record," she gasped as he slipped out of her, causing an aftershock to shudder through her body.

He held her tight against him as their breathing slowed to a normal rate. "You're right about one thing. Nothing feels better than this."

Chapter 27

EVERAL HOURS LATER, CLAIRE SAT AT THE GLASS-topped desk in the main room of the gallery. It was a typical slow Tuesday, so she had plenty of time to think.

Her relationship with Holly had reached a milestone this morning: her sister had allowed Claire to drive the girls to school for the first time, saying she would stay home and rest so she could pick them up at the end of the day.

Frank remained a touchy subject. Claire recommended that Holly bring Paul up-to-date on yesterday's events. She knew restraining orders weren't worth much, but she thought it would be good to have one in place. However, Holly vetoed that, saying she didn't want to provoke Frank further.

Claire let that go, since the police seemed pretty willing to offer Holly protection even without a legal document. In fact, Robbie McGraw had been sitting in an unmarked car parked two houses down when Claire drove up in the morning. She had waved and made a mental note to bring muffins the next morning.

She thought through all of those issues several times, trying to ward off contemplation of her relationship with Tim. She got up to straighten one of the Len Boggs paintings, and wiped down a black metal sculpture that showed every dust mote. She sat back down and sorted through a pile of junk mail Davis had left on the desk.

Then she folded her hands on the cold glass and gave in to Tim, staring at the Annie Nelson photo directly across from her without seeing anything in it.

Their relationship felt like a dance. A tense, steamy tango, full of advances and retreats. She was having a hard time keeping up with the choreography.

Had she pushed too hard by bringing up his dead wife a second time? As they grew more and more intimate, it seemed impossible not to. Yet Tim had been politely withdrawn as he drove her to the veterinary hospital this morning to pick up her car. It was a strange contrast to the explosiveness of their lovemaking.

No, it was sex, not lovemaking. She couldn't claim to love Tim, although sometimes she felt on the verge of it. He was a spectacular lover, a rock in a crisis, and a knowledgeable collector of art. It was actually amazing she *wasn't* in love with him.

Maybe the push-pull was deliberate on his part. When he felt she was getting too emotionally entangled, he pushed her away. In a way, he was doing her a favor. They both knew she was leaving in the not-too-distant future. Keeping their relationship uncertain would minimize the pain of parting.

"Who am I kidding?" Claire moaned as she contemplated returning to her empty apartment in New York. "I'll miss him enormously." She allowed herself a giggle at her choice of words. "Especially since he's so enormous."

"Care to share the joke?"

Claire jerked around to see Paul walking toward her as the gallery's front door swung closed behind him. "Oh, you startled me!"

"Talking to yourself is the first sign of insanity," he said, dropping into the chrome-and-leather chair beside the desk. He stretched out his long legs and stuck his hands in his pockets.

"No, answering yourself is."

"Then I'm totally off my rocker," he said with his flash of a grin. "Are you free for lunch?"

"I have to wait for Davis to come in before I can leave." She looked hard at Paul. "Didn't we have this conversation up at Chief Chipaway?"

"It's just a friendly lunch. No evil intentions or ulterior motives."

"You're a politician and a lawyer, so I don't believe you for a second."

He rolled his eyes. "That's right, I picked the two least respected professions on earth."

"You could try selling used cars."

"Funny. One warning, though. If you start throwing yourself at me, I'll take you up on it. No more Mr. Nice Guy."

"Thanks for the heads-up."

"Am I late?" Davis Honaker appeared out of the back hallway, his white hair perfectly combed and his beige linen trousers ironed to a knife pleat. "Paul, you son of a gun, I didn't know you were an art lover."

Paul stood and shook hands with the older man. "I'm interested in that horse painting you have locked up in the back room," Paul said with a wink at Claire. "I'll give you two hundred for it."

Davis snorted. "Two hundred *thousand* wouldn't even begin to touch it."

Paul whistled. "I'll settle for a postcard, then."

"No postcards," Davis said. "We tried to get permission, but the artist's agent said no. Can I interest in you some Len Boggs note cards? They were Claire's idea, and they're selling like hotcakes. Very tasteful and a nice little bit of cash flow between the art sales."

"Thanks, but I do all my writing on yellow legal pads," Paul said. "Can I steal Claire for lunch?"

Davis's expression turned speculative as he looked back and forth between them.

"We're old friends from high school days," Claire hurried to say.

"Just have her back by two," Davis said.

Claire glanced at her watch. It was a few minutes after noon. Usually, she took half an hour for lunch. She sighed at Davis's matchmaking. "Let me grab my bag, and I'll be right there."

When she returned, Paul escorted her out to a gleaming black Corvette. "I brought my car today because I want to take you on a guided tour."

"She's a beauty," Claire said, running her hand along the low, sleek line of the roof. "But I remember you always said your first sports car would be a BMW."

"When you're in politics, local or otherwise, you buy American." He held the door open for her.

"I like this car. It makes a completely different statement than a Beemer. It says, 'Look at me because I'm pure speed and power.' The BMW is just another sports car."

"And you wonder why I tried to kiss you by Chief Chipaway." He said it with the kind of grin that robbed it of provocation.

"What sort of a tour are we taking?" Claire said as Paul got in and eased the car onto the street.

"There are a lot of things you don't know about today's Sanctuary. Being the former mayor, I thought I'd show you a few."

The Corvette rumbled down Washington Street. "You've already noticed the old cracked cement sidewalks have been redone in brick."

"Yeah, they're not so great for walking in heels," Claire teased.

Paul ignored her, waving his hand toward a sparkling fountain centering a green square of grass. "Remember when that was a run-down parking lot?"

"I do."

"And you used to complain that Sanctuary didn't have a bookstore," he said, pointing to the display of colorful book covers in the bay window of Books, Books, and More Books. "Not to mention our permanent theater, right down around the corner in the former five-and-dime store."

Claire looked out at the Victorian storefronts lining the main street. Buildings that had been neglected when she lived here were now shiny with new paint and restored trim work.

"There's the new library, an annual concert series at Union Hall, and of course, Davis's gallery adds more artistic culture to town."

Claire slanted a teasing look at Paul. "It is so funny to hear you talking like a…a chamber of commerce video. You used to complain about Sanctuary even more than I did."

He looked out at the buildings scrolling past, and she saw pride in his gaze. "I discovered there was a lot to like here, and I could change some of the things I didn't like."

"Now that's the kind of attitude we need more of in politics," Claire said. "You're a good man, Paul."

"There's the kiss of death," he said, making a wry face. "You only hung out with me because I was a motorcycle-riding, hell-raising troublemaker."

"No, I hung out with you because I saw the future mayor behind the tough facade. And maybe a little bit because you rode a motorcycle. I had my goody-goody reputation I needed to overcome."

"Even hanging out with me couldn't overcome that," he said as he turned onto Battle Street. Once a residential neighborhood, the immaculately tended Victorian houses now sported discreet signs offering professional services from accountants, lawyers, and dentists. They seemed to be vying with each other for the most colorful flower beds and window boxes. Paul parked halfway down the block in front of an especially exuberant garden. The sign read, *Tammy's Place, Bring Your Appetite and We'll Satisfy It.* "Remember Tammy Hodges? She was a couple of grades behind us in school."

Claire dredged up the image of a girl with a mass of frizzy brown hair, freckles, and braces. "She used to bring homemade ice cream to school all the time. It was delicious."

"Well, she started with that and added breakfast and lunch. She doesn't do dinner because she wants to be home with her family in the evening."

"That sounds like Tammy. She loved babysitting," Claire said, joining Paul on the sidewalk. They strolled up the steps and snagged a table on the wide front porch.

After they ordered, Paul swept a hand around the scene, encompassing brilliant flowers, historic buildings, giant shade trees, and the murmur of contented diners. "All I'm trying to point out is, you might find living here more pleasant than you think."

Paul was right. Sanctuary had changed, and not just physically.

But could she be happy here?

She looked back at Paul. "You know how hard I worked to get to New York."

"Yeah, I do. You deserve all the success you found there."

"I have an amazing job waiting for me, opening a whole new gallery. Matching people with the right art is my passion. Here I'm sometimes lucky to sell two boxes of note cards in a day."

"And you have a man waiting for you back in the city. I understand. I get carried away sometimes."

Claire decided she owed her old friend the truth. "The man I was talking about isn't in New York. He's here."

"I see," he said, looking away from her and drumming his fingers on the tabletop. After a few seconds, he turned back to her. "Let me guess. Dr. Tim."

"Yes, it's Tim. I'm as surprised as anyone. We both understand it's not a serious thing since I'm leaving when Holly's better."

Paul's gaze stayed on her. "How not serious is it?"

She thought of all her questions and reservations from the morning. "It's too soon to tell."

His fingers went still. "Well, I guess that's between you and him, and none of my business."

The waitress arrived with their drinks, and Paul turned the conversation to other topics, much to Claire's relief. She was pleasantly surprised that he hadn't gotten angry with her about hiding her relationship with Tim. She slipped into the relaxed banter she and Paul had always shared.

Her sense of ease lasted through the sandwiches.

"Have you been to the Aerie yet?" Paul asked as the waitress brought two dishes of peach-and-pecan ice cream. "It's amazing what Adam Bosch has created up there. Just like a New York City restaurant but with a better view."

"I hear it's really expensive and hard to get reservations so I haven't tried," Claire said, remembering her aborted date with Tim. "How many times have you been there?"

"A couple, but always for political fundraisers," he said with a grimace. "You can't enjoy the food when you're glad-handing. How about I take you? Just a friendly dinner."

"Thanks, but I sort of owe Tim my first meal there. We were on our way to dinner when Frank showed up at Holly's."

Paul's angular face went tight. "For such a slow talker, he moves pretty fast. Maybe another time. Did you know this flavor of ice cream was voted best in the state?"

Once again, he dropped the subject, but Claire wasn't fooled. Paul had sent the metaphorical foosball spinning into the center of the table. He was in the game, and Tim was his opponent.

"I told Paul about Frank taking the children," Holly said as Claire stowed peanut butter and grape jelly in the refrigerator. She had fixed the girls an after-school snack before they went down the street to play at the Defibaughs'.

"You did? He didn't mention it," Claire said without thinking. "When did you call him?"

"This morning, after you left. I decided you were right about documenting everything that happens. He agreed and said he'd fill out the papers and take them to the judge today."

"You did the right thing," Claire said. "This way, the police have a legal justification for keeping an eye on you and the girls."

"What were you talking to Paul about, if it wasn't my divorce?"

"Nothing in particular. We had lunch together at Tammy's Place. It's fantastic." Holly was eyeing Claire in a way that made her keep talking. "Paul's proud of what he accomplished as mayor, so he took me on a tour to show it off."

"Sis, is something going on between you and Paul?" Holly's tone was like old times: affectionate, concerned, and teasing, without an ounce of accusation. "Because I thought you and Tim Arbuckle were an item."

"We are, sort of." Claire hesitated. Despite the previous day's confession, she wasn't sure where she stood with her sister. "I didn't really mean to get involved with anyone."

"And here you are with two men chasing you. Hey, enjoy it!"

Claire hesitated a moment, wanting to share her dilemma with Holly, but it was tough to trust her enough to open up again. "Paul and I are just catching up on old gossip. He knows everyone!"

She felt a guilty sense of relief when her cell phone rang. She snatched it up to check the caller ID. When she saw Tim's name, relief loosened the knot between her shoulders. Maybe she hadn't completely ruined things by bringing up his dead wife.

"Claire, I called to apologize for being a jerk this morning."

"You weren't a jerk." She put a smile in her voice. "Just brooding. I couldn't blame you. I brought up a difficult subject."

"If I provide dinner, may I invite myself to eat with you all?"

"Bribery always works. I wasn't looking forward to macaroni and cheese again." She loved his thinking he needed to bring food to make up for his withdrawn mood.

"Tell me what takeout you want, and I'll be there about six."

"How about the Aerie?"

His chuckle seemed to reverberate right through her. "Was I *that* big a jerk?"

"Let me consult with Holly and call you back."

She pressed the *End* button and stood staring down at the phone for a minute, savoring the pleasure of having Tim worry about her feelings. She turned to find Holly watching her. "Tim's going to bring us some grown-up food for dinner. What would you like?"

"Chinese! I have a craving for General Tso's chicken."

"Great idea! I keep forgetting we can get Chinese food in Sanctuary now. Pork lo mein would hit the spot."

Holly tilted her head. "You're grinning like a Cheshire cat, and I don't think it's about pork lo mein."

"It's relief. I said something stupid this morning, and I wasn't sure if he was angry. Turns out he's not." She tried to tone down the grin, but the corners of her mouth wouldn't cooperate.

"This morning?" Her sister was starting to grin too.

Claire wanted to kick herself. She'd forgotten that Holly had no idea she'd spent the night with Tim. "It's complicated."

The sound of approaching children's voices ended the conversation. As she listened with half an ear to the little girls' chatter, she debated what to say to Holly about Tim. Her feelings about him were hard to separate from her feelings about returning to Sanctuary. She had to tread carefully when describing those to her sister; she didn't want to play into Frank's comments about her attitude. She wasn't even sure how she really felt about her hometown anymore. It had been easier when she knew she didn't want to be here.

"I have five tickets to the 4-H fundraiser at the fairgrounds. Any chance I can persuade you ladies to join me? There's going to be live music." Tim sat back from the table littered with empty take-out containers. "It's a little greedy on my part, but I like the idea of walking in with four beautiful women. What do you say, Brianna, Kayleigh?"

"Yes, please," Brianna said, "if it's okay with Mama."

Holly nodded.

"I'll come with you too," Kayleigh piped up. "I'm going to raise a lamb for 4-H when I'm old enough. Maybe you can help me since you're an animal doctor. Do lambs need shots like people?"

"They sure do. I'll make sure your lamb gets all the vaccinations it needs." He looked at Claire. "How about you?"

"I've had all my shots already, thanks." She watched the smile slowly light his face. She loved sitting across the table from him so she could enjoy the lock of hair falling onto his forehead and the tendons of his forearms flexing as he reached for another food container. When he'd arrived carrying three large bags of Chinese takeout, she'd thought it was overkill, but he had polished off every bite no one else had claimed.

"They forgot the vaccination for being a smarty pants," he said, his gaze inviting Brianna and Kayleigh to join in his joke. The little girls burst into delighted giggles.

"Oh, you meant to ask if I would come to the 4-H event," Claire said, feigning innocent surprise. "Why didn't you say so? I'd love to come. Holly, if you think it would be too tiring for you, we'll take Brianna and Kayleigh ourselves."

"I'm coming too. It's been forever since I went out for fun."

Later, as Claire walked Tim out to his truck, she said, "That was really nice of you to invite everyone to the fundraiser."

"Truth is, I bought ten tickets to support the cause. Might as well use some of them." He came to a halt by the driver's side door. "Can I persuade you to come home with me again tonight?"

"Because you're worried about Frank?"

"Because I want you there with me."

She felt a twinge of unease as a jubilant "yes!" tried to wrench itself from her throat. Her response to him was too powerful, overwhelming all the reservations she had about him and the future of their relationship.

"I promise to behave like a gentleman in the morning," he said as she hesitated.

"Then I definitely won't go with you," she said with a grin.

His face lit with wicked intention as he backed her up against the truck. Applying just enough pressure so she felt every inch of his body from knee to shoulder, he sandwiched her between himself and the metal. He cradled her head between his two big palms and leaned down to kiss her slowly but thoroughly. He lifted his head and said, "Well?"

"You're very persuasive, but I want to stay with Holly tonight. We need some more sister time."

Tim's expression went from hopeful to accepting in an instant, which made it all the harder to resist him.

"Could you try to persuade me one more time before you leave?" she asked, running her hands up his chest and linking them behind his neck.

He obliged her.

Chapter 28

OESN'T HOLLY SEEM TO BE HAVING FUN?" CLAIRE asked as Tim handed her an ice-cold can of Dr. Pepper and sat down beside her on the hay bale. "I'm so glad you asked her to come. She looks much happier than I've seen her since I got here."

The 4-H fundraiser turned out to be a barbecue and barn dance in the huge covered livestock show ring at the state fairgrounds. The dirt floor was covered with fragrant wood shavings, while red-and-white bunting hung from the rafters. Hay bales edged the ring to provide seating.

Holly was sitting at one of the scattered round tables, laughing with a group of people that happened to include Officer Robbie McGraw. Brianna and Kayleigh were playing chase among the tables with some other children.

"Getting out of the house has done her good, but you should be taking the credit. She wouldn't have come without you," Tim said, tilting his head back as he drank his own soda, the muscles of his throat working. He pulled a baggie tied with blue ribbons out of his shirt pocket and offered it to her. "I bought us some brownies at the bake sale."

"Oh my God, Mrs. Estep's famous fudgies! Who did you have to bribe?" She looked past the dangling dessert to see his slow smile and the curve of hair on his forehead. The need to touch him surged through her. She knew she shouldn't because people would notice, but she reached out and threaded her fingers through the wayward hank of hair to comb it away from his face.

His smile never wavered, but his eyes went dark and hot. "I see I need to cultivate Mrs. Estep's acquaintance further," he said, running the back of his hand up Claire's bare arm to the ruffle of the embroidered Mexican blouse that slid off her shoulder.

It should have been nothing, the mere brush of his warm skin against hers, but it sent shimmers of heat whirling down to pool between her thighs. Her eyelids fluttered halfway closed as she gave in to the intensity of her response.

"If you keep looking like that, we're going to have to leave early," his voice rumbled in her ear.

"Mmm, not before I get my brownie," she said, shivering at the delicious tickle of his breath against the whorls of her ear.

"Claire, nice to see you here."

Her eyes snapped open, and she looked up to see Paul standing in front of her, wearing a cowboy hat and carrying a six-pack of Budweiser.

"Dr. Tim." Paul nodded to her companion. "I hear you made a very generous donation to the bake sale."

"Just a contribution to a good cause," Tim said, rising to his considerable height and shaking hands. His manner was easy, but his voice sounded tight.

"When you pay fifty dollars in advance for a half dozen brownies, it gets people talking," Paul said.

Claire shook her head with a laugh as she pushed up from the hay bale. "I knew he'd bribed someone to hold those for him. They always sold out first at our bake sales."

The loudspeaker broke in on their conversation. "Paul Taggart, you're needed at the barbecue pit."

He lifted the six-pack slightly. "My beer is needed at the barbecue pit." Flashing a grin at her, he said, "Save a dance for me later, will you? It's been a long time since we did the two-step."

As he walked away, she glanced up at Tim. He was staring after the other man with annoyance written all over his face. Paul's little barb had hit right where he'd wanted it.

"Paul's just joking around," she said, wishing she could give her old friend a good punch in the arm. "He never went to a dance of any kind when we were in high school. I doubt he's suddenly developed a desire to two-step."

Tim's gaze was heavy lidded. "I know I've suddenly developed a desire to two-step. Naked."

"Stop it, you wicked man," Claire said, grinning. "You don't need to remind me who I'm sleeping with."

"No, but I need to remind your old pal."

"C'mon, some food will make you less grouchy," she said, pulling him toward the snack table.

"I'm not grouch—"

"Dr. Tim, Mama said you got us Mrs. Estep's fudgies and to say thank you because they're our favorites," Kayleigh said as she came running up. "We can't have them till after dinner, though."

"You're welcome," Tim said, squatting down to the little girl's level. "Did I tell you what a pretty dress that is you have on?"

Kayleigh twirled so her pink skirt flew out and showed the lacy petticoat underneath. "You said we all looked beautiful. I like Aunt Claire's boots too."

Claire glanced down at the bright-red cowboy boots whose pointed toes peeked out from under her jeans. She'd bought them at an expensive boutique on the Upper West Side in Manhattan. The irony made her smile.

"I like Aunt Claire's jeans," Tim said.

"Really? They don't look fancy to me," Kayleigh said, eyeing Claire's classic Levi's.

"It's the way they fit," Tim said.

Claire cocked her hip into his shoulder, so he had to slap his hand down on the wood shavings to keep from falling over sideways. He slanted a reproachful glance up at her before he stood up, dusting his hands off on his jeans. "Kayleigh and I were simply discussing fashion," he said.

A sudden lessening in the general hum of conversation made Claire look around to see what was claiming people's attention.

"Oh hell!" she said under her breath as she saw Frank walking toward the table where Holly sat.

"Papa!" Kayleigh took off before Claire could stop her, running up to her father and throwing her arms around his legs.

Frank stumbled and looked down. "Hey, baby, how are you?" He swung his daughter up for a hug before setting her down and giving her a little push away, saying, "Papa needs to talk to Mama now." His gaze locked on Holly, and he strode toward her again.

When she saw the stricken look on Kayleigh's face, Claire could have strangled Frank. She jogged over to where he had left his daughter and scooped the little girl up in her arms. "Hey, Dr. Tim has a fudgie for you."

Kayleigh hid her face against Claire's shoulder, saying in a muffled and tearful voice, "I can't have it till after dinner."

"We can make an exception this time," she said as Tim came up beside her. "Kayleigh needs one of the brownies now."

He ripped the baggie open and handed the brownie to Claire. "I'd better go see what I can do to help."

"Could you find Brianna and bring her to me?" She didn't want the children to be involved in what might be an ugly scene.

Tim nodded, his gaze meeting hers with understanding. Claire kept Kayleigh's back to her parents and prayed Frank didn't start yelling. She was relieved that Robbie was still at the table; he could handle any physical threats Frank might make.

So far, Holly was unaware that her husband was bearing down on her, and Claire debated whether she should call out. Deciding it might set off Frank's temper if she brought attention to the situation, she bit her tongue and hoped Tim would find Brianna quickly.

She took an involuntary step forward when she saw Holly shrink back as Frank came up beside her. Remembering the little girl in her arms, she stopped herself and made sure Kayleigh was still engrossed in the brownie.

Frank had his hand braced on the table and was leaning down over Holly, but his voice was low enough that Claire couldn't hear what he was saying. She saw her sister put her hand on Frank's arm. She felt anger and nerves tighten the muscles in her shoulders when he threw Holly's hand off.

"Look who I found," Tim said, striding up to her with Brianna riding piggyback and Estelle Wilson trotting along beside them. He swung Brianna down off his back with a flourish that made her squeal with delight. "Mrs. Wilson here says she'd like to take the girls to see the draft horse foal in the barn next door."

"I think that's a great idea," Claire said, putting Kayleigh down gently. "You all would like that, wouldn't you?"

Brianna looked confused, but she said, "Yes, ma'am."

"I believe there might be kittens too," Estelle said, taking each girl's hand and leading them away from the scene developing by the tables.

As Claire hurried toward her sister, Tim easily matched her pace. "I thought you'd want to be with your sister now, and I knew Estelle would understand what needed to be done with the girls."

"Exactly right," she said, wincing as Frank's voice rang out.

"My wife claims she's too ill to even fix me dinner, and now I find her here, all dressed up to go dancing. I'd say she's been lying to me."

As Claire and Tim came up behind Holly, Robbie stood as well. A few seconds later, Paul pushed through the gathering crowd to add to the ranks around Holly.

"Now, Frank—" Paul began.

"I see you've joined her goon squad, Taggart," Frank interrupted. "I guess you've swallowed all her lies too."

With Frank's attention on Paul, Claire put her hand on her sister's shoulder; she could feel her shaking. She leaned down to whisper, "Estelle Wilson took the girls to the next barn. Let's get you out of here."

"No," Holly said, her voice cracking slightly. Then she stood up and said more firmly, "No! I'm tired of hiding and covering things up. I need to deal with Frank right here and now so everyone knows the truth."

Frank's gaze came back to his wife, and he raised his voice so the crowd could hear. "I tried to go to my own goddamned house, and two cops blocked me in front of my own front door. What kind of a wife won't let her husband in his own goddamned house?"

"An abused wife," Holly said, a slight quaver in her voice. "A wife you've thrown things at. A wife you've left bruises on with your bare hands. A wife whose children you've kidnapped."

Holly's voice grew stronger with every sentence, sounding clear above the gasps and murmurs of the crowd. Claire noticed that several people made a point of putting distance between themselves and Frank.

"Now, honey, you know the Lyme's makes your brain all fuzzy. You told me that yourself." Frank's voice became conciliatory as he scanned the crowd. "She's just ill and imagining things."

Holly swiped a napkin off the table and dipped it in the glass of water she'd been sipping. She scrubbed the damp paper across her cheek, wiping the carefully applied concealer off the ugly-colored bruise Frank's hand had left on her face. "Is this bruise my imagination, Frank? Are you going to expect me to tell these folks I ran into a door like you did the first time you hit me?"

Suddenly, Frank was standing alone in a circle at least ten feet in diameter. No one wanted to be anywhere near a man who beat his wife.

Claire's heart swelled with pride at her sister's courage, even as tears blurred her eyes for Holly's pain.

Robbie stepped forward, looking every inch a cop despite his jeans and Caterpillar T-shirt. "Mrs. Snedegar, would you like to press charges?"

Holly shook her head, her gaze still locked on her husband. When she spoke, her voice was low, as though she'd exhausted all her strength. "Just go away, Frank. Don't ever come near me again."

"Holly, our children—" Frank began.

"Paul will work something out with you about visitation," Holly said. Claire saw her start to droop and quickly put her arm around her sister's waist, bracing as Holly leaned into her.

Frank looked around at the stony faces staring back at him, opened his mouth and closed it, then turned to slink away.

Holly waited until Frank was out of sight before she spoke. "I'm sorry for that, everyone, but it needed to be done. Let's get back to having fun."

Then her sister sagged into Claire's arms, making her stagger. Almost instantly, Holly's weight was lifted, and Claire released her into Tim's strong grasp and helped him settle her onto the folding chair.

Claire dropped to her knees in front of her sister and looked up at her. "That was the bravest thing I've ever seen anyone do."

Holly managed a wavering smile. "I couldn't have done it if you hadn't been standing right beside me."

Claire gathered Holly's trembling hands in hers. "I'm proud to have been with you. I love you, Holl."

"Same here, sis."

Claire laid her cheek against Holly's hands before she let go and stood up. Arrayed in a protective phalanx around Holly's chair were Tim, Paul, and Robbie, all looking both concerned and formidable. Beyond them, the noise of multiple conversations was beginning to reach normal volume again. Suddenly, a fiddle struck up a country tune, and Claire blessed the musician for turning the partygoers' attention toward the temporary stage set up at the far end of the show ring.

Robbie leaned over so only Claire could hear him. "Ma'am, I'd like to go make sure Snedegar has left the premises."

"That would be great," Claire said. "You might check on the children in the draft horse barn too. They're with Estelle Wilson, so I'm sure they're fine, but just in case."

"Yes, ma'am, although I'd bet on Mrs. Wilson against Snedegar any day," he said with a hint of a smile as he moved off.

Paul watched Robbie jog across the expanse of wood shavings. "I have a feeling this is one restraining order that will be enforced."

Tim had been kneeling beside Holly, talking with her in a low voice. He straightened and said, "Holly wants to stay a few more minutes, to show she's not going to let Frank chase her away. Then we'll make a quiet exit and collect the girls."

"I'll go make sure the biggest gossips have the story straight," Paul volunteered. "We want the right version spread around town."

Claire sat down on one side of her sister while Tim hooked a chair over to sit on the other. A steady stream of friends and neighbors came by to chat with Holly, some offering oblique comfort in the form of a warm hug or a playdate with the children, while others flat-out said they were sorry for her situation and asked what they could do to help. Tim took on the task of deflecting any overly personal comments and questions with an easy joke and his unhurried smile.

As Claire watched the flow of support toward her sister, a glow of warmth bloomed in her chest, and tears brimmed in her eyes. This was her hometown the way she had always wanted it to be.

"Okay, I'm ready," Holly said when there was a lull in the procession. "Claire, I'm a little shaky, so can you give me your arm?"

"Why don't you let me do that job?" Tim said. "I'll have a beautiful lady on each side of me, and no one will think anything about it."

Holly cast him a grateful glance as he held out his hand and helped her up from her chair.

"Lean all you want," he said.

"He's used to wrestling six-hundred-pound sows," Claire said, tucking her hand under his other elbow.

"Are you calling me a sow?" Holly asked, leaning around Tim to make a face at her.

Relief flooded Claire. After all the drama, her sister could still make a joke. Claire started to giggle. She heard Holly snickering, which made her giggle harder.

"Care to let me in on the joke?" Tim said as he looked back and forth between the two convulsed women on either side of him.

"I have...no idea...what's..." Claire ran out of breath and had to stop.

"It's just..." Holly broke off as another fit of laughter bent her over.

"People will think I'm the funniest man alive." Tim gently led them toward the exit.

Claire sobered up first, taking several deep breaths. "The truth is, it's better than crying."

Chapter 29

*W*HEN HER CELL PHONE'S ALARM WENT OFF, CLAIRE bolted upright. Realizing it was morning and there had been no nocturnal visitations from Frank, she flopped back down with a sigh of relief.

"Ow!" she muttered as her weight flattened the flimsy mattress of Holly's sofa bed over the metal frame.

Last night, they had all been worried about Frank's reaction to his public humiliation, but evidently, he had gotten the message that Holly wasn't going to let him push her around anymore. Of course, having a police car parked outside the house all night didn't hurt. That was the only reason Tim had been persuaded to go home to his own bed.

"Hey, sleepyhead!" Holly walked into the living room sporting a denim skirt and a blouse touched with lace at the collar. Her hair was styled in soft waves, and she wore a splash of rose lipstick.

"Holly?" Claire sat up again. "You blow-dried your hair!"

"I know," her sister said, giving her head a flirtatious little shake. "I woke up this morning and felt like making myself look nice."

"It didn't exhaust you?" Claire swung her bare feet to the floor. "You should take it easy. You don't want to use up all your strength first thing."

"Well, I might have overdone it a bit." Holly sank into an upholstered chair. "But I feel so much better." She leaned forward. "I think Frank was keeping me from getting better. I mean, being scared of him and constantly worrying about doing something that would make him blow up. The worst part was I couldn't predict what would set him off, so I couldn't avoid it."

"It must have been awful," Claire said, perching on the chair arm. "Well, you've got guts, sis."

"I meant what I said. If you hadn't been there last night, if you hadn't gotten the children away from Frank's ugliness"—Holly's eyes brimmed with tears—"I couldn't have done it."

"Hey, you're the one who stood up to him where everyone could see and hear."

"Maybe it wasn't the smartest thing to do, but I couldn't hide anymore."

"Not smart? You have the whole town protecting you and the girls now." She sighed. "I wish I'd had the courage to confront Milo like that."

"He didn't hit you, did he?" Holly looked stricken.

"No, no, nothing like that. He just undermined me at every opportunity. He'd do it at parties, at work, in front of our friends. And I would pretend to laugh it off."

"He was jealous of you."

"Jealous? Why would he be jealous of me?"

"Because you knew so much more about art than he did."

"Are you kidding? Milo was much more knowledgeable than I was."

"Maybe book knowledgeable, but you could pick out what was good, even when no one else knew it. I don't think he could."

Claire moved over to the chair facing her sister. "Why do you say that?"

"Remember when you came to visit that weekend?"

"Oh God, yes. Milo was horrible. I was so embarrassed."

"We went to the Gallery at Sanctuary before dinner. You wanted to see if there were any artists you could show in New York."

"And Milo said it would be a waste of time."

"But when we got there, he followed you around and waited to see what you said about each picture. He never gave his opinion first."

"But that was because he didn't want to impose his views on me. He wanted to give me the chance to develop my taste independently of his." That's what he'd always told her.

"No, sis. I watched him. He would wait until you said whether the picture was good or bad, and then he'd put on the right expression to go with your opinion. When you asked him what he thought, he'd sort of jumble your words around to make it sound like he knew that all along."

"Really? But he hated the Castillos, and I thought they were great." Claire was trying to readjust all her ideas about Milo.

"Did he turn down the Castillos first?"

"No, he wasn't in the gallery when they came in. I bought them on the spot because I didn't want them to go to another dealer."

Holly sat back with a triumphant look. "That's it. You made a decision about art without him. He couldn't have that."

"But all the profit he lost when he made me get rid of them!"

"Doesn't matter. His ego was more important than money."

Claire shook her head. She couldn't quite wrap her mind around this new perspective. She was too used to thinking of herself as Milo's protégée, the unworthy student sitting at the master's feet. She scanned back through her memories of the decisions she and Milo had made at his gallery. She had always assumed he was being the generous teacher when he insisted she state her opinion first. When he endorsed it, she would glow with pleasure.

"Now that I think about it, he only turned down one artist who I liked," Claire said. "Other than Julia Castillo, of course. I always thought he was just being nice and indulging me."

Holly snorted. "He was taking advantage of a talent he knew he didn't have."

Claire's view of herself splintered and rearranged itself in a new pattern inside her head. She was examining it from different angles when Brianna appeared in the doorway, hugging her favorite stuffed pink unicorn.

"Mama? Aunt Claire? Isn't it time to get up?"

Claire glanced at the mantel clock and scrambled off the chair arm. "Oh goodness, yes! I'll get breakfast going."

"I'll do the girls' hair."

"Are you sure?" Claire hesitated at the kitchen door. Untangling and braiding the children's long hair was time-consuming.

Brianna's face lit up as her mother smoothed her hand over the little girl's messy bedhead before she dropped a kiss there. "I'm sure."

Claire unlocked the gallery's front door, dropped her handbag on the desk chair, and walked straight to the storeroom. Pulling out one of Kay Fogler's paintings, she set it on the nearby easel and stepped back to examine it.

"The colors are clear, no muddiness. Confident brushstrokes," she murmured to herself, "but the composition has weaknesses."

She leaned it against the wall and put another painting in its place on the easel. Two more paintings followed in rapid succession.

"Hmm, promising, but not quite there yet," she declared to the empty room. She slotted the paintings back into the storage rack and left the room with a confident stride.

Picking up the gallery's phone, she dialed her boss. "Davis, about those Fogler paintings, I took another look at them, and I don't think she's ready for a show yet. She's got promise, but it's premature to put that group out in the market. It won't be good for her reputation or ours."

"What made you change your mind?" Davis asked.

"I didn't change my mind. I just trusted it."

"All righty," Davis said, "we'll tell Kay maybe next time."

"Suggest that she concentrate on strengthening her composition."

Claire hung up the phone and did a fist pump. She had known all along that Kay Fogler's work wasn't ready for exhibition, but she kept hearing Milo's voice in her head, telling her she'd pick a Bob Ross over a Picasso if it weren't signed.

"Shut up, Milo." Her voice sounded loud in the quiet space.

It wasn't quite up to Holly's public performance, but it felt good.

She looked over at the best of the current Len Boggs paintings displayed in the gallery. "What the hell!" Rooting through her purse, she pulled out her cell phone and dialed her boss-to-be.

"Claire!" Henry's deep Brooklyn-accented voice transported her back to New York and the big white-walled rooms of the Thalman Art Gallery. "Are you ready to come to work?"

Damn. She should have known that's what he would think, but she'd been on a different mission, so she hadn't considered it. "Well, my sister had a breakthrough yesterday, but it's going to be a while longer."

"Priscilla has found a couple of possible locations she wants you to look at. Could you get away for a day? The plane flight is on the gallery, of course."

It was the least she could do. "How about next week? I'll coordinate it with Priscilla."

"So if that's not why you called, what is it?"

"There's an artist from this area I think we should represent. His name's Len Boggs, and he does impressionist landscapes. He's brilliant and sells extremely well both locally and to out-of-towners."

"Sign him up."

"You don't want to see any of his work first?"

"You say he's good, and that's all I need to know."

Claire felt the blossom of tears in her eyes. "If you were here right now, I'd hug you."

His big laugh boomed through the phone. "Give me a rain check for next week."

Ending the call, she sank down on the desk chair. Suddenly, she was sobbing in great gulps as the dark, ugly doubts Milo had hammered into her melted away in the warmth of her two bosses' trust.

The sobs subsided, and as she mopped her face with a Kleenex, she understood exactly why Holly had dressed up and styled her hair this morning. Energy surged through her, and Claire wanted to drag people in off the street so she could sell them the perfect artwork for their tastes.

She drummed her fingers on the desktop for a few minutes, then dialed Tim's number. "Want to meet me at Healings Springs Stables for lunch? I thought we could take Willow out with us in the pasture and have a picnic."

"How about we take Willow out to the pasture and have a picnic in her empty stall?"

The seduction in his voice made her breasts tingle and her insides turn liquid with heat. "I think we could relocate the picnic."

"I'll be there at twelve thirty. What do you want me to bring?"

"How about dessert?"

"I'll bring some for you, but I already know what I'm having for dessert."

The heat began to pool, and she crossed her legs. "I hope like hell Estelle Wilson can't hear you."

"Only three kittens and a parrot are within earshot."

"Does the parrot know how to talk?"

He laughed and hung up.

Claire led Willow out of her stall, smiling at the new spring in the mare's step. "Look at how much more energy she has now! Her coat has such a nice sheen to it."

"You want me to give her a quick checkup?" Tim asked as Claire paraded her whisper horse in front of him.

She nodded, stroking the arch of Willow's neck as Tim ran his hands over the horse's frame, probing for any tenderness or swelling. She knew what those big, capable hands felt like on her own skin, and a delicious anticipation shivered through her. Willow's eyes were heavy lidded too, and Claire leaned in to whisper in the mare's ear. "He's got a good touch, doesn't he, girl?"

The horse grunted.

"Does it hurt there, Willow?" Tim asked, dancing his fingers carefully back across the same spot.

When the horse didn't react again, Claire giggled. "I think she was agreeing with something I said to her."

Tim bent to slide his hands down the mare's hind leg, turning his head to look up at her. "Anything I want to know about?"

"She just had the same look on her face I'm pretty sure I get when you run your hands over me."

He straightened abruptly. "Willow's doing fine, and I'm feeling right hungry. Why don't you take her out to the pasture while I grab the picnic supplies?"

Claire grinned and murmured to the horse, "Sorry, girl! Didn't mean to shorten your time with the doctor. You'll enjoy the sunshine, though."

As she led Willow past Tim, she looked up and gasped. His eyes blazed with intention and heat. "Okay, girl, let's move it along," she said, tugging on the mare's lead line.

"Willow looked a little sad when I left her in the field." Claire teased as she spread a blanket over the thick straw in the stall. Instead of using Willow's, they had sneaked off to the foaling barn, which was active only when mares were near their delivery time. The mothers-to-be were out to pasture for the day, so Claire and Tim had commandeered a newly cleaned stall.

"Willow will continue to look sad until she puts on about fifty more pounds. She's just underweight." Tim set down the two bags Claire had ordered from Food and Folks and settled onto the blanket, pulling her down with him. His weight crushed the straw, sending a billow of newly mown scent wafting around them. "I want an appetizer."

He put his arm around her waist and snugged her up against his side, bending his head to touch her lips with his. She touched the soft, faded flannel of his shirt, loving the sheer expanse of skin-warmed plaid she had to slide her palms over to reach the column of his neck. She threaded her fingers into the straight auburn hair on either side of his head and pulled his face closer to hers. Their kiss started as a gentle tasting, but when his tongue traced along her lower lip and she opened her mouth to him, he rolled her onto her back under him, driving his thigh between hers. She bowed up against him in an arch of pure arousal, and he dragged his mouth down her neck and into the V of her blouse. He pushed up to kneel over her, yanking open the buttons of her blouse and unfastening her bra.

She rubbed against the hard thigh between her legs as he towered above her, gazing down at her as he cupped her breasts and ran his thumbs over and around her nipples. "So beautiful," he said.

"Please, your mouth...I want your mouth on me," she gasped.

"Yes, ma'am," he said. He leaned down and nipped at her shoulder, the side of her neck, her earlobe, her lower lip, while still continuing to tease her breasts with his fingers.

"You don't take direction well," she rasped before taking his head between her hands and pushing it downward.

The breath of his chuckle huffed against her sensitized nipple, and she came up off the blanket again so her breast brushed against his lips. He obliged her by taking it into his mouth and sucking hard.

"Oh. My. God." She grabbed his shoulders and held on as his mouth and hands sent bolts of pleasure searing straight down to sizzle between her legs.

She bucked hard against his thigh, trying to satisfy the longing inside her.

She felt his fingers at her waistband, and reached for his belt buckle. They helped each other yank at zippers and buttons until Claire's panties went flying in one direction and Tim's boxers went in the other.

Then he was inside her and his bare chest was crushed against her breasts and her legs were wrapped around his waist as he thrust in again and again and murmured her name against the hollow of her neck as he held her hard against him as though he were trying to merge them into one.

"Yes! Yes! Oh God, yes!" she cried out as an orgasm slammed into her. The muscles of her body clenched as it spread in an explosion of sensation.

His voice was loud in her ear as he called out in the throes of his own climax. As she felt his weight begin to relax onto her, he rolled them both over so she was draped across him. Her head rested on his chest, where his heartbeat thundered in her ear.

As she caught her breath and his heart slowed its pounding, she began notice the slightly rough texture of the hair on his thighs where they touched hers, and the warm spot where his hand rested on the curve of her bottom, and his breath ruffling her hair. She sighed and let the corners of her lips turn up in a contented smile.

"So you call that an appetizer?" she murmured.

"No, I call that a feast. I just wish I'd had some whipped cream." He feathered his fingers through her hair, making her purr with delight.

"Mmm, everything you do feels good," she said.

He slid his hand under her chin and lifted it so he could see her face and she could see his. He was smiling, but only with his mouth. "That's the best thing a woman's ever said to me."

She wanted him to smile with his eyes too. "Well, that's the best thing a man's ever done to me," she said, slowly scooting up the length of him, maximizing the friction of her skin against his, until she could reach his lips to kiss him.

"Oh hell!" The clop of horse hooves coming closer made her brace her hands against his chest.

His arms tightened around her so she was pressed against him from knee to shoulder. "Just one more moment of heaven," he said, sweeping one hand down her back and up again in a leisurely caress before he released her.

She tossed him his boxers before retrieving her panties and trousers. They were dressed fully, if somewhat messily, before they heard Sharon's voice coming through the window.

"Hey, Chuck, put that mare in stall three."

"Which stall is this one?" Claire whispered.

"Damned if I know," Tim said, "but we're just having an innocent picnic."

Claire stooped to fish his condom wrapper out of the straw and held it out with a grin. "If we're going to claim innocence, we need to conceal the evidence."

He crumpled it up and shoved it in the pocket of his jeans. "I always knew I'd be a lousy criminal."

The stable hand peered through the bars between the stalls. "That you, Dr. Tim?"

"Sure is."

"You come to take a look at Starlight here?"

"No, I came to have lunch."

"Oh, okay." Chuck sounded puzzled, but he asked no more questions. "See you."

Claire was doubled over behind Tim in a fit of laughter. As Chuck left, she straightened and gasped between her giggles, "I c...came to ha...have lunch. And he just let it go. How did you do that?"

"I kept it simple."

She reached up and smoothed his rumpled hair. "Words to live by." She sat down and patted the blanket.

He folded himself down beside her. "I don't care what's in those bags, this is already one heck of a good mealtime."

They ate the sandwiches and cold salads with Claire propped against Tim's chest so they were always touching. He opened the bakery box he'd brought and let her choose a cupcake before taking one himself.

Her eyes danced as he bit into it. "So a cupcake is what you planned to have for dessert?"

"No, this is just a temporary substitute because we both have to get back to work. I'm saving my real dessert for later."

"Oh." She felt a flutter of anticipation between her legs. "When were you thinking of having it?"

"Whenever my craving for something sweet gets the better of me." His eyes were dark again, but this time it was with sexual hunger. He brushed the top of his cupcake against her lips, leaving a smear of icing on them. Then he leaned over and carefully licked the icing off.

She wanted to rip her clothes off so he could brush the icing over her breasts and lower. "I had no idea a cupcake could be so sexually arousing."

"When I'm around you, anything can be sexually arousing."

"So I could make brussels sprouts sexy?"

He twisted a lock of her hair around his finger and gave it a tug. "They're my favorite vegetable."

They gathered up their lunch wrappers and folded up the blanket before heading out to collect Willow. As soon as they were out of sight of the main barn, Tim twined his fingers with hers.

As they walked side by side over the emerald-green grass, with the soft ridges of the mountains rising in the distance, Claire felt a swell of contentment. A pang struck at her as she remembered her conversation with Henry Thalman and her planned trip to New York next week. It was the first step in her departure from Sanctuary.

"You know, maybe I could be happy living here," she said.

Tim's grip on her hand tightened, then eased. "You can't beat the view, that's for sure."

His words were so carefully neutral that she blushed as she considered he might be thinking her change of heart was because of the sex. That contributed to her mellow mood, but it was more than that.

"I mean, last night showed me Sanctuary at its best—everyone supporting Holly, offering all kinds of help. It made me proud of my hometown, and I never thought I'd say that."

"Folks make a point to take care of each other here. That's the good and the bad of small-town living."

"You mean they know too much about you?"

"Or too little, so they fill in the blanks on their own."

Was he talking about his wife? Did she dare bring it up again? She sucked in a deep breath, then blew it out. She didn't want to ruin the pleasantly languorous awareness thrumming between them.

"Willow's over by the hickory grove," Tim said, starting to unlatch the gate.

"Just a minute. Before we go back to the real world, I want to do this." She climbed up the fence until her head was slightly higher than his. Grabbing his sleeve, she tugged him closer, smiling down at him as she skimmed her fingers over the planes and angles of his face. "I wanted to try a different perspective."

He stood without moving, letting her trace the arch of his brows, the strong line of his jaw, the slight bump on the bridge of his nose. Only the tension of his shoulders showed the effect her touch had on him. Finally, she buried her hands in his sunlit hair and leaned down to brush her lips across his.

He returned her kiss with the same gentle questing, and words welled up in her throat. As she pulled back to speak them, she realized what they were and gasped, setting off a coughing fit.

"Are you all right?" Tim asked, lifting her down from the fence.

She nodded as she cleared her throat. "Swallowed a bug."

"One of the hazards of sex al fresco," he said with a grin.

Claire managed a weak smile, but she was still reeling from shock. What she'd very nearly said to Tim as though it was the most natural thing in the world was "I love you."

Back at the gallery, Claire spent ten minutes in the bathroom, putting her clothes and makeup back in order. She'd seen the knowing look Sharon gave the two of them when they'd strolled into the barn leading Willow. Sharon hadn't said anything, but her raised eyebrows and sly grin spoke volumes.

The afternoon stretched before her as she stared out the gallery window, wishing someone would come in to take her mind off her close call with Tim.

What had she been thinking? The sex had addled her brain. Combine that with her sudden surge of professional self-confidence this morning and all was right with her world. It had been so long since she felt good about herself that it simply spilled over onto the man who had just given her a terrific orgasm.

And nursed her whisper horse back to health and rescued her sister from a violent situation and recovered the girls from their kidnapping father.

"No wonder I think I'm in love with him. He's like a knight in shining armor."

Except for the shadows in his eyes.

Chapter 30

*H*EY, EVERYONE, I BROUGHT CUPCAKES FROM Clingman's," Claire called as she walked in Holly's front door after work. A slight flush of heat stained her cheeks as she remembered what Tim had done with his cupcake. "Anyone home?"

"In the bedroom." Holly's voice had lost the vibrancy of this morning. She had probably overdone it because she thought she was cured. Claire left the cupcakes on the coffee table and hurried down the hallway.

Holly sat in front of her laptop, staring at the screen. Her position brought back unpleasant flashes of Claire's first weeks in Sanctuary. She shoved those memories aside; they were the past.

"You look tired," she said, not liking the lack of color in her sister's cheeks.

Holly looked up at her with an expression so bleak fear slammed into Claire's gut. "What happened? Did Frank come here? Are the girls all right?"

"He took all the money." Holly gestured at the computer. "There's enough for one mortgage payment and maybe a trip to the grocery store and that's it."

Claire glanced at the screen showing the bank account balances. "But that's not possible. Paul notified the bank that any withdrawals required both your signatures."

"Oh, he found a young, inexperienced female teller and sweet-talked his way right past that. He convinced her it was some computer error. That's the sort of thing he's good at—persuading people it's someone else's fault." Holly's voice was bitter.

"She just handed over all that cash?"

"No, a bank check, and it's already been cashed."

"That rotten bastard!" Claire slapped her hand over her mouth. "The kids aren't here, are they?"

Holly shook her head. "Playdate with the Dotsons. Annette told me she'd give them dinner too. Everyone's being so nice, and then this happens." Holly's voice quavered. "I can't earn enough money to keep this house. I haven't even got a college degree."

"Sweetie, don't worry. They'll find Frank and make him pay you alimony and child support and half of all the money he took. I can help you with the mortgage until then."

"I can't ask you to do that. I know how expensive it is to live in New York."

At the mention of New York, the little arrow of pain jabbed Claire again. Now that she had her sister back, the thought of leaving her, especially in her current situation, was wrenching.

"I don't think they're going to find Frank around here. I called his boss, and he's put in for all his accumulated vacation time, the time he wouldn't take with me and the girls because he was too busy. His boss thought he was going away with me—to Mexico." Holly looked away. "That's where we went for our honeymoon."

"Oh no, Holl!"

Her sister waved off the sympathy. "Frank loved Mexico. He used to talk a lot about how well you could live there on very little money."

Claire sat back on her heels. That sounded exactly like Frank. He'd enjoy flashing around his American dollars someplace where everyone else was dirt poor. He could disappear there for a month or two, and when he came back, who knew how long it would take to track him down and whether he'd have any money left? Especially if he took his girlfriend with him.

In the meantime, Holly would have no income.

"If I ever see Frank again, I'll…I'll…" Claire couldn't think of any punishment awful enough for her soon-to-be ex-brother-in-law.

"I'll do the same," Holly said with a bitter smile. "I can't even imagine how to explain this to the girls without making their father look bad."

Claire was more worried about how Holly was going to hold onto her house. As she cast around for options, the Castillo painting flashed into her mind. If she sold it, she could pay off Holly's entire mortgage and have plenty of money left over for her sister to live on until she found a job.

"You have a funny look on your face. What are you thinking about?" Holly asked.

"I was just…um…wondering what you could tell the girls about Frank." Claire needed more time to consider the possibility of parting with her treasured painting.

"I'm not going to say anything until I have a plan. The first thing I have to do is look for a job."

"I'm going to call Paul and ask him if there's any way to stop Frank from leaving the country with your money." She knew it was unlikely, but she couldn't let the bastard just waltz away unchallenged. "I guess the good news is that he won't show up here anymore."

"You know something, that *is* good news." Holly's woebegone face brightened. "I don't have to wonder if the car door slamming late at night is him coming home drunk and angry or just a neighbor on the late shift. That's really good news."

Claire winced at the thought of what Holly had gone through, but she summoned up a smile. "It's the silver lining. There had to be one."

Claire stood in the windowless quiet of the secure room at the gallery, her arms wrapped around her waist, as she gazed at Julia Castillo's beautiful creation. She felt as though she could hear the swish of the horses' tails, feel the late-afternoon sunlight warming her skin, and smell the scent of trampled grass.

She had spent the night with Holly, telling Tim her sister was feeling fragile. She knew she couldn't spend time with him and not tell him about the latest catastrophe. She wasn't ready to do that until she worked out what she intended to do, since he might be directly involved.

She picked out her favorite parts of the painting—the position of one horse's ears, the cocked hoof of another, the play of light on the chestnut's flank, the dappled light under the trees. She walked forward to savor the brushwork that created the grass in the foreground and the distant mountains. She even used her fingertip to trace the bold swirls of Julia Castillo's signature.

Then she stepped back and let her hands fall to her sides.

As miraculous as the picture was, it was only paint on canvas. Holly, Brianna, and Kayleigh were living, breathing human beings whom she loved, and whose lives were being destroyed through no fault of their own. The thought of selling the Castillo to help them evoked no regrets, only a bone-deep satisfaction. It was as though she'd fought so hard to keep this one painting because somehow she knew it would be needed.

She flicked off the lights and locked the door behind her. As she walked back to the main showroom, she realized that making the decision to sell was the least difficult part of the situation.

She had a lot of tricky negotiations ahead of her. It wouldn't be easy to convince Holly to take the money. And what should she do about Tim's offer to buy the painting? He had been serious, but she needed to get top dollar for the Castillo so she could secure Holly's future.

"It's good to already have a prospective buyer," she reminded herself. "I just wish I wasn't sleeping with him."

Tim slammed the door of his pickup truck and strode toward the door of the Gallery at Sanctuary. When he had called Claire to invite her to lunch, he could tell she was dodging him, which made him both worried and angry. He had fifteen minutes between the end of his morning office hours and his first farm appointment to find out what the hell was going on.

He was worried because he knew he hadn't responded to her comment about staying in Sanctuary the way he should have, and she'd probably been hurt. He'd panicked, not because he didn't want her to stay. God knows, he did. He just didn't want her to stay without knowing the whole truth.

For Claire, he was pushing himself, forcing himself to do things like say Anais's name out loud to her. He was battling to let go of his past, but for now, he couldn't offer her any assurances.

He ignored the fact that she hadn't asked for any.

As he reached for the handle, he glanced through the plate glass to see Paul Taggart standing too close to Claire. His mood grew darker, and he nearly growled. His self-restraint only went so far. He might not be able to claim Claire for himself yet, but he was damned if he would let anyone else do it. Yanking the door open, he stomped into the big well-lit space.

Claire turned, her long hair sliding over the shoulders of her pale-pink blouse, and he was struck nearly speechless by the urge to pull her into his arms and taste her mouth.

"Tim! I didn't know you were stopping by."

He watched a flush of color warm her cheeks. Was she flustered because of his unexpected arrival, or did she feel the same physical awareness he did?

"I was passing through on my way to do farm rounds, and I thought I'd drop in. Good to see you, Paul." He nodded to the other man, then bent his head to kiss Claire on the lips, a gesture of possession that sent a zing of heat straight to his cock. "You look beautiful."

Her blush went neon as she threw a quick sideways glance at him. "Th...thank you. Paul and I were just discussing the next step in Holly's divorce."

"It's an ugly business," Paul said smoothly, but Tim could see the tense set of his shoulders. Taggart didn't like seeing his old friend touched by another man. Tim couldn't blame him, but it didn't stop him from feeling a surge of satisfaction.

"So you think trying to track Frank down is a waste of our resources?" she asked Paul.

"If his plan was to leave the country, he's already gone," Paul said. "The best thing to do is have the police keep an eye out locally, in case Holly's wrong."

She sighed. "I guess so, but it's frustrating not to be able to *do* something to him."

"I take it Frank's skipped town?" Tim asked, relief flooding him. This was why she had bailed on him last night.

"Yes, with—" Paul began.

"Without telling Holly where he's going," Claire interrupted.

She was still hiding something. The question was why? She had shared all the details of Holly's disintegrating marriage with him after their first confrontation with Frank. His anger dissipated as his concern grew.

"Not with the children?" he asked.

"No, thank God!" Claire said. "But we need the creep's participation to move legal matters along. Otherwise, this is going to drag on forever."

"Which is probably part of his intention," Paul said. He glanced at his watch. "I've got to get back to work. Nice seeing you, Dr. Tim. I'll talk to you later, Claire." With a gleam in his eye, he snaked one arm around her shoulders and pulled her against his side. He looked straight at Tim as he planted a chaste kiss on her cheek and released her.

She stepped away from him immediately. "Thanks for your help, Paul."

"Don't mention it," Taggart said as he headed out the door.

As soon as the door swung shut behind the other man, Claire put her hands on her hips. "What was with the PDA? You've never kissed me at my office before."

"Don't you remember my list? Find more places to kiss Claire? Besides, you're a fine one to talk about displays of affection at the office after what we did in mine."

"You've got me there." She came up to him, wrapped her arms around his waist, and leaned against him, her cheek pressed to his chest. "Gosh, it's good to see you. I'm sorry about last night. I wanted to spend it with you."

He liked the sincerity in her voice, and he liked the soft, yielding feel of her in his arms even more. It proved she wasn't upset about yesterday, and it sent even more heat through his body. He tightened his hold and dropped a kiss on the top of her head. "Tell me why you couldn't."

She stirred against him. "Holly needed me."

"You said she felt much better after standing up to Frank."

He felt her rib cage expand and contract on a deep sigh. "She had another setback when Frank left town."

"Is that all?"

She pushed away from him, and he let her go. She took two steps backward and looked at him with a humorous twist in her lips. "Sometimes your persistence is really inconvenient."

"It gets results."

He saw her square her shoulders and take in another deep breath. This time she was going to tell him the truth. "Frank cleaned out all of their money. Holly thinks he's gone to Mexico with it, which means she'll never get it back."

"Wasn't the bank required to get two signatures on any withdrawals?"

"Yeah. Frank convinced the teller it was a computer problem." Her eyes flashed. "You know, the system doesn't do much to protect women and children in a situation like this. Holly never finished college and never worked because Frank wanted her to stay home after they were married. Now that he doesn't want to be married anymore, she's got two kids and no way to support them."

He wanted to pull her close again so he could feel all that fire and passion pulsing in his arms.

"Anyway, I refuse to let Frank ruin his family's lives." She looked away, then brought her gaze back to him. "I'm going to sell the Castillo, and I want to give you the first chance to buy it."

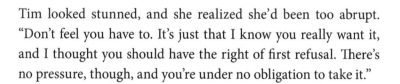

Tim looked stunned, and she realized she'd been too abrupt. "Don't feel you have to. It's just that I know you really want it, and I thought you should have the right of first refusal. There's no pressure, though, and you're under no obligation to take it."

"Shhh," he said, touching her lips with his callused fingertip. "I'm not feeling pressured. I know you could find another buyer for the Castillo in no time flat. I'm honored you would offer it to me first." He dragged his hand through his hair. "But I know how much the painting means to you. There must be another way to get the money. In fact, I'll loan it to Holly."

"I knew you'd say something like that." That's why she had let herself just lean against him for a few wonderful moments, to absorb his strength and kindness before she had to hold him at arm's length. "But, as much as we both appreciate it, neither Holly nor I could accept your generosity."

"We'll work something out with the bank."

She smiled and shook her head. "It's not necessary. I don't need the Castillo anymore. After my divorce, it symbolized the one time I stood up to Milo and won. Now I've rebuilt my confidence, and he no longer has any power over me."

A flash of insight exploded in her mind. "In fact, I feel as though selling it is my final step in the process."

"Then I'm a buyer. Name your price."

This was the awkward part. Claire had spent most of the day trying to come up with a price that was fair to Holly and to Tim. She'd even called Henry back and gotten his thoughts on the Castillo's value. Her future boss pointed out that she would get a lot more money for it if she sold it to one of his obscenely rich clients or went to auction with it. However, Claire wanted Tim to have it, if it was within his means.

Not that she had any idea what he could afford. He had mentioned owning a couple of pretty pricey artists, but the Castillo was not a small sketch or a study for a larger painting. It was one of the best examples of the artist's existing work.

So she had come up with a number that was slightly below a conservative market value, but which would cover Holly's mortgage and provide her sister with living expenses for at least six months. She named it.

Anger flared in his eyes, but he just shook his head. "I don't pretend to keep up with the art market, but even I know it's worth more than that. I give you credit for good intentions, but don't patronize me."

Damn! She should have known he was too smart for that. "I wasn't trying to patronize you." She put her hand on his forearms where he'd crossed them and gave him a penitent smile. "I want the painting to go to a good home, and I figure I can negotiate visitation rights."

"If visitation rights come with it, I'll hang it over my bed."

She felt her smile stretch into a grin of pure relief. "Works for me, especially since I'll still be able to sell you something else for the wall over your sofa."

"I'm pretty sure you could sell me the Brooklyn Bridge." He uncrossed his arms. "How soon do you need the money for the Castillo?"

It took her a moment to realize Tim was not going to argue any further about the painting's price. She was surprised and pleased. "It's not a rush. Frank was kind enough to leave one mortgage payment's worth of cash in the account."

"I'll wire it into whatever account you choose. Just e-mail me the information." He glanced at his heavy steel wristwatch. "I'm late for the Wallaces' ram."

She blew him a kiss because touching him would just frustrate her. He pretended to catch it before starting toward the door. His steps slowed, and he turned around. "I wish"—he took a deep breath—"I wish you didn't have to sell the painting."

"I don't mind. It feels good."

Tim sat in the pickup truck, gripping the steering wheel. Even though he was running late, he couldn't start the engine just yet. He was in the grip of a longing so powerful it nearly swamped him.

Claire had meant it when she said she didn't need the painting anymore. She had let go of all the pain her ex-husband had caused her. Her voice rang with the strength and hope of looking forward instead of back.

When he had turned around, he had been about to express his wish that he could do the same. But he couldn't voice that craving. When he opened his mouth, confusion swamped him.

Anais wanted the world to remember her; that's why she had chosen her path. Would it be a betrayal of her memory to put the loss behind him?

His knuckles went white as his hold on the steering wheel tightened.

He loved Claire, but his guilt kept wrenching him away from her. He could wrestle with it, shove it into the darkest corner of his mind, but it still hulked there. He was terrified it would ooze out and taint whatever they built together.

Hiding his guilt wouldn't work. He needed to drag it out into the light, and stare it down until it held no more power over him.

He had to find a way to do that so he could ask Claire to take the risk of loving him.

Chapter 31

WILLOW'S OUT IN THE SOUTH PADDOCK," SHARON SAID, checking the horse chart by her desk. "If you want, Lynnie can take the girls to visit the kittens while you go fetch her."

"Oh yes, please. I'd like to see the kitties again," Kayleigh said before turning to her sister, "if you don't mind waiting to talk to Willow."

Brianna took Kayleigh's hand. "Let's go."

Claire had promised Brianna a trip to the barn after she finished with work, and she'd persuaded Holly and Kayleigh to come too. A dose of sunshine and fresh air would do them all good.

Claire grabbed a lead line from the hook by Sharon's door. "Come with me, Holl. You can wait by the gate if Willow's gone too far away for you to walk."

Holly cast a glance at the children as they walked away with the young stable hand, Kayleigh's happy chatter floating back to them, before she nodded.

Claire basked in the comforting scents and sounds of the barn: the fresh smell of newly opened hay bales, the dull thud of hooves on pine bark, and the clang and splash of water buckets being filled. They settled and calmed her.

Outside, they walked between crisp white fences to the paddock where Willow was grazing no more than twenty feet from the gate. The horse raised her head and whinnied softly. She ambled over and stuck her nose between the boards to snuffle at Claire's pocket.

"She's got your number," Holly said, plunking down on an overturned feed bucket and lifting her face to the sun.

"Hey, sweet girl, can't wait for your carrot, can you?" Claire gave the mare a couple of treats. Then she wrapped her arms around the mare's neck and murmured in her ear, "I have a tough discussion ahead of me, so wish me luck." She inhaled the comforting scent of warm horse before releasing her hold and giving Willow a pat. "Go back to your grass because I need to talk to my sister for a minute."

"About what?" Holly's relaxation changed to tension.

Claire grabbed another bucket and flipped it down for her own seat beside her sister. "I've given it a lot of thought, and I'm going to sell the Castillo painting. We'll pay off your mortgage with the money and have plenty left over. You and the girls won't have to worry about losing your home ever again."

Holly shook her head violently. "No! I mean, it's incredibly sweet and wonderful of you to offer, but that's your painting. You kept it from Milo, and I'm sure not going to let my bastard of a husband force you to sell it."

"Here's the thing." Claire held her sister's gaze so Holly could see she was telling the truth. "I want to sell it. I don't want it anymore, because it reminds me of all the ugliness with Milo."

"Well, then you should keep the money. I know it's worth a lot. You could get a really nice apartment in New York."

"Oh, right, I'll live it up in my new condo while my sister is thrown out on the street." Claire rolled her eyes before she leaned forward. "Look, I love you and Brianna and Kayleigh, and I can't think of anything better to do with my painting than use it to help the people I love."

"But you always told me that painting is a masterpiece, one of the best Julia Castillo ever painted. You can't give up something that…that special."

"It's a lot less special than my sister and my nieces. Holl, just say, 'Thanks, sis,' and stop arguing."

"Th…thanks, sis." Holly buried her face in her hands. "This is too much, and I shouldn't take it, but oh my God, I'm so relieved that we'll have a roof over our heads."

Claire scooted her bucket closer, and the two sisters wrapped their arms around each other and sat there for a long moment.

Holly pulled away first. "You know what? I think this is a good time and place to tell the girls about the divorce. It's open and beautiful, and the mountains always make your problems seem smaller."

"I know what you mean." Claire raised her eyes to where the green-blue peaks touched the clear azure of the sky. "And Willow is here to listen to Brianna, if she needs it."

"There's a bench over there," Holly said, pointing to the place Sharon had prospective buyers sit while she put her horses through their paces.

"I'll get the girls and bring them back here," Claire offered. "Do you want me to stay or leave when you talk to them?"

"Please stay. It will help me."

Claire gave her sister a quick kiss, and jogged toward the barn. A warm glow spread inside her as she thought of Brianna and Kayleigh snug in their little rooms with the dancing unicorns and twirling princesses. The immediate future might be tough for them, but they had a safe place, a sanctuary.

She stumbled slightly as the impact of the word hit her. She'd never really thought about what the name of her town meant; it was just the place she grew up and wanted to leave behind. But all of a sudden, it had become something different. She had some serious thinking to do.

But first, she had to support three people through a very difficult conversation.

"So we're staying in our house?" Brianna asked, and Claire remembered what she'd overheard the little girl say to Willow about her friend's having to move away.

Holly threw a meaningful look at Claire before she turned to her daughter. "As long as we want to."

The tension seemed to go out of Brianna's small shoulders.

They had gotten past the first shock of Holly's explanation that Papa wouldn't be living with them anymore. Claire had stayed quiet, letting Holly handle the revelations. Now the girls' solemn, baffled faces tugged at her heart.

"Mama, could we take one of the barn kittens home?" Kayleigh asked.

The fist around her heart unclenched as Claire blessed the resilience of youth. Frank was allergic to cats, so Kayleigh had never been able to have one as a pet. That obstacle had been removed, and her niece was already taking advantage of it. The girls were going to get through this fine.

"How about if we take two kittens home?" Holly suggested. "You'd like one too, wouldn't you, Bri?"

Brianna's face brightened as she nodded. "Aunt Claire, can you ask Dr. Tim to give them their shots?"

Claire almost choked at the mention of his name. He seemed to have become woven into her life. "He'd be happy to. Why don't you go decide which kitten you'd each like, and we'll talk to Ms. Sydenstricker about taking them home."

The little girls trotted off toward the barn.

"You did a great job, sis," Claire said. "You kept it simple, and you didn't say anything mean about Frank. In my book, that qualifies you for sainthood."

Holly smiled with a sigh. "I'm sure they'll have more questions after they've thought about it. That's why I suggested they talk to you. There may be things they aren't comfortable asking their mother."

"I'm really honored by your trust. I hope I do half as well as you."

Holly pushed herself off the bench. "I'm going to go supervise the kitten debate. That will give you some time with Willow."

After hugging her sister, Claire walked back to the paddock gate and swung it open. Willow left her patch of thick grass and walked over to rub her head against Claire's shoulder.

"You're looking pretty good, sweet girl," Claire said, running her hand over the horse's coat. It was beginning to shine in the sunlight as the mare's health improved. She scratched behind Willow's ears, making the horse huff out a sigh of contentment.

"Willow, I have this crazy idea about staying here, and not going back to New York." There. She'd said it out loud. "Holly and I are just getting close again, and I've started real relationships with my two nieces. I adore those little girls."

She let her hand drift down the strong arch of the horse's neck.

"The way the town supported Holly when Frank got ugly at the 4-H shindig was amazing. You should see the number of casseroles stowed in the freezer."

Willow butted her forehead against Claire, asking for another ear scratch.

"But you know the real reason I'm thinking about staying. It's your vet." She looked the mare in the eye. "He offered to loan Holly the money rather than have me sell the Castillo. And he really, really wants that painting. I mean, how much more amazing can a man get?

"The problem is that I have no idea if he wants me to stay. When I floated the possibility yesterday, he didn't respond."

Willow shook her head, making the wisps of her mane fly.

"Are you trying to tell me something, or are the flies just bothering you?" Claire brushed off the annoying insects. "How stupid would it be to give up a fantastic job in the center of the art world if Tim doesn't want to have a relationship? I can't get a read on him. He likes my company—and other things about me." Her lips curved in a reminiscent smile as memories of the foaling shed floated back. "But he backs away when I try to go deeper, and I just don't see him as the kind of man who's in it for casual sex."

She stroked Willow's velvety nose a few times. "I'm intimidated by Anais Tremont. I see her memory claw at him. I'll say the wrong thing, and he gets that cloud of pain in his eyes. Maybe he's not ready yet, and that's a huge problem."

She hooked the lead line on Willow's halter. "I knew it was a crazy idea."

But she was already considering how she could tell Henry Thalman she was resigning.

The horse swung her head around so Claire could see one of her brown eyes. Claire could swear she saw a beam of approval in Willow's deep, liquid gaze.

Chapter 32

As Claire pulled out of Holly's driveway at nine, she hit the speed dial for Tim's cell phone. "I'm leaving Holly's house now. Your place or mine?"

"Did you notice it's a full moon?"

She peered up through the windshield to see the brilliant white disc hanging in a sky crowded with stars. "Yes, it's really pretty, but that doesn't answer my question."

"It gives me an idea. I'll meet you at your house in twenty minutes."

She couldn't stop a smile from curving her lips as she pictured Tim bathed in moonlight and nothing else. He would look like some pagan warrior with the light and shadow playing over his muscles. The speedometer's needle crept upward.

Once home, she figured she had about ten minutes before he arrived. She yanked off her work clothes and slipped into a bra and panties that were mere cobwebs of pale-blue lace. She'd bought them on impulse a few days before for an occasion just like this one. Over them, she tied a short cream-colored silk robe. Then she brushed her hair so it spilled around her shoulders like a cloud. She tried a look of seduction in the mirror, making herself laugh before she raced down the stairs to open a bottle of wine.

As she pulled the cork out, the doorbell rang.

"Who is it?" she called, her ear to the door.

"Tim," he said in his familiar low rumble. "You mean you were expecting someone else?"

She opened the door. "I was just making sure since I'm not dressed for just any guest."

"No, you sure aren't." His gaze traveled down to her bare feet and back up, and she could see the heat building in his eyes. "In fact, I'd be a little perturbed if you hadn't asked who it was."

He was wearing a rust-colored polo shirt and faded jeans, along with his usual scuffed tan boots. She was curious about what he had planned, so she didn't distract him by giving in to the temptation to plaster herself against him.

"I just opened some wine," she said.

"Bring it with you."

"What do you mean?"

"We're going moon-watching."

Claire looked down at her clingy robe. "I'll have to change."

"Nope. You're perfect just the way you are, and I'm looking forward to unwrapping my present." He gave the bow at her waist a playful tug.

"Tim, I can't wander around town in my bathrobe and not a whole heck of a lot else."

"We're going in my car, so no one will see you. You don't even have to put on shoes. I'll carry you."

She remembered what it felt like to be cradled by his strength and decided shoes were not necessary.

"Okay, Grog, I'll grab the wine, but I can walk as far as your car."

He chuckled, but it had ragged edge.

She retrieved the wine and handed it to Tim. "You go first, and make sure no one's around."

"All clear," he called.

She heard the chirp of his doors unlocking, and padded over the smooth slate sidewalk to his SUV, feeling wicked and daring in her state of undress.

The passenger door stood open, and Tim scooped her and slid her onto the seat, his hands lingering as he tasted her lips. She nearly burst into flames.

"Again," she breathed against his mouth.

He slid the robe off her shoulder and kissed her bare skin. His hand slid up her thigh to find the satin tie holding the lace over her hip. He made an odd strangled sound as his fingers tangled in it.

"The moon," he grated and drew away to slam the door shut. As he walked around the car, he scraped both hands through his hair.

Claire settled in the leather seat and let the delicious ache of arousal flow through her. She pulled the robe back up on her shoulder but let the lower edges fall open across her thighs. *Let Tim suffer too.*

He nearly leaped into the driver's seat. When he glanced sideways as he started the car, she heard him suck in a sharp breath. "I wish this were a shorter drive."

"So where are we going?" She grabbed the Jesus handle as he peeled out of the driveway.

"To a mountaintop where we can get closer to the sky."

"Wait! In my robe?"

"It's private, and I have blankets. And a telescope."

She peered at the road unspooling in the headlights, trying to follow the turns he was taking. "Okay, I'm lost."

"Sometimes making farm calls pays off." Tim swung onto an old dirt logging road, the SUV's suspension bouncing over ruts and rocks as they climbed through a dark forest. After a few minutes, they burst into a grassy clearing washed in silvery light.

"It's an old fire cut," Tim said, killing the headlights and the engine. "No trees to block our view of the sky, although I'm going to have a hard time tearing my eyes away from you."

He swung out of the car, and she swiveled in her seat as he went around to the back of the car and opened the rear door.

"Stay put," he called as he pulled a dark case out of the interior. "I'll be there to get you in a minute."

Her breath hitched as she anticipated the feel of his arms supporting her, his hands pressed against silk and skin.

The door beside her opened, and Tim leaned into the car, blocking out the moon and the stars with his shoulders as he lifted her. She put her arms around his neck and looked up as he carried her, watching the shadows make stark shapes under his cheekbones and jaw. He set her down gently in the back of the big vehicle, and she realized she was sitting on a quilt spread out across the roomy interior. In front of her was a telescope mounted on a tripod and aimed at the moon.

He sat beside her, the car dipping under his weight. She followed his gaze and saw that her robe had slipped so the lace of her bra was clearly visible.

She started to pull it back when his hand shot out to grasp hers. "Let me," he said, releasing her and then reaching downward to pull the end of the sash out of its bow. The robe fell completely open. In the moonlight, the lace looked silver, and she heard him pull in another deep breath. "Diana, goddess of the moon."

For a moment, it felt strange to be sitting almost naked in the outdoors. Then she saw the expression on Tim's face and felt power surge through her. She deliberately arched her back so her breasts strained against the lace.

"The hell with the telescope," he growled, toppling her onto her back as he came down on one elbow beside her.

He laid his palm on her bare stomach and began to skim it up over the thin fabric of her bra where her nipples peaked, then down over the same fabric at the V of her thighs. She gasped every time he grazed a nipple.

"Not a goddess, a witch, stealing a man's mind so he can't think."

"Thinking is not what I want from you right now," she managed to say as his fingers slid under the lace between her legs. She could feel how wet she was already, and he easily slipped inside her.

His mouth came down on her breast, and he sucked hard at the nipple. She bucked against him, driving his fingers deeper. Then his mouth and fingers were gone, and she opened her eyes to see him ripping his shirt off over his head. She enjoyed the magnificence of the view as he yanked off his boots, jeans, and boxers.

She started to unhook her bra. "Let me," he said, kneeling over her, again blocking the light with his shoulders. She trailed her fingertips over the flex of his thigh muscles as he flicked open the bra's front closure and peeled the lace away from her skin. He cupped her breasts for a moment and then shifted downward to untie the bows at her hips. He pulled the triangle of flimsy fabric from between her legs and then bent to kiss her where the tension was building to an almost unbearable pitch.

His tongue circled and flicked at her, and she planted her feet to tilt up to him. "Yes, yes, there, yes, again. No, wait!" She felt the orgasm coming. "I want you inside me."

He twisted to the side to get a condom, and then he was kneeling between her legs. He slid his hands under her bottom and tilted her hips upward, pulling her up onto his thighs as he drove into her. She grabbed fistfuls of the quilt and hooked her ankles around his waist.

He towered over her in shadow while the moon slanted through the car's windows to turn her skin nearly white. Only one strong thigh and his hands where he gripped her hips were brushed by the moon. It was a strange but erotic effect, like having a mystery lover.

His hands and hips guided their speed and rhythm, so he would bring her to the edge of climax and then ease back. It was exquisite torture, and she let herself relax into his control, the tiniest movement sending waves of sensation washing through her.

She felt his hands tighten and his pace quicken. He drove deeper, and she exploded in an orgasm so potent she thought her internal muscles would tear in the delicious agony. She felt him strain and pump against her and call out her name as he came.

Then he slumped forward, still holding her hips up against him, his breathing loud in the interior of the car.

Shivers of afterglow rippled through her as he stayed inside her, gradually softening. As his breathing quieted, she began to hear crickets and rustlings from small creatures moving through the woods around the clearing.

She unlocked her ankles from his waist, and he let her slide down his thighs to rest on the quilt. He stripped off the condom and lay down beside her, shaking out another quilt to drape over them.

"Tim?"

"Give me a minute. I have to come back to earth."

"Mmm, why?" She snuggled up against his big frame. "I'm still in the stratosphere myself."

He wrapped one arm around her and took such a deep breath she could feel his ribs move. A warm bubble of satisfaction floated inside her. It had been good for him too.

She closed her eyes and drifted, aware of Tim's scent and heat and pulse, yet not quite awake.

The feel of something in her hair made her stir and open her eyes. He had turned on his side and was looking at her while his fingers feathered over her scalp.

"How long was I asleep?"

"I don't know. I slept too."

She pushed up onto her elbows and saw the telescope. "Shall we look at the moon?"

"It's climbed higher in the sky, so we must have been out a while," he said, sitting up and throwing the quilt off.

She reached out to skim her hand up the beautiful planes of his back. His muscles bunched under her palm as he let her explore. "Is there a moon god?" she asked. "I think he should be called Timothy."

"Actually, you're not too far off," he said. "The Egyptians had a god named Thoth who had something to do with the moon and writing, as I recall. I also remember he had the head of a baboon."

"Hmm, I'll stick with Timothy, then, because I prefer your human head."

He took her hand and pulled her toward the open rear door. She tried to close the edges of her robe together with her other hand.

"Diana hunted nude," he said. "I think you should do the same."

"Didn't Actaeon get torn to shreds by his own hounds as punishment for seeing her naked?" She let go of the robe so it hung open.

"I'm sure he felt it was worth it. I would." He ran his fingertip over the curve of her breast, a touch as light as the brush of a feather.

"It would be a terrible waste to turn you into a stag, although it's better than a baboon."

He laughed and leaned down to kiss her. "Now scoot forward and look through this eyepiece."

She put her eye to the telescope and gasped as the silvery moon's craters and seas filled her vision. "It's gorgeous, and it looks so close I could touch it."

"Imagine walking on it."

She lifted her head to see him sitting with his head tilted back to look up at the disc in the sky. "Would you want to do that?"

"It would be mighty interesting. They say Earth is beautiful when seen from space."

"Did you dream of being an astronaut?"

"Doesn't every kid who likes science?" He brought his gaze down to her. "I outgrew a space capsule pretty young, though."

"Thank goodness," she said, making a show of eyeing him up and down. She turned back to the sky. "Do you know the constellations? The only one I can find is Orion with his belt."

He not only knew the constellations, he knew the myths behind them and entertained her with the stories of gods and goddesses wreaking their vengeance or showing their favor by tossing people and animals into the sky. She leaned against the warm, bare skin of his shoulder as he pointed upward.

After a while, she quit looking at the stars and just watched his face sculpted by the moonbeams, his hair shaded dark with silver glints. Certainty grew inside her; she wanted to stay with this man, to see what they could become together.

"Tim?"

He dropped his arm and turned toward her. "Am I boring you?"

"Never. I love listening to you." She shifted away just enough so she could see his full face. Nerves clamped a fist around her throat, and she had to force herself to breathe before she could speak. "I'd like to stay here in Sanctuary. To see what happens between us."

Her gaze was riveted on him; she wanted to catch every nuance of his reaction. That was the only reason she caught the look of yearning in his eyes and the tiny movement toward her before he looked away. It gave her hope before his words destroyed her.

"I can't ask you to do that. You'd be giving up too much." His hands were curled into fists on his thighs.

"You're not doing any asking. I'm staying by my own choice." Her heart began to crack open as she saw the resistance in his body. "If it doesn't work out, that's what I needed to know. But if it does…Well, can you imagine a whole lifetime of nights like this one?"

He shook his head without looking at her. "I didn't expect this to happen now."

"I never expected it to happen at all. I consider it a gift, a wonderful, unexpected gift."

Now he turned toward her, his face hardened into unreadable lines. "I can't accept this gift now, no matter how much I want to. "

The shock sent a spear of pain through her. She had made herself vulnerable, and he had rejected her utterly. She seized the edges of her robe and pulled them across her body as she wrapped her arms around her waist.

"Claire." His expression softened as he saw her withdrawal. "You know something about my past. I'm not sure I can change what it's made me."

"You can't change what's happened, but you can change what it means to you."

"Maybe, but I can't take the chance. Not at your expense." He shook his head again. "I'm sorry."

She turned her gaze up to the moon, tears making its shape waver and blur. She let them streak down her cheeks and drop onto the silk of her robe. "I'm sorry too. You're a wonderful man, and I could easily fall in love with you."

That was a lie. She was already in love with him, but she had to hold onto a few shreds of pride.

"You don't know me well enough to say that."

"And I'll never have a chance to." She used the sleeve of her robe to wipe the tears away before she looked at him again.

He sat staring straight ahead, every muscle in his body clenched. She wanted so badly to offer him the comfort of her touch, but he had taken away her right to do that. She shivered, and her involuntary movement seemed to bring him back from whatever dark world he had strayed into.

"Are you cold?" he asked, yanking the rumpled quilt forward to wrap around her shoulders. His concern brought tears to her eyes again. "I'll carry you to the front seat and turn on the heat."

There had been no need for artificial heat before. His body had given her all the warmth she'd needed. Her breath caught on a sob.

"Claire, please…" His voice was taut with pain. He stood and picked her up, quilt and all, striding barefoot through the tall, prickly wild grasses. He deposited her in the front seat. "The key's in the ignition. You can adjust the temperature here."

She just pulled the quilt tighter around her as she listened to him dress and pack up the telescope.

When he got back into the driver's seat, he turned toward her. "You're the best thing that's happened to me since…well, for a long time. I'm sorry I can't…don't deserve to have you love me."

She couldn't help it. She reached across and cupped his cheek. "Let's not talk about it anymore. I shouldn't have said anything. It's the full moon. It makes people do crazy things."

"That's why they're called lunatics." His voice was almost normal.

She gave a little puff of forced laughter. However, the rest of the trip passed in silence. He pulled into the driveway of her house and turned off the engine. He sat with his hands locked on the steering wheel.

"Just say good night," she said. "That's enough."

"No, it's not. I'll never forget tonight, never forget what you did me the honor of offering."

"Good night." She tried to open her door, to get away before she fell apart, but it was locked.

"Just a minute," he said, hitting the switch that freed her. "I don't want you walking alone."

Shedding the quilt and tying the robe tightly, she decided not to argue, but waited for him to open her door. Before she could swing her legs out, he had her in his arms, cradled against his chest. She gave in and stretched her arms up around his neck, letting her fingers twine in his hair.

He walked up onto her porch, but instead of setting her down, he bent his head and brushed her lips gently with his. Regret, pain, and love seared through her, and she pulled herself up so she could kiss him back with all the longing she felt. His arms tightened around her like steel bands, and for a moment, she thought he would respond in kind, but he simply held her until she let her head drop back against his shoulder.

"Good-bye, Tim."

He set her on her feet with heartbreaking care, and stood aside while she retrieved the key from her robe's pocket and opened the door.

As she stepped inside, she heard him draw in a breath. She waited a moment to see what he would say, but there was only silence. She closed the door behind her, leaned her back against it, and slid down onto the floor in a heap of misery.

Tim pulled the big car into the garage. He had no memory of
the drive from Claire's house to his. All he had seen were images
of Claire's skin illuminated by moonlight, of her body arching
under his hands, of the tears glistening on her cheeks.

He dropped his forehead onto the steering wheel. There had
been a moment of insanity—of lunacy, he corrected himself with
a savage smile—when he had nearly said, "Stay."

The word had leaped into his mind and onto his tongue. He
wanted desperately to speak it, to bind Claire to him.

But the enormity of her offer had hit him. He knew, better
than most, what she was proposing to give up. Her perfect job in
a place where what she did was considered important. The thrill
of having her finger on the pulse of the art world. The vibrant,
cultural life of New York City. She was going to leave all of that
to take a chance on him in a town she had fought desperately to
escape.

The sheer recklessness of it took his breath away. He flexed
his hands on the wheel. *What had she called him? Wonderful?*
Had Anais ever used that word about him? She teased him, she
leaned on him, she showed him off to her friends as her "giant
genius." But she had been the older, more worldly partner in their
marriage. He had been hugely flattered—and astonished—when
the famous actress chose him over all her many other admirers.

She had never called him wonderful.

How did he dare question their marriage now? Claire had
stirred up this maelstrom of guilt and longing. No, the guilt was
always with him—it was the longing that was new.

His heart would always carry the scar of the bullet that had
taken Anais's life. As a doctor, he knew scar tissue could grow
hard and insensitive. Maybe that would be a good thing, because
right now, his heart felt savaged by the pain. He tortured himself
with the dream Claire had conjured up, the fantasy of sleeping

without nightmares because she was in his arms, of watching her face as she absorbed the beauty of a painting, of seeing her skin bared to both sunlight and moonlight.

He cursed as he opened the door and swung his legs out of the car. Walking out of the garage onto the gravel of his driveway, his eyes were drawn upward to the moon hanging high in the sky.

With fists clenched against his thighs, he threw his head back to shout, "For God's sake, Anais, is this what you wanted?"

Chapter 33

"I'M ARRIVING LATE WEDNESDAY, PRISCILLA, SO YOU CAN set up appointments starting Thursday morning," Claire said into the phone. "Thanks for doing the legwork. I look forward to seeing the spaces you've found."

She hung up and dropped her head into her hands. All she had done this morning was lie. To Priscilla that she was excited about looking at possible locales for the new gallery. To Holly that nothing was wrong, she just hadn't slept much. To Brianna and Kayleigh that she couldn't wait until the new kittens could come home with them, since she was pretty sure she wouldn't be in Sanctuary by the time they were weaned from their mother.

The only person she hadn't lied to was Davis when she told him she was giving him the commission on selling the Castillo. He tried to turn it down, but she felt she owed it to him. She had also cleared Tim's request to keep the painting at the gallery until his house was finished.

She heard the front door open and quickly sat up straight. When she saw Paul stroll into the gallery with a devilish grin on his face, she nearly burst into tears. She was not in the mood for verbal sparring.

As he approached the desk, his smile vanished. He sat down in the chair across from her and said, "You look like your dog died."

She just shook her head.

He reached out to where her hand lay on the glass top and covered it with one of his own. "Claire, this is Paul, your oldest friend. Talk to me."

"I can't."

He frowned at her. "Is it about Dr. Tim? Because I was just yanking his chain yesterday. I saw you two at the 4-H shindig. I wish you looked at me that way, but I know when I'm beaten. It's the first thing you learn as a politician."

"You're sweet to try to make me laugh," Claire said, smiling as the tears broke loose and streamed down her face.

"Jesus, Claire, what is it?" He pulled a package of tissues out of his pocket, drew one out, and handed it to her. "You never cry."

She took the tissue and blotted her cheeks, her smile twisting as she thought of how many tears she had shed last night. "Life is full of irony. I've been counting the days until I could go back to New York, and now all I want to do is stay here."

"And you can't stay because…?"

She choked on a sob. "Tim doesn't want me to."

"Well, as a former mayor of Sanctuary, I can assure you that Dr. Arbuckle does not have the power to keep you away."

"Oh yes, he does. I offered to stay to see what happened between us."

"And he turned you down." He handed her the whole package of tissues. "Damn fool!"

"I know. I don't know why I did it, except I thought we might have something together."

"I meant Arbuckle is a damn fool." Paul sat back. "You know about his wife, right?"

"Of course. Everyone does."

"Think about it. The woman he's married to—and we assume whom he loves—chooses death over staying with him."

"But—"

He held up his hand. "I'm not saying he did anything to make her do that. I'm just pointing out what it must feel like to him. Guilt, blame, loyalty to her memory, the need to protect himself from being hurt like that again—it's all got to be boiling around inside him. Then you come along and offer him another shot, and he's too screwed up to grab it."

"So does that mean I should stay and wait?"

"No. It means you should make decisions that will protect you. He may never heal from that kind of mess. How badly do you love him?"

"Badly? That's an interesting choice of words." She looked down at the soggy wad of Kleenex in her hand. "Badly enough that I didn't sleep at all last night."

"That will pass." He considered a moment. "Do you love him so badly you would give up the career you've wanted your entire life on the off chance he might love you back someday in some possibly damaged way?"

"When you put it like that, it seems pretty unrealistic." Especially when she'd just gotten her professional confidence back.

"Here's the other thing to consider. You just came out of an ugly divorce. Could Tim be a rebound relationship? In my experience, those don't usually last."

"In your experience?"

He sat back. "My experience as a lawyer. I've handled a lot of divorces."

Everything Paul said was true, but then she thought of Tim cradling her in his arms in the moonlight, Tim touching Willow like she was worth a million dollars, Tim cooking pancakes with a Disney Princess towel draped over his shoulder, Tim driving like a madman when Holly was in trouble.

And she didn't care about careers or rebounds or wives who killed themselves. She just wanted to make him love her as much as she loved him. "Oh God, I don't know what to do."

"I can't give you an answer, especially since I'm not an entirely disinterested party." He stood up. "All I can advise is to take care of yourself. You deserve that."

"I appreciate the breath of sanity."

Walking around the desk, he gave her shoulder a comforting squeeze. "If you need a friend's company later on, call me. I've got some good bourbon."

The thought of drinking herself into oblivion was all too tempting. "I might just take you up on that."

A look of regret crossed his face before he turned and walked out of the gallery.

Claire made a quick trip to the bathroom to wash her face and repair her makeup. She finished just in time to meet some repeat clients. In less than half an hour, they had bought two of the largest Len Boggs canvases. Ordinarily, she would have been waltzing around the gallery at the thought of the commission, but she kept remembering Tim in his flannel shirt and jeans as he stood in front of one of the paintings she'd just sold. How little she'd known about him then, and yet she'd felt that tug of attraction, which had turned into a bond so strong it was tearing her apart to break it.

Her cell phone buzzed, and she grabbed it with a sense of relief.

"Ms. Parker? This is Maria Fannucci at Merrill Lynch. The wire transfer you were expecting just came through."

So Tim had bought the Castillo in spite of their rift last night. She had wondered if he would still want it. In any case, she certainly hadn't expected him to come up with such a large sum of money so quickly.

The broker went on to read the amount transferred, and Claire gasped. "Oh my God!"

"Is there a problem?" Maria asked. "Is the deposit incorrect?"

"It's too much. Way too much."

"I'll double-check it with the sending bank."

"No, that won't be necessary. I think I know what happened. Thanks."

Claire put the phone down gently even though she wanted to throw it across the room. Tim had paid her almost twice the price she'd asked for the Castillo.

"Damn you, Tim!" she muttered. "What the hell am I supposed to do?"

The pricing of art was very subjective. There was no fixed monetary value for any painting. It depended on a variety of factors ranging from something as straightforward as the size of the canvas to an idea as nebulous as the painting's perceived significance within the artist's entire body of work.

If she had put it up for auction, the Castillo might have brought even more than the amount Tim had transferred to her, mostly because there was a small, finite supply and a large demand for the artist's work.

However, that did not change the fact that he had taken matters into his own hands and overridden her determination of a fair price.

She also couldn't help wondering how he had come up with so much cash on such short notice. He had just bought a thriving veterinary practice and was building a substantial house. How could he afford to pay more than the asking price for an extremely expensive work of art?

She would have to call him.

Tim had snatched five minutes to wolf down a sandwich in the medications storeroom when his cell phone vibrated in the breast pocket of his lab coat. He swallowed and pulled the phone out to check the caller ID. When he saw Claire's name, he felt an almost physical pain.

He had spent the night staring at the ceiling, trying to convince himself he could offer her what she deserved from a man. He had failed. That didn't stop him from desperately wanting her to stay and take what little he had to give.

He knew why she was calling, and he had marshaled all his arguments about the money already. He punched the *Answer* button just before the call went to voice mail. "Hello, Claire."

"Hi, Tim." There was a second's hesitation before her voice came through strong and clear. "I just heard from my broker that the wire transfer hit my account. You paid almost twice what I asked for."

Her voice twisted the ache in his chest, and he leaned against the metal shelving with his eyes closed. "I did some research of my own. You asked too little for the painting, so I adjusted to the market value."

"There's no set market value for art. You know that. Castillo could release a hundred paintings tomorrow, and yours would plummet in value. Besides, you just bought a new business, and you're building a house. You shouldn't really spend all that money on a painting."

It warmed him to know she was worried about his finances. "You don't have to be concerned about me going broke. Before I went into veterinary medicine, I did cancer research. I have a couple of lucrative medical patents."

"Oh"—another slight hesitation before he heard her draw in a breath—"it doesn't matter. I'll send you a check for the difference."

"I'll tear it up."

"Fine, I'll deliver cash."

"It'll go in the fireplace."

"Tim!"

"Claire!" he echoed back. "I don't want to look at the painting and feel like I took advantage of a friend." It killed him to use that word when he knew she was much more than that.

"You're not doing this because you feel sorry for me after last night, are you?" Her voice was low, and he could tell that she was forcing herself to ask the question. "Because that would be ridiculous and unnecessary."

He had done it because this was untainted. He could present it to her with a whole heart, knowing he had done the right thing for the woman he loved so much he had to push her away. "No, this was a business deal, pure and simple. You have a painting I want, and I paid you the going rate for it."

He wanted to slam his head against the steel support to counteract the agony of lying to her. He had spent hours debating how much he could get away with giving her for the Castillo, both to assuage his guilt about hurting her and to help her in the future when he wasn't around.

"I don't really believe you," she said. "But I'm going to take the money for Holly's sake. Thank you for your generosity."

His shoulders sagged with relief. "You're welcome, but don't go back to New York thinking I overpaid. That painting's a masterpiece. It doesn't matter how many more Castillo creates."

"You told me persistence always pays off, didn't you?" she said, and her voice had softened almost as though she were smiling. "You got your painting, after all. I'm glad it's going to you because you understand why it's so brilliant."

"You still have visitation rights."

"We both know that's not going to happen."

Now he heard the hurt, and it sliced through him. "My door's always open. Whenever you feel comfortable coming through it, you'll be welcome."

She sighed. "I know you mean that. I'll let you get back to work," she said. "Thank you again. This will mean a lot to my sister."

"No more thanks. I'm getting exactly what I wanted." He was such a liar.

———————— ❖ ————————

"Frank's in Mexico—with his girlfriend," Holly said when Claire found her in the kitchen. The scent of warm chocolate chip cookies permeated the air, and Claire had a vague thought that her sister must be feeling better if she was baking. "The girls are out in the yard, so we can talk."

Claire dragged her mind back to Holly's situation. She'd been so busy wallowing in her own misery that she hadn't spared a thought for her sister's very real concerns. "How do you know?"

"Chief McClung has a friend in Immigration. They checked on Frank's passport and found out he'd flown into Guadalajara yesterday with a female companion. That means I'll never get the money back."

"It also means you won't have to worry about Frank showing up drunk and violent, and that's worth every penny of the money he stole from you." Claire had gone by her house to pick up the checkbook for her brokerage account. She held it up. "Besides, we're settled financially. Tim bought the Castillo, and the funds are in my account as of today."

"Already? How did he get that much money so fast?"

"Evidently he holds some medical patents that produce income. Anyway, I thought we'd go to the bank tomorrow and pay off your mortgage."

Holly put down the spatula. "I don't know how to tell you what this means to me. I feel free—and safe. I didn't realize how fear hung over me like this dark cloud all the time. And now it's gone." She looked around the room. "This is *my* kitchen, and no one can take it away from me."

Then she looked at Claire. "You are one amazing sister."

"Darn right I am," Claire said, turning away the compliment. All she had done was sell something she didn't want anymore.

"Claire? You don't look all that happy. Is something wrong?"

She couldn't tell Holly the truth. She was afraid it would hurt her feelings to know that Claire would stay in Sanctuary for a man, but not for her sister. Besides, Holly had enough on her plate right now. Claire shoved back the creeping misery and pasted a smile on her face. "Nope, I'm just a little tired. Nothing that a chocolate chip cookie wouldn't fix."

"Would you rather have dough? I saved you some because you always liked it more than the cookies."

As Claire dug her spoon into the thick, chip-laden dough her little sister had remembered she loved, she decided that Paul's bourbon couldn't possibly be any better for drowning her sorrows.

Chapter 34

CLAIRE ZIPPED UP HER RED OVERNIGHT BAG AND CARRIED it down the steps to her kitchen. She checked that the coffeemaker was unplugged and the washing machine valve firmly closed so it wouldn't flood the house while she made her quick visit to New York. She was leaving for the airport directly from the gallery after work.

She stood in the middle of the cozy room for a few moments, then sat down at the pine table and rested her head on top of her folded arms. Regret weighed so heavily on her it was hard to move.

The only bright spot in the past four days had been Holly's face when the bank representative had handed her the mortgage papers with *Paid in full* printed on them. Her sister was growing stronger every day now that Frank's shadow no longer hung over her. Knowing the house was hers seemed to speed the healing even more.

Other than that, all Claire had done was miss Tim and curse her own stupidity. She could be spending two more weeks of moonlit nights with him, and instead, she had pushed him into breaking off their relationship.

"Who am I trying to kid?" She shoved herself up from the table. "It wasn't enough for me. I needed to know if we had a future."

As she bent to pick up her bag again, her cell phone rang. Sharon's name came up in the caller ID. Claire debated not answering, but it was rare for her friend to call her so early in the morning.

"Claire, are you still in Sanctuary? I can't remember when you said you were leaving for New York."

"Yes, I'm here. I'm not leaving until after work."

"Then you might want to come down to the stable now. Willow's not doing so well. She's been colicky for over an hour, and I'm about to call Dr. Tim."

"Wait, why do you think I should come now? Isn't colic treatable?"

"Well, it depends on the cause. Thing is, I've seen lots of cases, and this one looks pretty bad, especially because Willow isn't as strong as she should be."

"You mean she could *die*?"

"It's possible."

Sharon was not prone to exaggeration, so Claire felt her words like a knockout punch. "I'll be right there."

As she raced back up the stairs to change her clothes, Claire was already making the first call to rearrange her schedule. She would stay with her whisper horse for as long as it took to save her life.

Claire pulled into the stable parking lot in a spray of gravel. As she charged toward the barn, she saw Tim's big tan pickup backed up to the open door. Dodging around it, she made sure to brace herself for the anguish of seeing him again.

It didn't work.

He was hauling a large metal case out of the back of the truck and didn't see her. She gave herself a moment to soak in the sight of him: the lock of hair falling over his forehead as he leaned forward, his focused gaze, the play of muscles across his back. Longing ripped through her, and she had to wrap her arms around her waist and force herself to breathe in and out.

After a couple of breaths, she dropped her arms to walk around the truck's back bumper. "Can I help?"

"Claire!" He let go of the case as though it had burned him and turned toward her. "What are you doing here?" He ran a hand through his hair. "I'm sorry, that didn't come out right. I just thought you'd be in New York by now."

"Sharon told me Willow was sick. How is she?"

His expression became grim. "I'm afraid it's a torsion in the colon. I want to do an ultrasound to make sure."

"If it is, what's the treatment?"

"Surgery." He went back to wrestling the case out of the truck. "And in Willow's condition, that's going to be chancy at best. It might be kindest just to euthanize her."

"No!" Claire couldn't bear the thought of losing her whisper horse without a fight. "You're a brilliant doctor, and I'll take care of her after the surgery. She survived everything her horrible owner put her through, so she wants to live."

"I reckon you have a point about that. She's sure made a comeback." He set the case down on its wheels and stood staring down at it as though he had forgotten what it was.

"Tim?" Claire was worried by his distracted air. "Is there something else I need to know about her condition?"

His gaze flicked to her face and away. "No, that's it." He grabbed the machine's handle and headed toward Willow's stall with it trundling along behind him. Claire got behind the box and helped push it through the thick sawdust.

As they approached the stall, she heard Sharon speaking in low, soothing tones. "Easy, girl, easy! Hang on, Willow, the doctor's coming. He'll make you better."

The mare squealed above the sound of hooves thudding rapidly against the ground.

"What's happening?" Claire asked Tim.

"Sharon's keeping her on her feet, in case her colon isn't already twisted. Willow wants to lie down because she's in so much distress."

Tim swung open the stall door and pulled the machine inside.

"She's getting worse," Sharon said. She was standing by Willow's head, holding onto her halter. "Claire! I'm glad you're here. We need to hold her still so Dr. Tim can see what's going on inside her. She responds to you better than anyone else."

"Hey, sweet girl," Claire said, starting toward Sharon. Willow swung her head around and whinnied, a shrill cry of agony. Her eyes were wild, but she stopped stamping her hooves as soon as Claire touched her. "I'm so sorry you hurt, my sweet Willow. So very sorry."

Claire put her arms around the mare's neck and laid her cheek against the horse. "Dr. Tim will fix you, don't worry."

Willow whinnied again, but the sound was less frantic. Claire came around in front of her and ran her fingers over the mare's nose and face. The horse lowered her head and leaned into Claire, whickering softly.

"The painkillers couldn't calm her down, but you can," Sharon said, shaking her head. "She's your whisper horse, for sure."

Claire kept stroking Willow as Tim scanned over the mare's belly and haunches with the ultrasound. The horse quivered and pawed the ground once but otherwise stood still.

Tim frowned at the machine and then turned it off before he looked up at Claire and Sharon. "We need to make a decision quickly. She's got a twist in one of the large left quadrants of her colon. The only way to save her is to operate immediately. But as I told Claire, she's not a good candidate for surgery since she's been malnourished for so long. Even strong horses can die of complications from a twisted colon."

Sharon looked at Claire. "You care about Willow more than anyone. It's your call."

Tim's eyes were on her too, and she felt pinned. "I don't want to cause her unnecessary suffering."

"I'll anesthetize her as soon as we get her to the operating room at my office," Tim said.

Claire shifted so she was looking into Willow's eyes. The mare moved restlessly, but her gaze was clear and trusting. Claire took a deep breath. "All right, girl, we're going to get you to Dr. Tim's office and make you better."

As soon as the words were out of her mouth, Sharon was shouting to bring around a horse trailer, and Tim was on his phone specifying operating room prep. Claire stood with Willow in the still, quiet center of all the drama, letting her horse lean against her and talking comforting nonsense to the mare.

"I'm going to ride with her in the trailer, just in case her distress becomes more severe," Tim said as the vehicle was maneuvered close to the stall.

"So will I," Claire said.

Tim didn't look happy. "It's dangerous to be in a moving vehicle with a large animal. She may strike out without meaning to hurt anyone."

"I can keep her calm." Claire sounded more confident than she felt. She knew that her control of Willow depended on the horse's goodwill. If pain clouded the mare's mind, she might not be able to recognize the human who loved her.

"All right, but if she becomes violent, you have to get away from her."

Claire nodded, and Tim left to collect his vet's bag from the truck.

"The trailer's ready," Sharon called. "Claire, bring her on out. I've got three hands here to help, if you need it."

But Willow didn't hesitate to let Claire guide her up the ramp into the trailer. "You are the best girl," Claire crooned as she threaded the lead line through a metal ring. She knew the moment Tim stepped into the trailer because it dipped slightly under his weight.

"Okay, close it up," he called before he came up to Willow's head. He patted the mare's nose, but he was looking at Claire, a frown drawing deep lines between his eyebrows. "You get behind me if she starts to thrash around."

"I will, I promise."

Sharon poked her head in the trailer's side window. "You ready to roll?"

Tim nodded, and Claire heard the truck engine rumble to life. "Hang on to the window grille," he said as the trailer began to move.

Claire grabbed a metal bar with one hand, but kept the other on Willow. The mare whinnied and thumped her front hoof on the straw a few times, but otherwise, she stood quietly.

"It's lucky for Willow you have an operating room for large animals," Claire said, just to break the silence between them.

"I had it built when I bought the practice. I figured if I was going to doctor farm animals, I'd better be prepared for the worst."

"How many times have you used it?" She noticed Tim was doing the same thing she was, gently stroking the mare's neck and shoulder. Her breath shuddered in as she remembered the feel of his hand on her own skin, and for a moment, she wanted to change places with the horse.

"Only about four times. All successfully," he added with a wry smile. "But that doesn't mean I can save Willow."

She raised her gaze to his. "I have total confidence in you."

The pain she dreaded darkened his eyes. "I'll do my best." He shifted his gaze to the mare. "It will be a couple of months before we can be sure she's fully recovered."

It hung in the air between them. Would Claire stay in Sanctuary another two months? She tried to read his expression, to see if he would feel the same exquisite torture she did at the prospect of having to see him and talk with him because of Willow. All she could find there was concern for the horse.

"I'll be with her until she's on the road to recovery," Claire finally said. That could mean almost any length of time.

Willow suddenly swung her head around to nose at her belly, knocking into Claire. She staggered, only to have her forearm seized in a grip of iron as Tim reached over the mare's withers to steady her.

"Are you okay?"

"Just surprised. It must be hurting her more."

"I gave her painkillers, but they aren't that effective with a twisted gut." He glanced at his watch. "We should be there soon."

Claire breathed out a sigh of relief, both for Willow's sake and for her own. Being so close to Tim and not being able to touch him was pure torment.

She concentrated on soothing Willow and tried to ignore the presence of the man she loved so much it actually hurt. It seemed Tim wasn't immune to the tension, because he looked out the front window and said with emphasis, "Thank God, we're here!"

The trailer rocked to a stop, the ramp was let down, and everything erupted into organized chaos. Claire simply led Willow where she was told and stayed with her until she was instructed to move her again. A scrubs-clad veterinary technician led her around Tim's office building to a new wing in the back where a large door stood open.

As Willow plodded through the door alongside her, Claire gasped at the expanse of shining metal surfaces and vast array of equipment. Tim had not stinted on his new operating room. Between all the high-tech machinery and her confidence in Tim's genius, she felt a sudden surge of optimism. "Sweet girl, you're going to come through this just fine."

"I'll take the mare now," the technician said. "There's an observation room upstairs, if you'd like to watch the operation."

Claire touched her forehead to Willow's for just a moment, then relinquished her. She walked up the stairs and found Sharon already in the room, sitting by the window. "I don't know if I can watch this," Claire confessed.

"There's Dr. Tim," Sharon said, nodding toward the far corner of the room. "Watch him. He saved my stallion two months ago when I thought the horse was beyond hope."

Tim was garbed in green surgical scrubs from head to toe. He wore safety glasses with a light attached to them and had his hair tucked under a cap. His movements were swift and capable as he injected Willow. It must have been an anesthetic because her knees soon buckled, and the surrounding technicians supported her as she collapsed onto a rubber mat. They winched her onto the operating table, rolling her onto her back and shackling her legs before they draped blue sheets over everything but her head and abdomen. One of the assistants shaved and swabbed Willow's belly, while Tim inserted a tube down her throat. Then Tim picked up a long, shiny implement.

At that point, Claire turned away from the glass and sat down in one of the folding chairs arrayed along the far wall. "Tell me when they're done."

"I'll do you one better. I'll tell you what Dr. Tim's doing as best I can. It's real interesting."

Sharon was right. It was fascinating to listen to her narration as long as she didn't have to see the blood.

"You know an awful lot about the insides of a horse," Claire observed as Sharon explained a technical term she'd used.

"Yeah, it's cheaper to do as much of the vet work myself as I can, so I've learned by watching and listening. It's a godsend Dr.

Tim built this operating room. Before he came, the nearest large animal surgical center was two hours away."

"Is Tim a good vet?"

"Best I've ever seen. We're mighty lucky to have him here. So what's going on between you two? It's something, but I'm not sensing it's good right now."

Claire closed her eyes and tilted her head back against the wall behind her. "It's over. Now that Frank's gone, Holly's improving every day, and I'll be leaving soon. So it's just as well."

"You don't say that with much conviction."

Claire opened her eyes to find Sharon watching her. "I fell a little in love with him, so it's hard to say good-bye."

"You could stay. See what happens."

"Yeah, I thought about that. I mentioned it to Tim, but he wasn't enthusiastic."

Sharon's eyebrows shot up. "You were going to pass up that great job back in New York and stay here in little ole Sanctuary?"

Claire nodded.

"Well, son of a gun! I'd say you're more than a little in love."

"I guess I am." Claire could feel the truth of that as her heart twisted in her chest.

Sharon folded her tall frame into the chair beside Claire. "Listen, hon, don't give up. He's got a big black cloud over the area of love and marriage right now. He just needs some more time to let the sun break through."

"But I don't have time. If I stay here, I lose the job in New York, and there's no guarantee Tim will ever get over his wife's death."

"Whoever said anything about a guarantee? It's like a race. You put your money on a pony and hope they fed him right that morning and the jockey isn't hung over and no one bumps him and the track conditions are perfect. But if he wins the race, it's a hell of a high. That's what I'm talking about."

"So you think Tim's worth betting on?"

"He's down there saving a broken-down, abused mare because she's your whisper horse. That tells you something."

Claire sighed. "I've just put myself back together after Milo took me apart. I don't know if I can take that kind of risk so soon."

"Whatever you decide, hon, I'll take good care of Willow."

"Thanks, Sharon. I know that's a safe bet." A sudden spate of raised voices came from the operating chamber. Claire half rose from her chair as Sharon strode to the window. "What's happening?"

"Looks like something's not right on one of the monitors."

Claire forced herself to come to the window. Since the blue sheets covered so much, Claire could almost forget that the exposed pink folds of intestines were part of her whisper horse.

She kept her eyes on Tim, who was snapping out a string of orders, even as his hands were deep in Willow's belly. Technicians scurried around, adjusting dials and checking screens. Tim's gaze was locked on one monitor, his posture still and tense. For a long moment, no one in the room moved.

Then Tim nodded and bent his head to begin manipulating Willow's internal organs. The technicians went back to their stations and calm prevailed.

Sharon let out a breath. "I think her blood pressure dropped. Probably a reaction to the anesthesia."

Claire dropped her head into her hands. "Thank you, God." She went back and fetched another chair. "I'm going to watch."

Seeing Tim in the epicenter of all the gleaming, complex equipment sent little shivers of pride through Claire. Gone was the slow country horse doctor. Here he was in command, his team responding to his direction like a well-oiled machine, his movements sure and efficient.

A sense of loss gnawed at her with razor-sharp teeth.

"Look, he's closing the incision," Claire said. "That must mean he found the problem and fixed it."

"Let's hope," Sharon muttered.

"Where are they taking her now?" Claire asked as they winched Willow off the table.

"To a padded recovery stall where she'll stay for the next few days."

"I'm going down there."

She was halfway down the stairs when Tim pushed through the door. They both came to a halt and looked at each other. He had taken off the lighted glasses and pulled the mask down from his nose and mouth, but otherwise, he was still dressed for surgery. She felt a little intimidated and oddly shy because he looked so different, so professional.

He smiled his usual deliberate smile, and her shyness evaporated. "It went well?" she asked, coming down two more steps so she was level with his face.

"Well, we had a bad moment when her blood pressure dipped, but we got it back up." He pulled the cap off his head and ruffled his flattened hair. "Once she was stable, I got the colon untwisted, and there didn't appear to be too much damage. So the surgery went well."

"Thank you," Claire said, putting her hands on his shoulders and leaning forward to press a soft kiss on his lips. "You saved my whisper horse."

She felt his stillness under her hands, and something like fear guttered in his eyes. "Don't thank me yet. For the next seventy-two hours, Willow is still in serious danger."

"I want to stay with her." She pulled her hands away and came down the rest of the steps.

"Claire, I have plenty of staff members who are trained to take care of her."

"But she doesn't know them. I don't want her to wake up and be afraid. I promised her she would never have to be afraid again."

"When a horse comes out of anesthesia, its behavior is unpredictable. I don't want you in the stall with her."

His arms were crossed and his feet planted wide apart. She laid her hand on one of his green-clad forearms. "She didn't hurt me when she was in agony, and she needs my help now."

"And you call *me* persistent." He shook his head in exasperation, then dropped his arms so her hand fell away from him. "This way."

Claire followed him down a wide, well-lit hall to a big sliding door with metal bars across its open top. Unlatching the door, he rolled it open.

Willow lay motionless on her side, her legs stretched out in the middle of a large stall with walls covered in thick pale-gray pads from floor to ceiling. There was no straw, just a rubber floor that felt soft and spongy as Claire stepped onto it and sank down on her knees beside Willow's head, stroking the mare's nose and neck, trying to pour all her own good health into her whisper horse's stricken body.

"She looks very peaceful," she finally said.

"She's still unconscious."

Claire resettled herself with her legs crossed and cradled Willow's heavy head on her lap. "How soon should she wake up?"

"Claire!" Tim tunneled furrows in his hair with both hands. "Even if she isn't violent when she comes to, she'll be disoriented. She may stumble and fall on you."

"I'll be careful, I promise." She gave him a serene look and went back to running her fingers gently around Willow's ears. "You like that, don't you, girl?"

He turned and stalked out of the stall. "Dave, keep an eye on both of these two. Call me if either one of them moves."

Claire smiled and bent down to lay her cheek against the mare's. "I'm here for you, sweet girl. I'm here as long as you need me."

Chapter 35

TIM WAS DRAWING BLOOD FROM A NEWFOUNDLAND, but his mind was down the hall with Claire. He could practically feel the strength and determination emanating from her as she stayed by the side of her ailing whisper horse. He envied Willow all that love and attention.

His hands went still.

He could have everything Claire was giving Willow and more.

He forced himself to take his time with the dog, even as his thoughts began to race. A vet tech opened the examining room door. "You asked me to tell you when anyone moved. The mare's trying to get up, and Claire's helping her."

Tim glanced at the clock and swore mentally. It was sooner than he thought the horse should be standing, and he didn't want Willow hurting herself or Claire. He also wanted more time to think. "Is someone in there with them?"

"Yeah, Ed went in when Claire asked for an extra pair of hands."

"Thank God she has that much sense," Tim muttered before he noticed the Newfie's owner listening avidly. "Mrs. Feury, I need to check on a very sick horse. Dave here will finish drawing Tiny's blood, and I'll call you as soon as we have the results."

With that, he was out the door and jogging down the hallway, his white coat flapping like wings behind him.

By the time he got to the stall, Willow was on her feet. Claire stood against one of the mare's shoulders, and Ed braced her on the other. The horse's eyes were still clouded and she swayed a bit, but she appeared calm and without any sign of acute pain.

"Tim, she's up and she seems fine," Claire said, her face radiating joy. "She hasn't tried to nip at her stomach or roll or stomp her feet. You did it!"

He wanted to kiss her, to taste all that happiness and hope. Instead, he pulled his stethoscope out of his pocket. "Those are good signs, but we have a long way to go."

"I know, but she's on her feet!"

He listened to the mare's heart and lungs, then moved back to listen to the digestive tract. "Everything sounds normal right now."

"Did you hear that, sweet girl? You're doing fine," Claire said, giving the horse a hug around the neck.

"Let's give her a quart of water," Tim said. "I'll come back in an hour to run an intravenous line with electrolytes."

Ed went to fetch the water, while Tim took his position by Willow.

"How soon can she eat?" Claire asked, her hands moving constantly over the horse's coat.

"In about twelve hours, we'll start hand-feeding her some soft first-cut hay and see how she does."

"That sounds good, doesn't it, girl? First-cut hay is the best!" She turned back to Tim, and he saw tears standing in her eyes. "Watching you operate on her was amazing. Willow is so lucky you're her vet."

"Willow's lucky you're her whisper human."

She shook her head. "You saved her life, not me."

Her certainty that Willow was safe worried him. He couldn't bear the hurt it would cause her if the horse took a turn for the worse. "Claire, her life isn't saved yet. A lot of things can still go wrong."

"I know, but I'm taking joy in every minute she's still here with me. If I don't think positively, she'll feel that. Even if you don't believe in whisper horses, you know animals sense human feelings."

The tears overflowed down her cheeks, and he had to clench his fists to keep himself from reaching across Willow's back to wipe them away. Fortunately, Ed rolled the stall door open as Claire swiped at the tears with the back of her hand.

The vet tech handed Claire the water bucket. She swished the water around so Willow could hear the sound, and the horse dropped her nose into the bucket and sniffed at it, but didn't drink.

"Don't worry about it. We can give her fluids intravenously," Tim said.

"I think she's just not awake enough yet to know what it is," Claire said. She put the bucket down and scooped up some water in her cupped hands, bringing it to touch Willow's lips. "You must be thirsty as all get out, sweet girl."

The mare whickered and sucked the water out of Claire's hands. When Claire offered her the bucket again, Willow drank it down to the bottom. She licked the last drops off the metal and nosed around looking for more.

"Can she have more?" Claire asked, her eyes pleading.

"In about fifteen minutes." He winced as he looked at his watch. He was already over an hour behind schedule, despite all the rearranging Estelle had managed. Perversely, he wanted to stay here and torture himself by being near Claire even though he couldn't touch her. "I have to go back to my appointments, but I'll see you in an hour."

"We'll be fine."

Somehow he knew she would make that true. And he began to think it could even happen to him.

Four hours later, he sat at his desk, eating a sandwich and watching the video feed from the recovery stall on his computer. Claire sat cross-legged on a dog bed someone had brought her, reading one of the magazines from the waiting room. She was wearing jeans and a light-blue T-shirt, with her hair pulled back in a messy ponytail. She looked so beautiful it made him ache.

Willow stood placidly in front of her with the intravenous line taped to her neck. Every now and then, Claire would reach up and pet the horse's nose, or Willow would arch her neck to snuffle at Claire's hair.

As he watched, Ed came into the stall and said something to Claire, who nodded, stood up, and stretched before she slipped out the door. She must be going home to get some much-needed rest now that Willow seemed stable.

Tim's pulse sped up at the prospect of Claire stopping to talk with him before she left the building. He wasn't sure what he would say, but it didn't matter. He wolfed down the rest of his sandwich as he watched Ed check over the horse and prop himself up against the padded wall. That was odd because Ed knew the video was constantly monitored, so no one had to stay with the mare.

Tim wiped his mouth and hands on a paper napkin and combed his fingers through his hair. Then he picked up a patient's folder and pretended to read it. Footsteps and voices passed his door, but no one knocked.

After several long minutes, he slapped the folder closed, disappointment clogging his throat. She had left without saying good-bye. He couldn't blame her. Now that the crisis was over, she probably preferred to keep contact with him to a minimum.

As he shoved away from the desk, movement in the monitor caught his eye. Claire had reappeared in Willow's stall, and Ed departed. Relief flooded through him. As he stood and shrugged back into his white coat, he watched Claire touch her forehead against Willow's before she settled back on her improvised seat.

Something seemed to shift inside him, making him feel off balance as he walked out of his office. He put his hand against the wall, resting a moment as he took a deep breath, then kept walking toward his next appointment.

Claire was wishing she had brought a book when the stall door opened and Sharon walked in. "I hear Willow's doing okay and you refuse to leave her alone."

Claire laughed as she stood up. "I guess that sums it up nicely. I'm glad you came. I've read every magazine from the waiting room, including *Ranger Rick*. I could use some conversation."

Sharon ran her hands over the mare, looking in the horse's eyes and putting her ear against her belly. "Why don't you take a break, and I'll sit with her for half an hour?"

"That's a really nice offer, but you have a stable to run. I was supposed to be in New York anyway, so I have no commitments here for the next twenty-four hours."

"Yeah, but it's making Dr. Tim crazy having you here."

"It is?" Claire was stunned. Tim didn't seem worried by her presence when he came to the stall. "I didn't mean to be a problem. It's just that Willow has been through so much, I didn't want to leave her all alone."

"Hon, she's not alone. Dr. Tim employs half the vet techs in the county. This place is crawling with staff."

"I know but…Well, I guess I should leave if it bothers him to have me here." Claire felt stricken. Tim found her company so distressing he didn't want to even have her in the same building.

"I didn't mean it that way. He's worried about you, thinks you need to get outside and breathe some fresh air. That sort of thing. So git!" Sharon made shooing motions, causing Willow to throw her head up before she dropped it back down. "See, Willow agrees."

"Oh, fine," Claire said. "I'll run down to the bookstore and get something to read. Do you want anything while I'm out?"

Sharon shook her head as she lowered herself gingerly onto the dog bed.

Ten minutes later, Tim rolled open the stall door, surprise and disappointment hitting him at the same time when he spotted Sharon. "Where's Claire?"

"I talked her into taking a short break."

His surprise mixed with a pang of injured pride. Claire hadn't listened to him when he suggested the same thing. "You're the only person who's been able to. How did you do it?"

"Used you for leverage." Sharon hauled herself up off the floor and dusted off her seat. "Couldn't you spare a chair for in here?"

"Claire didn't want anything Willow could hurt herself on, in case she started rolling. What do you mean, you used me for leverage?"

"I told her you were worried about her, so she felt guilty and agreed to leave for half an hour."

"I guess that's okay." He didn't like being the cause of any more distress to Claire, even if it was for her own good. He automatically went to the horse and checked her vital signs and bowel sounds. "It's extraordinary how well Willow is doing. I thought she would die on the operating table."

"You underestimated the power of love."

Something about Sharon's tone made him look up at her. She wasn't talking only about the horse.

"I'm going to stick my nose in where it doesn't belong," she continued, "but I can't help myself. I hear Claire offered to stay here to see how things worked out between you two."

He straightened and tried to stare Sharon down because he knew he wouldn't enjoy whatever she was going to say. She kept talking.

"All I'm going to say is this. When a woman like Claire is willing to give up the life she worked her butt off to build, you better think long and hard before you turn her down. Someone that special isn't going to come around again anytime soon."

He felt that weird off-balance sensation again, and suddenly, he was angry. "Why the hell do you think I told her to go? Because I know she deserves to have that life."

"Really? Is that why?" Sharon held his gaze with hers. "I'm thinking it might be something else."

He reined in his temper, even trying to put a little humor in his voice as he said, "You're right. You're sticking your nose in where it's not wanted."

"Fair enough," she said with a nod. "You're a smart man, so I trust you to consider what I said. Now I'm done lecturing."

"I wish I believed that," he said.

She laughed and started back toward the dog bed.

"Don't sit down," Tim said. "I'll watch Willow until Claire gets back."

"Promise? She'll never forgive me if she finds this horse alone."

Tim's gaze met Sharon's, and she saw something that made her nod and head for the door. As she slid the door open, she turned and looked over her shoulder. "More than one person can talk to the same whisper horse, you know." The door closed.

Tim snorted, and Willow raised her head to look him in the eye. "What? You expect me to bare my soul to you? I'm taking care of you, not the other way around."

The horse shook her head, staggering a little at her own sudden movement.

"Careful there, girl," he said, moving to brace her shoulder with his. She brought her head around to look at him again. "It's just because I'm holding you up. You're not really waiting for me to say something."

She blew out a breath and let her head drop forward again. He gently eased away from her, making sure her balance was steady.

He waited a few minutes before he lowered himself onto the dog bed. It offered little cushioning for his big frame, but he wedged his shoulders against the wall and tried to get comfortable.

Willow snuffled at his boots.

"Sorry, I know you're hungry, but they're not edible."

She took a little nip at one scuffed leather toe.

"Hey! That's not on your convalescent diet."

He tilted his head back against the wall, thinking about Sharon's words and then about his own. Maybe he was wrong about who took care of whom. "Maybe it goes both ways." He chuckled as he realized he'd spoken out loud. "So I'm talking to you, after all."

He reached out and touched one of the horse's sensitive ears. "What secrets has Claire poured in there? I wish you could tell me whether she'll think I'm worth the mess of trouble I carry around with me."

Willow flicked both ears forward. "She was going to New York today when you got sick, and I was going to let her do it."

A giant fist seemed to grip his chest and squeeze. He had to make an effort to breathe. He sat frozen for a long moment before he jumped to his feet. "But now I won't."

Willow threw up her head in surprise. "Sorry," he said, calming her with a touch. "I'm going to tell her all of it, ugly as it is, as soon as you're out of the woods, girl. She deserves the truth, and after that, well, we'll see what happens."

The horse whinnied softly.

Tim grinned as he slid back down the wall. "I'll bet that's horse talk for 'I told you so.' "

Chapter 36

WHEN CLAIRE WALKED BACK INTO THE BUILDING WITH a steaming cup of herbal tea in one hand and a bag of books in the other, an after-hours quiet had settled over the place. Estelle was gone, her desk as neat as pin. She nodded to a young woman who was stowing medicine in a refrigerator, but saw no one else on her journey to Willow's stall.

She juggled her tea and shopping bag as she shoved the stall door open with her hip. "Hey, Sharon, sorry I took longer than…" She realized it wasn't Sharon sitting on the dog bed. It was Tim, dressed in jeans and a green-and-gold plaid flannel shirt, his long legs stretched out and crossed at the ankles. He had a feverish gleam in his eyes. "Oh, sorry. I thought…"

He levered his big frame up off the floor. "I told her I'd wait until you got back."

"Oh, darn, I bought her a book." Claire winced as she heard how ungracious that sounded, but seeing Tim unexpectedly had thrown her. "Thank you for staying. I know you must be exhausted."

"Which made it pleasant to just sit still and do nothing." He shoved his hands in his pockets.

"Willow's okay, isn't she?"

"She's doing miraculously well. Sharon says it's the power of love." He looked away and then back. "Claire, I hope you understand that when I said you should go to New York, it wasn't because I didn't want you to stay here. It's because you've worked so hard to get there, and I didn't want to stand in the way of the dream you've built."

"Thanks for saying that," Claire said. So he was being noble and doing what was best for her. It lessened the pain of his rejection, but she didn't want self-sacrifice. She wanted him to yank her into his arms and kiss her until the hurt melted away.

He was still talking, as though he needed to get it all out at once. "When Willow is out of the woods, there's something else I need to tell you. But right now, let me get your dinner order."

She didn't want dinner, and she didn't want to wait to hear what he had to say, but she could tell by the set of his mouth he wouldn't budge on either topic. She sighed and gave him a wry smile. "Willow needs food worse than I do. She keeps trying to eat the magazines."

His chuckle was forced. "You can share your french fries with her."

As he waited for the food delivery, he felt like some sort of online stalker, but he kept glancing at the video stream on his computer. He would finish up a patient chart, then check on Claire and Willow. He had to push himself to go on to the next patient chart. Finally, he ceased pretending to work and pulled the computer screen directly in front of his chair.

Claire sat on the dog bed reading, and Willow dozed with her head drooping so her nose nearly touched Claire's book. Every couple of minutes, Claire would trail her fingers over the horse's blaze and the mare would swivel her ears in acknowledgment.

The peaceful scene remained the same for several minutes. He wanted to go sit beside Claire, to brush against her shoulder with his, to ask her about her book, and then to haul her onto his lap and kiss her until he forgot everything but the feel of her against him.

Sharon was right. He couldn't give Claire up. It was time to let go of Anais's secrets. Then he would be the kind of man who could ask this extraordinary woman to leave her hard-won life in the city, the kind of man who could offer her something worthwhile in return.

He was so engrossed in his thoughts he jumped when the stall door rolled open, and one of his vet techs walked in carrying an armful of dog beds and blankets. The vet tech and Claire proceeded to arrange them into a makeshift bed on the floor of the stall.

"Jesus Christ, she's planning to spend the night in the stall," Tim muttered, shoving back from his desk. His long stride ate up the corridors between his office and the stall, so Ed was just exiting as Tim walked up.

"I never seen anybody so attached to a horse," the vet tech said, shaking his head. "She's going to pull that mare through on sheer willpower."

"Until she collapses in a heap of exhaustion," Tim snapped as he went through the door.

Ed swiveled around to stare at his usually even-tempered boss and found the stall door closed in his face.

Tim stood just inside the stall and took a deep breath, trying to make his voice calm and steady. "Claire, you can't sleep here."

"Why not?" she said, straightening from where she was smoothing a blanket over her temporary bed. "You'd be amazed at how comfortable dog beds are."

"It's not safe."

She put her hands to the small of her back and did a little arch to stretch it. That brought his attention to her breasts, so his groin tightened.

"You keep saying that," she said, "but Willow is not exactly going crazy." She looked pointedly at the horse, who had lifted her head when Tim came in and then gone back to her drowsing, with one hoof cocked on its toe and her head hanging.

Now the desire to yank her T-shirt off so he could touch and taste her breasts ripped through his body. Frustration fueled the guilt-induced anger he was already feeling. "I'm sorry, but I can't allow it. I'm responsible for your safety."

She stalked up to him, the set of her shoulders telegraphing her own anger. "Do you think I'm going to sue you if Willow kicks me?"

"Of course not." At this point, he couldn't even remember why he was so determined that she leave. He just knew he needed to make it happen.

"Then stop being such an overprotective caveman." She gave him a little shove on the chest and turned away.

Her touch sent heat searing through his veins. "Claire, this is *my* veterinary hospital, and I insist you go home and get a good night's rest."

"No," she said, settling down on her nest of cushions and picking up her book. "I'm staying until Willow can go home to Sharon's where the people and surroundings are familiar to her." She opened her book and stuck her nose in it.

"You know I can make you leave, if necessary."

She lowered the paperback and tilted her head back to skewer him with her gaze. "Try it."

Suddenly, all the anger and lust and frustration were swamped by a flood of realization. *He was afraid.* It wasn't just loyalty to his dead wife's memory or concern about hurting Claire that held him back. He was terrified of loving someone who would choose to leave him when things got tough. He was trying to protect himself from ever feeling that agony again.

He looked into Claire's defiant glare and felt the fear dissolve like an April snow. He could toss her over his shoulder and carry her out of this stall without breaking a sweat, but she would not go quietly. She had made a promise to a horse, a creature who couldn't even understand what she was saying, and she was going to do whatever she needed to honor it.

If Claire ever left him, it would be his fault, not hers. He could work with that.

"Tim? Are you okay?" Claire dropped her book and pushed herself stiffly off the floor. He had a disoriented look on his face, like Willow's when she came out of the anesthesia. She wondered if she'd made him so mad he was having some sort of heart attack.

Suddenly, he dropped his head in his hands. "I'm such an idiot."

"What?" She glanced back at Willow, wondering if he'd just discovered some problem with the horse's condition. The mare stood placidly, her eyes half-closed. "Is it about Willow?"

He just stood there, shaking his head.

"Should I call someone?" she asked, coming close enough to tentatively touch his arm.

He lifted his head so suddenly that she took a step backward. "No, for God's sake, don't call anyone. In fact"—he scooped up a blanket from her nest and tossed it over the video camera that was bolted to the wall, then turned back to her—"Claire, I've been a coward."

"In what way?" she asked.

"In every way that counts."

She was beginning to worry about his mental state. "Um, I think you're pretty brave. You faced down Frank, and you saved Willow."

He shook his head again. "Those things didn't require courage."

"Hey, Claire, you in there? The video's on the fritz," Ed's voice came from outside the stall.

"Don't worry. I'm working on it," Tim called out.

Ed's steps retreated, and Tim locked his gaze on Claire. "What you did was brave."

"It was?" She understood now that he was talking about their relationship, but she had no idea where he was going with the conversation. She wasn't going to help him with this, because it was bad enough to be rejected once.

He came over and took both her hands in his. "You know what I thought when you offered to give up your job and stay here for me? I thought you were reckless, a lunatic, but I was wrong. You were courageous. You were willing to accept the risk of loving me, even with what you knew about my past."

"I thought you were a good bet," Claire said, remembering her conversation with Sharon. She was beginning to feel a tiny glimmer of hope, not so much from his words, but from the glow in his eyes when he looked at her.

"I was a losing bet, but I'm working on improving my odds," he said with a slight smile before his expression turned serious again. "I kept telling myself I couldn't love anyone again because of the memory of Anais and guilt about her death. But I was using that to hide the truth from myself."

His grip became almost uncomfortable as darker emotions crossed his face. Claire wanted to kiss away the pain she saw there, but she could tell he needed to keep talking.

"When you sat on that ridiculous pile of dog beds, daring me to physically remove you from this stall, all this fear I wouldn't even acknowledge just drained away. I didn't know it was there, and suddenly, it was gone. Because I knew you would never do what Anais had done."

He looked down at their joined hands. "I finally understood what the real problem was. I was terrified of being left again."

"Oh, Tim, I'm so sorry." Claire's heart was leaping and breaking at the same time. "I can't even imagine what you went through."

"You don't have to. I'm going to tell you the truth. Now." His voice was ragged but held an undercurrent of resolution.

"Please. You don't have to do this," she said, pulling one hand free to try to smooth away the harsh lines etched around his mouth and eyes.

He caught her hand again and kissed it before he tugged her down onto the cushions. He sandwiched her hand between his and leaned back against the wall, staring straight ahead. "Anais shouldn't have asked me to keep a secret that could do so much damage. I see that now."

"So that's why no one ever knew why? Because she asked you to keep it a secret?" Claire tried to understand all the implications.

He nodded, but she could tell he had returned to his past and was only partly aware of her presence. "She was diagnosed with cancer, an aggressive but not incurable type. I took her to the best specialists in the country." His mouth twisted. "I knew them all since cancer was my research field. She swore all the doctors to secrecy. She said she was worried about what the information would do to her career, but really she couldn't bear the idea of anyone thinking of her as less than perfect."

He shifted his shoulders against the wall as though the padding were uncomfortable.

"We worked out a course of treatment, which combined minimally invasive surgery with chemotherapy and radiation. She wanted to do it in Europe, away from the US media. I made all the arrangements."

"You don't have to go any further. I understand."

"I want it out of me," he said. "It's been locked away in the dark for too long."

"Then I'm listening." She snuggled in against him to offer him comfort.

He shifted and put his arm around her shoulders, pulling her even closer. "The night before we were supposed to leave, she asked me to take her to dinner at Sardi's at six o'clock, when all the theatergoers would be there. I was surprised, but willing to do anything to make her happy.

"She wore a gold satin dress that was much too fancy for the restaurant, but of course, it was intentional. She wanted to attract everyone's eye. It was her last performance, and she was brilliant, signing autographs on napkins and T-shirts and menus. Her audience loved her."

Claire had seen photographs of Anais Tremont, so she could picture the glamorous, dark-haired woman holding court in the restaurant while Tim stayed in the background, doing whatever his ailing wife wanted. It made her want to cry.

"When we got home, she was still on a high, glowing the way she did after a particularly fine performance. I was encouraged because she had been depressed ever since her diagnosis." He had that ugly, rasping note in his voice again. "It turned out she had borrowed the gun five days before."

"So she never intended to go to Europe?"

"It's impossible to know with any certainty. The fact is, I never had a clue as to what Anais was really thinking. She was an actress, through and through."

He went silent for a moment, and she felt him tense.

"The next morning she shot herself on the stage of the Marquis Theatre. She had sent me on a made-up errand so she could get out of the apartment without my knowing. She left the suicide note on top of her suitcase. She had sent another letter to her lawyer to make sure no suspicion was cast on me."

Claire couldn't find it in herself to give Anais much credit for that.

"Her note said she couldn't face what the treatment would do to her body, because it was the instrument of what mattered most to her. It couldn't be less than perfect because then her performance would be less than perfect, and she couldn't bear that. She asked me to keep her secret so her memory would be unmarred by the ugliness of the disease."

"Dear God!" Claire breathed. She wanted to rave about what a hideously selfish person his wife had been, but that would only add to his pain. She curled her hand around his.

"So now you know all of it, all the things I thought I would never tell another soul."

"She forced an unfair promise on you." She reached up and turned his face toward hers. "I swear never to tell anyone else."

"You needed to hear it." He lifted Claire away from his side and slewed around so they were facing each other. "I couldn't ask you to make this decision without knowing the whole truth."

He squared his shoulders and gazed straight into her eyes. "Stay. Stay in Sanctuary with me. I swear I'll make it worth everything you're giving up."

"Yes!" Claire launched herself against his wonderfully solid chest, joy surging through her. He caught her with one arm while bracing the other behind him.

Startled by the commotion, Willow jerked fully awake and whinnied.

"Sorry, girl," Claire said, laughing and trying to kiss Tim all at the same time.

He bent so their lips met in a butterfly's kiss as he shifted her onto his lap, locking his arms around her. When he lifted his head, his eyes blazed with relief and something much stronger. "If you said no, I was going to lock you in this stall until you changed your mind."

"There was no risk of that," she said, drinking in the power of his desire for her. She combed back his wayward lock of hair, then dropped her hand. "I'm not expecting any kind of a commitment from you. Just the possibility that something might work out between us."

"Then you're a better person than I am, because I intend to exert serious pressure on you to stay here for the rest of our lives." He cupped her face ever so gently in his big square hands. "I love you."

He leaned down and brushed her lips with his in a question and a promise.

She pulled away a fraction of an inch. "I love you so much it frightens me, because it happened so fast. But I'm going with it."

"That's the spirit." Tim pulled her back in for a soul-searing kiss that banished all fear, all caution, and all rational thought. Then he toppled them both over onto the dog beds so all she was aware of was his scent, his taste, and the feel of him against as much of her body as she could entwine with his.

In the video-monitoring room, Ed noticed the feed from Willow's stall suddenly come back to life.

"The boss got it fixed," he said, leaning forward to check the focus. The camera showed a blanket crumpled on the floor just below it, the mare staring into the corner with her ears pricked forward, and two people lying on the dog beds, entwined in an embrace that made him whistle with appreciation.

He was grinning as he reached over and hit the monitor's *Off* button.

Epilogue

"AUNT CLAIRE, WILLOW'S EATING MY BOUQUET!"

"Oops!" Claire laughed as she shortened the mare's beribboned lead line, pulling her nose away from Kayleigh's flowers. "She's making up for all those years she didn't have enough to eat."

"All right, everyone look this way and smile," the photographer said.

Claire could hardly stand to take her eyes off Tim. He looked so gorgeous in his pale-silver suit, yellow tie, and dark-blue shirt. The camera would never be able to capture the deliciousness of his slow smile or the protective strength of his arm as it encircled her waist.

"Now she's eating *your* bouquet," Kayleigh said.

"Well, the wedding ceremony did keep her from her dinner," Claire said, tugging a bit of freesia out of Willow's mouth before turning her gaze to the camera lens. No one had to tell her to smile. She couldn't have kept the happy grin off her face if she'd wanted to.

After all, here she was, surrounded by the people she loved most in the world. Her amazing new husband held her pressed tightly against his side. After a very hard-fought foosball match, Tim had asked Paul to be his best man, so her old friend was arrayed on Tim's other side.

Willow stood behind her on her right, with her head in its decorated halter poking out between Claire and Holly. Beside Holly, Sharon was holding her bouquet like it might bite her. Brianna and Kayleigh were posed in front of them in their adorable lavender flower girl frocks. All the dresses, including Claire's floating pale-peach chiffon, had been designed and sewn by Holly.

Behind them rolled the soft bluish greens of the mountains, as seen from the pasture behind Healing Springs Stables. She and Tim had been brought together by one very special whisper horse, so they had wanted to be married where Willow could be a part of it.

"One more and then you can go eat," the photographer said. "So everybody look their most beautiful."

Tim bent down to murmur, "You're doing that already."

She tilted her face up toward him. "You're no slouch in that department yourself."

"Perfect! The look of love!" the photographer said and stepped out of the way as Brianna and Kayleigh bolted toward the tables set up under a tent.

"You all go ahead," Claire said. "I'm going to turn Willow loose so she can eat something more substantial than wedding flowers."

"Are you going to leave all that froufrou on her halter?" Tim asked as he took the bouquet Claire handed to him.

"Why not? Everyone else still has their party finery on." She unclipped the lead line and gave Willow a pat and a push. "Off to your grass, girl."

Willow shook her head before she ambled off toward her favorite grazing spot. Claire watched her, marveling that the glossy creature swishing her long, flowing tail was the same horse she had first seen in Sharon's barn a little over a year before.

"She's come a long way," Tim said, wrapping his arms around from behind her as she leaned back against him.

"Kind of like us." She felt the ruffle of his breath in her hair as he dropped a kiss on top of her head. She let herself revel in the feel of him enveloping her. A horse whinnied from a far pasture, and Claire noticed Willow's amble had turned into a trot. "What's she doing, Tim?"

"I'd say she's celebrating the occasion."

Willow's stride lengthened, and she stretched out her neck as she broke into the powerful, fluid gallop of a true Thoroughbred, her tail streaming out behind her, eating up the ground beneath her hooves.

"She wasn't supposed to be able to do that," Claire breathed, "ever again. You told me that."

"As Sharon once said, I underestimated the power of love."

About the Author

Photo by Phil Cantor, 2003

Born and raised in the mountains of West Virginia, Nancy Herkness's passion for writing romance began the day her grandmother gave her a Georgette Heyer novel. After graduating from Princeton University with honors in English literature and creative writing, she had successful careers in retail, computer programming, and marketing before finally returning to her first love: writing. The author of *A Bridge to Love, Shower of Stars*, and *Music of the Night*, Herkness was named one of 2003's Best Up and Coming Authors in the *Affaire de Coeur*'s readers' poll. She is also a winner of the Golden Leaf Award, the Aspen Gold Award, and the Write Touch Readers' Award. She currently resides in New Jersey with her husband and two mismatched dogs.